EDGE
OF
HEAVEN

First published in 2016 by
Liberties Press
140 Terenure Road North | Terenure | Dublin 6W
T: +353 (1) 405 5701 | W: libertiespress.com | E: info@libertiespress.com

Trade enquiries to Gill & Macmillan Distribution
Hume Avenue | Park West | Dublin 12
T: +353 (1) 500 9534 | F: +353 (1) 500 9595 | E: sales@gillmacmillan.ie

Distributed in the UK by
Turnaround Publisher Services
Unit 3 | Olympia Trading Estate | Coburg Road | London N22 6TZ T: +44 (0)
20 8829 3000 | E: orders@turnaround-uk.com

Distributed in the United States by
Casemate-IPM | 1950 Lawrence Road | Havertown, PA 19083
T: +1 (610) 853-9131 | E: casemate@casematepublishers.com

ISBN: 978-1-910742-46-4
2 4 6 8 10 9 7 5 3 1

A CIP record for this title is available from the British Library.

Cover design by Karen Vaughan for Liberties Press
Internal design by Fergal Condon

EDGE
OF
HEAVEN

RB KELLY

LIBERTIES

For Jesse, with whom the future is an adventure

Acknowledgements

This novel was a long time in the making and wouldn't exist without the help, advice and support of some truly wonderful people. There are no words to express how grateful I am, but I'd like to try just the same. To my parents, John and Dee Kelly: thank you for believing in me and helping me believe in myself, and for encouraging me to do this thing that I love. Special thanks to my mum for putting a roof over my head while I tried to make my dreams come true: thank you, Mum, for always being my cheerleader and my biggest fan. To my brother and sister, Niall and Aine Kelly: thanks for being proud of me and my achievements (and for showing it through making up songs about my taste in coffee). To Jesse Durkan, my favourite musician and my constant pillar of support, whose presence in my life makes the sun shine brighter and the words flow easier: tá mo chroí istigh ionat. To Caoimhe Ní Chathail, Denise Kay, Robert Simpson and all my fantastic circle of friends: thanks for the emotional support, the laughter, the encouragement and the occasional wine. To my agent, Leslie E Owen, who read and re-read this monster novel and whose advice was always spot on: thank you for making this a far better piece of work, and for being gentle in the process. To Sam Taylor and Maeve Gorman, both of whom agreed to give up the substantial portion of their spare time that it took to critique the text and to offer the suggestions that helped shape it into its current structure: I am aware that the words that nobody wants to hear from an unpublished author are, "Hey, will you read my novel?" so thank you from the bottom of my heart for responding with an enthusiastic "Sure, no problem!" when a nervous "Um…" would have been completely understandable. Thank you to the Irish Writers' Centre for the colossal opportunity that is their Novel Fair (without which this novel might never have made contact with Liberties Press) and for being, in general, an outstanding resource for writers on the island of Ireland. And finally, thank you to everyone at Liberties for taking a chance on me and my novel – and for making this whole process such a pleasure.

29 APRIL 2119

0.1

It all started to fall apart on a clear, moonlit night in the Auvergne, in a quiet valley where the trees could still be persuaded to grow.

Héra walked briskly, burrowed into her jacket against the unseasonable chill that hung on the air. The day had been mild and dry, and the cold had only crept out of the shadows as the sun went down, but you weren't supposed to go out in the sunlight, this late in the season, and she didn't like the day-suits. They irritated her skin. So it was either walk after dark or stay indoors, and she could do plenty of that at home. She missed the green, at home. She always had.

It was a pleasant night, despite the whisper of frost in the breeze, and she was enjoying the hike. The moon was high in the sky and the dog, who didn't get out as much as he should, was mad with excitement, tearing off in a cloud of dust after a piece of bleached bone that she pitched into the middle distance. Sometimes she wondered if it was him she really wanted to see when she made these annual visits to an elderly aunt whose primary attraction, in Héra's opinion, was her residence on the edge of the Réserve Naturelle, where the trees were sheltered by a permanent UV haze-filter and the water table was stringently protected and, rumour had it, some of the bird life was creeping back. Héra was aware that you were supposed to work at creating bonds of social and familial connection, but she wasn't sure how you were supposed to be enthusiastic about it.

The path she had chosen followed an old river bed, dammed somewhere upstream and reduced to a shallow brook in the centre of a wide, arid trough. Trees and scrub bushed over the banks, tumbling down shallow ochre slopes, and ahead of her, reaching dark fingers of jagged stone into the night sky, the ruins of an ancient bridge caught the dog's barks and bounced them back to her in echoes. He was a mobile shadow in the gloom ahead as he worried around the base of an old circular lock on the embankment, relic of

a network of canals that wove through the place like cobweb, long-emptied now and left to crumble. The walls had collapsed under the weight of decades of neglect, cascading stonework onto the dusty river floor, and it was difficult to tell, even by daylight, where the lock left off and the bridge began. These things fascinated Héra: a window onto a long-forgotten past.

A light breeze stirred the naked branches as she passed, clattering them together like raindrops on a window. Shadows danced on the moon-bleached earth as wood rustled against wood, and the sound reminded her, suddenly, of rattling bones. Héra stopped, clapping a hand to the back of her neck, and glanced back over her shoulder at the empty path. The riverbed stretched out behind her, melting into darkness, still and quiet and undisturbed, a single set of footprints tracking her passage across the dusty scrub. She didn't know what had unsettled her, only that something felt suddenly … wrong.

Unease prickled in her belly. She was not a woman given to fantasy or flights of imagination, but there were still stories, even now, about the things that hid in the lonely places. Here, where the tourists went, the authorities were quietly watchful and airily dismissive, but you still heard stories.

'Sébastien!' she called. Her voice sounded uncertain and far too loud in the still air. 'Here! Come here!'

The dog's ears twisted towards her, but it was the only sign that he'd heard. He'd caught a scent, ears pricked and tail high, and followed it to the base of one of the struts, where he'd managed to scramble onto one of the unstable lumps of masonry at the bottom of the rubble pile. Héra picked up her pace.

'Hey!' she called again as he skipped onto a narrow ledge and almost lost his footing. She broke into a jog. 'Sébastien! Get down! Now!'

He circled unhappily on his shelf, tail thumping against an overhang at his flank and releasing a tumbling river of dust and scree that rattled down the slope. 'Get down here!' she shouted. Her breath was like sandpaper in her throat and her heart pounded against her ribs; where Héra came from, people only ran when they were chased.

A whine and a tentative step forwards, followed by a shuffling retreat. He was stuck. Héra rolled her eyes.

'Oh, for God's sake,' she snapped. 'All right, I'm coming, I'm coming.'

The footing was easier close to the bank, where the rubble was bedded in against the earth, and she heaved herself onto an uneven ledge near the bottom, snagging her trousers against the rough lip of the rock, feeling skin tear. Héra muttered a curse as she scrambled to her feet, curled awkwardly against a hip-level slab for support, and bent down to see what the stupid dog had made her do. Pale skin peeked through a fresh rip in a pair of trousers that were already well-patched, and she saw, half-hidden beneath the fabric, a crescent-shaped hollow, dotted with pinpricks of red where the blood was starting to flow. The cut was ragged but clean; it felt worse than it looked. She'd live.

Reassured, she straightened. And then she smelled it.

A sweet-foul smell, faint but unmistakable. A smell of mould, of decay, of meat left too long in the sun.

A dead smell.

A low growl from the dog crept through the shadows above her, and she realised that this was the scent he'd followed.

Her first instinct was to turn and run. Héra was neither delicate nor superstitious, but there was a lot of evolution behind the urge to get away from something that smelled like that. Her hand rose to cover her mouth as her stomach roiled; her legs twisted on their ledge, feet scattering white dust into the moonlight. Her thighs tensed, ready to make the drop onto the dark earth below and tear off blindly in the direction of civilisation. But she caught herself on the edge of balance, at the last possible moment before gravity made the decision for her and she found herself abruptly deposited on the hard ground with panic in her veins and the scent of death on the night air.

No. She was a forty-seven-year old woman. She needed to do better than that.

So she made herself drop to a crouch instead, fall back against the cool stone behind her, slide down against it into a sitting position that took the pressure off unsteady legs. She was an adult, a grown woman, a sensible woman. An ordinary woman in an ordinary life. The sort of woman who checks her facts before she allows her imagination to get the better of her.

Tourist calls police over dead rabbit. Héra could just imagine her aunt's face if *that* hit the papers. The smell was unmistakable, creeping in around the sleeve of her coat that she'd raised to her face as a makeshift mask, but death in the wilderness was not the stuff of horror stories: it was what happened to foxes who wandered too far in the midday sun in search of food; birds without water; dogs that clambered up unsteady slabs of masonry after an interesting odour. She needed to be *sure*.

So she tested her weight against a likely slab of rock, finding her balance against the angle of the stone, inching forward with cautious feet as it listed beneath her. Trapped on his perch, Sébastien circled and whined and watched her with unhappy eyes.

'Stay,' she told him, as though he was likely to listen, even as he tensed his back legs for a jump that he reconsidered at the last moment. 'Sébastien — stay!'

The lock wall had fallen in on itself at the weakest point, where the old gate used to open out onto the river. Héra shuffled across jagged stone to the lip of the overhang, clinging to the rock face for support. The basin was deeper than she expected, opening up into a syrupy, sucking blackness that almost unbalanced her as she found her footing and peered in, squinting into the darkness. Uncontained by the walls, the stench seared freely into her nose, and she retched, burying her face in the collar of her coat as her stomach heaved. It was an effort to keep her eyes open and focused on the gloom while they adjusted. They picked out the glint of moonlight on the detritus of decades, the shadow of ancient machinery, great beams of wood rotted to collapse in the uneven shadows cast by the crumbling walls … and a bright flash of white against black that drew her eye downwards, against its will, to a hollow beneath the arm of some kind of metal structure set into the centre of the well, where she could just see a figure in a pale shirt curled in on itself beside the ruins of a recent firepit.

Half-hidden by darkness, there was no way to tell if it was male or female, even if it was an adult or a child. It was only the sense of absolute stillness, the depth and the consistency of the silence, that made her certain that it was the source of the odour. Not a fox, or a bird, or a daredevil dog – Héra's life was not so ordinary, perhaps, as it should have been.

Enough. Whoever it was, whatever their story was, now she knew. She knew, and she needed to leave, right this second, and preferably sooner. Maybe the person in the white shirt had someone, somewhere, who was missing them. Maybe tonight's discovery ended somebody else's nightmare. She hoped so. It wasn't as though …

Something moved.

Something *moved.* At the bottom of the pit, where the dead thing was. *Where nothing ought to be moving.*

Héra's paralysed heart skipped painfully back into rhythm, drawing her breath back into her lungs in a ragged gulp, and she tasted death at the back of her throat.

Nothing moved, she told herself fiercely. She was a grown woman, a sensible woman. She was too old for ghost stories. *Nothing moved.*

'Hello?' she called softly, almost a whisper, but she had to be sure. If there was something moving, that meant something was alive. 'Hello? Is someone down there?'

Behind her, the dog let out another growl, soft with menace, and she turned her head to glare at him.

'Sébastien!' she hissed.

He shrank at the tone, flattening himself in submission, but his hackles were up and his eyes were fixed, not on her, but somewhere past her shoulder, in the depths of the ruined lock.

Behind her.

She couldn't look. She had to look. The dog growled again, head low, lips curling over his front teeth. She'd never seen him like this. Héra opened her mouth to snap at him, but terror had stolen her breath and her throat closed around the words before they could form. Her legs tensed, ready to scramble down the ragged slope; her neck was stiff, her shoulders were carved from marble. Panic whined in her ears as she made her head turn away from the moon-drenched scree, twisted her gaze back towards the silent shadows. But she *had* to look.

'Hello?' she whispered, soft words disintegrating in the sound-vacuum. 'Hello? Is there someone down there?'

It came sliding out of the blackness like a nightmare: two piercing eyes and a high, keening growl that sliced through the still air and the last vestiges of her self-control. Héra heard herself make some sort of noise – not words, but not solid enough to be a scream – and her knees buckled, loosening her footing on the ledge. The world refocused, narrowed to a point, and there was only the stench and the liquid darkness and the thing unfolding itself from the shadows, claws scrabbling against the dusty basin, fangs bared around a snakelike, predatory hiss …

It was a cat. For a second her brain couldn't process it, and then she started to laugh. It was a *cat*. It was a bloody wildcat, lips pulled back and snarling a warning through viscera-coated, broken teeth. It was a cat pulled from the vale of horrors, true: skin hanging loosely off its bones, mange poking through the matted fur; muzzle bloody and putrid where it had been buried in rotting flesh, feeding. But it was a cat. It wasn't a denizen of the underworld, rising like Death out of the black air and reaching for her with bony fingers; it was a starving animal protecting its dinner. And it just wanted Héra to go away.

She raised a hand in surrender and found it was shaking. The cat keened a warning note, body arched in rage, and Héra leaned back a little in her foothold, peering down the slope in search of a path.

'I'm going, I'm going,' she said unsteadily. Nervous laughter churned her stomach. 'Yes, all right, I'm going.'

But the cat's warning wasn't directed at her. Half a second too late she noticed, in time to snap, 'Sébastien! No, stay! *Stay!*' But he couldn't hear her. It wasn't his fault, he just knew his place in the universe, and part of it was to give cats a hard time. He was a big dog, his back legs were strong, and it was a good leap. It wasn't quite enough to clear the gap that separated them, but it was enough to unbalance her as he glanced off her foothold and tumbled down the slope in a torrent of shale and protest. For a second Héra hung, suspended in the air, hands scrabbling at nothing. And then she fell, pitching backwards, and she knew even as the sky moved above her that there was nothing she could do to stop it, that there was nothing to cling to, nothing to catch her or to soften her impact. She landed heavily on her back and for a moment the air was knocked out of her and all she could do was lie, helplessly, prostrated on damp earth that was thick with putrefying fluids. As the breath rushed back into her lungs, her mouth filled with stench and she gagged, rolling instinctively onto her side on aching ribs. The cat aimed a furious swipe at her cheek and disappeared into the shadows, and Héra was face to face with a week-old corpse, bloated skin mottled purple, bulging eyes staring blankly into hers.

The dark walls pillowed her screams and sucked them into blackness.

amnisonaut [am-**nis**-uh-ɴawt, -not] ***noun*** Any robotic unit with a direct processing link to the datastream. From *amnis* (Latin: stream), also the name of the first commercially available robots to follow the stream-linked model. *See also:* a-naut, Semi-autonomous Artificial Aide (S3A *abbrev.*), spark (*derog.*) - **From Oxford English Dictionary (2085 edition)**

MONDAY 1 MAY

1.1

Dawn in a bilevel city was not the kind of breathless wash of amber and coral that might send a poet spiralling into fits of literary greatness, even if Creo were the sort of place that had poets. On a good day, from the suburbs of the upper city, it might be a watery yellow smear across the haze where the horizon ought to be. The lower city, shrouded from the sky by a thick blanket of aluminoconcrete and a honeycomb network of supporting walls, was where the sun never shone at all.

Creo, as its residents would cheerfully agree, was a *shitty* place to live. Creo Haute was bad enough, with its permanent veil of smog and its disturbing tendency towards unpredictable pockets of subsidence that were liable to open up a road-swallowing crater in a vigorous rainstorm. The city was sixty years old, which was twice as old as it was ever supposed to be, and it was showing its age, in the manner of a functional human settlement that was built on top of another functional human settlement, with a four-thousand-foot gap between the foundations and the desert floor. Fissures and sub-surface collapse closed off a block or two every few months, and some of the older buildings were so structurally unsound that you wouldn't want to sneeze on the same street, let alone try and set up home. There was barely room up top for the people who lived there by the time the city fathers closed the doors to immigration, almost two decades ago. These days, when the transports arrived, new citizens found themselves ushered perfunctorily into Creo Basse, where the roof might be getting closer but the ground at least was solid.

For most of them, when the great northwestern gates closed behind them, it was the last time they saw the sky.

It rose out of the dusty scrubland of central France, a concrete mountain of Pythagorean precision, geometric slopes embossed in black against the gathering glow of a new day, still low on the horizon. A visitor approaching from the far distance would be hard pushed to measure the scale against the empty plains, but, drawing closer, the shadow-lines dissolved into louring, sandblasted walls, weathered by decades; a filigree network of arching roads that swept up from the desert floor and disappeared into the curtain of cloud that hung around the upper city; and, close to, dwarfed against the encircling walls of Creo Basse, like the entrance to a rabbit hole in the foothills of a vast, barren hillside, the seven-storey, eighteen-lane gates to the lower city.

As the sun crept softly across the desert floor, reaching fingers of watery morning light across the scree, a billion tiny sensors buried in the heavy aluminoconcrete skin flipped the city's circadian routines to *day*, and the dawn cycles kicked in across the dark streets. Scattered across the districts, peppered along the district walls, chasing the shadows up towards the high city roof, the light-bands that striped the paintwork of the upper storeys began the slow rumble up the colour wheel from syrupy blue-black to sunrise coppers, and daylight broke quietly across the sunless city. It crept over the street stalls of downtown Delphi, the seventh district, huddled in tight against the southeastern perimeter wall, and over the constant wash of freight trains through The Wharf in district eight. It climbed the high towers of Victoria's financial sector and the casinos of South District and Parnasse. It made its way lazily across the mobile city streets, across the permanent tide of human traffic that ebbed and flowed and never quite dried up – heads turned up into the holoscreen pergola that flashed a kaleidoscope of news and commerce above every thoroughfare, heads turned down towards the streets because you never quite knew what might be lying abandoned on the sidewalks of the lower city. It glanced off the teeming rain of Dog Island, poured through the south west wall of the twentieth district into Mère de Martyrs, where a scattering of burnt-out cars testified to an interesting evening's entertainment. It flowed north along smoke-dusted streets, through a set of aged gates that reached up past the light-bands and into the darkness, and into the nineteenth district, which was known to the locals, somewhat Byronically, as Limbe do Cielo. The edge of heaven.

Limbe do Cielo was not the worst place in the world to live. Granted, an objective observer might suggest that it would be possible to number the worse places using the fingers of one hand; two, if they were feeling generous. Some of those places were also in Creo. A charitable assessment might call it 'colourful,' and it would be difficult to tell, from context, whether that was colourful like an explosion or a bloodbath is colourful, or colourful like a florid, chimeric cultural melting-pot. Certainly, it was possible to walk the streets of Limbe and hear a different language every time you turned a corner. It was the sort of place where casual insults were traded as terms of endearment, where outsiders were met with a black wall of hostility and resentment, and insiders wore their belonging with the kind of pride that could start a war. It was the city in microcosm, like most of the districts, but in its own cacophonous, chaotic way.

And it was raining. It was raining with the sort of slow, focused concentration that spoke of a backed-up precipitation cycle that had threatened to empty for days: the kind of determined, persistent vertical wall of water that soaks through coat and clothes and skin and settles into the bones. It was raining *hard*. And it was currently falling on Danae Grant, who was glaring up at the ceiling as though sheer force of hatred could stop a downpour.

'Crap,' she hissed. 'Crappy crappy shitty crap.'

She'd made an *effort*. All morning she had hesitated, procrastinated, holding it off by inaction, but, once she'd begun, she worked steadily, pretending to think about work, about money, about the clamminess of the room and the way it nursed and ripened the street air that snuck in beneath the door. She had not thought about what she would wear, slipping the dress from the hanger with impassive hands, stumbling over the stubborn zipper and fastening the belt around her waist where the fabric gaped away from her narrow frame. She had not thought about brushing her hair, running bristles through perpetual tangles and tying it back for decency's sake. She had not thought about pulling on her shoes; about brushing lint off the good coat, the one that used to be Mam's; about folding her uniform into a geometrically perfect triangle and tucking it into her bag for later. She had worked methodically, carefully, drinking a glass of tepid water from the tap, scrubbing her face in the sink, using her damp hands to slick her hair back against her head so that the unruly blond troughs and whorls sat neatly. And she'd closed the door behind her before she had to think about anything at all, pulling it hard against the frame so as to shock the locking circuits into remembering what they were supposed to do. She wasn't sure why she bothered. It wasn't as though there was anything worth stealing, and, besides, as of three days ago, the population of the entire floor had halved.

Now it was just Danae.

Creo Basse was an all-weather operation, and its rush hour was pretty much all of the time. Danae, folding herself into a point, made her way out of the back streets and onto the main thoroughfare, burrowing through a heaving wall of humanity, elbowing where possible, and cursing as appropriate. Through the tumbling wall of water, colours streamed in every shade of the gaseous spectrum: the sixteen-storey sex shops, the virulent yellows and pinks of the street barrows punting everything from fried tomatoes to contact lenses, the holo-pane advertising boards that bisected the street and scattered like a mirage as she worried her way through them. Through it all, the light-bands, perched high on the walls and pretending to be sunshine, continued their battle against pigment, sucking the subtleties of hue and tone from the air and washing the streets with a uniform greenish-yellow glow.

The entrance to the underground was directly opposite a pleasure bay, where, for a price, a man could spend an hour with an energy belt wrapped around his frontal cortex, having his brain electronically coerced into euphoria. Danae usually stopped to watch for a moment, if only because the look on their faces was a sort of joy by proxy. She would stand across the street a little way, to avoid comparisons with the little boy that Santa Claus forgot, and watch while men and women whose lives were a conveyor belt of work and home and little else, found for a moment the ecstasy of being one with God. It set her up for the day.

She stood for a moment, buffeted by frustrated bodies and jostled by big hands at her shoulders that saw a fragile young woman of slight build and minimal street presence and expected to find her a whole lot easier to move. The pink-tinted window blinked behind the stream of bodies passing through her line of sight in all directions, but Danae stared through them, past them, lost in another time.

… look, Daddy, that man is smiling. Why's he smiling …?

Mam used to say that a person could get used to anything, given time and no alternative. Danae remembered her as a broad-shouldered, stocky northern matron, dark-haired where Danae was fair, ruddy-skinned where Danae was pale, tall and built for the outdoors, where her daughter was small, narrow-shouldered and a citizen of the dark. She'd thought about her often these past few days, memories rushing like floodwater out of some hidden spring in the depths of her recalcitrant brain: a smile, a faded scent, the feeling of folding into strong, soft arms. Danae didn't do nostalgia as a general rule, but lately, it seemed, nostalgia was happening whether she liked

it or not. Since last Friday morning, in fact, when she woke to find that her
father had slipped away in the night, and she was finally on her own.

★

The doors to the chapel were tall and ornate, in stark contrast to the bland,
bureaucratic minimalism of the vestibule outside. The last time Danae had
cause to be here, there'd been a modest, brass-effect plaque on the wall
beside them, advancing the extravagant claim that they were modelled on
the entrance to Notre Dame de Paris. It was gone now, replaced by a series
of tasteful images of lilies in soothing pastel shades, and, as she paid her
tokens into the slot by the door and accepted a memorial card from the
appointments terminal, she wondered if, perhaps, she hadn't been the only
person to question the likelihood that a fourteenth century cathedral would
be portalled in vacuum-set plastic.

   She hadn't been able to afford a casket, so she'd booked a nine o'clock
slot in the hope that the communal coffin would at least be clean and freshly
lined. So early into the working day, the waiting room — high-ceilinged and
tile-floored — had yet to shake off the night's chill, and she pulled her coat
tightly around her as she made her way across the cavernous silence to the
banks of wooden benches that lined the far end of the room. It was eight fifty-
five, and they were already packed, solemn-faced bodies clumped in parties
of ten or twelve, and divided on either side by a narrow circle of personal
space. Danae manoeuvred herself through the forest of legs and umbrellas to
a likely-looking spot in the corner, between a softly-weeping young woman
and her grey-faced companion, and a group of three elderly men, too alike to
be strangers, poker-straight in heavy, dark dress robes. A meaningful glance
and a quietly-cleared throat, discordant against the blanket of hush, cleared
the makings of a gap between them; enough to fit one small woman, at least.
Danae sat down.

   She wished she had some black to wear. The dress was her mother's,
and that had seemed appropriate, but it was a pale dove-grey, polished by a
faint sheen that wove through the thread like quicksilver. It was a dress for
a wedding, not a funeral. She wished it wasn't spattered by raindrops: dark,
steely stains spreading a Rorschach pattern across the thin fabric. She wished
her damp coat didn't smell musty with disuse. She wished she had a flower,
or a prayer book, or *something* to hold in her hands so they didn't feel so
redundant.

She wished she wasn't alone.

An audible hiss of ancient circuitry cut through the silence, and she looked up to see the great doors creak open on a party of twelve, dwarfed against ersatz medieval grandeur, making their way down the narrow aisle of the small chapel beyond. One of them, a man in his thirties, had his head bowed to disguise his tears, while a little girl clasped his hand tightly and looked up at him with worried eyes. Behind them at the altar, a conveyor belt slid forwards and a coffin disappeared through a hatch.

'Walter Grant,' said a tinny voice.

Danae rose. No-one else did.

1.2

Intimacy, it was called, home of the provocative uniform and the occasional questing hand, quickly slapped away. It was a cramped, three-room corner of the ground floor of a sprawling administrative block in Frain, the eighteenth district, where the long-distance lorry-drivers dropped off their cargoes, and it knew its core demographic. Food came *fried* or *deep fried*, coffee cups were bottomless, and the walls were papered with posters for films featuring mini-skirted women washing cars, sucking lollipops, or pouting for the camera, which animated when the air beside them was disturbed by a passer-by. That was often in Intimacy: its reputation for big plates and tiny clothes had a way of keeping the clientele happy and faithful for as long as they were in the area.

Danae slipped in through the kitchen door and into a wall of sound and heat and smoke, by which she guessed they had a full house again. Nadine, unsurprisingly, had failed to cave under the pressure. The cycler was piled high with dishes and the floor was sticky, but the processor showed only three orders outstanding, and nineteen of the twenty-five tables were eating. As Danae made her way out to the back office, she could hear her arguing with a customer about the availability of brioche, and the easy laughter of a couple of regulars who had cause to know why that just wasn't a good idea.

The office was tiny, just big enough to house a desk and a break table and assorted back room paraphernalia. Danae shrugged off her mother's dress and pulled her uniform from her backpack, contriving to scatter papers and smash a coffee cup as she did so.

'Danae?' called Nadine from the melee. 'That you?'

'Yeah,' she called. 'Two seconds.'

'Any time you like. I'm dying out here.'

'Coming.'

The uniform was barely big enough to cover public decency ordinances, let alone one human body. Nadine swept into the kitchen, arms covered in plates, as Danae was sidling through the break-room door, engaged in her daily pre-shift ritual of trying simultaneously to tug her top over her breasts and her skirt over her buttocks.

'Hey,' she said, decanting her load into the cycler with the care of a woman who'd been on her own in a crowded café all morning. 'How was it?'

Nadine wasn't much for the public displays of concern, which suited Danae just fine, but, she supposed, there were post-funeral protocols to follow.

'You know,' she said, with a flick of her shoulders designed to suggest that it might be okay, just this once, to bypass the niceties. 'It was fine.'

'Was it – yeah, in a minute, okay?' she added, turning over her shoulder towards a half-heard stream of invective. 'Sorry. Jesus. They're killing me.'

'Yeah, that's my fault. Sorry.'

'I think I can give you a morning off to bury your Dad. Was it a nice service?'

She could still feel the chill of his skin beneath her fingers, the light glinting off a weathered patch of funereal plastic. The memory of his voice had echoed in her ears as the coffin slid out of view and she'd had to wrap her arms around her chest, tuck her hands into the crooks of her elbows against a sudden, irrational urge to pull it back.

'Yeah,' she said. 'It was all right.'

Nadine nodded softly. 'When do you get the ashes?'

'Got them.'

'Yeah? That was quick.' A tilt of her head, eyebrows raised in approval, though whether it was directed at Danae or the crematorial prowess of the local authorities was hard to say.

'Yeah.' Danae tugged at her skirt, just in case it had grown an extra six inches of fabric since she last checked, and crossed to the cycler. 'Hey – did you get a chance to speak to Nigel?'

'Far too often. Yes – all *right*! In a *minute*!'

'Yeah, I mean, about me maybe making up my shift some evening?'

'As far as Nigel's concerned,' said Nadine, 'you were here all morning – All *right*!' A glare out onto the café floor that could freeze steel. 'Christ. Table seven need two burgers and a savage kick in the balls, whenever you're ready.'

'Is the hydrator fixed?'

'What you need to do is, you programme it to run twice as long at the next setting down from the one you want. And just kind of, I don't know, poke the hot food before you serve it, make sure it's cooked. It's mostly okay.' She loaded three plates up her arm, brushed a stray hair out of her face. 'And it's not freezing either,' she added. 'Nigel says he'll have a new one by tomorrow.'

'Nigel says he knows how to run a café,' pointed out Danae.

Nadine grinned and swept out into the smoke.

★

The rain had eased off by closing time, settling into a reproachful drizzle that misted the windows, twisting the streets outside into unnatural curves, and trailed liquid city dust through the door with every pair of feet. The last customers were regulars, light on tips but low-maintenance, the kind of guys Nadine never let Danae throw out if they were still nursing a half-full cup of tepid coffee when the clock chimed *leave*. The kind of guys who, when the café's ancient Hermes 4000 scuttled out of the store closet on its stumpy mechanical legs to begin the Sisyphean task of bleaching the detritus of the day out of the lino, just lifted their feet off the floor and kept on talking. Danae kept her smile in place for as long as it took to darken the windows and bolt the door behind them, then turned a scowl over her shoulder towards Nadine, who was emerging from the kitchen with a pot of coffee and a shrug.

'What,' she said, 'you'd rather have the guy who took a piss up against the radiator?'

'That was one time.'

'Wasn't me had to clean it up,' said Nadine, which was a fair point.

She pulled a chair down off the table and dropped into it, with the air of a woman who has forgotten what it feels like to sit down. '

Jesus,' she said. 'That was a hell of a day.'

'It's the rain,' said Danae. 'Can't keep them on the street when it rains.'

'Remind me to bar the door next time.'

Danae grinned. 'Hey, you're the one that wouldn't let me kick out Tomas and Jean-Luc.'

'Again: piss. Actual *piss*. On the radiator.'

'So, what, are you telling me we didn't suck up hard enough to the regulars that day?'

Nadine laughed, but softly, heavy with fatigue. 'When do we ever suck up to the regulars?' she said. A nod at the steaming carafe on the table. 'You want some coffee?'

Danae shook her head. 'I'm okay. I need to get going.'

A wide yawn tilted Nadine's head back on her shoulders. 'Yeah,' she said. 'Me too. Before I fall asleep in this chair. Hey,' she added, as Danae crossed the floor towards the kitchen, 'Check the cooler; there's a couple of stem-sheets in there are going out of date tomorrow. A couple of chicken, I think; maybe a bacon. Take them with you if you want.'

'Okay, thanks.'

'You want a lift?'

Danae stopped at the door, turned over her shoulder. 'A what?' she said.

'A lift.' Nadine peered into her coffee, picking an imaginary fleck of lint from the lip of the cup. 'You know.' A diffident glance up. 'Home.'

'I live on the other direction to you.'

'I know. But it's raining.'

'It'll take three quarters of an hour to clear the south east turnpike, this time of night.'

Nadine shrugged, but she looked away. 'I can go by North Gate, it's fine.'

'I'm okay,' said Danae. 'Really. It's fine.'

'It's not a problem …'

'I'm not going straight home.'

'Oh.' And then: 'Oh.'

'Yeah.' A beat. 'But thanks.'

'You don't want ?'

'No. Thanks. It's better if I … you know. On my own.'

'Okay,' said Nadine. 'Sure. Okay. But … you know. If you want … you know.'

'Yeah,' said Danae. 'Thanks.'

★

The rain cycle had almost flushed the system dry, but moisture still lingered in the chilled air, curling cool fingers around her ankles as she walked. Danae pulled her coat tightly around her, burying her hands deep in its pockets as she passed out of the concrete gullies of Frain and into the urban gothic of Kim Li, the thirtieth district, where the crowds were thinning into a mid-evening lull. Her feet knew the way by themselves and she let them carry her along the darkening streets without conscious instruction, head bowed against the swan-song bursts of drizzle that scattered from the distant ceiling, eyes lowered and unfocused, thoughts elsewhere.

At the gates of the graveyard, she looked up, and, for a moment, a stranger passing on the street might have caught her blank-faced disorientation and thought that she was surprised to find herself there. But only for a moment. She bent into the com link.

'Grant, Danae,' she said, swiping her card across her neck and through the little slot.

Grant, Danae, it fizzled, and flashed green.

'Yeah?' said a voice on the other side.

'Vault seven seven nine two three eight B six,' she said. 'Grant, Annelise.'

'And you are?'

The same Grant that's been here every night for the past thirteen years, she thought viciously. But aloud, since the voice was in charge of the gate and the gate was not yet open, she said, 'Grant, Danae.'

'Grant, Grant, Grant,' he muttered. 'Yeah. Grant. You have an interment?'

'Grant, Walter,' she said.

'Grant, Walter,' he said. 'Got it. The vault's open for you.'

'Thanks,' she started to say, but he was gone. As the gate swung open, an automated voice piped up, *Grant, Danae, PR 85682 BN. Thank you for visiting Kim Li Cemetery. Your visit has been logged and copied to the datastream. You may approach only your authorised vault. Acts of vandalism or desecration will be prosecuted. You are visitor number* Four. Hundred. And. Twelve. *To Kim Li Cemetery on* Monday. May. First. Twenty-One. Nineteen. *Have a nice day.*

Danae stepped inside, out of the damp chill of the street and into the warm, stale air of the vaults. The narrow, low-ceilinged corridors were brighter than the early evening city roads, and the lamps that lined the walls were stronger and better positioned than the dim, distant glow of the light-bands, hiccuping second-hand sunshine from their thirtieth floor stripes, but it always seemed darker here. There were no windows in the graveyard, just passageway after passageway of black walls and labyrinthine turns, square foot after square foot of drawers from floor to ceiling, each one marked with a simple plaque. In the evenings, the gates were closed and the vaults were seared with a jet of high-pressure steam to wash away the lingering odour of mortality, but still it was possible to tell which graves were tended and which abandoned. Dust would collect in the embossed black print of forgotten names, the plastic glint of the plaque would fail to dull under the regular brush of fingers, the satin sheen of the surface would be unsmudged. Danae was not sure which were more poignant – the banks of unremarked dead, or the aura of loss that hung about the graves of the newly departed. Or perhaps it was the stripped, unornamented glare of the occasional, half-blank memorial, scattered here and there among the sea of letters, that held three or five or ten names – and then no more.

The vault was open as promised. Danae rested her hand against the plaque, and wondered how it was that she always felt closest to her here, where there was nothing left but dust and words, as though the essence of a life could be rendered in black letters on brass.

ANNELISE CATHERINE GRANT
2062 – 2106

Nothing more. Not 'forever in our hearts', not 'safe in the arms of Jesus', not even a simple 'rest in peace'. Just a single name in inverse relief on a wall of letters and numbers, waiting for a partner.

Calm.

Danae never cried. She didn't see the point. But she lowered her head and breathed deeply for a moment, waited for it to pass.

Calm.

She was not his child, no matter what her birth certificate might say. They spent years pretending not to know that she wasn't one of them and it never seemed to matter when there was a future for the Grants. But it mattered now. It mattered that there was nothing left of Annelise's smile in the world.

You'll stay safe, Danae? he said, the night he died. *You'll stay safe? And you won't ever tell anyone?*

I won't tell anyone.

Not a soul, love. You stay safe. You don't ever tell a soul.

'All right, Da,' she said softly. 'Don't get yourself worked up.'

Her fingers cupped the box and it took a moment to persuade them to release it, to surrender him to the empty space behind two identical containers inside the narrow shelf. But, in the end, he slipped neatly into place alongside his wife, as though he'd always been there. She thought that, maybe, a part of him always had.

'Bye, Da,' said Danae quietly. With a click and a muted *whoosh*, the vault slid closed.

★

Her feet found their own way back to the apartment and left her head alone to drift into a kind of waking trance that carried her half way up the narrow staircase before she realised that she was walking, and had been walking for the three quarters of an hour it had taken her to get home. Typical: another two minutes and she'd be standing outside her door without having to confront the smothering fatigue that set in as her brain rebooted. She never used to be this tired when Da was alive, and now all she wanted to do was sleep – curl into a ball and hibernate for a week, a month. Maybe she could sell his leftover meds and buy herself a day off; Nadine would agree, being already mildly horrified that a person would turn up to work on the day their father died. Maybe there would finally be money, now that she was on her own.

At the door to the apartment, she stopped. She stood for a moment in the gloom, staring at it. Blinked, once, meaningfully; opened her eyes again. The universe failed to rewrite the glitch. Finally, Danae let loose a short, bitter laugh and went indoors anyway, leaving the fourteen-day eviction notice to flap in the displaced air.

1.3

Across the city, in a district called Chatelier, two girls slept in one of a pair of double beds crowded against opposite walls of a darkened room. Here and there were the trappings of care — blinds on the windows, a brightly patterned rug on the floor, flesh on their bones — and the air was heavy, peaceful and still. But for the med-patch on the older one's upper arm, peeking out from below the hem of a star-patterned pyjama sleeve, and that the younger one slept with her arms wrapped tightly around her, an observer might have missed the subtle undercurrent of tension in the room, as though both were poised to wake at the smallest movement or sound.

Theirs was a three-roomed apartment in a block of seven hundred identical homes: a bedroom, a bathroom, and a sitting room-kitchenette. It was inelegant, sparsely furnished, decorated in an off-white the shade of sour milk, but dotted here and there with signs of continuous occupation. Baby paintings, curling at the edges, hung from cupboard doors. A framed certificate of merit, dated some seven years earlier and awarded to Jocasta Turrow for excellence in spelling and language, perched on top of a hydrator, gathering dust and bathed in irregular reds and ochres from a defunct holobay diorama of the Martian polar north that had been built as a school project almost a decade ago and was now consigned to a glass display cabinet noticeably short on glasses. A series of photographs jostled for space along a section of wall: two dozen snapshots of four children in various stages of development, topped by a portrait taken many years earlier, from which a young boy offered a gap-toothed grin into the empty room, snuggled into the embrace of a seated woman with a toddler on her lap. Her clothes might be twenty, thirty years out of date, but, then again, it wasn't always easy to tell in Creo Basse.

The front door opened with its customary struggle and there was a pause, as though somebody were trying to moderate the mechanical protests by entering as quietly as possible. The room held its breath; the bedroom snapped to attention. Then a voice, soft, barely into its teens, called, 'Alex?'

'Boston,' came the reply. 'Go back to sleep, Cass.'

He was tired, and it showed in his walk as he shuffled into the apartment, stripping off his coat and slinging it over the back of the nearest chair. There was a mirror on the wall behind it, for no other reason than it had always been there, and the reflection that caught his eye as he passed was of a man who looked older even than he felt: thick, dark hair flattened by the rain, face drained of colour by a long shift and not enough sleep, eyes black with fatigue and glazed in a way that hinted of hundreds of years of the same old shit. Boston was a native of the lower city, and his skin was the clear, uniform white-grey of flesh that has never seen sunlight, but, beneath the pallor, there were shades of warmer, olive tones that hinted of an ancestry born on the shores of the Mediterranean. Perhaps his forebears had arrived from Corfu or Mykonos or as far north as Sicily, before they had been swallowed up by the swollen seas. But their origins had long since been written out of the family history; if asked, he would have said he was from Creo, and his first language was the language of the streets in which he had grown up.

He crossed to the kitchenette, feet scuffing against the plasticised surface, in the hope that a cup of coffee might keep him awake long enough to let his sister get back to sleep again before he hit the bedroom. The fact she thought he might be Alex was worrying; where the hell was Alex, if not here? A glance at the clock on the hydrator told him it was past ten thirty; way too late to be getting home from work, sure, and also too late to be wondering where his brother might be.

Someone — Cassie, most likely — had left a covered plate on top of the hydrator with leftovers from dinner, waiting to be heated up. Boston eyed it for a moment, then slipped it back into the cooler. He knew he ought to be hungry — he'd missed lunch, wanting the overtime —but the knowledge was abstract; the actual hunger itself was missing in the face of an overwhelming wave of fatigue. So, instead, he heaped a spoonful of coffee grinds and two spoonfuls of nutrients into a mug and shoved it into the hydrator, idly tossing a packet of mixed fruit in his hands as he waited for the cycle to complete.

Soft footsteps made him look up as his sister padded into the room, yawning widely and rubbing her eyes. 'You're late,' she said.

He punched the button on the hydrator a half-second before the high pitched whine announced it was done, and pulled the steaming mug onto the work surface.

'The A-38 broke down. I got a double shift,' he said.

'They paying you for it?'

'Time and a half.'

'Tight bastards.'

'Language.'

Cassie shrugged, contriving to invest the gesture with an infinite, world-weary insouciance, and settled herself on the sofa, curling her knees into her chest and resting her head against a cushion.

'You should be in bed,' said Boston.

'Can't sleep.'

'Cassie …'

'Yeah, I know, I know,' she said. 'But there's not much I can do about it if I can't sleep, is there?' Another wide yawn, half-hidden behind her sleeve. 'I thought you were Alex.'

'Yeah,' said Boston. 'About that …'

'He said he was going to call you,' she said. 'Said you were switched off.'

'Yeah, I was working. Where'd he go?'

'Med-hunting, I'm guessing,' she said. 'Caught him looking at the patch at dinner. I don't know; it's not like he'd tell *me*. I just heard the door close.'

'How long's he been gone?'

'About an hour and a half.'

'Jesus. And he just left?' Boston wrapped a dishcloth around the blistering handle of his mug, testing his purchase as he lifted it from the counter. 'Maybe I should go look for him.'

Cassie shook her head, shifting lethargically against the cushions to make room for him as he crossed to the sofa. 'He'll be back. Could be anywhere, anyway.'

'Good point.' Boston blew on the top of the steaming liquid, glancing sideways at his sister. 'It's late,' he said. 'Go to bed.'

'In a minute. I'm not tired.'

'Yeah. Bed.'

'I want to wait up until Alex comes home.'

'Alex could be hours.'

'I'm not tired.'

'*Cassie.*'

'Okay, I'm going, I'm going.' She stretched away from, nudging his leg with her foot and wobbling the surface of his coffee. 'You should sleep too, you know. You look like shit.'

'Thanks.'

'I'm not kidding. You look like you died three days ago.'

'I'll remember that, thanks. Go to bed.'

'I would if you'd stop talking to me, Boston.'

'Go!'

'All right, I'm going.' She grinned, standing slowly and with a lethargy that made a liar of her protestations. 'You're going to give yourself an ulcer, you know that?'

'Yeah, probably.' He yawned, stretched his arms over his head. 'Goodnight, kiddo.'

'Goodnight.'

Her stride was steady as she crossed the floor to the bedroom: no sign of muscle weakness, no hesitation or misjudged steps. He watched her disappear into the bedroom, listening absently for the sounds of her settling, contemplating the energy it would take to get to bed himself. Even footfall marked her progress across the narrow strip of floor between the door and the far bed, and Boston sipped from his mug as he listened to the sibilant rustle of bedclothes, the creak of a mattress distressed by petulant shifting, an exaggerated sigh that telescoped into a yawn. The gradual cessation of movement, a moment of silence, and a gentle rasp that was almost, but not quite, a snore.

For tonight, at least, she was fine. For tonight, she was safe. Boston sipped from his mug, and listened, and watched.

★

It was close to one in the morning before Alex returned. Boston had not moved since he'd passed out where he sat, arms still splayed on the cushions to either side of him, head tilted back, and so, when his brother dropped onto the sofa beside him with a flourish and an exaggerated sigh, it was enough to shock him awake with a poorly co-coordinated start that caused his head to jerk violently on its neck and his left hand to slam, reflexively, into the wall above him.

'Christ,' he muttered, as his affronted senses scraped themselves together, eyes hazy with sleep. His wrist throbbed reproachfully as he shook the ache out of his fingers. 'Did you have to?'

'Nothing,' said Alex by way of a reply. 'I've been round this city a hundred times, and nothing.'

'Did you try that pumping station off Thirteenth Street?'

'I've been everywhere, Boston. Nobody's selling vals. Not for less than forty-three hundred for a six-week patch.'

'What about Saville Street?'

'Gordie's moved on. Fredo thinks he might be dead.'

'Forty-three hundred?' said Turrow. He leaned his head forward, rested it in his hands. It had started to ache. 'Is *anybody* paying that?'

'Kenny said the market's gone dry. He said he's been trying to get oxitol for nearly two months now, but no-one's even taking orders. He said there'd been a crackdown in Paris.'

'But – forty-three hundred?'

'He said that's what he'd heard a couple of weeks back. But he didn't know who'd made the sale.'

'She's only got a couple of days left on that patch.'

'I can re-use the old patches. Maybe stick a couple of them on together. Maybe we can string it out a few more days. You know, it dries up from time to time. It always comes back.'

'Don't tell her,' said Turrow.

He shrugged. 'You know Cass. She won't ask.'

'Forty-three hundred.' It didn't get any smaller, no matter how many times he said it.

'You're going to have to go see her, Boston.'

'Not yet.'

'When, then? When we run out? When she seizes again? Or maybe when she ends up back in hospital and Child Protection want to know how we completely failed to medicate a thirteen-year-old epileptic kid?'

'Jesus, Lex! That's not going to happen.'

'Then you need to go and see her.'

'I know, I know. I just … I hate it. I hate asking her.'

'We don't,' said Alex, slowly, as though he were speaking to a small child, 'have – any – money.'

'I hate asking her,' he said again. 'I hate begging.'

'Boston,' said Alex. 'She's your mother.'

★

The first time Cassie almost died, she was seven years old. No warning, nothing: one minute she was sitting at the breakfast table, eating a bowl of cereal and complaining about a headache; next thing, she was on the floor, bleeding from a gash to the forehead she'd taken when she went down hard, and Rita was screaming and banging on the bathroom door to get Boston out of the shower. He remembered skidding to his knees at his sister's side, skin chilled beneath its cooling sheen of water, and he remembered the way he'd had to hold the ends of his towel together at the waist when the paramedics arrived, because he'd been on the floor, arms wrapped around her as she flailed and jerked and twisted, for the full six minutes it had taken them to arrive from the Acute Injury Pod on Thirty-Fourth Street Central, and he'd forgotten that he still needed to get dressed.

She was sleeping now, dark blonde hair fanned out on the pillow behind her as she curled in against her sister, chest rising and falling in the deep, measured cadence of sleep. Through the open bedroom door, a faint green glow in the shadow testified to the active working of the drug delivery system that had kept her functioning and healthy for the past six years, but already the circle of light was edged with amber. They had a week, he thought, if they were lucky. No more. And maybe less.

Alex made his way to bed, wobbling a little on his axis, and Boston pulled out the sheets and pillow and lay down on the sofa to wait for unconsciousness. Fatigue was like lead in his bones, but, now that the apartment was dark and silent and sleep was a definite possibility, his brain had kicked into a kind of restless overdrive that completely ignored the strenuous objections of his body in favour of dancing through the events of the day on an endless fifteen-second loop. For a moment, he considered just pulling the pillow over his face in the hope that his eyes got the message, and he lay for a long moment, deliberating.

Bollocks, he decided at last.

The remote control was on the floor underneath the sofa. He pulled it free and swiped it across his neck.

The last user had set the screen to *television*, and across the room, the darkened window that opened onto a vista of Chatelier apartment blocks, suddenly flickered, burped blue, and finally settled for screaming out an ad jingle with violent abandon. Boston, startled, bellowed a non-specific profanity and scrambled for the mute button.

In the pregnant silence that followed, Alex hissed from the bedroom door, 'Oops, that was me. Sorry.'

'Fuck sake,' whispered Boston.

'Sorry.'

'Any casualties?'

A beat. 'No, they're all still sleeping. Aren't you working tomorrow?'

'Yeah,' said Boston. 'Why?'

'Then go to sleep. It's nearly two.'

Nearly two. It wasn't the sort of thing he needed to know. *Nearly two* meant just a little bit more than four and a half hours until he had to get up, and the television shock had added a burst of adrenaline to his restlessness.

He rubbed his eyes, changed the display to *computer*, selected *laptop*. The window flickered confused blue haze for a moment, but settled back into a night-time panorama, and a shimmering screen materialised with an emphysemic splutter two feet from his face.

'Caumartin, Patrice,' he told it, as quietly as possible. '*Comparative Media and Communication Landscapes of the Twenty-First Century.*'

The screen flickered, died, flickered, coughed, died again, and then reappeared with the book open at page seventy-two, where he'd left it. Boston pulled the sheet around him and began to read.

EXTRACT FROM *COMPARATIVE MEDIA AND COMMUNICATION OF THE TWENTY-FIRST CENTURY* **BY PATRICE CAUMARTIN (RENNES: 2108)**

Unquestionably the most important event in the history of twenty-first century technological advance is the advent of the datastream, without which none of the communication technologies upon which we rely on a day-to-day basis could exist. The datastream has revolutionised our communications systems. It has powered the last century's Golden Age of construction. It has reinvented medical technology and has fundamentally challenged our notions of what it is to be conscious. As we stand here at the dawn of a new century, it is not an exaggeration to say: we are the datastream, and the datastream is us.

It is strange to think now, in a world so comprehensively fused with the sub-space phenomenon that powers our daily lives, that less than a century ago its existence was scarcely more than mathematical theory. A little-studied corollary of the Sheehan Interpretation, it was first proposed by Karolyi in 2038, in a paper presented to the Cowan-Bernstein Society, but it was not until the late-2040s, that its true potential began to be understood.

The basic principles are straightforward: Karolyi's theoretical model demands the existence of what is (to vastly oversimplify), essentially, a von Landauer membrane or, in layman's terms, a parallel, numeric universe.

Heger and Piscaretta's work not only confirmed Karolyi's hypothesis, but also speculated that the von Landauer membrane - or vLM — might be accessible via contemporary quantum engines, thus potentially creating an infinite processor, with capabilities limited only by human imagination.

That imagination has closed the gaps between systems in our galaxy, allowing us to reach out with virtual arms into the cosmos in search of intelligent life. It has put cities in orbit around the planet. It is in the process of sending the first human explorers to the moons of Jupiter. And yet, for all that the datastream has allowed us to achieve, no history of the medium would be complete without an acknowledgement of the dark shadow it cast over the close of the twenty-first century, for it was the widespread proliferation of datastream technology that directly precipitated the Insurgency of 2078-2095, during which more than 85,000 men, women and children worldwide were killed, and almost 250,000 more were injured. The violent, blood-drenched images of this period stand as a stark and salient reminder that, as with many of history's most significant developments, the advent of the datastream can be counted both in lives saved and lives lost.

TUESDAY 2 MAY

2.1

By the time a holiday entered its third week, Héra decided, the idea of going home became the best bit. Trees and fresh air and endless swathes of green, open space were all very well, but it inevitably turned out that there was no substitute for the peace and autonomy of one's own space, the privacy of one's own bathroom, the comfortable contours of one's own mattress. And, though she'd never had cause to consider it before, the reassuring familiarity of one's own medical professionals, too.

In the end, they'd kept her in overnight for the gash on the back of her skull, ostensibly to monitor her continuing levels of consciousness, but, as the night wore on and the endless parade of questions continued, she had started to wonder darkly if it wasn't an excuse to keep her awake so that half the damn county could talk to her. They'd drawn so much blood that she was almost surprised, when she finally looked in the mirror, to find that her skin hadn't shrivelled up like a peach left out in the sun, and they'd pumped her so full of organic and inorganic compounds that she felt as though she rattled with every step. Her aunt had been suitably unimpressed, but only because, Héra suspected, they'd decided, for reasons best known to themselves, that they needed to talk to her too.

No, she thought, as she let herself in through the door of her small apartment, you could keep your interesting times. Héra was quite content with monotony.

The flat was cool and musty, stale with disuse, and covered with the thin film of dust that seemed to settle on everything in this damn city the second your back was turned. But it was good to be home. Say what you like about Creo Basse – and Héra often did – but at least it kept up a pretence of normalcy in its diurnal cycle. Eighteen days of getting up during the hours of darkness had taken its toll, and she was tired: the kind of bone-deep weariness that pooled in her muscles and the inside of her skull and made her feel as though she was moving through warm fog. She needed coffee: at least two cups, maybe more. Half a pint of caffeine, Héra thought, and it was possible that she might start to feel like a human being again.

That, and a good night's sleep, in which she didn't wake three times an hour with the smell of the lock in the back of her throat and milky, dead eyes staring at her from a sea of shadow. That would also help.

She dropped her bags on the sitting room floor and padded across the thick pile of the carpet to sink wearily into the sofa, dropping her head back to rest against the thick padding of the cushions, feeling her muscles release. In a minute, she would have to get up, think about unpacking, think about breakfast, think about whether there was anything edible to be found anywhere in the apartment. But not right now. Right now, there was about an acre of soft sofa in which to lose herself, and the prospect of a hot, deep bath – to hell with the water tax – to scrub away the lingering scent of medicine, panic and death from her skin.

The discharge doctor had looked like he was too young to remember the turn of the century: a slightly built, fresh-faced youth with a shock of unruly hair in the most violent shade of auburn that Héra had ever seen. But he'd been surprisingly inflexible about the conditions of her release, and it turned out, apparently, that when one had come into contact with biohazardous material, in the form of a corpse of unknown provenance and mode of death, they had the right to hold you until such times as they'd satisfied themselves that you weren't going to go forth and contaminate with anything strange or startling that might have set up home in your blood stream. The things you learned. It took twelve hours for the initial lab work to come back clean enough to let her go, and even then he'd insisted on printing a scanner tattoo on her left arm before he would consent to send her away with enough prescription drugs to set up a black market pharmacy and an injunction to visit her local out-patient clinic this afternoon for follow-up serology.

She'd asked if they'd been able to identify the body yet, but he said no.

The remains of the coffee, it turned out, after a forty-five minute soak in warm, citrus-scented water had lulled her into a soporific stupor, had fused itself into a series of powdery clumps at the bottom of the jar, and a cursory search of the cupboards produced nothing more substantive than a couple of tins of dehydrated meat and a stem sheet that looked like it might be for blackberry coulis, though she couldn't imagine why she might have bought such a thing. The beginnings of a headache were building behind her eyes as she stood for a minute in the kitchen contemplating the merits of climbing into bed with some of the infinite variety of narcotics currently bursting the seams of her overnight bag: surely *one* of them at least had to be relevant for pain of the head, given that her head was the place where the pain was most likely to be? But that course of action did nothing to address the absence of coffee; it simply deferred the problem to a later hour, when she would, presumably, be in still greater need. So, with a certain reluctance, she pulled on a fresh skirt and blouse, wound her hair up in a thick black scarf to hide the naked furrow of scalp shaved around the line of sutured flesh at her crown, pulled on a coat, and headed out into the Thirty-Third district.

Downtown Victoria was in festive form as the human tide washed her up the subway steps and onto the streets of West Street, which made a change from its usual air of sullen hostility. A group of skinny boys had gathered around a lamp-post, making an impressive stand against the crowd that flowed against them from all directions, gripping several armfuls of floral bunting as the smallest and skinniest of them shimmied up the pole to the top. A line of fabric flowers dripped from his shoulder, connecting him to his friends on one side and every other lamp-post east of him along the street, where it arched and bowed in multicoloured procession at second storey height. Héra glanced to her right and saw that the other pavement was already decorated, and that women dangled out of their windows, fixing fireworks to the sills.

One of the boys caught her looking at him and animated. 'Sinjura, sinjura,' he said as she tried to drop her eyes a second too late. A tin was thrust into her chest. '*Parts xi flus għall-Marija?*'

Héra had grown up in the lower city and spoke four languages as fluently as she spoke her own, with a further six in which she could hold a slow and slightly non-committal conversation about the price of coffee or the distance to the nearest subway, but this was a new one for her. '*Pardon?*' she said, after a second's hesitation, just in case it was the sleep deprivation, and, without even missing a beat, he amended, '*Avez-vous un sou pour la Marie?*'

She couldn't fault that, so she asked, 'What's the collection for?'

'Sainte-Marie of the Sacred Heart of the Thirty-Third, madame,' he answered, in broken, urchin-y French, with his best urchin-y smile. Héra loved a player. 'Tomorrow is the festival. We are collecting for the procession, for the fireworks and the Marie.'

The Festival of the Virgin already. Did everyone else find that the days and the weeks and the years blended seamlessly together, or was it just her? Héra threw a couple of coins into the tin, spare change from her pocket, since she wasn't about to open her purse on the street, and kept walking. He called out a brief *merci*, but before it was even fully out of his mouth, he was on to another *sinjura*.

She thought of ringing Diana and asking her if she'd come over to Victoria for the procession. Diana was a church-goer, wasn't she? She'd had Pia christened, anyway, but what did that even mean anymore? Pia would want to come too, though, and if it was the Festival of the Virgin then that meant that Pia had recently had a birthday and Héra had completely forgotten. She checked her watch – nine thirty-five. The markets would still be open, and potentially slightly less insane than they might have been three quarters of an hour ago during the pre-work rush, though if it was Festival week, that probably wasn't a safe assumption. Still, there would be coffee there, coffee that could be consumed immediately, which was an improvement, actually, on the supermarket, where they made you go home and brew it first. It crossed her mind, as she turned left at Thirty-Third Lane West, which opened onto the Place du Marché, that breakfast might not be entirely out of the question as well, but only if it turned out to be possible to pass through the viral cluster of fireworks stalls that had sprung up, opportunistically, outside the market gates. In the end, she bought a couple of packets of sparklers, because Pia would like them, and, in fact, so would Héra, but they wouldn't do for a birthday present because they were obviously festival produce and purchased today, so bang went the alibi. Her head was really settling into a good old ache now, which was ample justification for judicious use of the elbows, and, if it happened that she caught a little old lady a whack around the ear, then it was excusable on the grounds that she hadn't realised that the little old lady was quite so old.

The market proper was quieter. Héra bought a coffee at the first stand she came to – over-boiled and thick as tar, but close enough to palatable to serve her current need – and sipped it as she walked. She wasn't even that certain what age Pia might have turned, but you couldn't very well ring up an old friend to say, *Come to the festival and oh, by the way, how many years is it now since you entered the state of motherhood? No reason, just curious* … It probably wasn't the sort of birthday that took one out of the realms of dolls and teddies, though. Even Héra would remember that sort of thing. She stopped at a promising *kiosque*, but the prices looked as though they were marked up, and the owner pretended not to speak French when she tried to bargain him down. Héra moved on.

Could one still buy clothes for children? Or did that cause them to hate you? She wasn't sure, but there was a pretty dress in a style that Héra thought she remembered Pia wearing once before, on a stall that also displayed a green silk blouse that would match the suit she was planning to wear back to work. And it wasn't as though she was overburdened with alternative ideas.

So she caught the owner's eye, nodded at them both. 'Ça fait combien, pour les deux?'

He shrugged. '*Desculpe, senhora?*'

Héra raised an eyebrow, by which she meant, *if I can do it, so can you*, and switched to Portuguese. 'How much for both?'

A wide, charming grin. 'For you, madam? Three hundred and ten.'

It was a good price, but she made a noise of contempt anyway, because this was how things were done. 'Three hundred and ten? I don't think so. Two hundred.'

'Two hundred!' he scoffed, and pretended to be offended. They finally settled on two hundred and eighty, including giftwrap on the dress.

Héra waited as his wife made an overly intricate show of wrapping, wondering idly if Pia had grown much since the last time she'd seen her and how you were even supposed to know what size dresses your friend's child wore, and flipping laconically through the ranks of folded jumpers on the table.

She sneezed. She sneezed again. And then once more.

'*Je m'excuse,*' she said, and reached into her bag for a handkerchief.

'*Desculpe?*' said the wife, and scowled.

2.2

'Yes — *Grant*. Danae Grant. With a *G*. No, no — God, don't put me on hold again ...'

She was holed up in the little office, crouched in the lumpy chair that Nigel used on his infrequent visits, and she was losing patience. The door was closed against the sounds of a high-octave carousal gearing up into full swing in the café beyond, but the floor was actually vibrating now under the onslaught of decibels, and Danae had been obliged to curl her legs underneath her on the seat to save her rattling bones and her concentration. Technically, it was her lunch break, but it had already stretched by ten minutes, and they were about to enter the busiest hour of the day – of the year, by the sound of it. Possibly of ever.

'Danae!' bellowed Nadine from the kitchen.

'In a minute!' she called back, contriving to spread a veneer of fatalistic apology over the necessary volume.

'You keep saying that!'

'One more minute, I swear.'

Something like a mutter – though it was loud enough to carry over the noise; this was the sort of thing you got good at when you worked at Intimacy – and Nadine was gone, leaving her erstwhile colleague to listen to synthetic pan pipes and watch a series of soothing images glisten across the shimmering screen in front of her as a smug-faced sim thanked her for contacting the Creo Housing Authority and assured her that her call was important. It was her third call so far that day: of the previous two, an extensive clatter of plates had drawn her swiftly from the first and the second had kept her on hold for the best part of twenty minutes before abruptly hanging up. Of course nobody wanted to speak to her, it was one of two things that everybody knew about the Housing Authority: they didn't take your calls. The second, of course, was that they didn't have any houses.

'Grant,' she now said. 'Danae Grant. PR 85682 BN. I need to speak to somebody about –'

'Please hold. *Thank you for contacting the Creo Housing Authority. Your call is important to us and will be answered as soon as a regulation port is available –*'

'Danae!'

'*You are number.* Three. Hundred. And. Ninety. Two. *In the queue.*'

'Coming,' she called.

★

It wasn't that there were no buildings to spare in the lower city. Accommodation really wasn't the problem. If there was a competition to find the city with the most free space, Creo Basse would win it hands down, with Creo Haute coming a close second. Every district in the honeycomb boasted at least three blocks worth of empty apartments or shops or warehouses. The trouble was, nobody could live in them. They could *die* in them, and occasionally did, when some brave or desperate soul breached the electric seal and made their way into an edifice marginally less stable than the San Andreas Fault, but for structural integrity, you'd have to look elsewhere. Subsidence on the second tier had rapidly destabilised the first, and, though nothing had actually fallen through the distant ceiling just yet – by dint of the erection of more pillars than the Temple of Karnak – most of the districts had an accommodation cut-off at the eightieth floor, just in case. Meanwhile, those unfortunate buildings that had the bad luck to be constructed under what was known affectionately as a bubble – a convex arc of aluminoconcrete that was the caved-in support structure of the upper city – were abandoned to the rats and the creeping damp to collapse in on themselves. Nothing could be built up under them, of course, once they had fallen or been pulled down. Mostly they became the site of a new pillar, the shaky props that held the city in place for a little while longer. Sometimes the old owners returned then, the electric seals broken with the final decay of their old homes, and set up a shanty-town in the shadow of the great joist. The Housing Authority tended to tacitly encourage it, though the bubble was usually the result of a burst pipe in the ceiling and the area was rife with damp and illness, because it was a solution of sorts to a problem they couldn't fix, and it kept people off the phone.

'Grant,' she said again, as the light-bands were winding down into a lazy evening blue. 'Danae Grant. No — *Grant*. Grant. G — R — A — yes, *Grant*. I've been trying to get through all day.'

'Please hold.'

She was aware of a movement behind her and turned to see Nadine, brandisher of coffee and cigarettes, and, now that the day was done and the café deserted, sympathy as well. 'Nothing?' she said.

Danae shrugged and accepted a mug, self-satisfied sim-smile rippling outwards across the screen as Nadine's hand stretched through its face. 'He'd kill you if he knew you smoked up here.'

Nadine arched an eyebrow. 'Then he should either haul his ass in here more often, or he should pay me for doing his job, shouldn't he?' she said, lighting a cigarette and passing it to Danae.

'*You are number*. Nine. Hundred. And. Four. *In the queue.*'

Danae closed her eyes, rubbed her forehead, took a sip of the coffee. 'I'm sorry about today,' she said.

'Forget it.'

'I'll make it up to you.'

'Forget it. You have to live somewhere.'

'I'm glad someone thinks so,' she said.

2.3

On the other side of the world, in an expensively appointed office set into the top floor of a building so exclusive it might as well have been invisible, there was an uncomfortable silence. An observer, had there been anyone in the room to observe, might have gathered from DiNetto's furrow-browed consternation that the news he had just received was not precisely consonant with his expectations. A really *observant* observer might wonder if this was the first time in a long while that this had happened.

'Well,' he said at last. 'That still doesn't explain why the tracking had stopped working.'

'No, sir,' said the young man whose face filled the screen above DiNetto's desk. Only the very faintest twang of distortion hinted at a secure line. 'We're still looking into that.'

'I don't understand how a data pocket can just disappear.'

'It can't, sir.' The man's voice was level, quietly confident, and DiNetto was inclined to trust it. His native environment might have been the clean, sterile white lines of the laboratory and not the clean, sterile black lines of the expensively appointed office, but the man at the end of the phonewave had been contracted to the project in a mandate handed down from head office, and the senior staff, pathologically risk-averse at the best of times, were taking no chances with this one. This one was too important.

'And yet,' said DiNetto, 'your report says otherwise.'

'We've lost access to the data pocket.' If the man was rattled, there was no sign of it in his tone. 'We're still looking into the reasons why.'

DiNetto nodded. 'Any word on the others?'

'We're continuing to monitor the area.'

He wasn't the sort of man who registered frustration. The first sign that DiNetto was annoyed was usually around the moment that his complicated programme of reprisals came into effect. But there were signals, for the initiated, and the gentle clearing of his throat before he spoke was probably bad news for someone.

He said, 'And your source is certain that the body is hers?'

'Yes,' said the man, who was just the messenger and didn't need to prevaricate. 'There's no room for doubt. It's definitely her.'

'Is anyone asking questions yet?'

'No, Dr. DiNetto. There are no questions to ask. There's no reason for them to look any further.'

'Good.' An unpleasant phone call was looming large in DiNetto's immediate future, and it was helpful to have something positive to add to a relentless barrage of news both confusing and outright bad. 'And you'll make … arrangements?'

'Already made, sir.'

'Good,' said DiNetto again. There was a miniature Newton's cradle on his desk, a gift from his youngest son, who understood that DiNetto did science for a living, and that physics was a thing that science did. He swung back two spheres on the far right and let them fly. The week was already shaping up to be the sort of week that kept him out of the lab for far too long, and the Third Law of Motion was likely to be as close as he got to any meaningful interaction with the immutable patterns of nature for a while. It wasn't how this phase was supposed to go, and DiNetto didn't like unexpected changes to his schedule. 'I'll be expecting an update if anything changes.'

'Of course, sir,' said the man. 'And I'll have the pathology reports with you as soon as they're available.'

DiNetto looked at his watch, calculated the time difference between the office and HQ, wondered how long he could theoretically put off the moment where he had to call it in. He sighed, pinched the bridge of his nose.

'Thank you,' he said as he leaned back in his chair, elbows balanced on the armrests on either side while the rhythmic *snap-snap* of steel on steel reminded him that, at least somewhere in the world, things behaved the way they ought to. 'So. That's one of them accounted for at least. Now we just need to find the other two.'

EXTRACT FROM DREAM STREAM: *THE EMERGENCE OF ELECTRONIC THOUGHT*
BY G J ROSE, (NEW YORK: 2125)

If the 2050s were the decade of the datastream, they were also the decade in which the S3A came into its own. From individuated, maladaptive task-engines, designed to perform within only one specific and limited arena, a rapid series of technological advances saw the S3A move, as one industry observer put it, 'out of the boutique and into the supermarket.' Whereas an S3A owner, at the beginning of the decade, might have needed a battery of aides to tackle a variety of domestic tasks around the home, the introduction of the Avix™ joint, which allowed for an unprecedented range of motion in an artificial limb, and an exponential growth, year on year, in cognitive pathway function, transformed the basic functionality of the unit, and expanded the S3A market penetration from a high-end, luxury item, to a basic household necessity available to a substantial portion of the developed world in only ten years.

The success of the 2050 Tycho mission to Mars, the first to trial the use of von Landauer signals in its communications array, led to considerable speculation about the possibility of expanding the nascent datastream engine technology to the rapidly evolving S3A processors, but, while public enthusiasm remained high, the cost of developing the technology continued to outweigh the perceived market gain as the 2050s came to a close. It would take a series of brutal skirmishes and a collapsing political situation to force the industry's hand, and set it, irrevocably, on the path to insurgency.

WEDNESDAY 3 MAY

3.1

'Boston! Baby boy! How are you?'

'Yeah, good,' said Boston, and submitted himself to one of Rita's hugs.

For a woman whose life was so perpetually mired in chaos, Rita had a quite the thing for routine. There was an order to her day, an order to her home, an order to her hair and make-up and clothes, and there was an order to her familial interactions. As Boston followed her into the apartment, surreptitiously scrubbing at the greasy red smear of lipstick residue on his cheek, he wondered what would happen if, just for once, he veered off script at the point of entry and said something like *fantastic* or *rapturous* or *well, as you can see, my life turned out exactly as I planned*: the words that came to his mouth every time he knocked on his mother's door; the words that died each time before he'd drawn breath to speak them. He'd long ago given up pretending that he was ever likely to find out. There was an order to everything in Rita's life, and that included Boston.

The sitting room was immaculate as ever: surfaces polished to a high shine, cushions plumped, floor so clean it practically glowed. The first time Boston had set foot in Rita's post-family home, that had come as something of a surprise, because his mother had been many things during her tenure at the head of the Turrow clan, but house-proud was not among them. It had taken him a while to understand that domestic splendour was not necessarily compatible with three-quarter inch scarlet nails, and then things had begun to make more sense.

'Tea?' asked Rita, as he lowered himself into an over-stuffed armchair. 'I made cake.'

His mother had never baked in her life, but she knew people who did. 'Great,' said Boston, who had learnt to pick his battles. 'How's Bill?'

'Oh, working away,' she called over her shoulder, as she disappeared into the kitchen. 'You know Bill. Caro's got a few words now, you know.'

Caro was his latest half-sister, offspring of Rita and her new husband, who regarded Boston with thinly veiled hostility, largely because the feeling was patently mutual. Bill wasn't the reason Rita left, but he was the reason she stayed away, and he wasn't a fan of her former family or their patchwork history of absentee fathers. Boston had unexpectedly made an appearance when Rita was fifteen and his paternity was never satisfactorily settled. Alex's father had turned out to be a violent alcoholic after eighteen fairly uneventful months, at the end of which his son had arrived and all hell had broken loose. Claude, who'd produced Tilly and Cassie, had been everyone's favourite, but he'd dropped dead one day before Tilly was a year old. He'd left them the flat and a hint of what normality was supposed to look like, but also a restless mother and two extra mouths to feed.

Boston missed him. Claude would have hated Bill too.

'She's getting big,' he said as his mother reappeared, crockery rattling on the gilt-edged tray that she reserved for company. She didn't bring it out for Tilly and Cassie; Boston wasn't entirely sure how to read the fact that it made an appearance for him. He'd have liked to ask Alex about it, but Alex hadn't visited Rita since she left. 'Caro, I mean. Talking and all.'

'Oh, she's a rascal,' said Rita pleasantly, swirling the teapot and lifting the lid to peer inside. 'She'll say *da da da*, but will she say *ma ma ma*? Bill thinks it's hilarious. Milk?'

'Please,' said Boston, because there was just no point in getting worked up about the fact that she never remembered. 'No sugar.'

Tea splashed into china with graceful decorum. 'It's a new blend,' she said. 'Forty-percent leaf; costs an arm and a leg, but you tell me if you can't taste the difference. How's Alex?'

'Good. He's good.' Boston accepted a cup, balanced precariously on a gilt-edged saucer, and swallowed a sigh as he reached for the milk. 'He's got his exams coming up in a few weeks, but he says he's ready.'

'He always was a bright boy. And what about the girls? How are Tilly and Cassie?'

'They're good.' In the absence of an overt offer, Boston reached for the tray and helped himself to a slice of cake, crumbs sprinkling the floor below him in tiny comestible starbursts. Rita's smile made a valiant effort not to notice. 'Actually,' he said, 'it was Cass I came to see you about.'

'Oh?' Now the smile was really strained. 'She was just here the other day. She's getting so tall — she'll be taller than me soon ...'

Of course, he knew she wouldn't make it easy for him, but he felt it every time. Every time, a part of him thought that she might capitulate, just say, *My goodness, aren't kids expensive — I bet you could probably do with some help, am I right?* and he could just agree wholeheartedly, maybe share a knowing little laugh, and take the money and leave. And so every time she didn't do this, every time she made him say the actual words, ask the actual question, she got to punch a hole right through his pride all over again.

For once, Boston would have liked to have pretended that it was a social call, that she'd sought out his company and he'd responded with pleasure. Just once, he would have liked to have thought that she saw him not out of duty, but out of affection. Once, he would like her to pretend that she thought any of it was her problem. But Alex and Cassie had turned up at the Authority after dinner, Cassie blanketed by a dark cloud of hostility and muttering, *I just dropped a fucking plate, Alex; you're acting like it's the end of the fucking world or something,* and Alex had leaned heavily against the wall and closed his eyes and raised his hands to pinch the bridge of his nose, and he'd said in a voice that was far, far too old and tired for a nineteen-year-old kid, *Ask her if she remembers dropping the fucking plate.* And that had been that in terms of options.

She was on full amber now; he'd seen it in the faint glow against her neck where her collar had gapped away from her skin. Nobody had mentioned it and nobody was likely to, because there was only one thing worse than knowing what that meant, and that was knowing that Cassie knew it too. They all remembered what happened last time she went to amber.

Boston brushed cake crumbs from the knee of his trousers, cup rattling in its saucer as he moved. 'Yeah, she grows like a weed,' he said. 'And her patch is about to run out. We need money for a new one.'

Rita took a sip of her tea. 'When does it run out?'

'Soon,' he said.

A tinkling laugh and a smile that stopped short of his mother's eyes. 'She goes through them so quickly, doesn't she?'

'A twelve-week patch,' explained Boston, 'lasts for twelve weeks. Then it runs out.'

'More cake?' said Rita.

He shook his head. 'I haven't asked you for money in nearly eight months.'

'I know that,' she said. Her gaze was fixed steadfastly away from him. 'Caro was just walking. She was into everything, do you remember?'

'Nearly eight months,' he said again. 'All I wanted was school books for the girls.'

'And you got them,' she said. 'You know, I want to help, it's just that Caro's growing so quickly these days, and Bill doesn't like me giving away his money …'

Boston could picture the scene the evening before: Rita answering the phone and Bill knowing, because she left the room before she opened the screen, who it would be. He wouldn't listen in; he'd just quietly watch the television, working himself further and further into a state of righteous indignation, so that, when she returned, smiling her fake smile, he could say with real venom, 'How much is he after this time?'

'I wouldn't ask you if I didn't have to,' he said. 'You *know* that.'

'No, I know.' One hand stroked absently at her throat, where a gold-plated locket hung on a chain that Alex had bought her as a birthday present three years before she left. 'I know, sweetheart. You do such a good job. Just — let me see. Tell me how much you need.'

'Four and a half thousand.'

Now she looked up. 'Boston, I haven't got that kind of money just lying around.'

'But you can get it.'

'Boston, I *can't*. Do you have any idea what Bill would say?'

'I don't actually care –'

'I *can't*.'

'She's got four days, maybe five …'

'I *can't*, Boston.'

'She's already having absence seizures …'

'Then take her to the hospital!' she hissed. 'God knows, it's only a matter of time before she ends up there anyway. I had to do it, Boston; what makes you so damn special?'

Rita was not the sort of woman to pepper her conversation with expletives; it was part of the veneer she'd lacquered over her former self when she'd met her husband. *Damn* counted as the height of agitation these days, and, not for the first time, Boston found himself wondering just how much of what had happened with Cassie had led to his mother's decision to walk out on them. If, in the end, the prospect of losing them all was so horrifying, so completely beyond the boundaries of what she could bear to contemplate, that the only way she could live with that pre-emptive terror was to be the one who left.

Maybe. And maybe she just felt like putting a new suite in the guest bedroom and didn't want to eat into the soft furnishings budget; it was really hard to tell with Rita.

So Boston squeezed his hands into fists, digging his nails into the skin of his palms, and stared at the floor until he was sure he could speak without yelling. 'Yeah, okay,' he said. 'That's fine. That's a fair point. Maybe I'll send her to live with you for a few weeks, and you can tell me later about how the visit to Emergency was no big deal.'

On the edge of vision, he saw her close her eyes, saw her chest rise and fall with a heavy sigh that hung on the still, quiet air. Boston looked up, fixed his stare on her face as the silence lengthened, drifted into *uncomfortable*. Rita was not beautiful but she looked as though she was, the more so as she got older and started to panic. She would be forty-five on her next birthday, but her face hovered perpetually somewhere in the mid-thirties: lips a scarlet stripe beneath powdery cheeks, lashes lacquered blackly beneath perfectly arched eyebrows, sculpted hair that alternated between the brightest points on the spectrum of red. He watched her, impassive, and, after a moment, she opened her eyes, dropped them, and reached for a pewter cigarette case on the occasional table.

She put a cigarette to her lips, lit it, inhaled deeply, exhaled. 'You know, you've never actually blackmailed me before,' she said.

Boston considered. 'Does that count as blackmail?'

'You know what'd happen if she seized on my watch,' she said. 'Yes, that counts as blackmail. You know it does.'

'But it's okay if she seizes on *my* watch?'

His mother sighed again, drew on her cigarette. 'Okay, fine. You've made your point. Four and a half, you said?'

'Thousand.' Just to be sure.

'Right.' Her smile was tight. 'You'll have it by tomorrow.'

'Good. Thank you.'

'Now,' she said, getting to her feet with an air that implied that he ought to do the same, 'Bill's going to be home in an hour, and I need to get his dinner on.'

The chances of Rita cooking anything that took longer than fourteen seconds in the rehydrator were minimal to statistically improbable, but

Boston couldn't really blame her, so he let that one slide. 'I should get moving,' he said, and watched his mother's face dissolve into relief.

She walked him to the door. They stood in silence as they waited for the elevator, but, as it opened, she reached up her palm to cup Boston's left cheek, rising onto her toes to press a kiss to his right with what felt like real affection.

'It was good to see you, baby boy,' she said.

3.2

The Blessed Virgin left the Sacred Heart of the Thirty-Third at seven o'clock as scheduled, to rapturous appreciation from the crowds, who lined the streets fifteen deep. Fireworks popped and flashed and a choir of altar boys made gentle music, while a trio of priests at the head of the procession waved purple-fragranced incense ahead of the towering plinth that wove through the melee, gold-leafed and glorious, glinting in the late evening amber light that spilled from the twentieth-floor light-bands. Maria of the Thirty-Third was neither the largest nor the most ornate of the lower city's religious icons but it still took fourteen men to carry the platform onto which she had been placed for the occasion, and they passed solemnly through the crowd, faces sober with the knowledge that, for one night only, they were very, very important people.

Diana hadn't been able to come up with an excuse when Héra rang and had spent the day trying to decide to cry off, but the fact was that she couldn't actually remember the last time she'd seen her, and it was a school night after all, which meant that they could leave early. All things considered, the thing to do would be to turn up, discharge her duty, and escape in the knowledge that the acquaintance had been sufficiently serviced for another lot of months.

Pia had rolled her eyes and made her 'Oh, *Mum*' last a full seven seconds, but Diana had catechism on her side and, besides, there would be fireworks.

'She'll make me talk French,' said Pia darkly.

'No she won't,' said Diana, but the fact was that she *would*. Diana promised ice-cream.

Héra was waiting for them outside the library, with kisses and effusive greetings. 'My friend!' she cried, arms thrown wide. 'It has been too long. How are you?'

Diana bent in for the double kiss. 'Good, thanks, H. How was the holiday?'

'Bof!' A Gallic shrug. 'Some day I will tell you, and you will not believe it. *Et Pia, ma petite! Comme jolie, ma cherie. Viens ici et de me donner une bise ...*'

Pia submitted to a cuddle, but made sure Diana caught her pointed look.

'And Con, how is Con?' Héra planted a final kiss on Pia's head and linked her arm through Diana's. 'Come – we have missed the procession, but we can find somewhere to watch Marie's return, I think. Does he still work for ... forgive me, the name of the place ...'

'Yes, he's still at the warehouse,' said Diana, who had learned long ago that when Héra wanted to move, it was easier just to let it happen. 'He was sorry he couldn't come tonight.'

'Ah, he works so hard,' said Héra absently, elbowing her way through a group of teenagers who had seen them coming but had miscalculated the speed of approach. 'It is sad that ... oh, *je m'excuse ...*' A violent sneeze, and she pulled up so sharply that Diana almost tripped over her own feet. Then another, and another as she was reaching for her handkerchief.

'You're not getting sick, H?' said Diana, in hopes of covering for the open-mouthed horror of her daughter, who had been caught in the initial spray.

'Me? No.' And Héra, for reasons known only to herself, laughed heartily. 'If there is one thing I can say with great certainty, it is that I am not sick. Just now, my friend, I am the healthiest person in this city.'

EXTRACT FROM *DIVIDED NATIONS, UNITED PLANET: THE FORMATION OF THE GLOBAL CONGRESS*, BY AMELIA LEAHY (LONDON: 2101)

The core of the problem, however, is to be found in the increasingly unstable global political situation in the face of the land crises in the second half of the twenty-first century. Rapid population growth, combined with rising sea levels, soil degradation, and higher peak summertime temperatures had led to unprecedented pressures on affected nation states, to which their governments struggled to respond. By 2050, changing rainwater and fluvial patterns had left approximately 80% of arable land reliant on artificial irrigation systems, and, in addition, many areas – both rural and urban – were becoming subject to catastrophic flooding on a scale and frequency that was financially untenable. As such, the percentage of land that was available to sustainable, productive human habitation was steadily diminishing, and the socio-political climate in water-stressed and/ or soil-degrading areas was increasingly tense. The first outbreak of overt hostilities did not occur until 2061, but, when they came, these conflicts were the culmination of more than a decade of factionalism, in-fighting and power-brokering under the rule of what became known as the Land Czars.

Initially a community effort towards policing the growing lawlessness and instability that had begun to plague viable non-urban areas, the Land Czars were the result of the gradual devolution of local power into the hands of one or two territorial 'chiefs,' and, eventually, substantial regions fell under the control of individuals whose concern was the maintenance and expansion of local interests and holdings, to the extent that skirmishes between rival territories became commonplace and ever-more violent. National governments, already stretched, were largely unable to mount a meaningful response, and, by the early 2060s, large portions of several nation states were essentially no-go areas, and agri-food distribution threatened to reach crisis levels.

The tipping point came on 14 September 2061, when authorities in Catalonia attempted to enter the territory of Land Czar Juan Luis Abelló to end Abelló's lucrative black market trade in olive products. Abelló, however, was considerably better armed, and his militia better trained, than anticipated, and three days of hostilities resulted in substantial losses on both sides before government forces were able to take his headquarters. Four weeks later, Abelló's second-in-command, Salbatore Vilaró, led a successful operation against the government incursion and regained control of the territory. This was to set the pattern for the coming decade, with clashes between Czarist militias and Congressional forces growing steadily more violent. The concomitant wave of refugees seeking asylum, in addition to the flood of economic migrants forced by environmental factors off non-viable land, would ultimately result in the construction of the bilevel cities of eastern and western Europe, Australia, and north America, and the trilevel cities of south-east Asia, in the mid-2060s -- a temporary fix that became permanent by default as it became clear that a lasting solution for the displaced populace was unlikely to be forthcoming

THURSDAY 4 MAY

4.1

It was the sort of building that was built for the sunlight. Not literally, of course: by the time it was built, the east coast was long past the days of standing carelessly around in the full glare of the daytime sun, and, these days, the vast majority of visitors came from the underground car park or after the hours of darkness. But it was a throwback to that earlier, less anxious age: rising seventeen stories into the air from the centre of a wide plaza of pale, immaculately scrubbed concrete, and possessed of not a square inch of surface material that was so much as opaque. It was a glass palace of a thousand nuances, for the highly-polished lacquered exterior was of steel-reinforced plexiglass – even now, there were extremists to beware – and it conspired to weave a guileless, open-handed fantasy of a multi-billion-dollar business with absolutely nothing to hide.

ReGen International was not the only company of its kind, but it was one of the first and certainly the most visible. It had been founded on dazzling scientific brilliance more than sixty years earlier, and it was the product of a certain type of mind: a mind that notices things, a mind that is bent towards a particular order. The sort of mind that understands that a hugely successful business must have a palace of glass that reaches for the sky, and when the sun shines upon it, it must reflect the light back in a gleaming hotspot glare, an effulgence that almost seems to go *bling*. And if the natural order renders the sunlight risky and ensures that no-one will ever see the glass palace go *bling*, then virtue must be made of necessity, and huge violet floodlights must be drafted in to drench the night with a tasteful mauve and ensure that the palace, since it will not *bling*, instead says a sort of futuristic *schwlang*.

It was the second thing a visitor noticed. The first was the logo, suspended in light above the top of the building: a coiling DNA double helix, locked in a perpetual two step, which resolved itself into ten-foot-high letters, visible three miles away, that spelled out the company's name and motto.

ReGen International
Live for Tomorrow

★

The glistening exterior pixellated, dissolved, receded into the wall of images, where it joined a thousand others. Painfully white rooms, where plasticised drones worked sub-cellular magic on Petri dishes and atomic mesh; gloomy, domed, flesh cathedrals where banks of darkened bell-jars filled with living human organs stretched towards the distant roof; bright staff rooms, where white-suited men and women stocked up on enough caffeine to see them through to lunch; innocuous, wood-effect doors that would stand up to the sort of explosion that would level a city ...

And a man, alone, because he liked to be so when there was no need for others, quietly making his way down an empty corridor towards ReGen's bespoke Press Room. Close up, it would be possible to see a smile on his face. Closer, the light of contented accomplishment in his eyes.

Someone was always watching.

He was good at it, he knew that. Better than his father, at least as the public face of the company. And yet it was too easy to excel: a call from the car on the drive in to find out who was scheduled to attend; a little bit of effort to recall their backgrounds; a moment or two to strategise, narrow down the possible questions, select a running order for the friendly and the hostile so that they seemed to segue naturally from journalistic curiosity. Done properly, ninety-nine percent of them wouldn't even know they'd been manipulated, and the sharper players, the ones who picked up on the gentle streamlining of the information flow, would be skilled enough to recognise and appreciate a virtuoso playing at the top of the game. Other people thought in muddy pools and eddies: it was too easy to make them love him. He saw it every day as he entered the building: always through the printing bays, and no-one saw fit to wonder why, when the executive elevator was at the far end of the building, the CEO used the everyday entrance. Muddy thinking. One phone call, a little background information, and it was too simple to breeze through reception, to call out a cheerful, 'Morning, Agnes,' and wait for the awed whisper to sibilate through the banks of assembled mothers: *That's ... isn't that him?*

At twenty-five, he'd been a handsome man; now, past fifty, he'd mellowed into a debonair, fading film-star glamour that did the work of a thousand friendly editorials, a year's worth of ad-buy. Even his father had tacitly acknowledged that Maurice Rademaker Jnr was the superior of the two at public relations; he'd taken that from his mother. He had the right smile – a sort of slow-burning *ting* – that gave him an air of sincerity and, more importantly, the sexual magnetism of a naked Adonis in a pheromone factory. Rademaker Snr, never exactly an oil painting, had found that fame and glory had attracted him the right sort of wife to add a pinch of matinee idol to the bloodline: beauty bred from old money, sharp as a gorgon and three times as terrifying in rage. As she got older and her son began to realise he was at least twice as intelligent as she, it had been fun to goad her into speechless apoplexies of fury.

He missed her. More than he missed the old man.

★

'I was wondering, Dr Rademaker, what your father would have made of the decision to sell off the Asian arm of the company?'

Ah, Matthews. As night follows day, as vultures follow carrion, Cornelius Matthews followed ReGen like a black and malevolent shadow. Rademaker had a sneaking affection for the man: fat and balding and habitually antagonistic – especially, it had to be said, towards ReGen. He livened things up a little, gave the folks from PR a chance to shine. It was never as much fun fighting with the others; they could barely muster a third of Matthews' bilious outrage.

First lesson in Hostile Members of the Press, The Management Thereof: do not take the bait. There *is* no bait. Maurice Rademaker Jnr, safe behind his ludicrous five-inch bullet-field, allowed himself an internal smile, and said, pleasantly, 'My father was a gifted businessman. He understood the importance of moving with the times. I think he would have wholeheartedly approved.'

'And there's nothing to the rumours that the sale is due to ReGen's current financial situation?'

'One question,' growled PR.

'It's okay,' said Rademaker, who loved to be able to play the good guy, especially when it got him off the back foot. He steepled his hands, caught his eye on a tiny dust mote that had wandered into the bullet field. It glowed green for a long second, then passed on its way. 'If you're referring to the company's recent investments, well, ReGen has bounced back from worse. Joe.'

'Joe Manfredi, Philadelphia Sentinel.' He *always* introduced himself, no matter that Rademaker made a point of calling on him by name. There was something strangely fascinating about Manfredi's determination to announce his familial and professional affiliation to every press corps in which he participated, and Rademaker was wont to entertain himself with little fantasies about having fun with that one day, when the stakes weren't quite so high. 'With all due respect, Dr Rademaker, doesn't the Congresswoman have a point? Wouldn't ReGen have been better advised to invest in cranial patching technology rather than gambling on an amendment that was never likely to pass?'

'Again, you're assuming that the failure of the Amendment has any bearing on the Board of Governors' decision to amortise the Hong Kong outfit,' said Rademaker, who wondered why anyone bothered to prefix an interruption with 'all due respect'.

He took a sip of water. He found it was a good way to look as though he were considering the question in hand. In truth, he would have been surprised if no-one had mentioned Congresswoman Velasquez, whose opinions of ReGen were only slightly south of Matthews'.

'The reason we haven't invested in cranial patches,' he said, 'is that cranial patches don't work. That's the bottom line. Patching over the faulty wiring in a degenerating brain is not only unethical, it's downright dangerous, and so ReGen will continue to campaign for the legalisation of cranial prostheses and campaign against patching on those grounds. But again, and I'd like to be clear: the failure of Amendment 6817 has had no bearing on the company's decision to withdraw from the Asian market. Let's move on. Okay, Andrew.'

Andrew Nazari, twenty-something, recently employed by the Chicago Democrat and eager to make his name. He had a habit of keeping his hand in the air as he asked his question, which shouldn't have made Rademaker's thoughts turn quite so decidedly towards murder, but it was what it was.

'Thank you, Dr Rademaker,' he said, arm waving like he was hailing a taxi. 'Could you tell us if ReGen will be continuing to campaign for the legalisation of brain printing?'

'Yes we will,' said Rademaker: short and firm. A faint nod from PR; good, solid answer, just the right note of confidence. 'It's the right thing to do for the millions of people worldwide who are suffering from brain injury or degenerative brain disease. We happen to think that if there's a chance to give people their lives back, then Dark Age thinking and moral panic shouldn't be allowed to get in the way.'

'But with all due respect, Dr Rademaker.' He should have worn glasses. If he'd been wearing his glasses, he could have rolled his eyes unnoticed. Instead, he had to lean forward and not look irritated as Nazari went for the kill shot. 'Isn't it true that ReGen's fortunes have been in a cycle of decline since the Insurgency itself?'

'No,' said Rademaker, 'that's not accurate at all.' And if this wasn't entirely true ... well, it was part of a larger truth that had informed the whole damn press conference anyway, and he wasn't sure he wanted to engage with anyone who didn't understand that. 'The manufacture of amnisonaut cranial technology was only ever a subsidiary venture. It has never been all that ReGen was about, and the Insurgency had very little effect on our bottom line. These days, we're back to being a market-leader in the international PharmaTech industry and that's where we'll be staying.'

Across the room, blended efficiently into the shadows in a manner that rendered her at once inconspicuous and perfectly placed to overhear any interesting *sotto voce* conversations that might spring up in the back rows of the assembled company, Rademaker saw his assistant put her hand to her ear and turn into the wall, lips moving quietly. She didn't, he noticed, activate her visor. That could mean a number of things, he knew, but, given the circumstances, it was likely to be Option A.

'ReGen continues to lead the way in pharmacological innovation,' he said without missing a beat, even as he caught her upward glance, the nod that told him his instincts were correct. 'Last year alone we invested more than two hundred million credits in nanopharmaceutical research and we continue to push the frontiers of organ printing technology in order to fulfil our vision of a world where disease is a thing of the past. Okay, everyone. Thank you very much. Dr Young will sum up.'

A sine wave of hands spiked the air as Rademaker ceded the stage to his younger colleague, stepping down from the podium and breezing through the electrical drape behind the speaker's platform that served as both a reminder of the company's logo and a sound-proof security field as she started to speak. Young knew her job and today her job was to science two dozen inquiring minds away from the idea that selling off the company's Asian arm was a sign that ReGen's finances had taken a hit when the 6817 gamble had failed to pay off. It wouldn't work, of course, because there wasn't a single inquiring mind in the room that gave a damn about science or finance, but it might keep the scent of blood out of the water for a little longer. And all Rademaker needed was a little longer.

His assistant was already waiting for him in the corridor beyond, heels snapping against the highly polished floor as she fell into step beside him.

'Don't tell me,' he said as they walked, Rademaker at an easy stride, Alenka brisk and clipped as she kept pace on legs a full four inches shorter without any visible evidence of effort. 'There's only one man in this company with timing like that. Is the line secure?'

'Yes, sir,' she said, eyes focused on her visor as her hands sifted through data on the screen that hung in the air in front of her. Rademaker wondered, vaguely, if there was some kind of sixth sense gifted only to extraordinarily accomplished assistants that kept her in a straight line, or if she practiced when the corridors were empty. 'I've stepped it up to Protocol 6, and he's buffered at his end. He's ready when you are.'

The executive elevator was set into the far wall of a white marble lobby, alongside the staff elevators and distinguished only by a small, tasteful plaque below the ID scanner. Rademaker swiped his hand across the auric sensor, stepped inside as Alenka transferred the call to his phonewave, waited for the doors to close behind him before he spoke.

'Frank,' he said. 'Don't ruin my morning. Give me good news.'

The image on his visor flickered, pixellated for a second as the man at the other end dropped his gaze in a manner that was the opposite of promising. 'There's … news,' he said, and, if the pause was supposed to gloss over the absence of a qualifying adjective, Rademaker was forced to wonder if he needed to include some kind of basic oratorical training in his company's induction programme.

He resisted the urge to roll his eyes. 'Frank,' he said. 'I've just come from my third press conference in two weeks and I'm scheduled to meet with the congressional subcommittee in four hours to update them on progress that we haven't made. It's the wrong morning to try and pretty things up for me. Have you found the uplink or not?'

'Yes, sir.' A lengthy pause did the work of half a dozen sentences. 'We've found it.'

'So you've located the beacons?'

'No, sir.' A purse of the lips; this was not a man accustomed to being wrong or uncertain, and it didn't sit well on his face. 'Not exactly.'

Maurice Rademaker Jnr was the genius son of a genius, but it was amazing how often people forgot that. He'd given up reminding them. It just came off as uncouth.

'Frank,' he said, with his best semblance of an affable smile. 'This elevator is going to come to a stop in less than thirty seconds. I need you to have finished speaking in the next twenty-five. Where the hell are my tracking beacons, Frank?'

And DiNetto looked up, met Rademaker's eye with the same granite-faced obduracy that had, once upon a time recommended him to the project, and said, 'Red Space, sir. We have no idea how it happened, sir, but at least one of our data pockets is now in a-naut controlled datastream space.'

Red Space. Rademaker loosed a soft puff of breathless laughter. It seemed like the only sane response.

The morning had started so *well*. The sun was low on the horizon when Rademaker woke up; scattered, wispy clouds freshened the air and the flowers on the veranda were just coming into bloom. He'd drunk two cups of good coffee and skimmed through the papers and headed out into the world to lock horns with Cornelius Matthews with a spring in his step and the knowledge that, whatever else might happen, the wheels were turning and the circle was closing. Even Senators Lawrence and O'Neill and their subcommittee of anal retentives hadn't been able to take the edge off the good mood; he'd thought it was bulletproof. But that was one thing you could say about Frank DiNetto: the man was full of surprises.

'Frank,' he said, and there was no trace of the smile in his voice and no more blanket pretence of cheerful camaraderie. 'I need you to track this, and I need you to have a definite answer for me by four thirty today. I don't care,' he added, as DiNetto opened his mouth to voice the obligatory protests that such a thing was outside of the realms of possibility. 'Everything else is on hold until you can tell me how the hell we lost our data pocket to the a-nauts. Now, get off my phonewave – I have a call I need to make right now.'

'Yes sir,' said DiNetto, and there was something in his tone that made Rademaker look up sharply in the act of cutting the phonelink; something in DiNetto's carefully blank expression that made a little warning light start flashing in the back recesses of Rademaker's brain.

'Jesus Christ,' he said. 'What else?'

And DiNetto said, without looking away, without hesitation or prevarication, 'Sinon has also disappeared, sir. We've lost the uplink to Sinon.'

EXTRACT FROM *DREAM STREAM: THE EMERGENCE OF ELECTRONIC THOUGHT*
BY G J ROSE, (NEW YORK: 2125)

Two factors over the next two decades would have a major impact on the industry. The first was the recession of the early 2050s, which limited the buying power of the general public and significantly reduced demand for high-end or luxury items. Telectronics firms that had been established for twenty years or more were suddenly obliged to find new and more cost-effective manufacturing methods in order to remain competitive, and there was a strong sense within the industry that current production models were unsustainable in the long-term.

In 2059, then market-leading a-naut firm AGR entered into partnership with organ printers Møller-Kjeldsen to begin to explore the possibility of incorporating some percentage of organic matter into the a-naut production model, and to lobby for a relaxation on legal restrictions then in place that prohibited large-scale printing of human genetic material for a non-human host. It would be a further five years before the law was overturned; however, prototype design specifications developed during this period clearly indicate an awareness of the enormous cost-saving benefit to replacing complex synthetic components with living material, whilst also identifying potential logistical issues with blood supply through a partially synthetic system, and in particular the question of how to institute a pathogenic response facility within the organic tissue, given the complexities of replicating even a semi-functional immune response outside of a living system. The latter was never satisfactorily resolved and, indeed, accounted for a great many a-naut casualties after the Insurgency, when their organic tissues were unable to respond to a pathogenic invasion following trauma.

The second was the outbreak of the Land Crises, during the first term of the new Global Congress. Military losses were substantial, but, no less significantly, the exercise was a PR disaster for the nascent governing body, who made minimal progress against the Land Czars with each military venture, but were obliged to contend with widespread images of civilian casualties, an ever-increasing demand for agri-food products that the Czars were able to leverage against further incursions, and the growing perception, in the public eye, that they lacked the authority to take meaningful, restorative action against threats to global governance. Drone warfare, while effective at reducing military casualties, lacked the necessary autonomy to make critical, battlefield decisions, and a number of high-profile debacles – including one in which eleven schoolchildren were killed when their transport was used as cover by a fleeing platoon of Czarist militia – looked set to derail Congress' future viability, as member states hurried to distance themselves from the rising death toll.

However, the success of the Tycho 7 mission led many to speculate that a more widespread application of the new datastream engines had been in development for some time. Rumours abounded that Calator, a minor player on the global telectronics market, but one with close links to several national militaries, were close to marrying S3A technology with datastream-uplink capability in a new breed of S3A that would have the capacity to think semi-autonomously and, more importantly, to make value judgements, in line with a strictly defined set of protocols. The new model premiered in late 2062, but, contrary to commonly held opinion, the first commercially available models, which arrived in stores in early 2064, were not known as amnisonauts, although they were marketed under the brand name Amnis. In the wake of the Insurgency of the late twenty-first century, many have sought to criticise the haste with which the global military developed and deployed stream-linked autonomous units within an active combat zone, linking this to the eventual catastrophic loss of human life, but it is important to remember that, at the time, the move was considered a resounding success.

FRIDAY 5 MAY

5.1

Dr Ravi was a man of comfortable years, which was one thing that Héra found eminently reassuring. He'd also been her primary physician for almost thirty of them, and this was another. He had told her many times that his nature was to worry about something until he'd been proven wrong, and that this was what she paid him for: to lose sleep on her behalf, so that she didn't have to. All things considered, the arrangement was extremely satisfactory, and a far cry from the child-doctors of Aurillac, which she'd had no hesitation in telling him on Tuesday. This was Friday, however, and it was starting to look a little different now that it was causing her to miss work.

The scanning chamber was padded at least, but it was still a narrow tube of plastic, hermetically sealed and wide enough to accommodate nothing more expansive than the occasional shuffle from side to side, and she'd been inside it now for almost fifteen minutes. Moreover, this was the third time in less than a week. Héra could understand caution, and, given the circumstances, she was inclined to approve, but the fact was, she'd been scanned and scanned and then scanned again and, quite apart from the lingering suspicion that she was one more battery of tests away from glowing in the dark, she had the beginnings of a chest cold, and that was bound to start throwing up the kind of anomalies on the vitalic readouts that would lead to more scanning. And her chest was sore and her nose was running and she'd needed the bathroom for the past ten minutes, and what she wanted now, more than anything else, was a patch and a cup of coffee and a radiator to sit and feel sorry for herself beside. She just did not feel like she had the energy to explain to a computer and a fractious medic why a watery cough was not always cause for concern.

'How are we doing in there?' said Ravi's disembodied voice, and for the briefest of moments she considered actually telling him. Apart from anything else, he'd startled her out of an idle moment of reflection and she'd jumped so badly that she'd banged her head on the roof of the chamber.

But he was, after all, paid to worry on her behalf. So she allowed herself a disapproving purse of the lips, knowing he'd see it on the monitor, but she kept her voice neutral as she said, 'I'll just be glad when this is over.'

A chuckle. 'Just a few more minutes,' he told her. 'There are a couple of anomalies I'd like to check out.'

Well, of course there were. Héra cleared her throat in what she hoped was a meaningful manner, but stopped short of rolling her eyes.

'I thought we'd covered all of this on Tuesday?' she said.

'What do I always tell you?' His voice reminded her of her father's: a rich, warm baritone, utterly imperturbable. Héra wondered if that was the reason he tended to get his way so often. 'You let me do the worrying for you. I see a feedback blip from your monitor, I want to check it out. This is what you …'

Pay me for, finished Héra in the privacy of her own head. In no other industry, she thought, did the customer's opinion matter so little.

The feedback blip, the cause of all this fuss, was a slight temperature rise, tracked over the past twenty-four hours. In vain had she protested that this was not precisely unheard of in a woman who was clearly in the process of developing a rhinoviral infection, but apparently it was also not unheard of in a woman who was in the process of developing something slightly more worrying, and, since the body in the lock had been carrying several blood-borne pathogens that fit the bill, nobody was taking any chances. The fact that Héra's own system was, as of Sunday evening, possibly the most cytotoxic environment in the lower city, and the fact that she had repeatedly and comprehensively tested negative for anything nasty, was apparently the only reason she wasn't in an isolation ward right now.

'Your serology's still looking good,' said Ravi now, as the lid of the chamber hissed open and Héra, eyes protesting, squinted into the sudden shift in light. 'I'm seeing a minor infection, some inflammation in the nasal mucosa, some congestion in the upper respiratory tract, all consistent with a dose of the common cold. But you already knew that.'

Héra sat up, swung her legs over the lip of the chamber. 'Yes. I did.'

'I just …' he added thoughtfully, turning back to his feedback screen, and Héra's heart sank. Nothing good ever came of the trailing sentence. 'I think it might be worth bringing in my colleague to have a quick look at some of these counts,' he finished. A glance back over his shoulder as she dropped her feet onto the steps that led back down to the treatment room floor. 'I don't think it's anything to be concerned about, but I'd rather be safe than sorry.'

She didn't sigh, but only through the exercise of extraordinary willpower. 'And how long will that take?'

'Oh,' he said airily, 'it's just a couple of tests. Not long.' A beat, in which she allowed herself to be lulled into a false sense of security, before he added, 'I'd prefer to admit you overnight, though.'

An eyebrow arched. 'Dr Ravi ...'

'There's probably no reason to be concerned,' he said in his velvety voice, and she was about to protest that this rather wilfully ignored the substance of her complaint – which was less about his propensity towards excessive caution and more about the fact that not everyone's employers allowed them the latitude to drop everything for a twenty-four hour sojourn in hospital on the whim of their doctor – when the *probably* registered.

Probably. Probably changed the landscape a little. Not significantly, perhaps, but he'd been her doctor for almost three decades now, and she had been practicing the subtle art of decoding his euphemisms for a long time. He had a way of using words, and a way of making them mean things that they didn't necessarily mean – the trick was to work out the disingenuous from the figure of speech.

So she said, carefully, 'I thought you said it was just a cold?'

'Oh, yes,' he said mildly, and flashed her a distracted smile. 'Almost certainly nothing to worry about.'

A beat, while Héra waited for him to drop the final clause onto the end of his sentence. 'But...?' she said at last.

The doctor pursed his lips, shook his head. He was good at this. 'But,' he said, 'we've loaded you up with thirteen different prophylactic treatments in the past five days.' An expansive shrug. 'I'll be happier when I can explain why I'm getting any viral readings at all. That's all.'

5.2

It was the end of a long day, though the Housing Authority never actually closed: regulation ports would take calls well into the night for anybody that cared to hang on that long. But somewhere around eight thirty, nine-ish, the indignant general public started to trickle away, so that, by the end of Boston's shift, the great hall was empty but for the ranks of the really, really determined, and they weren't going anywhere without making sure that someone understood just how committed they really were to their indignation. This was the moment he spent his whole day trying to avoid, for all that it meant that he was going home soon, because long years' experience had proven time and time again that people preferred to rant at a human figure, and Boston was the only one going. He was sure it was deliberate. He hated his job.

But it hadn't been bad day, all things considered. People came, people seethed, people went. People accosted him, as though the whole stupid system were his fault, as though one man with a mop were the root cause of all ill in Creo Basse, and then they took their stress-related heart attacks outside and let him get on with the cleaning. Some days there was violence and he had to get rough with them. Once, he'd been set upon by the three oldest members of a family of brick shit-houses and security had had to peel them off him, then peel him off the floor. Boston *hated* his job.

The Housing Authority was close to the western wall of Cilicia, an urban wasteland of quangos and Departments and Associations, where ambitious people went to learn how to be important. Somewhere above him, in the network of dark and cramped offices that stretched forty storeys towards the ceiling, important-people-in-training put in thankless hours trying to reorganise space-time to find a couple more rooms for two hundred and fifty thousand homeless, but here, the Authority's sprawling public face, was a cavernous ground-floor chamber, paved with great slabs of marble-effect plastic, supported by post-aestheticist concrete pillars and walled in stripped white breezeblock. It was possible that, when it was constructed, it had represented the height of sophistication, but, more importantly, there were no awkward nooks and hollows down which a mop might become stuck, nor were there tedious hulks of furniture or potted plastic plants to be shifted or cleaned around. From the point of view of a mop and bucket, it was a dream come true.

The constant trample of feet trailed dust and dirt and rubbish across the floor, so he was kept busy as the day seeped by, but his real job, of course, was avoiding the dead-eyed glares of the dispossessed. Usually, he kept close to the walls when the queues were at their longest, trailing the length of the hall towards seventy-two regulation ports at the far end. By night, the hall was vast; by day, with six dozen queues stretching the full half-kilometre span from the ports to the doors, it became impossibly small.

Boston *hated* his job. *Hated* it.

Cassie was waiting for him out back, in the little bolt hole he'd commandeered years ago from an old storage closet and gradually outfitted to meet his specifications. He'd left her doing homework and complaining about a lack of food, daylight, and entertainment, while he got on with the task of repeatedly sluicing water across 20,000 square metres of tile, but he'd crept back seven times in the past two hours to check on her, just in case. The last time, she'd been staring into space as he edged the door open, and he'd heard the panic in his voice as he called her name, but she'd snapped back abruptly with an eye-roll and a scowl, and it turned out that she wasn't absent, just avoiding trigonometry. That was fifteen minutes ago. There were three patches on her neck now, because Alex was the kind of guy who saved things like old patches just in case they ever came in handy, but two were flashing orange and one was flashing red. Boston didn't know how much time that meant they had, but he guessed that he probably ought to be checking in on her more often than once every quarter-hour.

Another forty-five minutes and his shift was done. Boston straightened slowly, arching his back away from the central buttress of his mop and bucket, aware that three nights without sleep were catching up on him. He looked like the walking dead. He'd noticed people in the queues looking at him strangely, giving him a wide berth. It was a good look for the Housing Authority, he thought: people didn't hassle a perambulatory corpse.

Two on amber, one on red. It was getting harder to pretend to ignore it.

*

It was raining again. But, then again, it was always raining in Creo Basse.

Danae pulled her coat around her shoulders as she walked, eyes down, head bowed against the deluge. Nadine was trying to be sympathetic, but her patience was wearing thin and the look she'd given Danae as she crept down the stairs after an hour and a half of soothing music and smug green letters could have fractured marble. But what could she do? She had to live somewhere.

'Maybe you could try one of the hostels, huh?' Nadine had suggested with a thin veneer of composure. It was her way of saying *get off the fucking phone*.

'Yeah,' Danae had answered. 'I could try that.' It was her way of giving in.

She wasn't often in Cilicia; it was strictly a cut-through for when trouble flared up on the way home. Trouble never flared up in Cilicia. It was the anti-flashpoint. Maybe it had something to do with the soporific deadness of the air, the sense of thousands of industrious minds beavering away at jobs too tedious to sustain intelligent thought, that sucked the fire out of the most impassioned malcontent and turned their thoughts to shades of beige and magnolia. Even the rain was boring: a monotonous stream that fell in civil service precision from the distant ceiling, coating the dark grey floor with regulation-consistency damp.

And it was *always* raining in Cilicia. Danae shrugged further into her coat and elbowed her way through the thick crowds in the general direction of the sprawling concrete leviathan up ahead.

The Housing Authority didn't answer calls. She had decided to stop phoning.

★

There were few sights in the world more depressing than Cilicia in the rain, Boston thought, running his mop over the dark streaks of wet street dust trailed in by the three dozen or so bodies that had trickled through the doors since he had checked on his sister. The rain made people stay away, which was good, but it also meant that the few who did arrive were the really focused ones, which was bad. There were about twenty of them in all, spaced regularly across the far end of the hall. Funny, that: how they found their own pattern when there were ports to spare. Never grouping together, never punctuated by anomalous spaces, but always a regular distance apart, spaced across the wall.

He wasn't the sort of cheerful janitor that whistled while he worked. He'd found that a certain type of temperament tended to regard conspicuous good cheer as both an affront and a challenge, and so he was used to a cavernous, empty quiet by the doors at this time of night. After twelve hours of continuous auditory assault, it was almost a pleasure to sink into a kind of dissociative fug and let muscle memory take over while his brain checked out. The entry locks were set to one-way, the important-people-in-training were either at home now or else drowning in quiet desperation in their own personal corner of hell, and Boston was far enough from the last of the hangers-on that he was generally left in peace and to his own devices. So the sound of his name, cutting through the silence in a way that had never happened before, was enough to make him start so severely that he jolted the bucket, which sent a tidal wave of brackish water careening over the lip and onto the floor. Boston swore, and looked up in search of the sound.

It had come from outside, so he followed it to the first doorway, reasoning that the sort of person who would return to beat seven kinds of shit out of him for not being able to help with their enquiry wouldn't be calling him by name. His badge said *Turrow*; the voice had called *Boston*. It had sounded like Alex.

It was.

His brother was standing on the top step of the portico, face pressed against the darkened glass, hair plastered to his head and slick with rainwater. 'Let me in?' he suggested.

The trouble with that, of course, was that there were at least six other shadowed figures on the street behind him, loitering with focused nonchalance, whose collective gaze had unmistakably turned to the question of whether or not the door was going to open. On the other hand, it had been nearly thirty-five minutes since Boston had been back to his bolt-hole, and a lot of things could change in that kind of time. He slid back the lock back and let the hordes tumble through.

'Stop. Alex,' he said, as his brother paused in the doorway to shake a week's worth of city water out of his coat. 'Wipe your feet, at least. Jesus.'

A pointed glance at the seven sodden figures trailing a smear of street and downpour across the faux marble tiles took care of his brother's objections to niceties. 'Is she ready to go?' he said. 'I'm starving.'

'Out back,' said Boston. 'I'll let you through.'

Alex's shift had finished more than three hours earlier. If the first thing he said when he set foot inside the hall wasn't, '*I found the meds*', then he hadn't found the meds. But there was no harm in checking, just to be sure. 'Did you find the meds?' asked Boston, as his brother dripped his way across his clean white floor.

Alex shook his head. 'Nothing,' he said. Corrected himself: 'No, not nothing. That guy on Flass thought he might have a lead, but it's in fucking Fiore. Maybe if we go together, see if Aaron and his brother are up for making up a four … but I don't know, Boston. Even then …'

'You're not going to Fiore,' said Boston evenly, swiping his wrist chip across the scanner by the service door. 'Give me the address. I'll go when I get off here.'

'Yeah.' Alex huffed a humourless laugh. 'You head over to Fiore on your own; that's a great idea. I'll tell the undertaker to put Captain Fucking Sensible on the casket, will I?'

'Hey,' said Cassie as the door slid open onto the corridor beyond, 'how come he gets to say 'fuck' and I don't?'

'He's not thirteen years old,' said Boston automatically, but there was no authority to his voice, and no conviction. He was just too damn pleased to find her still standing.

★

The entrance to the Authority was closed and locked when she arrived, which came as a blow, but there was a crowd huddled into the shelter of the portico that looked like it knew what it was doing, so Danae found a spot as far out of the rain as she could squeeze herself without violating the laws of matter, and tried to exude an air of casual familiarity while she waited to see what would happen next. The colonnaded roof was more of a gentle suggestion than an active barrier against the rain, and the slow passage of traffic on the road beyond whipped the street-wash into a stinging mist that saturated her coat and hair and sucked the heat from every pore. But light spilled through the glass panes of the doors, broken now and then by the passage of shadows, and there was an attitude of expectation to her companions in idling that Danae was inclined to trust. They looked as though they knew what they were doing, and, in any case, she was here now, and she was already as wet as it was possible to be. It wasn't like she could get any *more* drenched by waiting a few minutes.

The man who opened the door was young, maybe a few years older than Danae, though his eyes were old, and he wore his exhaustion like a cloak around his sloped shoulders. He looked like he was planning to close the doors again soon, though, so she slipped past him while he was still talking to the younger man, the one who'd got got him to open up, and drizzled her way across the hall to the regulation ports before they could fill up with her associates from the street outside.

Greyish-brown street water streamed out behind her as she crossed the bright white tiles, and she cast a penitent glance back towards the man with the mop, but he wasn't looking at her. He was talking to the younger man, heads close together, deep in conversation as they walked. She wasn't sure he'd even noticed her, and, though she'd cheerfully have killed the man, woman or child who'd tracked dirt and rainwater across Intimacy at closing time, hers certainly weren't the only wet feet smearing the lobby right now.

Danae let it go. She had bigger things to worry about than somebody else's clean floor.

★

Alex and Cassie left amidst a cloud of thirteen-year-old profanity that might have turned the air around them blue, had it not already been so comprehensively filled with water. Boston watched them to the end of the street, where a clip around the head from his brother testified to an ill-advised effort to exert some manner of fraternal authority, and led to a fresh stream of invective that carried all the way back to the stoop where he stood. Well. While she was swearing, she wasn't fitting, and that was something at least.

Alex had given up the address only on the condition that Boston wouldn't take it upon himself to check it out alone, but he had to have known. Had to have. It wasn't like they had any other options, and one of the patches was on red.

He stopped for a moment, leaned on his brush, surveyed the wreckage of his clean, shiny floor and the bodies that were about to trample through it on their way out of his clean, shiny doors. Maybe two thirds were family groups, and two of those were losing steam now; he could hear it in the dull, distorted speech-sounds that bounced off the high walls and disappeared into shadow and air. A quiet word would shift them, and then, once they were gone, the ones and twos would trail after them: they never stayed long once the groups started to leave. One final glance at the clock, and Boston darkened the door glass and drifted down towards the regulation ports with what he always hoped was an air of easy authority.

'Closing time, folks,' he said neutrally. 'Finish up. Doors are closing in ten minutes.'

Three of the families broke away without comment. He wondered what it was like to be so utterly lacking in hope that they couldn't even muster the will to fight anymore. One had small children, one elderly parents. How long, he wondered, did a person have to struggle to get so beaten? He liked the quiet ones, but their dead-eyed stare unnerved him.

He moved along the port wall. 'Finish up, please,' he said again.

'Yeah, in a minute,' snapped one man, thirty-something, neatly groomed, well-dressed. That was a long way to fall when the Housing Authority slapped on an eviction notice. Boston fingered the handle of the switchblade he kept in his pocket just in case.

'Ten minutes,' he said. 'Okay, folks, finish up, please. Closing time.'

At the furthest port, a blond-haired woman – maybe early twenties – was hunched over the screen, talking quietly with poorly leashed fury. He could have told her to save her breath, but no-one listened to him.

★

'Closing time,' said the man again. 'Come on, folks, let's move it on out.'

Danae carried on ignoring him. He'd be at her port soon enough, and then she could ignore him to his face.

'No, no, wait a minute,' she said. 'I've been calling for *three days*. I'm about to lose my job. The least someone can do is come down and talk to me.'

Were the regulation ports artificial? Or was there some harassed organic perched in a remote room, paying no attention to what she was saying and wondering what it would take to get her off the line?

'Locking up in ten minutes, folks.'

'It's not that we're not sympathetic, Ms Grant, it's just that there are protocols to be followed in these cases. The Housing Authority can't classify you as homeless until the eviction has actually been carried out …'

'Wait, wait,' said Danae. 'So what are you saying? That I have to actually be kicked out before I can go on a housing list? How long is that going to take?'

'Well, it's true there's a waiting list for re-housing. However, in line with new government guidelines, we're reviewing our core efficiencies, and we hope that – '

'Are there any houses?' snapped Danae. 'Just tell me that: are there any houses for me to live in?'

' – As I said, there's a waiting list – '

'And how long is the waiting list?'

' – And once we've carried out an assessment, you'll be contacted in due course – '

'In due course?'

'Ms, time to move out.'

'Wait a minute - due course? What's that? A year? Two years? The rest of my natural life?'

'I don't think there's anything to be gained by getting hysterical – '

'No, I actually think I'll get hysterical!' she shouted. 'I have eleven days left on an eviction notice and nowhere, *nowhere* to go, and so what the hell am I supposed to do now apart from get hysterical?'

'Miss, time to finish up.'

'In a minute!' she shouted.

'The Housing Authority will be closing in five minutes,' said her screen.

'Hey, wait!' she shouted. 'I'm not finished. I'm not finished!'

But she was talking to dead air. In frustration, she slapped the palm of her hand against the retinal pad, but all that achieved was the activation of an opaque, protective casing that emerged from the wall to cover the port. Now her call was twice as over, and she had a sore hand to add to the day's excitement.

'I'm not finished!' she said again, but more softly now. Her head dropped to rest against the wall, her eyes closed. 'I'm not bloody finished ...'

Calm.

Calm ...

When she could trust herself to look up again, she saw that she was alone in the hall except for the janitor, who was looking at her with barely concealed impatience. It wasn't his fault, she supposed; she guessed he put up with plenty like her. She imagined she'd be wearing the same expression, in his shoes.

'In a minute,' she said quietly. She turned so that she was facing outwards, leaned her back against the wall, slid downwards to the floor. 'Just give me a minute.'

'The ports are closed,' he said.

'I saw that.'

'So ... time to leave.'

She closed her eyes, bit her lip. Shook her head. 'No. I don't think so.'

'I'm locking up.'

'Yeah, you said.'

'Lady, I have a home to go to even if you don't, okay? Move.'

Danae opened her eyes, fixed them on his face. His skin was grey, slack with fatigue; he looked like he needed to sleep for a week. She knew the feeling.

'Mister,' she said. 'My dad died last week, and when I got home from burying him on Monday evening, someone had landed me with an eviction. And I don't have anywhere else to be right now, so I'm staying put until someone sorts me out with somewhere to live.' She reached into the pocket of her coat, withdrew a cigarette and cupped her hands around it to light it. 'I'll squat in a sewer if they want, but I'm *not* going on the streets.'

'You can't smoke in here,' he told her.

'Yeah, well,' she said. 'They're not my cigarettes.'

She sucked in a long draw, picked a fleck of tobacco from her tongue. His head flicked towards the door, back to her.

'I'll call the police,' he said.

'Yeah, okay, that would do.' The cigarette flared, ash curling from the tip as she inhaled. 'Maybe I could smash up my cell and do some real time. Maybe by the time I got out my name would have made it to the top of the waiting list.'

Hesitation, and then he dropped down into a crouch in front of her. His hands were chapped, she saw, as he rested them on his knees: strong, square, blunt. Workman's hands.

He said, 'Do I know you from somewhere?'

Danae had been wondering the same thing herself. But she shrugged. 'Maybe. I'm not sure.'

'I feel like I know your face.'

She took another long draw of her cigarette, eyes locked on his. He sighed.

'Look. You can't stay here,' he said. 'When I lock up, the cleaning cycle's going to start. That's scalding water.'

Her eyes dropped to his chest, to the badge above his heart. '*Turrow*,' she read. Back to his face: 'You have a home to go to, Turrow.'

'Yes. I do.'

'And a family.'

'Yes.'

'Well, I have nobody. Nobody.' She pressed the balls of her hands into her eyes. 'And I don't know what to do.'

5.3

'Coffee.'

Her head flicked up, as though the word had startled her out of a trance, but she reached out and took the cup from him, silently, with a blank-faced nod of thanks. She'd curled herself into one of the two chairs that comprised the entirety of the furniture in Boston's bolthole, shoulders hunched, one arm wrapped around her ribs as she hugged the cup to her chest. Her face, dropped towards the floor, was shrouded by shadow. Boston had given her his coat to wrap around her, and it seemed to shrink her as she burrowed deeply inside, choking off a shiver with the determination of a woman who wasn't used to being vulnerable.

He'd left the door open onto the dark corridor outside. She didn't seem like a woman that took kindly to having nowhere to run. Nor was he certain, when it came right down to it, that she was the sort of woman with whom he wanted to be shut into a tiny room.

He had no idea what he was doing. He had no idea why he'd asked her back here, no idea why she'd accepted. She was small, slightly built, fragile, a woman who looked like she'd blow away in a stiff breeze, but she wore a cloud of hostility around her like a wall of broken glass and razor wire. Only her eyes betrayed her: dark, hooded, and ever so slightly broken, and he wondered if that was what he'd recognised in her. Boston knew that look.

She raised the mug to her lips, sipped carefully, glanced up at him. 'Good coffee,' she said. 'Thanks.'

Boston lowered himself into the spare seat, wrapped his hands around his mug. 'You want sugar? There's sugar if you want it.'

'No. Thanks,' she said. 'I'm good.' A beat. 'I'm sorry; I'm keeping you back. You have places you need to be.'

He shrugged. 'Not yet. I'm killing time until nine thirty anyway.'

'What's at nine thirty?'

'The place I need to be.'

The woman dropped her eyes and, unexpectedly, a smile washed the shadows from her face. 'Touché,' she said. 'Just tell me to mind my own business.'

'Does that ever work?'

A soft laugh. 'You tell me. I guess that was your sister, before?'

Boston felt a grin tug at the edge of his lips. 'So, that'd be a no, then? Yeah, she's my sister. I didn't know you'd seen her.'

'I didn't know there was a door there until you brought her out,' she said, as though that explained everything. He'd thought she was preoccupied with the regulation ports; tried to remember if he'd said anything he'd rather nobody overheard. 'She looks like you.'

'She does?'

'Your face structure.' A narrow hand gestured vaguely at her own. 'It's the same.'

'No one ever thought we looked alike before.'

A shrug. 'Does she work here?'

'Cassie? She's thirteen.'

'I got my first job when I was twelve.'

He didn't doubt that. She had the air of a woman who preferred to be beholden to nobody. 'No,' said Boston. 'She doesn't work here. It's … kind of complicated.'

'Hey, who am I going to tell?' She glanced up, met his eyes, half-smiled. 'I'm just some crazy lady that wouldn't leave at kick-out time.'

'True,' he said, and grinned. 'But that's not why it's complicated.'

'Fair enough.' Another shrug. 'Not my business.'

That was certainly true, but she hadn't meant it the last time she said it either. Besides, it wasn't polite to agree. So, instead he changed the subject: 'You're not from the lower city.'

'Bloody accent,' she said. 'I can't seem to lose it.'

'Why would you want to?'

'That,' she said, 'is also complicated.'

'You've been here a while?'

'Nearly nineteen years.'

'Ever go back?'

'No chance,' she said, and laughed, but there was no humour in it. 'We used to go for daytrips to Châteauroux when I was a kid; that's about it.'

'Would you believe,' he said, 'that I've never been outside the city walls?'

An eyebrow arched. 'Never?'

'Nope. Never wanted to. Probably the only person in Creo Basse, but there you go. It's home.'

'It's certainly something,' she said.

'Hey,' he pointed out, 'you're the one staging a sit-down protest at the Housing Authority.'

Her fingers flexed against the mug, straightening and closing, as though they were stiff. 'Yeah,' she said. 'Sorry about that. I bet you get it all the time.'

'Normally, I just get punched,' he said. 'At least you didn't punch me.'

She smiled, and it seemed like it reached her eyes. But she turned it on her coffee.

'I'm Danae,' she said. 'Grant. Danae Grant.'

'Boston Turrow,' he said.

'Thanks for the coffee, Boston Turrow.'

'No problem,' he said. 'I always make coffee for people who don't punch me.'

She smiled again, this time let it linger on him. Again, tracing his face as though the contours were a key. He couldn't place her.

She said, 'You smoke?'

'No.'

'Me neither,' she said. 'I found these in my dad's stuff – when I was going through it.'

'I'm sorry for your loss,' he said, and realised how trite it sounded, how vapid. He tried again: 'You must miss him a lot.'

Inexplicably, she barked a laugh that was only fifty per cent amusement. 'Yeah,' she said, gently. 'Yeah, I miss him.'

She lit another cigarette, blowing the smoke upwards, away from him. He watched it curl towards the ceiling and hang there. He said, softly, 'There must be somewhere you can go.'

She didn't answer, but tilted her head to the ceiling and he saw the light change on her eyes as they filled with water. Her lower lip depressed. And then it was gone.

'Yeah. Probably,' she said. 'There's always somewhere.'

'How old are you?' he asked suddenly.

She turned her eyes on him. 'Are you serious?'

He grinned at the smile that was hiding behind her affronted tone. 'Yeah, I'm serious.'

'I thought a gentleman never asked a lady her age.'

'I thought a lady didn't punch out the regulation ports,' he said.

She sputtered laughter. 'You're lucky your coffee is good, Turrow. I'm twenty-four.'

'Not school, then.'

'What's not school?'

'I want to know where I know you from.'

'Oh.' She smoked, impassive. 'Hardly.'

'Huh.'

The silence lengthened. He sipped. Then she said, 'How can you *never* want to see the outside?'

A grin split his face. 'I *knew* that had to piss you off!'

'But – *never*?'

'What's to see? Water and dust and a couple of scruffy trees. I'll take Creo, thanks.'

She said, 'I had a place to live on the outside.'

Softly, he sidestepped. 'You think it's still there?'

She shook her head. 'Not anymore.'

'What was it like?'

'What, my house?' She glanced up and he saw that her eyes were gleaming with remembered belonging. It lit up her face, as though a minor sun shone out from behind her cheeks.

'Yes, your house,' he said, carelessly, provocatively, wanting the light to stay.

She grinned, hugely. 'Big,' she said. 'Great big thing, fields all around it.' She shifted, animated, sitting a little taller in her chair. 'It was blue, like this really light, pale blue, on the outside. And it had this big, massive kitchen out the back, and my bedroom used to be just off of it, just out the back of the house. And I remember I used to stand at the bottom of the bed and look out the window, and you could see all the way down to the lake and it used to shine when the moon was out. It was like a big plate of silver. God, I used to love it when they'd let me out and I could run down to it. It was down this big steep slope, and the wind would kind of bounce my hair and you'd almost feel like you were flying ...'

She trailed off, and he realised that he'd been watching her when he found her eyes on his: steady, amused. He returned her grin; he couldn't help it. Her smile was magnetic: it radiated warmth and smoothed her brittle lines and cold, sharp edges. He wondered if he'd been staring at her the whole time, and if she'd noticed.

'Nah,' he said, 'sounds rubbish.'

She exploded into disbelieving laughter and he joined her easily. 'Give me Creo any day,' he said. 'You know where you are in Creo.'

'Bullshit!'

'You know how far away the sky is.'

'That,' she conceded, 'is true.' A beat. 'You're scared of an infinite sky, then, Turrow?'

'Scared? No.'

'Sounds like you're scared to me.'

'Of infinity?'

She considered. 'It doesn't feel like infinity when you're there.'

'How can it not feel like infinity?'

She shrugged. 'Now that,' she said, 'is why you need to leave the city. I can't help you there. It just doesn't.'

A tiny, certifiable, utterly unfamiliar part of him wanted to say, *Okay – show me. Show me your sky.* But his habitual self was too ingrained. Before the words would come out, the moment was gone: the fire behind her cheeks had faded, and she was back in the lower city. Damp, cold, and alone, sitting on a stranger's floor with a cup of coffee and her dead father's stale cigarette.

So instead he said, 'Danae Grant. *Where* do I know you from?'

She barked her fifty per cent laugh. She said, 'I'm the crazy homeless lady that tried to punch out the regulation port, remember?'

'Oh, *her*,' he said. 'The one I had to give my best cup of coffee to.'

'This is your *best* cup?'

'Turrow's finest.'

'That's tragic,' she said. 'Didn't your mother teach you better?'

It was the wrong thing to say, and she saw it as soon as it struck his smile, though he buried it quickly. That tiny moment, that flash of something unknown, sank like weighted concrete between them, and she dropped her eyes to the floor. He felt the shift and knew that she'd seen.

A beat. And then they both spoke together:

'I should probably ...'

'Maybe there's something I can ...'

But her eyes darted quickly back up to his face, and something –– not quite hope, but close –– flashed behind them and died quickly. And he realised that he'd said the words just to say them, to try and make it better, and now they were out and there was nothing to be done.

There was nothing for it but to take them back, and kill whatever that flash was.

He said, 'But there's somewhere ... you said there was maybe somewhere you could go.'

And it was gone. Whatever had been hovering in the room was gone, like a flip of a light switch.

'Yeah,' she said briskly, too briskly. The atmosphere shifted another notch to the right. 'I owe you a coffee,' she said, raising her mug, but not her eyes, to him.

'All part of the service we offer,' he said quietly, and he knew she was leaving.

Still she didn't look at him.

'You need to get moving,' she said presently. 'It's nine-twenty.'

'Finish your coffee. I can wait.'

'I'm finished.' She scrubbed her hand across her cheeks, obliterating, for a second, the lines of worry that crowded her eyes. She took a deep breath, which drained her face of energy, and she said, 'It's okay, you need me to go. You've got places to be.'

There was nothing to say to that. 'I'll walk you out,' he said.

5.4

The front doors were locked, darkened and shielded, but there was a staff entrance at the back that opened onto a quiet side street. Danae paused at the door, unwilling to step out of the shelter of the stone canopy and into the rain, and tossed the end of her cigarette onto the saturated road, into the burgeoning tide of waterlogged street debris.

'I swear, this city has rained for five days straight,' she said.

'You have far to go?' he asked.

'Limbe,' she said. 'You?'

'Fiore.'

'Fiore?' She slid her eyes sideways, expecting levity, but his expression was neutral. 'You don't look like a Fiore kind of guy.'

He grinned. 'No? What does a Fiore kind of guy look like?'

'Usually, there's more knives. And scars. And not so many limbs. Seriously — you live in Fiore?'

'I live in Chatelier,' he said. 'I just have some stuff I need to do in Fiore North.'

'At this time of night?'

'You know Fiore. Doesn't come alive until ten. Come on, I'll walk you to the subway.'

The last time Danae took the subway, she was nine years old and at her father's side as Walter, never exactly a bastion of moral guardianship, took it upon himself to teach her how to ride the subway for free. It had been a rare moment of quiet understanding for them, a chance to shine in her father's eyes, to show him what she could do. '*You did good, pet*', he'd said when she slipped through the barriers, cheeks flushed and eyes gleaming, and he'd scuffed her hair with one hand, guided her off into the throng. Annelise went ballistic when she found out, of course, and it became a Thing, and they'd always walked after that, because three tokens were three tokens and she had a perfectly good set of legs to carry her.

But it didn't seem like the sort of story you told to someone you'd met twenty minutes earlier. 'Okay, sure,' she said. 'It's not like the rain's stopping any time soon, anyway.'

She'd given him back his coat, though he'd tried to refuse, and, as they stepped out of the shelter of the Authority's louring shadow, as she pulled her collar tight around her neck and squinted her eyes against the sudden wash of rainfall on her face, she caught him shooting a furtive glance in her direction, as though he were worried that she might short-circuit or start to dissolve. Danae shrugged.

'Can't get any wetter,' she said. 'One of us might as well stay dry.'

Cilicia emptied after business hours but, here and there, gated residential estates broke up the industrious grey brick precipices and spread viral clusters of shops and restaurants into the streets around them. Danae set the pace as they made their way down the backstreet towards the main thoroughfare, moving at a rapid walk that was almost a run, but she could see, through the dark alleys that bisected the buildings across the road, that they were on the edge of a pocket of bustling light and life. The subway was on Thirty-Sixth Avenue and Turnpike, close to the southwest border with Fiore; an easy fifteen minute walk by day, but by evening, as the roads filled up with the dinner crowds and the rain slowed traffic to a crawl, it was like moving through silt.

It'd be quicker to walk; to take the empty Thirty-Sixth Street North up to Kim Li and hit the Turnpike through to the northeast gate with Limbe. By the time she'd wasted the price of a day's water fare on a forty-five minute trolley ride through six districts, with changes at two, she could be wrapped in a towelling robe and warming her hands around a cup of hot milk in the silence of her apartment. She was getting up for work again in ten hours; her evenings were precious. And so there was no good reason to turn right instead of left at the end of the street and let a man she barely knew lead the way into the colourful throngs of Cilician nightlife, no good reason at all. But she did it anyway.

'You meeting someone in Fiore?' she asked, as they stepped out onto a gridlocked roadful of cars to a chorus of affronted horns and yells. He didn't move like a man used to the festivities, and that made sense: Chatelier was the opposite direction.

Turrow shrugged. 'There's a guy I know on the Avenue.'

'Wow.' She sidestepped a tumbling current of street water as it rushed along a hidden channel beneath the kerb. 'Nice part of town.'

'It's kind of a business trip.'

She'd guessed that much. One didn't visit the Avenue for its ambience or its collection of artisanal breweries. 'Hell of a night for a trip like that,' she said.

A brace of pedestrians barrelled past, headed by a matronly woman carrying tiny, yipping dog in the cradle of her arms, and they moved back into the overhang of a covered doorway to let them go by. Turrow grinned, and said, 'Yeah, but if we all waited for the rain to go off, this city'd grind to a halt.' He stood back to let her step out onto the street again. 'It's not so far. Half an hour's walk, tops.'

Thirty-Sixth and Parkway were linked by regular alleyways, narrow canyons between soaring walls of rain-washed concrete, across which a legion of local entrepreneurs had hung brightly coloured cloths and rugs as a kind of makeshift mall. Cilicia proper might close at six, but that just funnelled the crowds into a series of hyper-kinetic bottlenecks where the action was, and Parkway, curving along the length of the border walls with Kolasi and Fiore, was its western nerve centre. Elbows jostled them as they pressed through the multitudes: traders, patrons, families, workers trying to get home; a restless tail of wet, uncomfortable bodies massing and shuffling in every direction as Danae folded herself into a point and scrambled through the wall of people towards the street beyond. A glance back over her shoulder placed Turrow a few paces behind her, and he caught her look, grinned, rolled his eyes. Definitely not a Fiore kind of guy, and she knew he knew what she'd meant. He didn't belong on the Avenue, and the Avenue wasn't a place to be if you didn't belong.

Parkway was the sort of street that came into its own after dark, when the street-side tapas bars lit up their artificial candles and piped music hung on the air, tangling together in the no-man's land between eateries, where heavily-moustachioed men stood in the street to banter with prospective diners. This was the eating street, and it was time to eat: most of the crowd clung close to the shop-fronts, reading menus, bartering with maître d's, waiting for one of the wall-ferries that shuddered up the faces of buildings, carrying diners to the high-level eateries where balconies spewed plastic tendrils from cast-iron railings. Danae made for the roadside, where the going was easier, and Turrow fell into step alongside her as she dodged a parking car that disgorged a swarm of oblivious passengers, talking animatedly in a language she didn't understand.

She said, above the howl of a lone guitar that blasted from a shop-front, startling a flock of birds off a nearby canopy, 'You don't seem like the kind of guy who has business on the Avenue.'

'Thanks,' he said. 'I think.'

'I'm just saying, Turrow.' What? That he had kind eyes, the sort of face that made a person want to trust him? That he was a man who'd make coffee for a stranger with a sad story, who'd wrap her in his coat because she looked cold? That these things, as best she could figure, were the reason she was here, now, instead of hiding from the rain on her way back to a life she'd spent twenty years creating, but that they were the sort of things that painted a target on a person's forehead on the streets of Fiore North? 'Maybe you might want to think about doing this another time.'

But Turrow shrugged. 'Now's good,' he said, and, when she chanced a glance sideways at him, she saw that his smile was gone.

There was a steady stream of bodies massing towards the subway's northbound exit, flanked by a billow of hot air that geysered up from the platform below. A screech of metal, sharp enough to cut through the white noise and chaos of the street, signalled the arrival of a trolley, and the crowd surged forwards, buffeting Danae as she sought the temporary shelter of a rain shield erected above a nearby troupe of musicians competing for money from the apathetic take-out crowd. The trumpeter caught her eye and glanced meaningfully at a coin-filled hat on the pavement at his feet, but she ignored him, turned to Turrow instead.

'I'm just saying,' she said again. 'There's only one reason a guy like you has business on the Avenue.'

'A guy like me?' he said, and he was trying to smile, but rainwater was running from his hair into his eyes; he had to keep blinking it away. 'We just met. How do you know what kind of guy I am?'

Because she knew his face. 'Somebody's sick,' she said. 'Right?' The trumpeter was firing little dagger-loaded looks in her direction between phrases, edging her towards the perimeter of the shield. 'Believe me, Turrow — I know a few things about the stuff you buy in Fiore North.'

A beat. He stared at the ground. 'Your dad?' he said.

'Yeah,' said Danae. 'Your sister?'

'Yeah.'

'She seemed okay.'

'She's not.'

There was probably some way to answer that, but she didn't know what it was. 'Okay, then,' she said. 'I guess you've got to go.'

It sounded lonelier spoken out loud. Turrow combed a hand through his hair, scattering a mist of drizzle, and nodded without looking up. 'Yeah,' he said. 'I guess so.'

'Well. Thanks for the coffee.'

'Any time.' A hesitant half-smile played at one corner of his mouth. 'Seriously,' he said, 'Any time. I'm at the Authority every day. You keep not punching me, maybe I even throw in milk and sugar next time.'

The words were casual; the smile was not. It would be so easy to answer with a grin, to say, *Hey, unless someone found me a place to live in the last half hour, count on seeing me again tomorrow,* see what happened, see what he said next and take it from there. Danae wondered what it would be like to be that person. She wondered what it would be like to be the sort of person for whom these things were possible.

But she wasn't. She was closed in a way that needed to stay closed, and his life, as it turned out, was complicated enough already. So she said, 'Yeah. Okay, thanks,' and watched the half-smile fall away.

To her left, the subway entrance opened onto a subterranean world of light and humid heat; a crush of damp bodies and steam. To her right, the south-western arc of the Thirty-Sixth Turnpike disappeared into the border wall with Fiore North in an embolism of traffic and fraying tempers. Opposite directions. Danae pulled her collar up tight against her throat, offered an awkward nod to Turrow, and stepped out of the shield.

'Hey,' he called as she moved into the crowd, and she turned back over one shoulder to see that he'd raised a hand in send-off. 'Don't give up, okay?'

'You too,' she said, and turned her head away, kept walking.

It would have been easier, she thought, if the street had been empty; if there'd been no human tide to buffet and fight her every step; if she could have just dissolved into shadows in the knowledge that, if she were to turn her head, she'd find him gone, disappeared back into a world of sisters and care, to write over a half hour in the company of a stranger whose face he thought he knew. Maybe it would be better if there was something more interesting than the great faceless hulks of building that towered above her on either side to distract her from the sense of inertia; the sense of a stasis; the sense of a life lived entirely on *what if*.

It would certainly be better if she hadn't found herself pulled up short at the entrance to the subway, pushed back and to the side by a surge of discharging commuters, and caught sight of his head in the gateway crowd as he waited to pass into the bowels of a district where he didn't belong, where a gentle face and a predisposition towards kindness could knock years off a person's life. Fiore, of all the godforsaken holes in the ground. One of a handful of places in all the world that could make Limbe look upmarket. And, because he was a good man, a decent man, with a sister that needed help, he kept his head bowed against the blistering rain and pushed his way through the pedestrian turnstiles, because on the other side of that wall he thought he could find the help that she needed, even though he knew, and she knew that he knew, that he was just one man, a decent man, stepping into an ocean of danger.

The subway steps had cleared of their outgoing traffic, and the hordes pressed forward again, like water rushing towards a drain. Danae stepped back, out of the flow, and watched him disappear into the shadows of the Twenty-eighth district: quickly, decisively, without looking back. Elbows jostled her, bodies slammed her from all directions, complaints were offered and ignored. Danae stood, immobile and immovable, in the path of late evening multitudes, and watched the space where he had been.

'Shit,' she said at last.

5.5

The air was different here, Boston thought. It smelled, if such a thing were possible, of thwarted hope. And danger, of course. Mostly of danger. The backstreets of Fiore were so erratic and nasty that even the gangs refused to patrol some of them. But it was possible to walk the streets in safety; the trick was to look as though you were meant to be there.

People rarely made eye contact in Fiore. Dark-eyed women with babies fastened to their chests by threadbare scarves walked, heads down, past sharp-featured men who were trying to look rugged. It was impossible to tell by sight who was in charge: Boston had seen men built like a nightmare step hurriedly out of the path of a guy who could not comfortably unscrew a jam jar. People who belonged in Fiore just knew. He had seen the jam-jar men leap out of the way of some of the dark-eyed women once before, and one of the men, who didn't move fast enough, took a blow to the head that knocked him off his feet. The safest thing was to defer to everybody.

One thing you definitely didn't do, though, once you were off the main thoroughfares, was move at anything approaching speed. Set a pace beyond a gentle stroll, and somebody might think you were running, which was not a good thing for somebody to think: if you were running, you were either running at or running from, and neither one of those things boded well for your long-term future prospects. What that meant, in real terms, was that, if it happened to be the case that the rain in Fiore fell like bullets, drumming a tattoo on your head that was one pointy edge away from open brain surgery; if your coat was carrying half your body weight again in water and the skin beneath your sodden clothes felt as though the heat were being scraped off the surface with a pallet knife with every single step; if you'd just worked almost thirteen hours straight after your third sleepless night this week and all you wanted to do was go home, fall facedown onto the sofa, and pass out for a couple of days; allowing any of this to show on your face or in your stride was not only out of the question, it was too dangerous even to consider. And it meant that, no matter what, no matter how many hidden senses screamed *watchers* and internal violence monitors sounded blaring klaxons inside the privacy of your head when you turned the deserted corner on Twenty-Eighth Street North and Avenue, you did not pick up your pace. And you definitely did not turn back to look.

This part of the district had once been a trade centre for Creo Basse, but in years gone by it had fallen into disuse. Commerce steered clear of Fiore North. Everything steered clear of Fiore North. The *weather* steered clear of Fiore North, apart from the rain. Under the shadow of the district wall, Twenty-Eighth Avenue snaked its desolate trail across a perimeter of deserted warehouses, waiting to crumble into the street, and elderly hangars that reached into the gloom with scrubby, windowless walls, on which light-bands flaked and crumbled into erratic patches, punctuating the darkness like spreading stars. Away from the noise and thunder of the district's arterial routes, the roads were unnervingly quiet, and only the steady stream of rain on concrete kept the silence at bay.

The street stretched out ahead of him, disappearing into the shifting shadows, feeding into a network of alleyways. From somewhere in the darkness ahead, unseen figures barked sudden laughter that skittered up the high walls, bounced back in watery echoes. The rain was easing now, but that didn't mean much, beyond the fact that he was getting wetter less quickly. Boston pushed down hard on the unease that prickled in his stomach, made himself walk forwards on steady legs, spine straight, face blank. The address Alex had given him was about a mile to the south of the gate, close to the border wall with Parnasse; he'd be surprised if he'd covered a quarter of the distance yet, and wondered, for the first time, if he might have been better to stick to the main road a while longer, cut down a side street when he thought the house numbers might have reached the high thousands.

Too late now, at least for a while. The alleys that linked the Avenue back to the Turnpike were narrow, dark and labyrinthine along this stretch of the route; his hackles rose even as he turned his head to check. And that small action — innocuous, almost coincidental — was almost certainly a mistake, he realised, as he felt unseen eyes zero in on his back; felt them watching, biding time, waiting to see what he'd do next.

He'd known, even before Alex had turned up this evening, damp and dispirited, that one of them was going to have to go to the Avenue. It'd been too long without a lead, which meant that the market had run dry again, which meant, usually, that the folks on the Avenue had found a way to dam the stream. Never let it be said that the folks of Creo Basse were without enterprise or ambition. There were parts of the lower city where crumbling tenement walls hid luxury of such staggering excess as to rival the courts of the Ptolemies, and that didn't come from shady black-market meds deals. The market ran dry from time to time, when it suited certain parties to make it so. It came back eventually. Trouble was, Cassie didn't always have *eventually* to wait.

The last time Boston had gone to the Avenue, Cassie's meds had cost them three times what he paid on the corner of Saville Street, and that was only because two men with faces like a behemoth's bad dream had picked him up and shaken him to make sure he wasn't carrying anything else he could use to trade. The time before that, Gordy had gone in his place and come back with two extra scars and a deficit of one and a half grand that it'd taken them nearly a year to pay back. But she'd been on red that time, too. They were out of options. You didn't go to Fiore North unless you had to.

The glow from the light-bands pooled in watery yellow circles beneath Boston's feet. As the rain eased off, the roar of the silence rushed in to fill the space, and the prickling on the back of his neck stepped up a couple of notches. It was no longer a question of whether someone watched him from the dark side streets — it was a question of how many of them there were, and what they were planning to do. By the edges of the alley mouths, he felt the shadows reaching for him, following him, and he stepped out into the empty road, into streetwater an inch deep that pooled and flowed over his shoes and knocked another few degrees off his core temperature. His danger meter was off the scale.

Alex was waiting for him back at the apartment. Alex knew the address, the name of the man who might or might not have a patch to sell them to keep the wolf from their sister's door for another few weeks. Alex would leave it until midnight, maybe one o'clock, and then he'd find Aaron and Aaron's dad, see if they couldn't rustle up Jean-Paul and Bernard as well, and some of them would come looking, and maybe it'd be enough and maybe it wouldn't, and if Alex didn't make it home either, what happened next? Rita might take Tilly, but she wouldn't take Cassie, because Rita had almost lost her once already, and now there was Caro to think about too. Cassie had maybe three days left before the last traces of meds cleared her system, and Boston was in the back streets of Fiore North with at least two and maybe three unseen figures following him from the darkness.

872 read the plaque above a gaping loading bay door. He needed 1196. And that was the sound of footfall on the street behind him: even, measured, and confident.

It was the confidence that made him stop, steady himself, turn to look.

'It's you,' said Boston, because he had known they were there all along.

They were a-nauts. One of them had a gaping wound bisecting his chest; the other had a heavy, festering bandage across his forehead. And he knew they were looking for blood.

5.6

When Boston was six years old, a pair of swollen hands tried to snatch him from a crowd while his mother walked him home from school one afternoon. After Rita got finished beating their owner half to death with her handbag, she bought him an ice cream and made him cover his eyes when the Rens arrived, so that all he remembered from the aftermath was the sound of a single gunshot and a cheer from the circle of onlookers that had gathered in the corner of the little square. An old man scuffed Boston's hair affectionately, told him he was a lucky boy to have such a sensible mum, and gave Rita a handkerchief to clean the blood off her bag and hands.

Bad men, she told him when he asked, and, since that was her stock response to everything from glass shards scattered on the pavement to bomb scares on Thirty-Fourth Street Central, he didn't question it until much later, when, researching a history project with a girl he was trying to impress, he came across an Op Ed from the earliest days of the Insurgency that read, *Paper Cuts and Grazed Knees: Why Experts Predict It'll All Be Over by Christmas.* That was the first day he began to understand.

Because the problem with a-nauts was that inorganic bones held no marrow, and a fully functional immune system was costly to replicate. A rudimentary blood stream kept genetically modified tissues alive from the inside, but that was about it. With the early, fully synthetic models it was easy: there was no organic matter for a virus to attack, but what made the later series stronger also made them weak.

It was quite simple: they couldn't fight off infection.

They had the basic checks and balances. A nanosynthetic haemolytic compound held off bacteria and the commonest viruses, but it couldn't adapt, couldn't recognise a foreign body. So they were fitted with cytotoxic a-cell virus filters over every mucous membrane, and in a subdermal layer beneath their toughened skin, and, in the normal course of events, that should have been enough. Military units had specialist repair-shops assigned to platoons; domestic units took care not to impale themselves on things or plummet from third storey windows. A complicated warranty covered accidental damage.

The Insurgency changed everything. After the blood-soaked sixth month, the Renegade Elimination Network was given tacit approval to do what it did best, and the a-nauts started to drop. The lucky ones died quickly, taken out by a shot to the head or chest, but the ones who crawled to safety found their systems overloaded with microbes and died in agony over many days.

There was no way to stop it. Immunoglobulin therapy, when they could lay their hands on immunoglobulin, worked best, but it wasn't exactly available over the counter, and, as a wound lay open, it began to fester. Antibiotics were designed to support the immune system, not start it from scratch. Nanocytes did a better job, but they had to be programmed, and you needed a *lot* of them to kill the kind of infection that took hold inside a compromised a-naut system. And so for a long time it looked as though they would peter out ignominiously, drift into history, undone by creatures too small to see with the naked eye.

It was in the ninth month of hostilities that organics started disappearing. It was another three before anyone worked out why.

The thing was, a-nauts couldn't respond to an infection; their bodies didn't even realise they'd been breached. But humans could. Humans were positively swimming with antibodies, and, what was more, their immune systems were adaptable. They were mobile immunity factories, covered with the flimsiest of sheaths, and they were all over the damn place.

And so it became known as blood-farming, or harvesting.

It was far from foolproof; even the complex human system couldn't cope with the really nasty stuff like tetanus or botulinum. But it gave them a fighting chance, and a wounded a-naut was generally happy to concede that the same chance as an organic was better than no chance at all. Humans were raided on the streets, in their cars, at lonely outposts. A broken neck kept the heart beating while the organic immune system was stimulated with a shot of a-naut blood and the swarming t-cells were collected, to be fed intravenously into the dying a-naut. Sometimes it even worked. It was better than nothing.

Organics died, one after another. Hundreds. Thousands. Tens of thousands. And the ones that didn't were the ones that were scared enough to keep one eye constantly turned over their shoulder. That was what Boston understood, ten years after the fact: blood on a handbag, ice cream and a gunshot, and a cheering crowd of onlookers, all symptoms of an ingrained, visceral fear.

It seemed like a reasonable response.

5.7

He raised an eyebrow, tried to look as though they were just one more obstacle on the long path home. 'I don't have any money, guys,' he said.

They said nothing, just fanned out in front of Boston so that he couldn't pass. There were only two of them that he could see, but he thought that he wouldn't get far if he tried to run. He could yell, but would anyone hear? Would they care?

'Maybe you can help me,' he tried. 'I'm looking for 1196.'

The taller one, the one with the head wound, arched an eyebrow, glanced sideways at his friend. If he recognised the address, there was no sign of it in his face.

'Almasad Cavus' place,' said Boston. It was a long shot: if the street number meant nothing, there was no reason to think that they'd care about the name. And even if they did, he didn't look like the kind of guy that Cavus was likely to miss. But it was worth a try. 'Maybe you know it? They're expecting me.'

Nothing: not so much as a disbelieving shake of the head; Boston might as well have saved his breath. The first one, the one with the head wound, took a step forward. Instinctively, Boston stepped back.

'Don't,' he said. 'Please.'

The one with the chest wound was failing. The gash was maybe two days old already, Boston guessed, and it stank of rotting flesh. He stared levelly at Boston, eyes narrowing into points as he peered at him, blinked, shook his head. The reek from the bandage shifted in the air.

'You need to come with us,' he said.

If Chest Wound had been on his own, he would be absolutely wrong about that, but there were two of them and one of Boston, and Head Wound's eyes were still sharp. Boston might outrun his friend, but Head Wound would catch him in three blocks, and by then he'd probably have a half dozen groupies on his tail, eager to see what the fuss was about. You didn't run in Fiore North, and, if you did, you didn't run far.

'You know what they sell at 1196,' Boston tried again. 'You know my blood's no good.'

It was a lie with virtually no chance of success. Head Wound acted like he hadn't heard.

'I can shoot you in the leg,' he said. 'Or the arm. You won't die for days. You should do this the easy way.'

Boston's brain was working on overtime. If he followed the two of them into the alley he was dead, no question about it. But if they shot him, he was helpless, and he was dead anyway. He glanced Chest Wound, who was having trouble standing. Could he take him? Were they both armed or just his friend? How much of Head Wound's wide-shouldered stance was posturing? How much was real strength?

Head Wound raised his gun, levelled it at Boston's face. '*Now*,' he said.

Out of time.

Boston's hand slid into his pocket with what he hoped looked like casual nonchalance, found his knife, gripped the handle. 'Okay,' he said. 'Okay, sure,' and he took a tentative step forwards. Another. Then a third. One three-inch blade against a projectile weapon wasn't much, but it was better than nothing; might even nudge the advantage in his direction, once they were in close quarters. Another step forward, and now they were lowering their guard, thinking he was complying. Boston dropped his eyes, hoping they took it as submission, hoping they couldn't see him tighten his shoulders, readying himself. Another step. The stench from Chest Wound's bandages was overpowering; Boston thought that he couldn't have long to live, with or without a blood-harvest. One more step, and they were level with the alley, directly in front of the men, the narrow space between them humming like the air before a thunderstorm. Boston tensed.

'Go on,' said Head Wound, and he waved his gun towards the shadows, and, in that second of distraction, Boston's body made the decision for him.

He lunged before he knew he was going to do it, slamming his shoulder into Head Wound's sternum with all the force of his downward momentum. The blow caught the other man off guard, but Boston had misjudged: Head Wound moved more quickly than he thought he would, and the impact, which should have carried him to the ground, sent Boston flying into the wall instead. He hit badly, head grazing concrete, and the world flashed white for a second, pain howling at his temple, blood pooling behind his lips where his teeth had connected. Boston crumpled, stunned, and, before he could check his slide towards the ground, rough arms had lifted him by his collar and heaved him to his feet, cutting off his air supply and trailing him deeper into the alley.

Boston lashed out with his hands, punching and slapping at the other man's arms and, but his angle was wrong; there was no force behind the blows. The dim glow from the light bands was receding as the fists at his collar dragged him backwards, and, even as he twisted and struggled for breath, Boston was aware that movement was bad, that movement away from the street was worse, and that wherever they were going was somewhere he didn't want to be. He couldn't see which one of them held him, but he could see that the other man was limping, arms wrapped around his rib cage in a manner that suggested Chest Wound, which made the dragger Head Wound, and that made sense. It also made it less likely that any of Boston's struggling would be effective, but Boston was nothing if not a glass-half-full kind of guy, and one man's limping rear guard was another man's easy target. Head Wound was out of reach, but Chest Wound was within kicking distance, and one sharp jab to the knee toppled him mid-stride with a yell that caused Head Wound to twist in place, seeking out his friend. It wasn't much, but it was enough to buy Boston half a second to find a little purchase against the alley floor, to thrust upwards against the grip at his collar. It was enough to break him loose.

He took off at a run as Head Wound staggered backwards, knocked off centre by the sudden shift in balance. Chest Wound was down, clutching at the wall and struggling for breath, and Boston passed him without a sideways glance, which, in retrospect, was a mistake. He wasn't expecting a hand to reach out, catch at his coat as he went by; he certainly wasn't expecting there to be any strength left in a man who'd been bent double by a blow to the knee, and so he wasn't prepared to correct against the sudden tug of fabric, the snap of gravity as it took hold, dropped him to the ground. Boston twisted as he fell, and it was enough to land him on his shoulder instead of his back, but his face grazed the alley floor, filling his mouth with street slime and sodden garbage dust and he choked, gagged, struggled for breath. Head Wound had righted himself; Chest Wound was already on him, and, though Boston rolled, dodged his first lunge, spitting mouthfuls of black grime, they were both on him before he could get to his feet.

He went down again, face forced into the alley, streetwater flowing freely into his nose as a knee pinned him to the slick ground. Boston struggled, scrabbling at wet concrete, and the pressure at his lower back slid sideways, hands clutching at his hair as Head Wound lost purchase and toppled. His fingers twisted against Boston's scalp, and Boston yelled as his head was yanked sideways, pain clouding out his vision, hands coming up instinctively to punch and slap at Head Wound's wrist as he struggled to right himself.

If they'd pressed their advantage then, if Head Wound had dragged him back down the alley by the hair, there would have been nothing Boston could have done about it, and it would have been over. But it was a poor hold, lacking purchase, and Boston felt it loosening already as Head Wound pitched him forward instead, skidding his face along three inches of alley dirt as he scrambled to his feet. Boston was half a second behind him, but that half a second was enough to knock the advantage back into Head Wound's favour, and he was on Boston before Boston was fully upright, knocking him backwards and into the wall. The force of the impact knocked the breath from Boston's lungs and he sucked at the air, arms flailing in front of him as Head Wound pinned him to the brickwork with an elbow at his throat. The gun was in his hand again, and Boston saw for the first time that he'd been bluffing: it was a volt gun, and if he'd run, he'd have been safe. He was coughing, struggling against the pressure at his throat, the foul taste of alley water in his mouth, trying to make his lips form the words to cry for help, and he knew that, whatever he might have been able to do while they were still out on the street, at this range, gun pressed to his shoulder or his chest, even set to the lowest voltage, he'd be out before he hit the ground, and if he came to — if — he'd be as good as dead already.

Boston's hands were at his throat, but he struck out downwards with his left, knocking the gun off target. Head Wound was trying to find a way to get it under Boston's shirt, wrestling with layers of sodden fabric, and that meant that they were trying to keep him alive for now, and relatively unscathed — nobody was going to risk anybody's clothes going up in flames, even if it would be like trying to set fire to the rain itself; damp cloth was unlikely to burn. It might hold a charge though, and Boston didn't feel particularly inclined to wait until that thought occurred to Head Wound, too, just in case the other man was in an experimental mood. He kicked out blindly in front of him, finding only air, and then air, and then more air — and then skin, soft flesh and bone; not Head Wound's groin, as he'd been hoping, but Head Wound's upper thigh, and with force enough to knock the other man sideways.

The sudden leverage almost threw him off balance, but Boston's hindbrain was in charge now and it knew this situation of old. An ancient, primal response threw all his failing strength into one headlong rush forwards, slamming into Head Wound's shoulder, and they fell together: Head Wound crashing backwards into the rough brickwork of the wall behind and folding in half like a shattered ruler, Boston falling solidly onto him and sliding sideways onto the sodden alley floor. For a long, terrifying moment, his legs did not remember how to work and he lay, helplessly, scrambling at the ground like a freshly-landed fish. And then his brain rebooted, panic firing his muscles, and his hands splayed in the street slime beneath him, struggling for purchase, struggling for the momentum to get himself back on his feet. Hand in front of hand. Nails digging into the mud, fingertips bloodied and broken. Up onto his knees, staggering to his feet, every laboured breath like knives slicing at his throat.

And then a hand on his ankle.

Boston toppled, foot sliding as it went out from under him and adding momentum to his fall so that he struck the ground hard, chin slamming into concrete, hands crushed beneath him. The world flashed black, and when he opened his eyes, he saw that he'd been turned on his back and Head Wound filled his line of sight, blocking out the last of the faint light from the street beyond. Somewhere by the alley mouth, Chest Wound was struggling to his feet, bent double with the effort of drawing breath, but Boston had only half a second to notice before the first punch hit, striking his right cheek bone with force enough to slam his left against the ground. Head Wound was perched awkwardly above him, squatting on slick ground to rain blows from above, but at such close quarters, Boston had no chance of deflecting, no chance of dodging; he could barely block them with both hands, and that left him nothing with which to scramble free. His feet scrambled in the dust-slime, struggling for purchase. Blood trickled freely into his left eye from an open wound on his forehead. He couldn't find leverage, couldn't push himself upright. All he could do was shield his face so that one strike out of every three glanced off, struck his wrist, his elbow, the ground beside his head.

And then there was a dull thud from the direction of the street, a muffled cry and the sound of something falling, and Head Wound was turning, eyes moving instinctively to seek out the source of the noise. Boston didn't think, didn't waste the second it would take to work out to do next, but let his hands move of their own accord, thrusting upwards and forwards so that Head Wound went flying backwards, skidding along the slick alley floor and colliding with a stack of bins set along one side. They toppled under his weight and he rolled with it, backwards, as Boston found his feet, found the knife in his pocket with shaking, bloodied hands, flicked the blade free. Head Wound saw him coming, but he'd landed badly and he couldn't rise. Boston saw his eyes widen, whites crowding out the pupils as panic spiked, as Boston's hand rose, arched, halted at its apex.

He'd been carrying the knife for seven years, since the first time someone had thrown a punch at him that he couldn't counter. It had sat in his pocket for all that time: a comfortable weight, insurance against the situation that he couldn't handle, the assholes, the casually violent. The Bad Men. He'd never used it, not once.

And then there was a hand on his shoulder, and he turned to see a slight blond woman, hair coated in streetwash and plastered across an angry scarlet graze that ran the length of one cheek, pockmarked with algae and bits of brick. Her eyes were black and filled with something he couldn't read, something he didn't completely understand, but just then, in that moment, the things that Boston didn't understand were basically uncountable.

'Leave them,' said Danae urgently. 'It's not worth it. Let's go; let's just go.'

He didn't ask her where she'd come from, why she was there, how she'd found him. Those were questions for another time, and none of the answers were as important as the fact that she was there. 'Okay,' said Boston, but they were already moving, taking off from the alleyway at a sprint across the rain-washed streets of the Avenue.

You didn't run on the streets of Fiore. But, Boston thought, for every rule there was an exception, and when your future prospects unquestionably disappeared a little further into shadow with every second spent *not* running, it seemed like a good time to get flexible.

He ran.

★

At the edge of the Turnpike, she grabbed for his arm, pulling him to a halt mid-stride, and he swung blindly at her, instinct overriding conscious thought. But she was too quick for him, side-stepping his clumsy right hook with humiliating ease, and all she said was, 'Easy. Easy, Turrow — it's just me.'

He was shaking. He hadn't noticed it while they ran, but now, crouched in a side street, head thrown back and chest heaving as he struggled for air, he could feel it in every muscle. And she was shaking too; he could feel it in her fingers, though she pulled her hand back from his elbow as though she'd been stung, wrapped her arms tightly around her chest. It could be the cold; it could be the way rainwater filled her coat and ran out of her hair, trailing a smear of watery blood down her right cheek. And it could be the spreading purple bruise across one eye, the tremble in her voice, and the way she held her wrist as though it ached.

Danae caught his look, shrugged, looked away. 'If we run out onto that street at this time of night, looking like this, we'll have a whole other set of problems,' she said. 'Take a minute, catch your breath. You look like hell.'

He could have said the same to her. 'Are you okay?' he asked. His voice sounded like it belonged to somebody else.

'I'm fine,' she said. 'How about you?'

'Yeah,' said Turrow. 'I'm okay.' It was a little sentence and it wasn't true, but it was the best, the very best thing he had ever said.

5.8

He dipped a cotton ball into the steaming water, sharp with the scent of antiseptic and healing hormones, and pressed it against her eye. Danae winced.

'Sorry,' said Turrow, but he didn't move his hand.

She had followed him back to his apartment: it was closer than hers, and she was exhausted, and he was moving awkwardly — unsteady and uneven — and so, when he asked if she wanted him to have a look at the ragged tear across her cheekbone, she hesitated only for a moment. Just long enough to let him see the moment's indecision, let him register her reluctance, let him know that the decision was hers and not his. He could make of that what he wanted. Danae wasn't even sure herself anymore.

Cassie, the sister, the reason for the trip to the Avenue, was sleeping solidly in the small bedroom, next to another girl that he told her was called Tilly. Alex, the brother, was not home. Turrow's eyes betrayed him but his face was set in stone, and so she hadn't asked, just watched him watching his sisters for a long moment, listening to the regular susurration of their sleeping breath. He'd closed the door, but she'd seen the red glow from the patch on Cassie's neck: a tiny, scarlet beacon in the darkness, and she knew what it meant.

She'd said nothing. Danae knew a thing or two about fear that ran too deep to speak aloud.

'Is it bad?' she asked now as he dabbed at the abraded skin beneath her eye, as much to break the silence as out of any desire to know. She hadn't looked in a mirror; it had seemed a little redundant.

'No,' he said, eyes fixed on the wound. 'Just big. There's a lot of dirt in it. Does it hurt?'

Danae shrugged. 'It stings,' she said. 'Could be worse.'

His own face was bruised and swollen, lower lip rising in a fat, purple blister, and he moved his jaw carefully, as though it ached, but, when he'd washed the layer of grime from his skin, she'd found only one break beneath it: a long, deep gash over one eyebrow that she'd flushed clean for him and pinned closed with sterile healing glue. He'd live. They both would. Though not, she couldn't help thinking, for want of trying on Danae's part.

His hands at her face were gentle: left touching careful fingers to her chin, tilting it upwards towards the light, right dabbing softly at the hot, angry skin above her upper jaw. Three discarded cotton balls lay on the floor at his feet, and, as he dropped a fourth, she saw that it was clogged with dirt and dust, but only a little blood. He dipped another, held it to the gash, and his hands trembled but his body was still.

'Was it a harvest?' she asked softly.

Hesitation. And then he nodded. He said, 'Were you ever in a raid before?'

'Once,' she said. 'You?'

'Yeah, once.' He nodded. 'Nothing like that. It was the middle of the day on a crowded street. Rita had them beaten to a pulp before the Rens even got there.'

'Rita?'

'My mother.'

Danae nodded slightly. An uneven breath agitated his shoulders. She carefully failed to notice.

'I was four,' she said quietly. 'They tried to raid our farm.'

His hand moved against her skin. His eyes held back, gave her space. 'What happened?'

'The Rens showed up.' She shrugged, but it came out wrong – less insouciant, more defensive. 'They'd been watching the house.'

'That was lucky.'

Lucky? she almost spat. But he hadn't been there. He didn't know.

So she shrugged again, better this time. 'There was a lot of a-naut activity in the north then,' she said. 'They were getting ready to shut it down.'

A wry smile twitched the corners of his lips. 'Good thing you made it here, then.'

'Speak for yourself,' she told him. 'You're the one that keeps attracting the damn things. I'm just an innocent bystander that got caught in the crossfire.'

'Yeah,' he said. 'The things that happen to an upstanding citizen on a quiet evening stroll along the Avenue.'

'I told you,' she said. 'You're not a Fiore kind of guy.'

'You did tell me that,' he admitted. And then, quietly: 'Is that why you came back?'

It was a fair question. It deserved a fair answer. The trouble was, Danae didn't have one to give him.

She smoothed at a crease in her skirt, where the fabric was drying at the wrong angle, dropped her eyes, fixed them on the pile of cotton balls on the ground. 'You made me coffee, Turrow,' she said. 'That's the best I can do.'

'Okay,' he said. The word was loose, breathy: the tail end of a sigh. 'That must have been one hell of a cup of coffee I made.'

'Must have been,' she agreed.

He cleared his throat, loud in the quiet room. 'If I'm not thanking you … properly …' he said, and paused. Tried again: 'If I'm not … it's because there aren't any words for it. You know.'

Still she didn't look up. 'You seem like the kind of guy who'd have done it for me.'

'I would,' he said quickly.

'Why?'

'Because,' he said, as though it were an answer. But, then again, Danae thought, it was as good as hers.

A deep breath broke the silence, and he started picking up discarded cotton balls. 'Maybe we should find a Ren tomorrow,' he said. 'Let somebody know, I guess. I don't know.'

Danae raised an eyebrow, chanced a look upwards now that his gaze was elsewhere. 'Not really their kind of jurisdiction,' she said. 'You ever see a Ren in Fiore?'

'No.' He dumped the cotton balls into the bowl of antiseptic, walked it over to the kitchen. 'But, you know, I'm not a Fiore kind of guy.'

'Not enough scars.' She tried for a smile, felt it stutter half-way. 'But I guess you're working on that.'

'You and me both,' he told her. 'How's the wrist? You want me to have a look at it?'

It was swollen and tender, but it was healing. And she could still feel the echo of his touch on her face.

'No, leave it,' she said evenly. The bones ached in protest. 'I'll see to it later. You should sleep.'

Turrow shook his head. 'Not until Alex gets back,' he said. He upended the bowl into the sink, water rattling against the steel surface as it drained. 'Coffee? I'm told I make a pretty decent cup.'

'No,' said Danae. The smile was getting easier to maintain. 'Thanks.'

'Gin?' He looked over, saw that he had her attention, and laughed. So did she.

'My mother used to say there was nothing worth fixing if it couldn't be fixed by gin,' she said.

Turrow grinned. 'She was right.'

Danae watched as he pulled a bottle out from below the sink and poured two generous measures, gaze drawn to the flow of the liquid into the glass, the settling crack of the ice cubes. Her eyes followed their movement, liquid in liquid, as carried them over to the sofa, settled himself at the far end, passed a glass to her across the boundary distance. She accepted it with a soft word of thanks, clinked it against his, sipped.

Gagged. 'Dear God, who called that gin?'

'Get your own next time,' he said pleasantly.

She winced, took another sip, shook her head, 'No, I'll take it. It's better than nothing.'

'Your face doesn't believe you.'

She turned an arched brow on him, but his eyes were dancing, and something had changed; some little tiny part of the universe had shifted.

She said, 'I'm not good at this.'

'At what?'

'This. Being taken care of. It makes me nervous.'

He held up his hands. 'Care is done. This is gin.'

Danae grinned. 'Turrow, this isn't gin. I thought we'd established that.'

'Right,' he said. 'The quality of spirits is much higher in Limbe.'

'Not Limbe,' she told him. 'Outside.'

Turrow laughed, smile spreading out and across his face, and the effect was startling: like the sun breaking through layers of cloud. A rebellious tingling in Danae's fingers wanted to trace the lines of it, to see if it felt as warm as it looked.

'Yeah,' he said. 'I hear everything's better when it's not in Creo Basse.'

'Most things,' she agreed.

'Is that where your mother is?'

'Oh,' said Danae. The glass twirled in her fingers, shards of light shattering on the ice as it moved. 'No. She died.'

Heavy silence. 'I'm sorry,' he said at last.

'It was a long time ago.' A sip of gin; subject closed. 'So — what's your story? How did you end up ducking punches in the Housing Authority?'

'Naked ambition,' he said. His sunlight smile flashed and her answering laughter cleared the clouds from the air. 'A job's a job. I'm trying to get my Higher Certificate. One credit at a time. Maybe by the time I'm forty I'll have a qualification.'

'Now that,' she said, 'is naked ambition.'

His lips twitched upwards and he cradled his glass against his chest, staring into the middle distance. Gently, without malice or regret, he said, 'It wasn't exactly the plan.' A slow, silent beat. 'But, you know, Alex'll finish school in a year, maybe I can go back if he gets a good enough job.'

'That's a good plan,' she said softly.

'I wanted to have a choice.' He shrugged, took a drink. 'And I did. I chose to be here. I chose them.' A beat. Then, decisively, 'It's more important.'

'Yes,' said Danae quietly. 'It is.'

EXTRACT FROM *DREAM STREAM: THE EMERGENCE OF ELECTRONIC THOUGHT*
BY G J ROSE, (NEW YORK: 2125)

Considered alongside later models, the Amnis is ungainly, but at the time of its release, and certainly in comparison to the leading S3A models of the day, the Amnis series was hailed as being the first artificial humanoid to breach the so-called 'Uncanny Valley'. The earliest models were entirely synthetic, covered in a modified dermal substitute, similar to the prosthetic skin temporarily grafted onto human burn victims during this period. This allowed for an unprecedented range of movement, but, while Calator's earlier, industrial units were designed primarily with functionality in mind, the Amnis series was the first commercially available model to actively attempt to replicate the full range of human movement, up to and including non-verbal and facial communication. This was in part a relic of their military design brief, which had stressed the importance of integrability, and in part indicative of a desire to capitalise on the novelty factor in attracting a new high-end customer base. Calator's initial promotional programme was aimed at high-income households, and emphasised the customisable features of the Amnis model, which allowed customers to select for anything from hair colour, to weight, height, and build, but such was the level of demand for the unit that, by the end of the year, they had released the Amnis Vision and the Amnis Effects, aimed at middle- and low-income families respectively. This business strategy would set the pattern for Calator's competitors: accessibility, affordability, and, above all, customisability. Indeed, the marketing campaign for Ovation's oMega Solo stressed the individualism of the model, claiming, with some justification, that 'No two are alike!'

Such was the enthusiasm for cosmetic modification among the domestic lines that it was estimated that, during the Insurgency, the ratio of successful operations against domestic versus industrial (non-modified) units was 1:37. The visual diversity of the former allowed them to avoid blanket detection methods such as were used with, for example, the Saber or Helot military lines, which were created to a blueprint and comparatively recognisable. Moreover, this diversity increased with the introduction of the semi-organic models...

SATURDAY 6 MAY

6.1

There was a Ren check on Eighteenth Street North. Because of course there was, given that they'd spent fifteen minutes that morning debating the relative merits of going overground to North Gate and walking the mile or so into Frain, or taking the tube to Omicra and transferring, and decided on the latter on the grounds that traffic in the thirty-first district was always unpredictable in the mornings, and Boston still had to get to Cilicia after he'd walked Danae to Intimacy. He wasn't sure why he'd offered, or why he'd pressed the point after she'd pointed out, quite reasonably, that she didn't need an escort and he didn't work in Frain. Neither was he sure why she'd conceded. Maybe she was pleased? It was hard to say.

'You should go on,' she said now, as the queue advanced another couple of shuffling footsteps. 'No point in both of us being late.'

Boston shrugged. 'If I leave the queue, they'll arrest me anyway. It's fine.'

She hadn't planned on staying the night, he was certain of that. She'd let him pour her a second glass of gin, and when she'd finished she'd started making noises about going home, but she hadn't moved from the seat and her hands were still shaking. He decided not to notice that; offered her a third, which she refused, but she still hadn't moved. And somewhere in the hours that followed, her eyes had closed, or his had, and the next thing he knew, he woke to the sensation of being watched and looked up to find Alex standing at the kitchen counter, white-faced with fatigue and staring at the sofa's somnolent tableau.

Seriously? he'd said, and Boston had no answer for that but a slack-shouldered shrug. He couldn't explain to his brother what he didn't understand himself.

The morning air was dry but cold. Danae hugged her coat a little tighter around her ribs as they shuffled forward in the line, glanced at her watch. 'Fucking Rens,' she muttered. 'I'm going to get fired.'

'Wow,' said Boston. 'That'd be the end of a perfect week for you, wouldn't it?'

She glared up at him, then laughed. 'Sensitive, Turrow. Thank you.'

'Just saying.'

Another step forward. Boston watched her move, watched her watch the queue advance with furious eyes as though mentally swearing at it could make it go faster. Her face was not as messed up as it had been the night before, but he thought it would be an explanation all on its own if she walked in late. A livid bruise painted one eye purple, spreading up to her hairline and down across her cheek, where it met a ragged stretch of abraded skin. It had seemed worse last night, but he'd been high on shock and adrenaline then, and, in the morning, she'd shrugged it off.

'I'll live,' she had said, and her manner, locked-down and distant, advised against pursuing it.

At least the queue was moving quickly. There were six Rens, he saw now, as they neared the checkpoint. Six Rens meant that they were just looking for a way to kill a slow morning; it didn't take more than three, four at most, to do a spot check. One to swipe, one to usher down the street or into a waiting van, and a sniper in a nearby window to pick off the ones that ran. Maybe someone had found a couple of dead a-nauts last night in Fiore North, maybe not. The guys at the checkpoint didn't have the air of men under pressure, or even men labouring under any kind of particular concern. That made sense. He'd be surprised if the bodies in the alleyway had surfaced so quickly. He'd be surprised if they surfaced at all.

Another shuffle forward brought them, finally, to the head of the queue, and Boston swiped his palm against the dermal code in his neck, pressed his hand to the offered sampler. The man on the kiosk was a full head shorter than him, dressed ostentatiously in a balaclava and a heavy black coat that showed the lines of his concealed weapons to best advantage. But he was happy to let the hardware do the intimidating for him, and he gave Boston a companionable smile as he squinted at the name on the readout, glanced back up.

'Boston Turrow,' said Boston.

A cheerful nod. 'Where are you headed this morning, Mr Turrow?'

'Work,' he said, as the man took Boston's shoulder and pressed a CP meter to the back top of his spine. It was cold against his skin. 'I'm walking my friend to rue de Quartier Borne first.'

'That's your friend?' A nod towards Danae, who was staring towards the ceiling as the scanner was pressed to her neck, eyes vacant, face pale. Boston nodded.

'That's her.'

'Name?'

'Danae Grant.'

'And where do you work, Mr Turrow?'

'Cilicia.'

'Cold morning for a walk like that.'

'When is it not cold in Creo Basse?'

'That's true enough.'

A light pressure at the back of his neck where the meter clung to his skin as it was pulled away. Pale green light bounced off the man's eyes as he checked it, and Boston's guts unknotted. Of course it was clear; he knew it would be clear, but you always worried about the day when you got a faulty meter and a bad readout. They said they swiped you again at the centre, but who'd come back to tell the tale?

'All done,' said the man amiably. 'You have a nice day. And stay warm.'

'Will do,' said Boston.

Danae was standing a little way away, freshly scanned and picking at a hangnail. She glanced up as Boston approached, greeted him with a raised eyebrow.

'Still not an a-naut,' he told her.

'Good to know,' she said.

'Do you ever worry,' asked Boston as they fell into step alongside each other again, 'that one day the meter won't be working and you'll get a red?'

She huffed a soft laugh in the direction of the concrete, and her eyes, when she lifted them to meet his, were dancing. 'Every bloody time,' she said.

6.2

'This is me,' said Danae.

'*Intimacy*,' he read.

'Good old fashioned food and a friendly ear,' she told him.

'Clearly.'

'Well,' she said, 'nobody punches *me*.'

He grinned. 'I'm going to be late.' But he made no move to leave.

'I *am* late. And my boss is watching me out the window, planning what to scream at me.'

'Can I see you again?'

It was out before he knew he was going to say it, and he watched, horrified, as her smile froze in place and her eyes died. Suddenly, the familiarity of the previous night receded to the vanishing point, disappeared over the horizon. He looked down at his feet; she did the same.

But instead of saying no, she said, 'I was thinking ... I could ask Nadine — about your sister. She knows just about everyone in the lower city. You know? If there's anyone can get what you need, it's probably her.' A beat. 'You know? I could ask.'

'Yeah,' he said. 'That'd be great. I'd appreciate that.' And then, because the moment clearly wasn't finished, but, for the life of him, he couldn't work out how it ended: 'You know where I am.'

Danae nodded, but she wasn't looking at him; he couldn't see her eyes. 'Write it down,' she said. 'What you need. She'll know who to ask.'

'You have a pen?'

'I'm a waitress, Turrow. Of course I have a pen.'

She had three, which was three more than Boston reckoned he'd ever owned. He took one, found a scrap of paper in his pocket, scribbled down his phonewave and a couple of names, underlined the one at the top of the list. She looked at it as he handed it back to her.

'Valproisol,' she read. 'What about these others?'

'Valproisol is best,' he told her. 'Sometimes people have lamotrigine when they don't have valproisol. Sometimes they have zonisamine-activated cellulides. I'll take what I can get right now.'

'Okay,' she said. And then, quietly: 'Turrow ... is she okay?'

He remembered her face last night, her eyes on the side of his head as she watched him watching Cassie. He'd felt the weight of her scrutiny like a blanket on his shoulders, and thought that the quality of silence in that stare said more about her than she'd like him to know.

'She will be,' he said, and Danae nodded.

'Okay,' she said again. Another nod, eyes fixed on the paper in her hand. 'I'll come to the Authority tonight, then. Let you know.'

'Okay. Great. I'll see you then.'

'About eight-thirty?'

'I don't get off until nine.'

'I remember,' she said. Her eyes swung upwards, and, unexpectedly, she grinned. 'I reckon I could find some way to occupy myself at the Housing Authority for half an hour.'

*

'You're late. Again.'

'I know, I know. I'm sorry. There was a Ren check outside the tube station. I'll make it up at the end of the shift.'

'Jesus,' said Nadine. She pulled up sharp in the middle of the kitchen, arms piled high with plates, and stared at Danae. 'What the hell happened to your face?'

'Nothing, I'm fine.' Danae brushed past her on the way to the stares, head low. 'Give me three seconds to get changed ...'

'Nigel's upstairs.'

'Perfect.' She shrugged off her coat, began the impossible task of trying to shrug on a glorified bikini in two square feet of kitchen.

'Somebody leap on you?'

'I said I was fine.'

'If you're so fine, why're you late for work? Again?'

'There was a Ren check, I told you.'

'Yeah, well, Nigel came in and I couldn't exactly lie. He's docking you half an hour.'

Danae closed her eyes, made a face. 'Fuck,' she hissed.

'Table three needs two full English, a pain au chocolat and a pot of coffee. I tried to talk him out of it.'

'Yeah, thanks. Hey,' she added, as Nadine was about to sweep back out into the café, 'you know anyone selling a thing called valproisol?'

'Valproisol? Jesus. Who needs valproisol?'

'A mate.'

'Why does he need valproisol?'

'His sister's sick.'

'And he needs valproisol?'

'That's what he said. Why?'

Nadine shrugged. 'Not much call for it, these days, is all. Is your mate loaded?'

Loaded wasn't the adjective that came to mind, but Danae would like to think she hadn't spent an evening picking bits of Fiore plasterwork out of her face for a guy who didn't have sense enough to bring cash to a meds deal. 'He has money,' she said.

'If he has money,' said Nadine, 'there's a couple of places. I can ask around.'

'Would you mind?'

'No, I don't mind.' She turned, headed out into the café, calling over her shoulder, 'I'm not promising, but I can ask.'

'Okay,' said Danae, 'thanks.'

But she was talking to herself. A glance towards the back stairs, a glance back out towards the fog-choked diner, a glance down at her creased, shop-stained uniform. Her eye throbbed reproachfully, reminding her that she had, effectively, as of twelve hours ago, abdicated responsibility for her own life. And that she had more or less just agreed to continue doing so.

'Fuck,' said Danae again, and followed Nadine onto the café floor.

6.3

Angelo had lived his early life many miles from the lower city, and spent as much time as he could outside its walls, but every time he came back it was as though he'd never left. Literally: every single time he'd disembarked the bus in Punta Oeste, every single time he walked out of the Terminal doors and onto the streets of the fifteenth district, it was raining, and surely to God it couldn't rain constantly? He was starting to think it was just for him.

The woman across the room from him called herself Miriam, but it had taken him the best part of the journey to even get that much out of her. *Why do you need to know?* she'd asked, and he didn't have a good answer for that, so he'd just shrugged, introduced himself, and left her to her misdirected aggression. The other one, the one with the wide, frightened eyes, who looked like she was maybe seventeen, eighteen years old, told him her name was Alice and claimed that she was Miriam's sister. She wasn't, of course, but he took her point: they were a unit. They hadn't expected to be parted on arrival, and there was almost a scene at the Terminal gates, but the elder one had fixed the younger with a glare so glacial that the air between them seemed to freeze, and that was the end of it. And then she'd turned her head and shared it with Angelo.

'Standard procedure,' he'd explained, and tried not to shrink under her eviscerating stare. It had been unexpectedly difficult.

That was yesterday evening, the end of a long ride from Montpellier on an elderly bus full of returning tourists, and he wasn't supposed to be the one to take her to the safe house, to spend the night watching over her and watching the door, but Micheline had cried off at the last minute, and there wasn't anyone else. So he'd walked with her through the teeming downpour, through the backstreets of Punta, to the door that didn't look like a door, up the million steps that led to a complicated series of false walls and crawl spaces, and finally into the tiny room with the damp, fungal beds and the window that looked out onto brickwork and rainfall. She'd paced the floor for eight straight minutes, scanning the walls, the furniture, the ragged boards beneath her feet, with the eyes of a woman who had recently looked directly into the depths of Hell, and when she was done, she'd dropped onto the bed, cast him one last glare, and closed her eyes. He had watched her sleep for a long time: the thick, comatose sleep of a small child; the sleep of a woman who was allowed to delegate responsibility to someone else for the first time in too long to remember. He'd watched her sleep, and he'd watched the door, and he wasn't sure which one made him most uneasy.

She was standing by the window now, gazing out as though there was something to see beyond the grey-streaked, cobwebbed pane besides the side of another building, black with algal damp. Her back was to him, but he knew she knew he was watching her. It was in the rigid line of her neck, the tension in her spine.

'So,' he said, and tried to make it sound casual, like he was used to the scrutiny of people whose eyes weren't even facing him. 'I got the all-clear. Ready to move?'

She nodded her head slightly, but her shoulders tightened. 'Where are we going?'

'Can't tell you that until we get there,' he said. A beat, and then – because she was the sort of person that created these little sucking silences that demanded to be filled – he added, 'Sorry.'

'No, it's all right.' Her voice was high and clear, and she didn't waste it. 'That makes sense.'

He wondered, vaguely, who she'd been. Her manner and bearing spoke of power, tightly coiled, but the ex-militants never wanted to talk about days gone by. He sort of understood that. He'd heard stories.

There had been three of them, Alice had told him, before her sister silenced her with one of those withering glares, but that much he knew already. Three of them, all women, taken together almost three weeks ago from a safe house in Swangate that turned out to be not just as safe as they might have hoped. He didn't need to ask how long they'd been travelling together; it was in their faces, in their movements, in the stoop of their shoulders. Three of them, for years at least, and now there were two. He knew they knew they were lucky to have escaped, but he also knew it was hard to feel lucky when the memories were so raw.

The rain had stopped, but the streets were cold in its absence now, chilled by the thousand little drafts that liked to sneak up through the gutters and down from the ceiling when the water was gone. She was buried in her coat, arms wrapped around herself, and her lips were bluish, but, for the first time since he met her, they were curling faintly upwards. He caught the tail end of her smile and offered her one of his. 'This your sort of weather?'

She shook her head. 'No. No – just … I didn't know how much I missed it, that's all.'

Three weeks. He wasn't sure that would be long enough for him to start getting nostalgic for the stink, but maybe it depended on the circumstances of the departure. He said, 'You know, they're going to ask how you got away.'

'I know,' she said.

'They're good guys.'

'I know,' she said.

'Just …' he said. 'Just don't get offended if they look sceptical, that's all.'

She turned her head now and quirked her lips again. 'I'd imagine they'll do a bit better than that,' she said.

Her tone was light but her eyes were not. He wondered if they'd always looked like that, or if it was a consequence of having stared into the face of death. He'd thought he'd seen his own coming too many times to count, but she'd been *there*. She'd felt the bony fingers close around her arm and the cold breath steal her final scream, and then, for no reason at all, death had let go. *I don't know why*, she'd said. *They had us, and then they let us go.*

Three weeks of sleeping in ditches, scraping out a living from the parched earth, wandering circuitously and constantly watching. Three weeks of waiting for the axe to fall, of waiting for the shadows to mass and take form, of waiting for the lights and the guns by night, of waiting for some sort of reason to manifest itself. They had them, and then they let them go. They *never* let them go.

'Will Alice be there?' she asked now, suddenly. 'At the safe house?'

'She'll get there later today. Omar likes to stagger new arrivals.'

'Makes sense,' she said. A beat. 'Especially ones like us, huh?'

He hadn't been going to say it, but there was no sense in denying it. 'Hey,' he said, 'You've got *me* nervous, and I can run away.'

'They're not following us,' she said. 'I'd have known.'

Yes, she would. She was the sort of woman he'd like to keep close by, as insurance against the day when he missed something. But she'd been taken in a raid, held for a day, and then released. It made *no* sense, and so she frightened him.

He said, 'I'd kind of prefer it if they were.'

She glanced sharply sideways, but the anger that had flared was gone almost before it registered. 'Yeah,' she said, 'I know what you mean.' A beat. 'You can't run from an enemy you can't see.'

There was exhaustion in the words. He didn't think she was the sort of woman to ever concede defeat, but her voice had an air of resignation to it, as though she saw shadows hovering in her peripheral vision that scattered every time she looked at them directly.

'When Carina got sick, I thought, maybe ...' she began, and then stopped. He glanced sideways to see that her face was lowered, rain running freely over her cheeks and pooling in the line of her tightly-pressed lips. 'I thought that was it. I thought we were all sick, and that's why they let us go. It wouldn't exactly be hard to do. I thought maybe they just wanted to see how long we'd last. Or something. I don't know.'

'You and Carina were ...?'

'Yeah.' She ran a hand roughly over her face, and he wondered if she was hiding tears. 'And all I thought was, *what if I'm next?* And every day I was still alive, I was glad.' She sighed. 'I never thought I'd be glad.'

There were words he could say, but what would be the point? She didn't want to hear them. So he let the silence linger while their synchronised footfalls carried them along streets, cratering last night's shallow rainwater and casting fractals in the swirling eddies of water-borne dust.

The car was waiting on the corner of Zelyenike and Stansfield, engine idling and steam rising from the bonnet where it trembled with motion. As they approached, the passenger window rolled down and Fredo poked his head out. 'Hey, buddy,' he called pleasantly. 'Cold enough for you?'

She paused on the street, and turned bodily towards him. She said, 'I'm guessing you're not getting in.'

He laughed. There was almost humour in it. 'Nope,' he said. 'Lucky me. I get to walk back.'

'Well,' she said. 'Good luck.' She leaned forwards suddenly and pressed cool lips to his; parted them and let them linger a moment longer than he expected. 'And thank you. You've been kind.'

'Stay safe,' he said.

She raised an eyebrow to that, and climbed inside. The door closed, and she was lost behind shadowed windows.

'Hey,' called Fredo as he turned to go, 'hold up. Gordie's been looking for you.'

'*Gordie?*' He turned back, leaned in and lowered his voice. 'I thought he was in Mexico?'

'Yeah, well, *I* thought he was dead,' said Fredo. 'Turns out I need better friends. He went by Ana's, nearly scared the shit completely out of her. She wants to kill you, by the way.'

'Tell her to get in line.'

'Funny. She said to give you this.'

'Do I want it?'

'Just take it.' The hand proffering the crumpled sheet of paper waved irritably. 'Yes, yes you want it, don't be such a paranoid freak. It's business.'

'What business?'

'*Other* business. Money business. Some chick's been looking for you.'

'Not Ana?'

'Just read it. Not Ana. Some chick that doesn't want to kill you – that ought to narrow it down.'

'No-one springs to mind.'

'Your life makes me sad. Now get your arm out of my window. You're letting the cold in.'

He stepped back, misjudging the distance to the curb and planting his foot firmly in the swirling currents of ankle-high water that ran along the edge of the road. Tepid street-soup filled his shoe.

'Good hunting, buddy,' said Fredo, and the window slid up, obscuring the occupants as the car drifted out and into the tide of traffic. He could taste the faint flavour of her on his tongue, and his lips tingled with remembered touch.

Alone on the street, he unfolded the paper in his hands, scanned it quickly as it twisted in the slipstreams of a dozen passing cars. And then he grinned.

TELECTRICITY MAGAZINE, FEBRUARY 2065

And finally, it looks as though last year's relaxation on laws governing the use of human genetic materials may, as expected, impact upon the telectronics world. Organ-printing giant Genesis had been campaigning for the lifting of restrictions prohibiting the growth of human tissue for a non-human host, arguing that lives could be saved if replacement organs could be printed before they were required, and kept alive in an artificial 'body', ready for transplant as needed, but had been hampered by concerns from both religious and human rights groups. This month's announcement by a-naut design market leaders AGR that they have developed a semi-organic S3A model is likely to come as little surprise to industry watchdogs ReServe, who have consistently argued that the immediate beneficiaries of any less stringent restrictions on human tissue growth would be the a-naut industry, as organic products are likely to be cheaper and more straightforward to produce.

SUNDAY 7 MAY

7.1

It was late evening in Montréal, which meant that Creo was well into the small hours of the following morning, but Pasachoff wasn't altogether sure the doctor had noticed. Ravi had the look of a man who hadn't slept for a few days.

'Slow down, Isaac,' he said, raising a hand. Liver spots glowed darkly in the thin light from an anglepoise lamp; Eunice had already taken one of her tablets and he hadn't wanted to wake her. 'It's a long time since I've practiced general medicine.'

He'd known Ravi for many years, and long acquaintance had matured into a comfortable, mutual respect. It wasn't friendship exactly: more the kind of default familiarity that comes from four decades of attending the same conferences and knowing the same people. Their sons had been at Princeton together; they shared a passing interest in golf; both had, at various times, worked as peer reviewers on the same journal; and, occasionally, when Ravi was in Montréal or Pasachoff was in Creo, they would meet up for dinner and reminiscence about the things that it was acceptable for men who knew each other slightly to discuss. They drifted in, drifted back out of each other's lives.

It certainly wasn't the sort of relationship where one of them called up the other at 10PM on a Saturday evening. Pasachoff wasn't even sure he *had* Ravi's home number, and he didn't remember ever handing out his.

'Apologies,' said the doctor now, and his hands came up to scrub at his temples. He'd gotten older since the last time they'd talked, or maybe it was just the exhaustion, draining his skin of colour and tension, so that it hung off his cheeks like folds of old sackcloth. 'Sorry, Theo. I know it's late. I hope I'm not interrupting anything …'

Pasachoff was due to play golf with an old colleague at nine the next morning, and had been planning to put in an early night to make sure he was fresh, but he didn't suppose that counted.

He waved a dismissive hand. 'No, my friend. But perhaps you'd start again? Any one of those pathogens you mentioned could have triggered sepsis …'

'That's just it, Theo.' Ravi spread his hands. 'Her serology was clear. All I've found – all we've been able to find on fifteen separate scans – is a mild rhinoviral infection. And there's no way a viral load that low could cause sepsis – look at the titre.'

Pasachoff glanced towards the shimmering lines of green text that floated above the second screen to the left of the doctor's face. It was a while since he'd been required to know this sort of thing, but, if memory served, he'd have been surprised if numbers like that could have shuffled a fever past 99.5.

He said, 'And she wasn't showing any signs of infection?'

'There was only the cough and the slight temperature. Nothing on the scans.'

'But the samples from Aurillac showed *Bacillus anthracis* and *Clostridium tetani* – the early symptoms of either could look like that.'

'And a host of other opportunistic infections too – the Aurillac body was a catastrophe. But she's been vaccinated against both, and she's not immunocompromised. And she's had prophylactic treatment for all of it – targeted and broad spectrum, whatever anyone could think of. And even if she hadn't, Theo, we're treating her now, for *everything* – and she's still getting worse. I don't … I know what it looks like. But I don't see how it can be sepsis. I don't see how this can be caused by an infection.'

'It was my understanding,' said Pasachoff, 'that in 0.1 per cent of cases, no infectious agent is ever discovered?'

'Yes,' said Ravi, 'and I could believe that, Theo, if there'd been any chance for an infectious agent to take hold. But we've been *looking* for infection all week. We've been treating her for pathogens we haven't found. And there doesn't have to be an infection present for a severe inflammatory response to occur.'

'Ah.' Pasachoff crossed his arms and leaned back against the padded headrest of his chair, thinking, *this is why he called.* 'You're wondering about the possibility of a drug interaction.'

A disconsolate shrug. 'Theo, what's my alternative? The CDC has a team en route, and I'm supposed to hand them over a patient that I've known for half my life because they're convinced it's more likely that my machines aren't working properly. You're a nanopharmacologist. Isn't it possible that this is something we did?'

Pasachoff sucked in a deep breath, considered his answer. 'It's … not *impossible*,' he said at length. 'Thirty, forty years ago, I might have said yes. But, Isaac – you realise we're still talking about machines failing? Because if anything you've given your patient has caused an inflammatory response so severe, then your therapeutic programmer has malfunctioned. Her immune system shouldn't even know the delivery agents are there.'

'It's reacting to something, Theo.'

'You've treated her before, presumably? The machine has her code on file?' A sharp nod. 'And she's never experienced such a reaction to a nano delivery agent in the past? That's because the code is working, Isaac. And if it was a reaction to the drug itself – surely you've cleared the toxins from her system by now?'

'I looked for information on the stream,' said Ravi. 'I looked for precedents. There were a few.'

'Not in the developed world,' said Pasachoff, as kindly as he could. 'And not in the past fifteen years.'

'Theo,' said Ravi, and, if he hadn't already had the look of a perambulatory corpse, Pasachoff might have said his face was getting greyer as the conversation progressed. 'I had a healthy patient thirty-six hours ago. She had … There was nothing … I brought her in because she had a mild upper respiratory tract infection, and now there's a machine doing her breathing for her. She's in an isolation suite with acute respiratory distress syndrome and she's showing the first signs of renal failure, and whatever we do, all it does is hold off the inevitable for another few hours. Will you … would you just have a look at her workups? Please? Just have a look at the agents, and the response, and tell me … just tell me what you think?'

'Of course,' said Pasachoff. 'I'll look, of course. But you understand, Isaac, that, even if I find something, the chances of reversing it are … minimal? Anything I'm likely to suggest, you're likely to have done it already.'

'If there are productive suggestions still to be made,' said Ravi, 'at this point, they're going to come from you, Theo. Thank you.'

'And you understand,' said Pasachoff gently, 'that the CDC aren't sending a team out because they think your machines aren't working.'

A deep, sigh, and Ravi's shoulders sagged. 'No,' he said. 'That's why we've got her in an isolation suite.'

'Are you ...' said Pasachoff, and stopped. He tried again: 'How are you feeling, Isaac?'

'Oh, you know me, Theo.' A weak smile, but it failed to reach the doctor's eyes. 'Strong as a horse. They've asked me to stay on the ward until the CDC arrives, though – as a precaution. But the thing is, Theo ...' said Ravi, and Pasachoff revised his earlier assumption: the doctor looked like he hadn't slept in *weeks*. 'The thing is ... I've been tracking a slight temperature rise over the past couple of hours. On me. On my own readouts. I think ... I think there's a chance that I might be symptomatic too.'

EXTRACT FROM *DREAM STREAM: THE EMERGENCE OF ELECTRONIC THOUGHT* BY G J ROSE, (NEW YORK: 2125)

Notwithstanding, the issue of brain printing — the functional replication of human cranial matter — remained divisive. In the end it was Dr Lena Decker's work on the stabilisation of synaptic transmission pathways, for which she was, controversially, awarded the Nobel Prize in Medicine, that demonstrated the feasibility of the programme and paved the way for the work that followed. It was, however, a legacy that she bitterly regretted, and she would eventually become a staunch campaigner against cerebral replication, devoting the final years of her life to attempting to having the practice recriminalized. On hearing the news from Zakynthos, she is reported to have said, 'A person can send an idea out into the world with the best of intentions, but they can't prevent it from becoming their prison.'

Decker's work made possible the replication of the complex neurological pathways that would ultimately facilitate the construction of the semi-organic cranial processor, an innovation that improved a-naut motor functionality by a factor of more than 300 percent and, for the first time, brought their cognitive capacity into line with the human brain. The semi-organic processors were lighter, more efficient, and cheaper to manufacture than the synthetic models, and, after Yamazaki Jotaro, a leading telectronics researcher at JAIST, was able to demonstrate the stabilising influence of the datastream uplink on the coherence of the neural network, the processors were cleared for use in artificial units.

Emancipation immediately condemned the move as unethical, claiming that it set a dangerous precedent for the personalisation of a unit that remained, to all intents and purposes, a labour-saving device with few protections under law. Insisting that it was unethical to install a functional, pain-bearing neurological system in an appliance that had no ability or right to self-determine, an extract from an interview given to the Nexus show in February 2070 now seems disturbingly prescient. 'We're playing with fire,' said North American spokesperson Adeline Macchiarolo. 'Let's just hope it doesn't come back to bite us.'

8 MAY

8.1

'We're closing,' said Danae, without looking round.

'I know,' said Boston.

She was still sweating from the last, frantic hour, grease-matted hair tumbling loose from its low ponytail, apron smudged with globs of yellow, red, and, worryingly, green. Danae had been working for Intimacy for more than a decade; she was one hundred percent certain that nothing they served came in green.

'Oh. Hi,' she said.

'Good, old fashioned food,' he said, as his eyes ascended valiantly from her uniform.

She grinned. 'And a sympathetic ear. I thought you didn't get off until eight?'

'There's a riot brewing in Mère de Martyrs west. We shut early. Should I come back?'

Danae shrugged. 'I don't know. Nadine's friend is going to give her a call. Nadine!'

'In a minute!' she shouted from the kitchen.

'Turrow's here for the meds.'

'Yeah, in a minute!'

'Sit down,' said Danae, nodding towards an upturned chair as she moved past on her way to the kitchen. 'I need to finish up.'

She looked better than she had last night, as though she'd slept, and, though there was still a faint purple shadow across the line of her brow, it had faded back into her skin, and the graze was almost healed. She'd come over after work to tell him the news about the meds, spent a half hour shouting into the regulation ports, and then she'd left before his shift finished. Boston couldn't blame her; staying behind hadn't worked out so well for her the night before. Though he couldn't help but notice that she could have phoned, and didn't.

He pulled a stool down from its table-top perch, disturbing the air in front of a poster on the wall behind him and causing a buxom redhead to animate suddenly with a lascivious grin and a peal of deep, sultry laughter that she threw over her shoulder onto the empty café. 'That would be the sympathetic ear, then?' he said.

'Shut up, Turrow,' she called over her shoulder. 'At least it's not the Housing Authority.'

He had to concede the point.

From the kitchen drifted sounds of plate-stacking, the hiss-whir of a hydrator cleaning cycle, the low murmur of conversation, almost inaudible. 'How's your sister, anyway?' she called at one point, to which he answered, unsure as to whether she could hear him,

'Not great.'

If there was a response, it was lost in the kitchen sound. He stared at the redhead, no less terrifying for all that she was stationary again. She looked a little like Rita, as he remembered her when he was small. That *was* terrifying.

'Nadine, Turrow. Turrow, Nadine,' said Danae, emerging at last, wiping her hands on her apron. Boston regarded Nadine carefully as he debated the relative merits of extending a hand in greeting. Tall and angular and possessed of a face you didn't want to fuck with – almost androgynous, but strikingly beautiful.

'Yeah, I saw you out the window yesterday,' she said. He decided against the handshake. 'Maybe Danae wasn't late enough, yeah?'

He couldn't tell if she was brittle, furious, or joking. 'Sorry?' he tried.

'Forget it. She made it on time today.' He was no wiser. 'Right. I'm waiting for a call from a guy I know, some time in the next hour. He'll need the money up front.'

'He'll have it.'

'You're walking around with four and a half grand in your pocket?'

Her arch-eyebrowed incredulity was the opposite of flattering. But Boston said, levelly, 'I'll make a call, as soon as I see valproisol.'

'You'll see valproisol.'

It was an effort to keep his face from creasing into a beatific smile, but something told him she wasn't the hugs and lip-quivering type. So he kept his expression neutral, his voice even, as he said 'Yeah?'

'Yeah,' she said.

A beat. There was no way it was this easy, not after the week he'd just had. But Boston got no more than ten seconds into the stare-off before he realised he just wasn't in her league; the woman could have out-glared a Gorgon. So he arched an eyebrow instead, inclined his head.

'Okay, then,' he said. 'I'll make the call.'

She took the concession with good grace. 'Come back in an hour, okay? They'll be here.'

'Okay,' he said. And then, as she turned to leave, 'Thanks. Just … you can't get valproisol. Anywhere. So — thanks.'

She nodded, and her face softened, though you'd have to be looking really closely to notice. 'Any time,' she said. 'Any friend of Danae's – you know.'

'It guess it pays to be Danae's friend, then.'

Danae laughed. 'Of course it does,' she said lightly, but, when he looked up her eyes dropped away from his in a way that wondered, quietly, *are we friends?*

Boston didn't know what to do about that, so he pretended not to see.

Nadine, who hated an awkward silence, said, 'So, are you leaving, or what? Maybe you want to hang around and start up a nightshift?'

'You know me,' said Danae. 'I love my job. Which way are you going, Turrow?'

'Chatelier,' he said. 'That direction, anyway. I need to call Alex.'

'I'll walk with you to the subway.'

It was unexpected, but he'd take it. 'You want to share a train?'

But Danae shook her head. 'I'm going to Kim Li. Wrong direction.'

'What's in Kim Li?'

'Nothing,' she said.

It was a significant *nothing* — he could tell by the way Nadine's eyebrows suddenly climbed to her hairline — but before the silence could lengthen, a determined thumping rattled the shuttered door. Boston, startled, jumped in his seat, and his only consolation was that Nadine and Danae did too.

'We're closed!' yelled Nadine, with the fury of the recently disconcerted.

'I know,' called a disembodied voice. 'I'm looking for a Fuck You? A Miss Nadine Fuck You?'

'Oh my God,' said Nadine. And then, to Danae, 'Get out of here, okay? Just — come back in an hour with the money.'

'Hey!' called the voice, and now he was at the window, peering through the darkened glass. 'Getting wet out here!'

Danae's face was a mask of artless innocence. 'You're not going to let him in?' she asked.

'I swear to God,' said Nadine, whose cheeks were mottling with patches of red, 'if you are not out of here in the next thirty seconds, you are so completely fired, I can't even tell you.'

'I think he has *wine* – '

'Get out!'

'Okay,' said Danae, whose mouth was twitching with the effort it was taking to restrain her grin, 'I'm going, I'm going.'

'An hour, okay?' Furious eyes decided to scatter some of the vitriol Boston's way. 'And don't be fucking late. I have stuff to do.'

'One hour,' said Boston, and followed Danae out of the café before Nadine could decide he was an easier target.

★

'She's terrifying,' he said.

'She has a way with people,' Danae conceded.

She had wrapped her jacket tightly around her, but her legs, exposed to the rain, were mottled purple with cold and spattered with smudges of liquid street dust that had been kicked up from the pavement as they walked. Boston wondered if he ought to offer her his coat, for all the good it would do either one of them in the three blocks to the subway entrance, but decided against it. It didn't strike him as the sort of gesture that would go over well.

'Have you known her long?' he asked instead.

'Twelve years,' she said. 'Since I started at Intimacy.'

'Twelve years.' He shot her a glance as they pulled to a stop on the edge of the pavement. 'I'd better not be at the Authority that long.'

'In twelve years, you'll be forty-one,' she said. She grinned sideways. 'You'll have a qualification.'

They were on Eighteenth Avenue Central, right in the middle of the Greek quarter, which meandered through the heart of the district like a wide, welcoming smile. Boston liked Frain. Even in the rain, it felt warm.

'So, I got up to one hundred and seventy-eight in the Authority queue today,' she said. 'It's a personal best. Then they hung up.'

'Good work.'

'I might throw a street party.'

'Street parties are for people who get in the top one hundred and fifty,' he said. 'Keep trying.'

'It's not like I have a choice.' The tone was light, but there was bitterness in her eyes. She turned away.

It was early for the evening rush, late for the afternoon exodus, and the street was comfortably full, absent its habitual air of rampant marketeering. Restaurants were idle, waiters smoking quietly beneath sodden canopies, holo-ads pixelated and washed out by the rain. Danae walked quietly beside him, eyes fixed on the ground.

He said, 'You can always come beat up the regulation ports.'

She half-smiled, but it was pointed at the pavement. And then, out of nowhere, she asked, 'What happened to your mam?'

It wasn't so much that the question was unwelcome, it was more that he felt like it came from uncertain ground. But when he glanced sideways at her, she was busy scanning streetside menus as they passed.

'No way,' he said carefully. 'You don't get a non sequitur after five minutes' walk.'

Her eyes didn't leave the shop fronts, the garlanded eateries, the rain-spattered windows marked with letters in an alphabet he couldn't read. She said, 'How many minutes?'

'What?'

'How many minutes' walk until I get a non sequitur?'

He stared, levelly, at the back of her head. She did not look around. 'The question is moot,' he said, 'Since we've stopped walking.'

She took a step away from him, towards a shop window, and said something he couldn't hear. He stepped closer. 'I missed that.'

'I said, my mam used to love baklava,' she said, smearing a circle of rainwater on the window with white-blue fingers narrowed by the damp cold. Now she turned her head a quarter towards him, nodded it towards the shop. He closed the distance to stand beside her and saw that, whatever the arcane lettering might proclaim, it was, in fact, a bakery. 'We didn't buy it very often,' she said, peering through the water-distorted glass at the glistening pastries inside. 'Birthdays, mainly. Hers. I'm not that fussed. Never had it again after she was gone.'

He risked a sideways glance, uncertain of how to respond, and she met it with something like triumph glinting in her eyes.

'There,' she said. 'Now it's not a non sequitur anymore.'

He laughed, and an answering grin released the minor sun behind her cheeks.

'Well played, Danae Grant,' he said. 'Well played.'

'Well?'

'Well what?'

'What happened? You don't just end up alone. Is she gone?'

'Dead?' She didn't answer, held his gaze evenly. 'No, she's not dead.' Still the gaze: it was a question by itself. He gave in. 'Long story for another time. She left.'

She acknowledged the hidden words in that sentence with a flicker of something dark, familiar, in her eyes. 'Do you see her?'

'Occasionally,' he said. 'When I can't avoid it.'

'Does she know about your sister?'

She'd had two days with the name of Cassie's medication du jour. Danae was a woman who valued privacy like it was armour or a bulletproof vest, Boston thought, but there was no way she *hadn't* asked the questions. He would have, in her place.

'She knows,' he said.

Danae nodded, dropped her eyes. 'How's she doing?' she asked quietly. 'Your sister. Is she …okay?'

Boston shrugged. 'Yeah,' he said. 'She's okay. I mean … she disappeared for three hours last night, turned up drinking stolen beers in an alleyway with some kids she knows from school, but, you know. As long as Alex hasn't killed her before I get home, I guess she's okay.'

'Sweet kid,' said Danae, but her voice was warm, amused.

'Yeah,' said Boston. 'That's Cassie.' He glanced sideways, tried to imagine Danae at his sister's age, came up short. Danae Grant, he thought, had never really been Cassie's age.

'I don't know,' he said. 'I guess she's used to this whole thing by now, but she gets … angry sometimes. She likes *angry* better than *scared*, I suppose.'

A couple of quiet footsteps carried them past a maître d' scattering phosphorescent light balls among the branches of a pair of laurels that fronted his empty restaurant front, and, absently, Danae brushed the residue from her sleeve. 'It's pretty bad, then,' she said.

A statement, not a question. He guessed she'd done her homework on the dosage, too. 'Yeah,' he said. 'It's pretty bad.'

'She can't get the …' A hand rose, gestured vaguely at her head. 'The surgery. The … implant thing.'

'She can get it,' he said. He thought of the doctor's faces, the second time his sister almost died. The way the blood drained from his mother's skin when she realised they weren't going to let her take Cassie home again this time, and why. The way her knees buckled and the sound she made, like a wounded animal. 'As soon as they stop being seventy thousand credits, she'll be first in the queue.'

'Yeah,' said Danae, and the word was soft; almost a sigh. 'There is that.'

The gaze faltered; dropped. And suddenly he thought of her father, of the Avenue, of the things you bought in Fiore North. He thought of her face by the entrance to the subway on the corner of the Thirty-sixth Turnpike and Parkway, of the sadness in her eyes, and he realised that he understood.

'Kim Li,' he said. 'The cemetery. That's where you're going.'

She didn't answer immediately, but shaded her eyes and stared up at the distant ceiling.

'I was,' she said at last. 'But the rain, I don't know … I don't think I feel like it anymore.'

'Fair enough,' he said neutrally.

She smiled a sad smile, dropped her eyes again. 'I've gone every night for thirteen years,' she said finally. 'Since Mam died. So why not tonight?'

Another lightning sideways glance. Still she didn't meet his eye. 'Do you want to get a coffee?' he said.

'No,' she said. Her smile was fixed, plastic. 'You need to call Alex.' A beat. 'You need to get back to Nadine.'

'I have an hour,' he said.

'It'll take you an hour to get there and back.' She waved a hand. 'It's fine; I'm just tired. There was this group of truckers came in at a quarter to seven and ordered a fucking banquet …but they left a massive tip …'

He watched her for a moment, but she kept her eyes bowed. 'So,' he said at last. 'I'll see you at the Authority tomorrow.'

'Count on it.'

'Nothing I like better than a really difficult customer at the end of the day.'

'Unless,' she said suddenly, 'you need any help? With, I don't know — maybe your sister? Maybe we could talk, or something?'

Still she wouldn't meet his eye. He could picture Alex's face: worn with worry, frayed with Cassie's constant low-level fury at the world; the yelling; the acrimony; the fear. He could picture Tilly, locked in the bathroom with a towel over her head, waiting for Turrow to come home and make it better. He could picture raised, irritated eyebrows; cold glares predicting difficult, hushed conversations once the girls were in bed; the exact quality and texture of Cassie's disdain.

'Yeah,' he said. 'That'd be great. Thanks.'

8.2

He'd brought wine. An hour after Boston had returned and left again, with the money sitting companionably on the table in between them, they were into the second bottle. 'So, who'd you mug?' said Nadine.

'A little old lady,' said Angelo. 'On her way home from the off-licence.'

She stared at him for a moment. His faced creased into wry amusement.

'Fuck you,' she said. She was definitely getting pissed.

'You still say that a lot,' he observed, topping up her glass.

'People irritate me,' she countered.

'Yes. I remember that.'

'Where've you been?'

'Around,' he said.

'Seriously, I asked everyone. No-one knew where you were.'

He smiled his supremely irritating smile and topped up her glass. 'You still seeing that guy?'

'Which one — Werner? Christ. No. That was, what, three years ago? It hasn't been three years, has it?'

'You tell me. I only remember his stupid name.'

'He sent a lot of business your way.'

'I didn't say he wasn't a good customer.'

She sipped from her glass, watching him, a smile playing around her mouth. 'You cut your hair,' she said.

'Yeah … There was a bit of an incident last year.'

'A hair-related incident?'

He cocked his head. She raised her eyebrows and shrugged. 'An identity-related incident,' he clarified.

'And, what, you think you're Clark Kent with your head all shaved?'

'There may have been' — he stared into his glass — 'glasses and a false moustache involved.'

She sputtered, spraying wine. 'Please tell me you still have them.'

He stood up, moving easily across the café floor as he always did, with that same air of proprietary efficiency that had once helped him to move firmly into her life and her head. He disappeared into the kitchen and called back to her, 'I still have them. But you'll never see them.'

The wine was warm in her blood and the world was beginning to bend. Angelo emerged from the kitchen, wiping at his shirt with an old cloth, moving to the counter to lean against it, no more than a foot to her right. She swivelled slightly to look at him, back in her head after a lengthy absence. She said, 'You don't play fair.'

He had the decency to grin a wide open grin that exploded any artifice. 'And you're still surprised.'

It wasn't the answer she'd wanted. But he *had* come back. She said, 'Danae's friend was pretty pleased. You turning into one of the good guys?'

'I had what he needed,' he said, and there was a tiny emphasis on the *he*. Or maybe it was just the wine, making the world bend.

'No one has valproisol,' she said. 'Where did you get valproisol?'

'*No one* does not have valproisol,' he said. '*I* have valproisol.'

It was good to see him again. And there didn't seem to be any point hiding that from him, so she said it. Not softly, not like a lovesick teenager, not like she'd missed him. But he smiled anyway.

'Are you busy tonight?' he said.

8.3

Danae hadn't helped much. She knew she hadn't. She'd regretted asking almost immediately, as soon as she'd seen his face and understood that it would be difficult for him, that he would say yes because he thought she was too fragile to say no. Maybe he thought he owed her. Maybe that was it. Either way, she'd followed him back to his apartment, where the transferred sound of Alex and Cassie's screaming match had sawn through her teeth from the moment the elevator doors slid open. At the end of his corridor, a woman opened her front door as they passed.

'I've called the police,' she said.

'Great,' said Turrow, and ignored her.

'It's not just me!' she'd shouted after him. He kept walking.

She'd tried to back out at the entrance to his apartment. The lock wouldn't recognise his wrist scan on the first three attempts, and the yelling from the other side of the wall was turning the air fifteen shades of azure, and she'd said, *Hey, you know, this is a bad time for you guys, maybe I should just …* And he'd turned to her with helpless eyes, but at that moment the door had swung open, and he'd shut down, switched straight into peacekeeper mode, and barrelled into the sitting room to break up the fight. And what was she supposed to do then, just slink away? Maybe. Maybe that was exactly what she ought to have done, but it felt wrong, just that little bit more wrong than stepping inside and letting the door close behind her as Cassie screamed an impassioned *fuck you* to all concerned and an interior door slammed. And then Alex was pushing past her, head bowed in rage, on his way out of the apartment, and there was a hissed and heartfelt *Jesus fucking Christ* from the living room, and the sound of crockery shards rattling: a lonely sound, a solitary sound, the unmistakable sound of Turrow trying to fix things. If she'd wanted to, she could have slipped out then, just stepped back and out through the open door and left him to his complicated life, the one that did not need Danae and baggage and her thousand and one exciting ways to make everything worse, and she'd spent a long moment deliberating, frozen in indecision, as his footsteps on lino marked the passage of his feet into the kitchen, the clatter of porcelain, the sweep of a dustpan and brush.

In the end, it was a close-run thing. She'd almost taken that first step towards the door when her feet moved her forward instead, unbidden, out of the hallway and into the living area, where he was crouched in the centre of the room, picking up bits of plate from the floor. But then he'd looked up at her with eyes that were black and hollow with exhaustion, and, though his face was ashen and his shoulders were loose, as though he couldn't spare the energy to uncurl them, he'd made himself smile. And she'd realised that, yes, maybe it was a little bit wrong to be here, but it was also a little bit right.

She'd put the room back together while he talked to Cassie, tossing cushions back onto the sofa, scraping soil back into the pot of an up-ended gerbera, tidying away the last fragments of pottery from its impressive spray across the sitting room floor. She'd run a glass of water for Tilly, found biscuits in the cupboard and fed her three while they waited for Turrow to re-emerge from the bedroom, sat beside her in silence while she ate, because it seemed less invasive, less patronising, than trying to make small talk with a kid she'd never met before today. She'd watched a sudden rainburst spatter the windows with force enough to startle them both, shared a quiet smile with the girl beside her, fixed her eyes on the darkening cityscape outside from behind a mobile wall of water.

And when the bedroom door slid open, Cassie, red-faced and swollen-eyed, had pushed her way past Turrow to her sister on the sofa, wrapped her arms around her, and led her back out of the room, and Turrow had stood for a moment on the threshold, watching them go, before he lifted his gaze to Danae's. He swayed a little, and then crossed the floor to the sofa and sank onto the cushion beside her: one fluid, boneless movement, like a puppet whose strings had been cut.

Danae watched, waiting for him to do something she understood. His face was drained grey, his eyes black. She watched him lift his palms to his cheeks, fingers pressed tightly into his eye sockets as he scrubbed away layers of fatigue; she watched his shoulders rise, halt, release on a deep, heavy breath. She watched him roll his head back against the sofa, eyes closed, and she let her gaze trace the heavy light that settled on his forehead, his cheek bones, the ridge of his eyes, his mouth, as his breathing evened, as his shoulders relaxed.

She thought, *I know this face.*

Later, when the others were asleep, he brought pillows and sheets and set them on the sofa but stared at them instead of making them into a bed. Danae, who was now sitting beside a pile of sheets and pillows, glanced up at him.

Finally, he said, 'I'm glad you're here.'

'Why?' she said, softly; softer than him.

He shrugged. 'It feels different with you here.'

In the end, they sat on the floor, backs resting against the sofa, wrapped in thin sheets and shivering as the darkness sucked the heat from the air. Their shoulders brushed, but after a very little while there was nothing more to say, and so they sat in silence as the night melted through the hours. In the morning, when the habit of a lifetime woke her before dawn, she found that they had slept as they sat, and that her head had fallen onto his shoulder, and his head onto hers.

THE DEMOCRAT, 14TH MARCH 2065

... Nevertheless, the extent to which organic and artificial matter can be combined in a non-human is presently the focus of a great deal of debate. A spokesperson for Emancipation, who are opposed to the development of a-naut technology on the grounds that it blurs the distinction between human and non-human lifeforms, announced today that the group intends to take the case before Congress in a bid to have a clause written into Amendment 6313 that would specifically prohibit its use by telectronics firms. However, it seems likely that the crucial determinant will be in the order of combination. If, as expected, the new a-naut line is more than 50% organic, then it will match surviving human prosthetics patients, who can potentially live for ten years or more on prosthetic organs. Therefore, potentially, units will be covered by the Human Rights Act, and, by definition, classed as human. However, by creating first the metal skeleton and grafting the organic components to it, a loophole in the law prohibits the resulting combination from receiving human status, presumably on the grounds that prosthetics patients receive their artificial components the other way around ...

9 MAY

9.1

Diana hadn't even realised that she was Héra's next of kin until the hospital called, but the soft-faced woman on at the other end of the line left limited space for considering the wider implications of what that meant for Héra's conception of their friendship versus Diana's. The woman wouldn't tell her much over the phone, but there was something in her voice, the sympathetic cant of her eyebrow, the way she looked away, just for a second, when Diana asked if it was serious, and she knew then, really, that whatever was waiting for her at the hospital, it was going to change things.

But it never occurred to her to think that Héra was already dead. That came as one hell of a shock.

She was surprised to find that she was crying. Diana and Héra had known each other for years, the sort of casual acquaintance that you don't quite know how to shake: snatched coffees and the occasional lunch after months of silence, birthday cards and a cheap bottle of wine at Christmas; not quite friendship, not quite indifference, not somebody whose absence was going to leave the sort of hole that can never be filled. But she'd asked to see her just the same, because it felt like something she ought to do, and there was something so tragic, so awful, about that tiny, slender body, covered to the neck by a thin sheet, wasted by illness and so utterly, pathologically alone in the world that there was nobody to claim her but a woman who made time for her only when the mutterings of her conscience got too loud to ignore. Diana had burst into tears, and she had no tissues in her handbag, because she hadn't expected to cry.

'Did she …' she tried, and stopped, because it sounded trite, tired – detached, almost – but she had no idea what people said in this situation, and this felt like it was the sort of thing that might be acceptable. 'Did she suffer?'

The doctor, a wide-bellied, middle-aged man whose jowls rested solemnly on his downturned neck, passed her a freshly laundered handkerchief. Diana took it with a nod of thanks and pressed it to her streaming eyes. She was not, she supposed, his first weeping relative.

He said, 'She was kept as comfortable as possible.'

Which was not, Diana couldn't help but notice, an actual answer.

The body was in an isolation ward, hermetically sealed while it waited for post mortem. Diana thought, disjointedly, that Héra had never looked so small.

'There are a couple of questions we'll need to go through with you,' said the doctor quietly, and cleared his throat, hand rising elegantly to his mouth. A reflex gesture, Diana thought – the sort of thing a mother instils into muscle memory early in life – because his face was entirely shrouded in a gel hazmask, features stretched like a bag of butter behind a sheath of transparent latex. Two tubes snaked from either nostril, curling over ample cheeks and disappearing behind his head to the filter box on the side of his neck, where an osmotic field sieved poisons from the air and a voice modulation panel did his talking for him.

'Of course,' she said, dabbing the linen square to her nose. It smelled of lemon and roses, the scent of the ward around her. 'Whatever you need.'

He nodded, eyes cast respectfully towards the floor. 'And I'd like to take some bloods as well.'

'Bloods?' She felt her forehead crease. 'From me?'

'And anyone else in the family that might have had contact.'

'I'm sorry …' Her head was fuzzy with unexpected emotion, and he'd veered off the script she'd been vaguely sketching in her mind. 'Contact? I don't understand.'

'It's just a precaution,' said the doctor. 'There's almost certainly nothing to be concerned about.'

'Concerned?' Diana shook her head, folded her arms across her chest. A defensive gesture, she realised, a second too late to correct it. 'I'm sorry – I think I've missed something …'

And then it hit her: he was wearing a hazmask. She hadn't thought to question it; it was a hospital after all.

'I'm going to print you and your family with scanners, and I'll proscribe a prophylactic course of p-cytes, just to be on the safe side,' he was saying now, but his voice had receded into a kind of fuzzy white noise behind a rising wail of alarm that sounded somewhere on the edges of hearing. 'I'll ask you just to stay home for a few days while we track your signs. And if you'll step into my office for a moment, we can talk about the sort of things I'd like you to be watching out for. Like I say, there's probably nothing to worry about — it's protocol, really. We have to go by the book …'

He was wearing a hazmask. He was wearing a hazmask, and his hands were gloved. But Héra was in an isolation suite, sealed into an airtight room by a heavy-duty pathogen field and blast-proof glass four centimetres thick. Why did he need a mask?

'Oh God,' whispered Diana, in a voice that trembled on the edge of hysteria, as cold panic trickled into her belly and her chest forgot how to breathe. 'Oh God — my daughter's been ill …'

9.2

'He's just some guy,' said Nadine as she opened a beer, before Danae could ask the question that was manifestly hovering on her lips.

The café was not clean, but it wasn't going to get any cleaner, and there had just been too much crap all day to worry about what the hell that was on the floor. The fact that there was beer at all suggested that no one was *just some guy*, but Danae was not going to point that out and risk the retraction of beer.

'Will you see him again?' she asked as she eased herself into a chair across from Nadine and accepted a drag from her cigarette.

Nadine shrugged. 'Angelo will show up if and when Angelo wants to show up. What?' she added in the face of Danae's smirk.

'"Angelo will show up if and when Angelo wants to show up",' said Danae, in a voice that was designed to provoke.

'That's what Angelo does. I don't see you complaining that I managed to find valproisol in a town where there is no valproisol.'

'Nice pet name he has for you,' said Danae, who was beginning to seriously enjoy herself.

'Oh God,' said Nadine, but she arched her neck backwards and laughed. 'Yeah. He pissed me off the first time I met him, and when he asked me my name I said *fuck you*.'

'How sweet of him to remember,' said Danae.

'Listen, you,' said Nadine. 'I gave you beer.'

Danae smirked, and raised her bottle.

'So,' said Nadine, 'no Housing Authority tonight?'

That was a good question, and one that Danae hadn't settled yet. So she said, 'Are you trying to get rid of me?'

'Possibly,' said Nadine.

To Turrow or not to Turrow? There were a number of very good reasons to go straight home and spend the rest of her natural life on the telephone instead. One really *fantastic* reason, in fact, that she wasn't quite ready to give voice to just yet. It was just that anything was better than the flat these days, with Walter's imprint fading from the bed, but the lingering scent of him still in place and a box of clothes and assorted things that she didn't know how to get rid of. And then there was last night in Turrow's house, cross-legged on the floor; the fading light on his paper-white skin and the rise and fall of his shoulders as he scrubbed the weight of the day off his face…

Danae noticed the exact moment that Nadine mistook her silence, and tried to speak first, but Nadine was quicker. 'So,' she said in the tone of voice that says, *brace yourself: sympathy is on its way*, 'Is everything okay? I mean … You know …'

'Fine,' said Danae neutrally.

'You know, when my dad died –' she began, but Danae, who couldn't bear it, said quickly, 'Yeah, I know. It's fine.'

'Okay,' said Nadine. 'It's fine.' A beat. 'Good.'

Danae drained her beer. There was more of it left in the bottle than she'd thought and it almost choked her, but she swallowed as best she could in a manner designed to convey insouciance and, if at all possible, pretend that she meant to do that, summoned her remaining dignity, and said, 'Angelo will show up if and when Angelo chooses to show up. I'd better go and let you get ready.'

'No rush,' said Nadine, but her face said otherwise.

'I should go,' said Danae.

★

She turned left at the bottom of Nineteenth Street Park, crossed Via Occulat at the Nineteenth Avenue junction, and walked, head down, eyes unfocused. At the end of the Avenue, the adverts ceased their relentless assault, and she felt the tiny pinpricking sense of being near to home. Cars thinned, faces became familiar, her feet knew the crests and troughs of the warped concrete paving slabs by touch. From somewhere far above, she heard the lyrical wail of a fight breaking out and knew that she was back in Limbe. The edge of heaven: not quite close enough.

Rainwater runoff was lying on the sodden concrete, mingling with dust-slime and all manner of unmentionable detritus of a hot, busy day as Danae turned the final corner into her street. It wasn't so much the ties of belonging that bound her to the place, she thought, because there was only one place that had ever claimed her and it was long gone, receded out of sight into the mists of memory. But it was the fact that it was familiar, in both senses: in the sense that it was a place where she had been someone that mattered to somebody, and in the sense that it was known, and that was important. She could read the air in Limbe the way she might read another person's face; she could feel the beating heart of the district pulsing just below her skin. She could hear the far off wails of sirens and guess, from the timbre and the Doppler shift, where they were coming from, where they were going. She could scent fried onions on the air and know from the accompanying bouquet of spices what time of day it was and which street was waking up. And she could hear a shout break out somewhere in the shadowy heights above and know that a window had been opened; flick her eyes upwards in time to see a coat catch the city thermals on its descent, papers, coins and pocket things scattering on the breeze as unseen hands threw it from a window.

And so it was that, looking up to follow the flight of someone's jacket from the twenty-fifth floor, she saw the men for the first time.

You walked with your head down in Limbe, especially if you were on your own, and that was why she didn't see them until she was almost level with her front door. Three men in dark coats, like an executioner or an undertaker: men enlisted to pronounce the final sentence of death upon a person's home.

For a moment, shock rooted her to the ground. Afterwards, she wondered why: it wasn't as though she didn't expect them, only that she hadn't expected them so soon. Perhaps it was just that, scattered on the street, flimsy fabrics ruffled by the breeze of their exertions, everything she owned in the world looked diminished, less even than she had thought. Later, she would ask herself if, given the circumstances, any of the other residents of the street, some averting their eyes in tacit sympathy, others staring wholeheartedly from their windows, could have produced a more impressive bundle to show for all their years of living in a cramped, crumbling square of limbo, but by then it didn't matter.

'What the hell are you doing?' she said at last, and was surprised to find her tone so calm, so even. As though, with the next breath, she might ask if they wanted a coffee: milk? Sugar?

Two of the men were leaning against the pillars on either side of the entrance to the apartment block, smoking laconically. This was the sort of job they liked: no heavy lifting, no lawyers, no fists. The third was rifling absently through a plastic box of keepsakes that had spent the last seven years gathering dust under the bed. 'Working,' he said.

'These are my things.'

'That's why they're out here. Your floor's been closed.'

'I have another nine days on the notice,' said Danae, and her voice was creeping up the octaves as panic prickled her throat.

Calm.

Calm.

But the man only shrugged. 'Not my problem,' he said, and he was right.

9.3

The bag was too small to carry much, too big to be inconspicuous. If she had to sleep on the street it would be gone by morning. Some clothes at least: a pair of her father's work trousers, sturdy and warm. A pullover. A knitted hat. She forced them into the small canvas sack, cheeks burning with hot, furious shame. Her father's ID card, the last evidence of his life, tucked into the battered wallet that he'd carried with him for all the years he'd been well enough to walk. Her parents' wedding picture; a scrapbook that Annelise had kept for years, filled with newspaper clippings and notes scribbled down from books that she'd read. Her father's watch, to trade if she had to. A couple of old microcards, obsolete and unwatched in decades: she wasn't even sure anymore what was on them. The farm? Her baby years, captured on camera for posterity? Their wedding, even? Her grandparents? A birthday? What? But they went in the sack anyway, because somewhere in the midst of the plastic sheeting was a dot link to the datastream, and on the link existed images of her family, moving and talking, maybe even smiling, and the knowledge was enough that the cards became the final link between then and now.

Some food. A couple of cans of meat, some fruit, some coffee, a few packets of stem sheets in apple, baked beans, and Cajun chicken. A blanket, so threadbare that she could see the street through it when she held it up to the light. She left the rest.

As she stood up and walked away – slowly, confidently; let them think, in defiance of all common sense, that she had somewhere better to be – she saw, from the corner of her eye, the shapes moving in, from doorways, windows, alleys. Centring on her boxes, as though she might have something that they wanted.

★

'Turrow, it's me again. Hope you got the message I left with your sister. Still trying to get you. I'll try again in a while.'

It was almost midnight, and the road outside the café window had settled into a thick, inky blue, punctuated by the sodium spots of streetlights. Why they didn't just keep the light-bands on permanent sunlight was a mystery that had bothered her in her first years in Creo, until someone explained to her about the circadian rhythm, and how it was important in stopping certain sensitive people going mad with guns and knives.

She was holed up in a café that she didn't know, sipping tar-like coffee that she hadn't wanted and couldn't afford, because her data pocket was, as ever, out of credit and the waitress wouldn't let her jack their bandwidth unless she bought something, and foul coffee and the faintest twinkle of hope that she might yet manage to stay off the street that night was preferable to staying three tokens richer and bedding down in an alley. Turrow's phone had been off all evening, and whatever he'd been doing, he was almost certainly now asleep, probably dreaming of streamlink alerts and cursing people who called after 10 PM. There was no point even trying Nadine.

The waitress was shooting her the same sort of prickling psychic rage she used herself on customers that *would not leave*, but Danae had years on the other end of that gaze and it was easy to zone it out, focus her attention on the street outside, disassociate herself clean out of the way of the coruscating waves of telepathic hate. She'd made her way as far as Cilicia, reasoning that the streets would be safer there, but apparently thirty gazillion other destitutes had had the same idea, and they'd been there longer. In vain, she'd searched the faces for some sort of solidarity, even pity for the new girl, and had found only apathy, extending to vicious territorialism when she tried to set down her bag. So she'd moved to Frain, where she knew some of the down-and-outs, and found flick-knives and violence, and finally a café with a telephone.

Turrow wasn't home. Nadine was with Angelo. She knew nobody else in the city, and was beginning to wonder how it was possible to spend most of one's life in Creo Basse and know precisely two whole people. She sipped her coffee, absorbed the hate-daggers on the back of her neck, forced down the panic that was straining at her throat.

And suddenly thought of the graveyard.

★

The light flashed green. *Grant, Danae*, it chirped. *PR 85682 BN. Thank you for visiting Kim Li Cemetery. Your visit has been logged and copied to the datastream. You may approach only your authorised vault. Acts of vandalism or desecration will be prosecuted. You are visitor number* Seventeen. Hundred. And. Thirty. Three *to Kim Li Cemetery on* Monday. May. Eighth. Twenty-One. Nineteen. *Have a nice day.*

It was always warm in the graveyard. Strange, she thought as she made her way through the gate and into the darkened halls, when death itself was materially cold, that a house of death should be the warmest place in the city at midnight on a rainy night. Stranger still – as, caught off-guard by a tidal wave of accumulated fatigue, she lurched violently in the empty corridor and brushed against a bank of vaults, which bleated out a protest in a wash of red light – in a city in which a person could be casually murdered for the laces in their shoes, that the never-sleeping eye was saved for those who had already passed out of harm's way.

Exhaustion dragged more heavily with every step. Perhaps it was the sensation of finally being warm, perhaps the knowledge that sleep was imminent; so she dismissed the first flickering shadows as a trick of an over-worked brain. A flash of movement in the corner of her vision closed her throat around a strangled intake of breath: it couldn't be rats – the area was vermin-free and hermetically sealed. It had to be her imagination, heightened by the glowering darkness. But then, on the edge of hearing, the half-glimpsed motion was joined by a gentle susurration, like the rustle of wind in leafless trees. The image conjured up her childhood in stark relief, like freeze-framed microdisks, and for a moment she had to stop, catch herself, remember where she was.

In the graveyard, and not alone.

9.4

It was a building that was built for the sunlight, clean lines of glass that sparkled and glistened like an earth-bound star, but the sun had long since set. Night had crept under the blinds while Rademaker's attention was fixed on the report that hovered on a shimmering, green-tinted glow above his desk, and he hadn't noticed the lengthening shadows until his secretary had stepped inside to see if there was anything he needed before she left for the day, switching on the lamps as she was walking out the door. He'd switched them off again once she was gone: his screen was light enough to read by, and he wasn't sure it was the sort of information that ought to be digested in the comfortable yellows of a warm evening glow. Besides which, his phonewave had buzzed as he was finishing his third inspection of the closing paragraphs, and he was now holding a spirited discussion with an empty space where his conversational partner ought to be. That definitely felt like the kind of thing one ought to do under cover of darkness.

Gerald was the sort of man that knew the right people and the things that the right people got up to when they thought nobody was looking, and he had a gift for self-interest that could be extremely useful, as long as you made sure your interests lined up with Gerald's. He had been a part of Rademaker family history for more than forty years — almost as long as Maurice Rademaker Sr had been involved in ReGen — and he'd helped ease the company out of the upheavals of the Insurgency with a couple of well-timed governmental contracts which had certainly benefitted Gerald more than they'd benefitted ReGen. Lena Decker, who had opposed the move into amnisobiological production in the first place, had never trusted Gerald — Rademaker remembered her words, half-heard through an open door as he approached his father's office on his return from a research trip to the UK early in his ReGen career: *Be careful, Morrie.* Nothing more, then she'd turned and brushed past Rademaker as she stalked out, and even then, in the years before he really knew her, his twenty-two-year-old self had called her *haunted.* But Decker's control over the company she'd helped to found was well into its final decline by then. Rademaker Sr was her heir apparent, and he was young, ambitious, hungry for prestige, and he'd wanted what Gerald could offer.

But Rademaker Sr was a poor judge of character. His son knew that. Decker had known that.

Gerald knew that.

'Yes,' he said now, and the blank screen where his face ought to be, testament to a slightly unhealthy obsession with confidentiality, seemed to flicker reproachfully, in the manner of an elegantly arched eyebrow. 'You've mentioned that. Several times now, in fact. But I'm still not clear on how the data pocket was lost.'

Nor, in fact, was Rademaker, despite several pointed conversations with his project leader and the company's Head of Stream Security, but his sole advantage in the conversation was as the imparter of knowledge, and it was important to retain the tactical high ground.

'There are a number of theories,' he said, which was a variation on a theme he'd been singing for almost fifteen minutes now. He was tired, and he was hungry, and there was a decanter of a particularly fine fifteen-year-old Swiss single malt on his sideboard that he'd really like to unstopper and empty in generous measure into one of the cut-glass snifters on the tray beside it, and then proceed to drink until the whole damned day disappeared beneath a comfortable blanket of whisky fumes, but none of that was going to happen while Gerald remained unhappy. Gerald was good at being unhappy, though, Rademaker thought, you'd never know it from his demeanour. Until very recently, Gerald had smiled for a living; these days, he smiled on a consultancy basis. It was a good smile, designed to put people at their ease. He could even make it reach his eyes.

'I don't need theories,' said Gerald evenly, because Gerald's voice was seldom other than even. 'And I can't help thinking I've heard all this before, Maurice. When you came to me with this project, if you recall, the first thing — the *first* thing — I asked you was, how do you propose to control this? Because if you can't control it, it's worse than useless and I won't take it to the committee. Do you remember? And you told me — you told me, unequivocally — that Sinon was safe.'

'Sinon *is* safe, Gerald.'

'You'll forgive me if I'm inclined towards scepticism just now.'

'Gerald.' Rademaker was a hand-steepler. It was the sort of visual he liked to encourage. 'This call is a professional courtesy. Your involvement with this project is limited — at your insistence, I might add — to making the introductions that got it off the ground. So you'll forgive *me* if I'm inclined not to give much of a damn what you're inclined towards, now or at any other stage up to and including delivery of the final product. We've lost the

data pocket but we will retrieve it again. Let's keep things in proportion —
this is just a temporary glitch.'

'I think,' said Gerald, 'that the loss of the uplink to Red Space counts as a
little more than "a temporary glitch".'

'We have no evidence that Sinon has moved to Red Space.'

'Because you don't want to find that it has.'

Well, that was undeniable, but Rademaker decided to have a go just the
same. 'That's categorically untrue. And I resent the implication that my team
is anything other than …

'Your team represents the best and brightest minds working in
PharmaTech today,' said Gerald mildly. 'That's why I took your idea to the
committee.'

That, thought Rademaker, and the promise of the kind of return on his
investment that exceeded even Gerald's wildest dreams, and he doubted that
Gerald dreamt in under six figures. But he said nothing. The more unhappy
Gerald got, the longer the conversation was likely to take.

'The committee's satisfied that we're delivering according to schedule,'
said Rademaker. It wasn't a lie, as such; it was only that it glossed over the
parts of the meeting where all the shouting happened. 'I'm not happy about
the uplink either, but we have it under control. I see no reason not to move
to Phase Four trials next month. And let's remember, we have a confirmed
success in the field. Subject One is down.'

'True,' said Gerald, with such a pleasant inflection to his voice that
Rademaker knew what was coming before his conversational partner had
drawn breath to launch the offensive. 'And if we knew what had happened to
Subjects Two and Three, then I might be prepared to agree with you. Then
again, I might not. Forgive my vulgarity, Maurice, but I'd need to see a lot
more bodies before I call Sinon a success.'

'Gerald.' Rademaker could do granite-faced obstinacy too; it was just that
the effect was slightly spoiled by an audio-only connection. 'You've read the
reports — we observed cellular breakdown in every single in vitro culture
to which Sinon was introduced. We observed replication. We observed
transfer. Phases One and Two of the clinical trials did exactly what they
were supposed to do, and now one of our Phase Three subjects has turned
up dead. According to the terms of the trial protocol, that's practically the
definition of success.'

'And where in the trial protocol,' asked Gerald amiably, 'does it specify the terms for losing the uplink to Red Space?'

They could go on like this for hours. Rademaker knew, from painful personal experience, that Gerald did not tire like normal people, and that he had an insatiable appetite for worrying away at a person's reserves of patience until they lost their temper or their will to live and just told him whatever it was they'd been trying to keep quiet about. It was one of the reasons, apart from Gerald's obsession with distance, that Rademaker never let him talk directly to project leaders.

'Under "Contingency Planning," Gerald,' he said now, with the finality of a man whose blood whisky levels were running dangerously low. 'I have my people on this 24/7; nobody is sleeping until the uplinks are restored, including me. So, if you'll excuse me, I need to wake my assistant and make her put another call in to my wife to tell her I won't be home tonight, because believe me, Gerald, if I make that call myself it will be the end of my marriage. You'll know more as soon as I do. Good night.'

In the darkness of his office, washed silent and empty as he cut the connection, Rademaker sat back in his chair and loosed a long, weary breath. There were bunks in the on-call room on the third floor, and a cheerful smile and the fact of Rademaker's presence would clear them in the time it took a handful of scientists to recognise his face, but he wasn't ready for sleep yet, no matter how thick the exhaustion might hang behind his eyes. Whisky would help settle the uneasy corners of his mind, he thought, and in a moment he'd get up, cross the floor to the cabinet, and pour himself the drink of champions — just as soon as he could work the energy back into his muscles.

Be careful, Morrie, she'd said, and stormed out of the room. She'd been right, of course, but not for the reasons she'd thought. She was afraid their bodies wouldn't work, that they'd start to fall apart without a functional immune system, that the blood that stained his father's hands would be artificial. Decker died four years into the Insurgency, and Rademaker often wondered if she'd have been surprised to learn that, in the end, the problem was not that the a-naut body was ill-adapted to survival in a microbe-rich world, but almost exactly the opposite: they just would not die. Forty years on, and they still wouldn't die. That was … unexpected.

He stood up slowly, darkening his screen with a word, and crossed the room to where the decanter caught the faint starlight trickling through the window in a thousand points of white. He'd read DiNetto's report three times now, top to bottom, and the only thing he'd learned was that he had entirely too much faith in his staff's ability to problem-solve. No solutions, no suggestions, just a catalogue of issues that were the same issues with a slightly different haircut, and Rademaker was supposed to think that meant they were making progress.

This, he thought, was something that Gerald didn't need to know.

The thing in Creo was another. It had taken him a moment to recognise the name and make the connection, and then one more to leash the cold wash of disquiet that tightened his chest. But in the end he decided it was overkill: DiNetto had fucked up, and now he was covering his back with a tidal wave of detail, just so that nobody could come back at him two weeks from now and ask him why he didn't say anything at the time. It was nothing: a byline in a report that was full of bylines.

Sinon was safe. They'd proven that many times before they'd moved to Phase Three testing. There was no way it had put a woman in hospital, no matter what she'd found in Aurillac.

EXTRACT FROM *THE STREAM RAN RED: THE A-NAUT INSURGENCY* BY OSCAR LUNDELL (LEXINGTON: 2131) – INTRODUCTION

3 February, 2076: it has been three years since the rains fell in any measurable quantity on the Ionian island of Zakynthos. Along with a sizeable portion of the Peloponnesian peninsula, the island populations are being evacuated to temporary accommodation in the north of the country, where they're told that they can apply for compensation for their lost ancestral lands and find a way to start again. But rumours abound that the north itself is too water-stressed to cope with the influx of dispossessed; there are whispers of slum conditions in the refugee camps; the grapevine has it that the only resettlement option is Creo and the waiting list to get in is at least five years. Zakynthos is not the first and it won't be the last, but the people are organised and they are determined: they're not going anywhere. A dispute turns into a standoff, which turns into a riot. To this day, the identity of the first shooter is contested, but on the island paradise of Zakynthos, on 3 February 2076, the question is moot. Somebody shoots first, but the gunfire doesn't stop.

For almost fifteen years, Congressional military policy has been to lead the vanguard with a platoon of a-nauts. A-nauts do not experience fear or pity, they don't question orders, and their lightning-fast reflexes have saved countless lives on the battlefield and beyond. The team on Zakynthos are eight-year veterans of civil disturbances across Europe, and in all that time, they have discharged their weapons on only four occasions. Why they open fire on Zakynthos, killing twelve civilians in the initial volley, remains a mystery. Nor can anyone explain why they stop.

At 1302 hours, local time, Mission HQ in Athens receives the following cryptic message from the island: Interference registered. Reconfiguring. Unknown modus. No further communication is intercepted, but, within hours, Central European Command reports that a-naut units in southern Spain appear to be malfunctioning. Then Corsica. Then Hungary. Then the Urals ... And they keep coming.

The amnisonaut series is self-aware.

10 MAY

10.1

Danae was sitting next to a man called Robert Charcot, whose grandfather had died half an hour before Annelise. The late, lamented M Charcot now rested two slots above the Grant family repository, and the grandson rested on the floor five feet below him.

'One day, I will join him there,' said Robert in broken English, on the edge of a hacking cough that threatened to rip his lungs out and eject them from his throat. 'Maybe soon, eh?' He laughed, a hoarse, throaty sound, and nudged her none too gently in the ribs.

It was twenty-past twelve on a Tuesday morning, and Danae was sitting in the pitch-black of Kim Li graveyard, in the company of multitudes. She counted maybe eighty in total, though in the dark it was difficult to tell. It obscured their features, blanched them moonlight white, so that, from across the hallway, they looked like ghosts, half-formed and faceless. Some were in families; some were alone. They whispered amongst themselves in the shadows, and Danae was put in mind of a horde of bats, clinging to the roof of a cave.

They'd made way for her easily enough, though space was at a premium by the more recent graves, for the simple reason that more of the relatives were still alive and were morally – if not legally – entitled to claim their place on limited floor space; the vaults, after all, stretched to the ceiling. Down the corridors, into the heart of the graveyard, lay the dispossessed, afforded shelter for the night by dint of a dead relative.

'Do you sleep here every night?' she had made the mistake of asking her neighbour, who had turned out to be the loquacious and astoundingly drunk Robert.

'Every night,' he said. 'It's warm and dry, and what more do I want?' He had laughed his painful laugh and she'd thought even then that it was a terrible sound and hoped it would stop soon.

'It is like family,' he continued, warming to his theme, though she had turned pointedly away from him and closed her eyes. 'You can sleep safely here, little one. No one will pick your pockets while you sleep. We watch out for each other. You will too.'

'I'm only here for one night,' she reminded him, which provoked another lacerating laugh.

'Nobody here ever meant to stay for two,' he said.

She could feel the presence of their plaque above her in the dark; could almost trace the outlines of the letters with her hands. Now with its second name, letters and dates: WALTER ORMONDE GRANT 2059 – 2119, less familiar, like a new structure on an old landscape.

Calm.

On the edge of sleep, she wondered vaguely if any part of her father existed in a way that was able to see her, and what he thought of her bed for the night. Her mother would have laughed, had she been able to bypass her horror, but Walter she wasn't so sure about. Perhaps he would have been proud of her for coming up with a sensible idea; he wasn't so much about strict adherence to the letter of the law where self-interest was concerned.

Perhaps it would have broken his heart.

You won't be lonely, Danae? he'd said, in the hour before he slipped into the final sleep that had gently segued into death as dawn began to streak a jaundiced yellow light through the flimsy curtain.

No, Da, she'd said, because what were you supposed to say?

And you'll look after yourself?

Yes, Da.

You won't tell anyone? You'll stay safe and you'll never tell a soul?

No, Da. I'll never tell a soul.

Not a soul. Promise me.

I promise.

You're a good girl. Not a soul, our Danae. You stay safe.

10.2

'Look what the cat dragged in,' Danae said, depositing her bag in a cupboard before Nadine could see.

'Look who's talking,' said Nadine. 'You look like you slept in a hedge.'

Danae shrugged and started pulling her long clothes off her short uniform. 'How was your evening?'

'Great. You know.'

'I can guess. I don't want details.'

'I wasn't offering details. Mind your business.' She danced a plate of scones into the hydrator. 'So what's your story? Did your bed catch fire? You do know you're early?'

'I couldn't sleep,' said Danae.

'Yeah, well, why don't you mop the floor before the shock gets too much for me?'

'What,' said Danae, 'is the point of mopping the floor?'

'So that the dirt crusts on one layer at a time,' said Nadine. 'Otherwise you'd be out there with a hammer and chisel at the end of the week, trying to separate the chairs from the ground.'

'Just curious. It's not like anyone notices.'

'They'd notice when they stuck to the lino. Are you okay?'

The question caught Danae by surprise. She pivoted on her axis.

'Fine. Why?'

Nadine stared at her, narrowing her eyes. 'Not fine,' she said.

Danae shook some soap flakes into the mop bucket and shoved it in the larger hydrator. 'You're just buzzed from last night,' she said, careful to focus on the dial and not Nadine's face. 'Not everyone's on cloud nine this morning.'

'You have a hangover? What?'

'Yes, I have a hangover.' If passive drinking were possible, that would be true. 'What? Quit staring at me.'

Nadine's stare was like a hot knife on Danae's scalp. 'Seriously,' she said, and Danae rolled her eyes.

'Seriously,' she said, mashing the hydrator button with unnecessary force. 'Drop it, Nadine. Please. I'm early for work. I'm mopping the floor. You should be thrilled.'

'Yes, I can barely contain my excitement. My life is complete.' A loaded pause. 'I'll find out,' she said. 'You know I will. Just give me a while.'

See you tonight, he'd said as she gathered herself to leave. She'd grabbed all of about an hour and a half's sleep, afraid every time she closed her eyes that she'd wake up to robbery or rape or murder.

Don't count on it, she'd said. He had laughed.

'Is this hydrator on the blink again?' she called after Nadine's retreating back, as the machine wheezed half a pint of lukewarm water into the mop bucket.

'Is it ever not?' Thrown over her shoulder, their conversation relegated already to a mental filing cabinet.

'Perfect,' she muttered.

He had laughed. He'd laughed because everyone came back in the end. When he'd stopped laughing, he said, *I never speak to a newbie who thinks they can't get their life back before anyone notices. Arnaud, my friend, how long are you here?*

Tonight only, Robert. Laughter.

There is no hiatus, newbie. Tonight, I will say, welcome home.

Nadine breezed back in. 'Seriously,' she said. 'What?'

'Nothing,' said Danae. A beat. 'Does Nigel know about the hydrator?'

Suspiciously: 'Nigel always knows about the hydrator.'

'Then he should get a new one. Christ.'

There is no fear in the graveyard, newbie. See? You can sleep. We are your family now. See how peacefully this little one sleeps. She knows that she's safe.

Soap suds floated listlessly on the brackish water. She stirred them in with the mop, but it made them slimy, didn't dissolve them. Who would notice? Who would care? She slapped a damp puddle on the floor and started spreading the dirt around.

Welcome home.

'Not me,' she told her reflection in the water-bright lino. Furiously: '*Not me.*'

10.3

The rain started on the way to Cilicia, and the wind got up three blocks later. By the mouths of the subway stations, it was almost like a hurricane: the wash of warm air rushing to meet the brisk cool bluster and locking together in a violent two-step that tore at Danae's coat tails and sculpted her damp hair into tangled spikes. Every time, she looked into the sodium-lit depths, through the emerging throngs and wondered if she could, if she still had the courage.

You did good, pet.

But those were the easy days, when she was small enough to scam tokens with impunity. Now – what? Arrest? They'd ask where she lived, and she'd have to tell them, and that would be it: hiatus over. Everyone thought that they'd stay in the graveyard until they got back on their feet. They'd leave before anyone noticed.

Welcome home.

She bore down against the wind and struggled on.

Someone was shouting near the regulation ports. Danae could understand that. But as she dripped into the cavernous lobby, she saw that the anger was directed, not at the faceless screen, but seventeen places back in the queue, at a cowering wife and crying toddler. A purple-faced man, shaking with rage, screaming incandescent abuse while the woman cried silent tears and gripped her child. Faces in front and behind and from the queues to either side had turned to watch. A dark-skinned man two rows to the left had tightened his grip on the shoulders of the two small girls that stood in front of him, white eyes wide with fascination, and watched the scene with something approaching enraptured disgust. Danae turned away. The fight continued.

Turrow was leaning on his mop handle, standing in a corner as far distant from the argument as the laws of physics would allow, watching absently for signs that the purple-faced man was about to escalate. She stood at a little distance from him, waiting for him to notice her, watching him while he didn't. He looked tired, but perversely, healthier. Colour was creeping back into his flesh; his eyes had lost their hollow, sunken shadows. He leaned on the plastic handle as though it were an extension of his body, his shoulders slack where he had transferred his weight, his back arched to meet his centre of gravity. A hangnail on his index finger glowed red against the whiteness of his skin and she wondered if the cleaning fluids irritated it.

Danae watched him as he stiffened, alerted by a sixth sense to the presence of eyes on the back of his head, and turned to find the watcher. His face dissolved into a contented smile as he registered her presence, and he straightened, turning his body to face her.

'I've just mopped that floor,' he said, glancing at her feet.

She followed his gaze and found that she had drizzled a puddle of grimy street-water onto the polished tile; glanced back at a trail of translucent grey footprints that tracked her progress from the door. 'Oops,' she said.

He shrugged, grinned in the direction of the screaming fight. 'Better than street theatre, this,' he said.

'Just what you need at the end of a shift.'

'I wish,' he said laconically. 'He's been there for hours.'

'You need a hand with the cleaning?' she said, in lieu of actually apologising for the mess.

He shook his head. 'Go through to the back room. You're freezing.'

'I'm all right,' she said.

'You're dripping on my floor.' He straightened, suddenly weary again, and called, 'All right, folks, time to wrap it up. Closing in five minutes.' To Danae, he added, 'Make yourself a coffee. Make me one too. I'm not leaving 'til the rain goes off.'

★

He found her hunched in on herself, grey-white fingers curled convulsively around a steaming mug and shading to purple at the tips. He covered her hands with his own before he realised he was doing it, and then, embarrassed, said, 'Your hands are freezing.'

'Bloody rain,' she said. She had shed her wet coat but the jumper beneath it was no less saturated. 'I'll be all right in a minute. Your coffee's by the kettle.'

He lifted it, set it on the floor by his seat, and wrapped her in his coat before he settled. She burrowed into it.

'I'll soak it for you,' she warned.

'It'll be soaked as soon as I go outside anyway.'

'Did he leave?'

'Who?'

'The shouty guy. Did he give you grief?'

'A little.'

'Don't you just hate it when people won't give up?' She looked up, treating him to a wry smile. 'Got any cigarettes? I'm frozen to the bone.'

'They don't actually warm you up,' he pointed out. 'Drink your coffee.'

'You need to get back.'

'In a while. I got your message last night. I was going to come by when I got off.'

'Oh,' she said. 'Forget about it. It's nothing.'

'Cassie said you called a bunch of times.'

'Maybe. I can't remember.'

'She said it sounded important.'

'It's fine, Turrow. Don't worry about it.' She sipped at her coffee, eyes lowered, closed off. Boston opened his mouth to speak, but on his indrawn breath she said, suddenly, without looking up, 'I suppose you get all sorts in here.'

He squinted at her, trying to decide where she was going. 'You get enough,' he said.

'I heard a block in Dog Island fell in last week. The top three storeys just crumbled.'

'I heard that. We had a load of families in from the bottom floors.'

'Maybe it would've been better to be on the top floors,' she said, and he thought, *she didn't check the regulation ports when she came in*. 'I heard the Authority started closing off the entire street after that.'

'Sometimes they panic,' he said. 'There's a lot of lawyers in Dog Island.'

'Would it be better to be on the top floors?' she said.

'No,' he told her softly.

'How many of those families are going to last a year on the streets? When it rains? I was in the rain for twenty minutes tonight and look at me.'

'Not everyone died straight off,' he said. 'They can't get to the ones that were buried. Maybe they're still alive.'

'I heard that. That bubble's been there a while.'

He shrugged. 'What can you do?'

'Shut down the block five years ago,' she said. 'The street's nearly a half a mile long. Bubble's only at the east end. There's a lot of blocks like that, I reckon. Shut down while they're still good.'

He looked at her for a long moment but she didn't meet his eye. 'Dog Island's in bad shape,' he said carefully.

'Yeah, but what about that one in Kim Li? Do you remember – about five years ago? They said the one block was relying on the other for structural support, so they closed them both down. They're still standing.'

'I don't go through Kim Li.'

'But you hear about them?'

'Sometimes …'

'Turrow, you work in the Housing Authority. You hear about them.'

'I push a mop about the floor,' he said, holding up his hands in supplication. 'I'm a janitor. What does a janitor know?'

'Places?' she said, and now she looked up at him, eyes veiled by her lashes, afraid to meet his gaze. 'Places to go. Safe places.'

'If I knew that …' he started to say, but his voice fell away when she dropped her eyes. 'You mean sealed blocks?' he said. 'Condemned places.' With the emphasis on *condemned*.

She shrugged, shook her head. 'Forget it,' she said. 'Just forget I asked.'

She didn't check the regulation ports.

'Safe places,' he said. He exhaled. 'They'll be sealed.'

She shrugged again, kept her eyes low.

'I can't get the access codes for the seals, you know,' he added.

'Did I ask for the codes?'

He sighed. 'How safe are we talking?'

'Maybe a block fell down and the Authority panicked,' she said. 'It happens.'

She was trembling in his coat, her fingers were blue. She didn't check the regulation ports. He said, 'Yeah, it happens.'

10.4

The Hilton, it was not. But it wasn't a cemetery.

He'd given her a few names, streets she knew and streets she didn't. She wondered if he'd had the same idea himself, whether it was his contingency plan in case the worst happened. If that was his idea, he'd have kept the best back for himself, but, then again, he was only a janitor. Maybe five names was as many as he knew. She'd wandered in the rain, sizing up distance over area and decided at last on Parnasse. Not near the centre, where the tourists went searching for the good life on a roulette table, but out around the edges where there was actual money. Money meant big apartments, which meant high security when they were shut down. Which meant a little extra effort getting in, but it also meant anonymity, privacy.

Near the bottom of the street, the blocks were haggard and crumbling. Some of them had crumbled already. Their electric seals had been damaged in the fall and they'd been set upon by vandals, presumably furious that, now they were accessible, they were uninhabitable, and the louring walls were charred with the smoke of a hundred fires. Idiots: the available oxygen in Chatelier was already on the low side. Danae passed them by as she traced the rivulets of foetid water, cascading from the roof into the beginnings of a street-river, past the cankered shells to where the real houses were.

She chose a block close to the commercial end of the road, where the desolation began slowly to dissolve into life and chaos. Across the road, the fragmented light-band spewed a yellowish glare up about seventeen storeys, enough to cast some kind of glow into the dim windows beyond, where light sources were scarce. A wall-ferry, relic of earlier prosperity, hung immobile close to street level, tilting rakishly, threatening to collapse. Up the outer walls, as high as the vermin shield and as wide as the block, snaked a colossal advertising board, entreating her to vote yes on Amendment Sixty Eight Hundred and Seventeen. These days it was falling into disrepair: frayed patches allowed green-grey wall tiles to show through, and the electrical supply was intermittent, but she thought that it was a good sign. It meant that the building's circuitry wasn't completely defunct.

It was good. It would do.

*

The darkened main doors opened onto a large atrium, centred by an ostentatious courtyard effect complete with miniature water feature. The water wouldn't have been real, of course, when the building was in use: it would have been a shimmering trick of the light. And the lazy sunlight that had once conjured images of a vanished Mediterranean countryside would have been a solar mist, cast downwards from the photic paint now peeling from the plasterwork ceiling. Shorn of its *trompe l'oeile*, the atrium was dark, dank and claustrophobic, the courtyard fouled by real water that pooled in lines of weakness, the fountain cheapened by years of abrasion and encroaching algae, its plasticised veneer erased. In the dim light that seeped through from the street, Danae could almost make out a trail of beads on the marble-effect floor, running the length of the lobby and stopping, abruptly, by the fountain's edge. She imagined the owner on a distant day, harried from the building by stone-faced men, in fear of imminent collapse, twisting fretfully at her necklace and watching in dismay as the string snapped, the beads scattered…

She chose the third floor. There was no reason for it, no significance to the number, only that she hadn't eaten since lunchtime the previous day and three flights of stairs was as high as she went before her head began to spin. It wasn't high enough to be rid of the pervasive stink of the street below, but it was enough to escape the creeping damp that climbed the lower walls and threatened to suck the block down with it in a decade or two. The apartments were large: three bedrooms, she would guess. At least one bathroom, maybe two receptions, with space unstinting. As she walked down the dark corridor, seeking a door that was at least still locked, she measured the spaces between

entrances. Two hundred, two hundred and fifty feet? Limbe had *blocks* that
were smaller than that.

You didn't move through the districts in Creo Basse. You took your space
and you set down roots, and you were bloody glad at the end of the day that
you had them at all. As her hand rested against a random door – *3319*, it
said – she realised that she felt severed now, as though the act of taking new
quarters had erased those that went before. She pushed, testing the lock, and
found it firm.

She was home.

10.5

Doctor Kabede's orders had been specific, but, in any case, Diana was
glad to note, as the trolley broke through the pathogen field and burst into a
world of white light and antiseptic, that they'd arrived at the main hospital
campus in downtown Saint-Julien. She'd been afraid they'd divert to one
of the smaller Acute Injury Pods in the district centre, and she knew, even
if Con was still quite manifestly invested in the idea that it wasn't as bad
as it looked, that they were some way beyond triage now. A mother has an
instinct.

The paramedics' faces were hidden behind hazmasks, pulling their
skin into animalistic contortions as they ran behind the trolley, barking
information to the doctors at whose heels they trotted, and Diana had to
blink to clear the sudden sensation, fringed with the edges of hysteria, that
she'd wandered into some kind of surrealist nightmare in which the city had
emptied of human beings and repopulated with plastic-faced, computer-
voiced simulants. It felt as though her life had narrowed into a tunnel, as
though these past, terrified fifteen minutes had telescoped into infinity, and
it was getting more and more difficult, with every passing moment, to think
clearly. They were talking urgently in low voices around her, whispering
numbers in tones of great urgency, as though a person's life could be reduced
to a series of digits, as though a body on a trolley was the sum of a serology
count and a temperature reading, and she felt her hand reach out to catch
the nearest arm, to remind them that she was here, she had ears, that she
needed to know what was happening. But it fell away of its own accord and
she turned her head instead, searching for Con and finding him running
alongside Pia's stretcher, hand pressed against the thick plastic coating that
sealed his child inside with whatever had spiked her temperature to 105

degrees. His skin slipped against the surface as he moved, and she saw the flesh flare white against the dark, coarse hair that covered his knuckles as he tightened his grip.

He caught her gaze, twitched his lips upwards into a faint smile. Diana had never seen her husband so close to tears.

'I should have …' she said, and stopped. It was getting so hard to hold a thought in her head. She tried again: 'I should, I should have called earlier. I'm sorry. I'm so sorry. I thought …'

'It's all right, Diana,' said the dark-skinned girl, the one who had smiled at Pia and told them all her name, but it had slipped through the cracks of Diana's mind in the crowded moments that followed. 'It's not your fault. We're doing everything we can.'

'I want to stay with her,' she said, but the voice that forced its way out of her throat was coarse, sandpaper-rough. It didn't sound like Diana's. 'Please. Let me stay with her.'

But they were already bustling away from her, coffin-like stretcher fizzing through another pathogen field as two heavy doors slid out of its way, opening onto a room so bright with artificial light that Diana had to close her eyes against a sudden sensory overload.

'She's in good hands, Diana,' said the dark-skinned girl –- Blessing, Diana remembered suddenly; that was her name. How could she forget a name like that? 'Con will stay with her. We need to take care of you now.'

And Diana wanted to say more, wanted to argue with them, scream at them if necessary, make them understand that this was her daughter, her sick child, the child whose fluttering heart – the heart Diana had felt beating inside her own body for the first nine months of Pia's life – was trying to tremble its way out of that small chest. Her child whose eyes were rolling in her head as her core temperature soared into the danger zone. Her child whose body, even now, was being hooked into a machine that would strip it of everything that made it autonomous, everything that made it human, until all that was left was a brainstem and an unconscious mind, for as long as it took them to stabilise her. But it was getting so hard to think, so hard to talk. So hard to breathe.

Con was with her. Con would stay with her. Con would make sure she wasn't alone.

Diana closed her eyes and felt a soft curtain of static brush her skin as her stretcher was wheeled through the opening doors of Emergency Room B.

THE COURIER, 6TH FEBRUARY 2076

Sources on Zakynthos are today refusing to confirm or deny recent reports that an a-naut expatriation force that three days ago refuted their protocol and laid down arms have been deactivated. Emancipation, the a-naut rights organisation, claim that the Zakynthos Group have been shot, and that this is an infringement of the basic corporeal rights afforded to them by virtue of their semi-organic status. The head of the Peloponnesian expatriation outfit could not be reached for comment.

11 MAY

11.1

'It's nothing, I'm fine,' said Nadine.

It didn't help that the Rens had raided that morning: three of them, with nothing better to do with themselves, brandishing a warrant card and lining up the customers against the wall. Danae had protested a little, but it didn't do to make too much noise about it. They could just as easily leave the place in pieces.

Two of the customers had walked out. The rest had pushed their luck, trying for free coffees or a reduction on the bill, and she'd had to hand them out. No point in protesting that it wasn't their fault that they were the first store in eyeline when the Rens got bored, because there were plenty of other cafés in Frain and most of those weren't getting raided that day. Tips were down, a couple of plates were smashed, and someone had ground a cigarette into the face of one of the buxom redheads on the wall, but it could have been worse. At least there hadn't been any a-nauts in the assembly. You heard stories.

She'd had better Wednesdays, and most of the morning was spent in a haze of stress and frustration, three steps behind herself and running to break even. So it was lunchtime before she noticed that Nadine's colour was up, that her eyes were dull and that she rubbed her throat when she spoke, and that the mood, which Danae had assumed was Ren-induced, had failed to improve in the absence of Rens.

'You okay?' she asked at last, when she came into the kitchen to find her leaning heavily against the hydrator, eyes closed and thumbs massaging deep circles into her temples.

'Magnificent,' said Nadine.

'You don't look okay.'

'I'm fine,' she said.

'Why don't you take the afternoon off? I can manage.' True enough: word had spread, custom was slow.

'Nigel's coming in tonight.'

'So come back tonight. Get a couple of hours' rest.'

'Danae …'

She knew that tone. It was the tone she would have used herself the other night, but for the fact that Nadine was still her boss. Danae held up her hands.

'Okay, okay,' she said, and beat a strategic retreat onto the empty café floor. 'I'm just saying.'

Nothing. No answer, no snarky comeback to follow Danae out of the kitchen, no injunction to spend more time thinking about the state of the floor and less about the state of the shift manager. That was nearly as worrying as the mood itself.

Turrow came over in the afternoon, while they were still clearing up the lunchtime debris, caught Danae's shredded look of low-level panic, and almost shrank straight back out the door. 'Bad timing?' he suggested.

She shook her head minutely, in the hope that it would convey just how prodigiously accurate his assessment of the situation was, while in no way attracting even a small portion of Nadine's attention. 'How come you're off early?'

'Someone shot out a regulation port,' he said. 'We closed for repairs. I'll make it up at the end of the day.'

'And you couldn't think of anywhere better to go?'

He ignored that and said, 'Have you had your break yet?'

If Nadine had been in a better mood, she would have laughed that off, made some joke about the wicked and their typical rest allowance, but a glance at the counter told her to think again. Nadine was watching them, eyes darkly hooded, decanting tray-bakes onto a plate as though they were made of evil and had recently insulted her family. She looked away quickly when Danae met her gaze, and pretended to absorb herself in arranging the snack bar.

'Now's not a great time,' said Danae.

'Take half an hour,' said Nadine. Her tone was neutral, her face sour. 'We're not busy.'

'No, I'm fine,' said Danae.

'Half an hour. Go.'

'Honestly, I'll stay,' said Danae desperately.

Nadine glared. There was a lot of conflicting information in the glare, but what it mostly communicated was the velocity with which the shit was currently approaching the fan. 'Danae …' she began.

Danae grabbed her coat.

★

'Shit, sorry,' he said when they were outside.

Danae rolled her eyes. 'I don't know what's up with her. I'm about ready to bloody well murder her this afternoon.'

'Slow today?'

'It's not that. She usually likes slow. We were raided this morning.'

'Ouch,' he said.

'Someone shot out your regulation port,' she pointed out.

'Five of them, actually. One of the bullets bounced back and hit him in the gut. I've been shifting blood stains out of concrete for the past hour.'

'Did he die?'

Turrow shrugged. 'Maybe.'

'You're all heart.'

'He had a *gun*.'

His voice was steady but a note of something indefinable betrayed him, and she shot him a sideways glance. She realised that his skin was white, shaken; realised that he'd known, for a brief moment, that there was a very real possibility that he would die. She pictured him standing on his highly polished floor in the second that he understood, blood draining from his face in a rush as though he'd been shot already, with no time to run, nowhere to duck for cover, only the creeping knowledge that his life was about to end for the least worthy of causes. He was smiling now, trying to erase the revelations that had slipped free in tone of his voice, trying to pretend he was a regular superhero, relaxed in the presence of death, and all it did was tear a jagged line of sadness along the inside of her throat.

Without thinking, she reached towards him, found his hand, and locked her fingers through his.

He glanced up sharply, as though her touch had burned. Danae shrugged and made a *so what* face, although *so what* was not what she was thinking.

'Half an hour,' she said. 'Where do you want to go?'

They settled for coffee from a street stall, thick as tar and slightly less nutritious, and carried it to the back of a night warehouse, empty in the afternoon, where discarded boxes in the yard made for a makeshift picnic ground. Danae, who only ever saw the afternoon through the windows of Intimacy, was dizzy with freedom, overly inclined to laughter.

'If I turned this cup upside down,' she said, 'would any of the coffee fall out, do you think?'

'Buy your own next time,' he told her, but he was smiling.

She dipped her finger experimentally under the filmy surface of the liquid. 'You need a new job,' she said.

'I'm holding out for an executive position.'

She nodded. 'Something with a company car.'

'And dental.'

She smiled, but it tailed into a sigh. 'Do we ever know how to pull the short straw, you and me,' she said.

'Speak for yourself,' said Turrow, but carefully.

'How'd we end up in this stupid city?'

'Some of us were born here,' he reminded her, but she only rolled her eyes, shook her head.

'Look at you,' she said. 'Stuck in this crappy job that you hate, just to get by, just to try and deal with the shit you got handed, and today someone nearly kills you just because — I don't know. Because you're *there*. And me: no home, no family. Crappy job' — an expansive nod of the head to illustrate the pattern — 'and so broke I need my mate to buy me a cup of coffee.'

'It won't always be like this,' he said.

'Yes it *will*, Turrow. That's the point.' He said nothing, just swirled the coffee in his cup: a regular, concentric circle. So she continued, 'You know what I heard today? They're closing down a school in Fiore for bacterial meningitis.'

'They're always closing *somewhere* down,' he said.

'It's this stupid city,' she said, as if he'd settled an argument. 'It breeds disease, Turrow. Doesn't matter what you do, or what you say, or what you want — this stupid city's always got something else it can do to you.'

So leave. It hung between them, but she knew he wouldn't say it. You thought about it, but you didn't say it, in case you made it not come true.

Finally he smiled. 'I'm glad, I don't think like you,' he said.

Yeah, thought Danae, *So am I.*

She closed her eyes, pressed the tips of her fingers into her sockets, scrubbed her hands up and over her temples. 'Ah, ignore me,' she said. 'It's been a shitty, shitty few weeks.'

'That,' said Boston, 'may be the understatement of the century.'

Laughter burst out of her, catching her by surprise. She risked a sideways glance at him, but he wasn't looking at her; his eyes were fixed on some point in the indefinable future, unfocused and distant. He was smiling, but whether it was in response to her laughter or to something she couldn't see was anyone's guess.

She watched him for a moment, enjoying the private joy that warmed the air around him, and she thought that this part of him, of being near him, had become familiar. There was a little ineffable *something* about Turrow that radiated from him and made you feel better just because he was there, and she wondered what on earth it was he saw in her that made him seek her out, again and again, when surely the opposite was true of Danae.

'How do you do it?' she asked quietly.

Turrow shot her a glance. 'Natural hypnotic allure?' he said. 'I don't know, Danae Grant. I don't know what "it" is.'

'You just ...' she said, and hesitated. 'You always just assume everything's going to be okay. I don't know how you do that.'

He shrugged. 'What's the alternative?'

'Life?'

Warm laughter, and the sun broke free again behind his eyes. He said, 'Maybe I should've stumped up and bought you a shot of cheer-the-hell-up in that coffee. Sometimes it sucks, and sometimes it doesn't. You know? Cassie's meds ran out, and I met you. Things just work themselves out, one way or another.'

The words were light, but there was something beneath them, she thought: a question that needed an answer. And she was, abruptly, aware of the tiny distance between them, aware of the heat that drifted off his body and jostled against her personal space. His skin smelled of chemicals and exhaustion and second-class coffee left brewing too long: the scent of the city, of the Authority, of his life, and it filled her with a sudden urge to lean her head across the small distance between them and rest it on his shoulder. Sit easily for a few minutes. Let go.

But she didn't. She couldn't. So, instead, she sucked in a breath — but quietly, so he wouldn't hear — and said, 'I should be getting back,' and the moment was gone, dissolving into the dark city air like sugar in water.

He glanced at his watch, and, if he noticed the evasion, he gave no sign. 'Don't want you getting in any more trouble.'

'I don't think she's feeling well,' she said. 'I thought it might be a hangover, but, you know.'

He shrugged, as if to suggest that it was all one to him. 'Hey,' he said. 'Before you go.'

She turned, afraid of what he would say next. In Danae's experience, nothing good ever came of a last minute call-back. But he only reached out his hand, caught hers in his, tightened his grip and gently let go.

'Just ...' he said, and hesitated. 'Just remember: it's not all bad.'

11.2

In the end, it was a relief when Nadine agreed to allow Danae to close up alone, and the last hour and a half of the day was able to be spent in the absence of a mood that presaged the Apocalypse. Late in the afternoon, a bomb scare in the south of the sector – which might or might not have explained the raid that morning – closed twelve blocks to human traffic and Intimacy mopped up some of the spill-over trade, which was enough to put grey hairs on a person's head, but not enough to make them actually pine for the presence of Nadine. The rain cycle kicked in half an hour before closing time, smearing the grime of days down the windows in grey-brown stripes as the shadows lengthened, but, because Nadine wasn't there, it was okay to actually ask people to leave at closing time when they were disinclined to surrender a warm, dry seat for a cold, wet pavement. None of them were regulars and nobody ever needed to know.

Alone, finally, Danae darkened the windows and switched on the cleaning lights, locked the doors and the till, and sank into one of the chairs with all the grace and aerodynamics of a damp sack of sand. The apartment, with its patina of dust and regret, was not enough incentive to get her moving quickly; she might, in fact, never move quickly again. If Nadine had been there, they may have sat for half an hour, eating leftovers and easing out some of the tensions of the day, and Danae considered the possibility of heading over to her place for an hour or so, making sure she was all right. She hadn't been asked and wouldn't be welcome, and if Nadine had turned up at her bedsit while *she* was ill she would have been seriously unimpressed, but Danae had never been ill, so it was a moot point.

Maybe. Right now, all she wanted to do was sleep, and the apartment was like a morgue; it bred hideous dreams that nibbled away at the back of her brain when she woke. Maybe she should swing past the Authority on her way home, make sure Turrow wasn't dead. Maybe there could be another coffee, maybe even a street-stall dinner, eaten on the move, between smiles and careful distance and the easiest conversation she'd ever known. Maybe he'd have thought of another bunch of names, places that didn't smell so manifestly of dereliction and lost hope, places where a body could sleep and forget to be constantly on its guard. Maybe he could make her feel that sense of possibility, the one that nobody had ever managed to persuade her to feel before, and she could hold onto that for however many minutes they spent in each other's company, and guard it like a candle flame into the long and restless night.

Maybe.

She cleaned the floor, threw out what leftovers couldn't be reused, scraped the crumbs off the ones that could. She cleaned out the display cases — after all, Nigel would be round that night — restocked the cooler, switched off the lights and the Hermes, programmed the Mod to start propagating a new batch of stem sheets, sent a quick message to head office to say that she didn't think Nadine would be in the next day and could anyone cover? In the absence of a second body, the work took nearly twice as long, but, hey, as long as her chip showed activity, she was getting paid for it. In any case, it was pouring outside, and the café was warm. The streets and, more importantly, the apartment were not. And nobody was paying her for either of those.

It was dark outside by the time she finished, with no sign of Nigel yet, but that was one of those small mercies for which she was prepared to thank any beneficent deity that might be interested. The Authority would be closed by now; possibly still within the hours of cleaning, but locked from the outside and too far out of her way to justify the probability of a wasted journey. In the silence of the empty kitchen, Danae was pulling a long skirt over her uniform and trying not to think too hard about whether or not she was bothered about the de facto absence of Turrow from her evening, when a thumping at the front door startled her abruptly into the coffee machine. It wobbled reproachfully on its axis but failed to break in any noticeable manner that could be attributed to her.

'We're closed!' she snapped. It was fortunate that she had to shout to be heard through the café and the closed doors, because it permitted her to fragrance her tone with a satisfying soupçon of *fuck the fuck off*.

She fastened the clasp on the skirt, shrugged into her coat. The door thumped again.

'I said we're *closed!*' she shouted, possibly veering off into the psychotic at the end, but these things couldn't be helped. There was one door out of Intimacy, and she was about to have to choose one of two equally unpalatable options: remain until the invisible door-thumper gave up, whenever that might be, or else attempt to get past the sort of customer that thinks banging on the closed door of a darkened café is the path to a late-night coffee. She sighed and squeezed her eyes shut, in case that might help. The door thumped again.

Danae crossed the floor in six strides and pressed her face up against the door. 'We. Are. *Closed*,' she said, loudly and in a tone that, at the very least, ought to make the thumper question whether his need for coffee really outweighed his need for testicles.

'Yeah, I worked that out all by myself,' said a voice just familiar enough to oblige the common courtesies, even muffled by a door thick enough to withstand Frain's finest when things got a bit colourful. 'Can I come in? It's *pouring* out here.'

Danae sighed again, and slid back the retainer bolt.

Angelo, to be fair, looked as though he'd swum there. It was exactly the sort of look — dripping with the kind of water that passed through the filters in a Frain rain cycle — that did not recommend access to a recently-cleaned floor. 'Nadine's not here,' said Danae, without moving.

'Perfect,' he said, and rivulets of brackish water rolled off the tops of his lips and into his mouth. 'Can I at least, please, and for the love of God, come inside?'

Danae regarded him levelly. 'Are you *kidding*?'

'Uh …' He looked at her, looked at the rain, spread his arms and shrugged. 'No. No. Not really. I think I might drown.'

'She's at home, Angelo,' said Danae, with the moderate tone of desperation that recognised a person who just did not understand the rules of social interaction. 'I'm closing up, no-one's coming in.'

'Uh — Danielle?'

'Danae,' said Danae, who suspected he knew her name very well.

'Danae. Right. Danae. Listen, I'm standing in the rain here. I've never been this wet in my entire life. Can I at least come in and jack the phonewave? I will clean the goddamn floor after me.'

She stared at him. He did indeed look miserable, shoulders hunched against the downpour, collar turned up, apparently, to better funnel rain water down his neck, skin shading to the greyish pallor of a man who has been in the cold for too long. But he was a man she had met once, and the café was deserted.

She said, 'Angelo, the till is closed. I've buzzed the takings to head office already.' Which was a lie, but unless Nadine had actually shown him the unlock key, there was no way for him to know that. 'Strictly streampoint only.'

He blinked. Fractured raindrops scattered from his lashes. 'Are you *serious?*' he said.

'I'm closing the door now. I'll tell Nadine you were looking for her.'

'Are you serious?' he said again. She started to close the door, but he slipped his foot into the jamb.

'I'm not kidding,' she said, 'I'd bet on this door over your foot any day of the week.'

That made him laugh, which she wasn't expecting. 'It's a nice door, but it's not *that* nice,' he said.

'Goodbye, Angelo.'

'Wait a minute …'

It came as a surprise to her to find that she was, apparently, going to wait a minute. Mostly because his foot was still in the jamb. It had been a long day, and Danae just did not care about a severed foot anymore. She pushed harder.

'Okay, so that actually hurts now,' he said.

'Of course it hurts,' said Danae. 'Move your fucking foot out of my fucking door.'

'Hold on a minute,' he said. Danae considered giving up, throwing the door open, and kicking him in the groin. See if he could jam his foot in the door *then*. And then he said, 'Do you actually not know?'

The obvious response was, of course, *do I actually not know what?* But then he would be entitled to tell her. So she went with, 'Angelo, I'm two seconds away from calling the police.' Which was not original, but was at least thematically consistent.

'Good,' he said. 'Call the police. At least you'll have to let go of the damn door and I'll get in out of the rain. Seriously, how can you not know?'

He had a point about the door. Danae was tired, hungry, pissed off, and out of options. She gave in.

'One phone call,' she said. 'You have two minutes. And don't fucking drip on my floor.'

The *dripping* comment lacked finesse, because there was absolutely nothing either one of them could do about that, but he was good enough not to mention it. She released the door just far enough to allow him to squeeze himself through, and he stood close beside it, regarding her thoughtfully. And, naturally, dripping all over her floor. He said again, 'How can you not know?'

While he showed no inclination to get the phone call over with and get out, she stood, defensively, close by — near enough to act, if action was needed, but far enough away to oblige him to declare his intentions first. She said, 'Angelo, I'm not playing. I'm in no mood for this. Phone call and out, or I'm calling the police.'

His smirk was arrogant, and she wondered how Nadine tolerated him, but his eyes were confused. He said, slowly, 'I clocked you in three seconds, soon as I walked in that night. But you really don't … how can you not know?'

Danae, who had a really good stare, met his gaze and held it. But the tiniest kernel of panic had taken root in the pit of her belly. When she spoke, her voice was not as confident as she would have liked, and she could hear the smallest trace of the faint but insistent whine of anxiety in her head. She said, 'What don't I know, Angelo?'

'About me.' Inexplicably, he waved a finger between both their heads. 'Seriously. There's no way you don't feel that.'

'Your waggling finger?' But the whine was making its presence felt; the question was more like a request: *please mean your waggling finger.*

His eyes narrowed; he was obviously struggling to understand. He said, 'I know what you are.'

11.3

Her first thought, ridiculously, was to run. Her second thought was, *there is no way he knows. He cannot possibly know.*

So she said, 'Phone call, Angelo. I haven't got time for this. And you're dripping all over my goddamn floor.'

He took an uncertain step towards her. Danae got the impression that Angelo never did anything uncertainly, so even his uncertain was uncertain. Instinctively, she took a step back, but, even as she did so, it occurred to her that this was the wrong thing to do – it looked defensive.

It looked frightened.

He said, 'I'm not going to spell this out, Danae. You *have* to know what I mean. I *know* you know what I mean.' But, of course, for a man so declaredly certain, he was protesting a lot.

Danae was suddenly, acutely aware that her hands were shaking. She balled them into fists and shoved them in her pockets, where little treacherous tremors batted the fabric against her skin. If she said, *I don't know what you're talking about*, did that resonate with every clichéd denial in the history of trite? Did that make her look more or less like she had something to hide? But if she brought up the phone call one more time, did that make it look like she was wilfully ignoring the question?

He could not know. He could not possibly know.

And then, in confusion, Danae did the worst thing she could have done under the circumstances: she opened her mouth, took a breath to speak, and closed it again.

Angelo didn't miss it. Of course he didn't. It was that sort of day.

He said, 'You know.'

'Phone call,' she said, but she knew she'd lost, and she knew her voice lacked any kind of authority.

'I don't get it,' he said.

'Just go, please.'

'I don't get *you.*'

'I want you to leave. Right now.'

'I know what you are, you know what I am. What's happening here?'

He'd taken another step towards her. An elongated puddle of greyish water tracked his progress across the floor. Danae took another step back, but there was no point in pitching for control of the situation anymore; stepping backwards was pretty much all she had left. The whine had become a heady, terrified wail, and, because she was no longer in any semblance of control, she went for the comfortable option.

'I don't know what you're talking about, Angelo,' she said, but she could hear the uncertainty beneath a tone that pitched valiantly for brusque and came out laced, instead, with poorly restrained panic. 'Get the hell out of my café.'

His eyes narrowed again. He was, manifestly, completely and utterly mystified. He said, 'I'm standing three feet away from you. You have to be able to feel it. I'm *three feet* away.'

'What?' she said. 'What do I feel, Angelo?'

Again, he waggled the finger between their heads. 'You seriously ...' he said, and his eyebrows arched. Danae would have sworn, on the basis of two short encounters, that he'd never worn an expression of such complete and abandoned bewilderment in his entire life. It was a face with which he had clearly had no practice. 'Where are you from?'

Shock and confusion almost forced a laugh out of her. 'Where am I *from*?'

'How can you actually not know this?'

'Do I look like I have the faintest idea what you're talking about?' she snapped. 'Is this the expression of someone who has the faintest idea what you're talking about? And I've already asked you to leave, about a dozen times. Just – get out, Angelo.'

'You genuinely don't know,' he said, as though it was something that she hadn't been trying to tell him all along.

'I'm calling the police,' she said, and turned her back on him to cross the café.

He let her get a step and a half, which was further than she expected. 'There's a disturbance,' he said, softly, although the sudden silence of the café made the words sound huge. 'I know you can feel it. Like butterflies in your brain.'

And Danae stopped sharp, pulling up in the middle of the floor as though her legs had forgotten, mid-stride, how to move.

Back turned to the door, she couldn't see his face, but she felt his eyes on her as her shoulders slumped, as the tremors in her hands set up a visible trembling in the fabric of her coat, and she couldn't tell if they were from the panic, or the sudden chill that had shut down her motor systems. Silence settled on the café like a blanket of ash. She let it lengthen, deepen, until it was so heavy that it twisted her throat and stole her breath, until her ears rang in the absence of sound. And somewhere in the middle of it, in the centre of her skull, was the delicate fluttering of a thousand gossamer wings.

'We are what we are,' he said.

Get out, she wanted to say, but the words lined up in her head, got jumbled. So she kept quiet, stared at an ancient, irregular stain on the floor, thinking that if she moved, if she tried to make one more denial, she would disturb whatever it was that was holding her together. She knew without looking that his eyes were level on the back of her head, impassive, unspeaking, confident in what they saw, and she thought, *he knows.*

'Like butterflies,' she said softly, nearly a whisper. Absently, as though she were talking to herself. 'I felt it. I didn't know what it meant.'

He said, 'I don't get it.'

She didn't turn around. 'You don't have to get it.'

'So, what – all this time, you've thought – what? That you were alone?'

Alone. Yes. No. Excluded, perhaps. Peripheral. Perhaps there was no identifiable word for what she'd thought or what she'd felt. She shrugged.

'Your whole life?' he said. There was something indefinable in his voice, some mutant offspring of horror and pity and rampant disbelief.

She said, 'Like I'm in a moving car, looking out the window, and I'm trying to focus on something in the distance. Is that it? I had no idea what it meant.' All those times. All those dozens and dozens of times.

'Will you turn around?' he said. 'I feel like I'm talking to a wall.'

'I don't want to watch you fuck up my clean floor,' she said, but she turned around all the same. His face was blank, but his eyes were relentless.

'The floor will survive,' he said. 'You – I'm not so sure.'

'Nobody knows but you,' she said.

'Understood.'

In the cemetery: every time that big hulking man and the tiny, very pretty woman moved, her brain had buzzed and they'd looked at her and he'd winked once and she'd just thought that he was pissed or crazy or both. How many times in the café had a head suddenly snapped up as she passed and she'd just thought she was tired or stressed? On the streets and in the subway, on her mother's cookie stall. Walking through Limbe or Cilicia — in the Housing Authority, for Christ's sake — or Chatelier or Fiore or Nebe. Buying groceries or getting her shoes mended or sheltering from an unexpected downpour. Stealing a pretzel on the way to work one morning and catching the vendor's eye and instead of shouting and popping a blood vessel he looked surprised and then smiled as she backed into the crowd. The caretaker at her old school, who had studiously avoided her eye and never passed her in the corridors when there was an open door to duck into. All those faces over all those years.

She wiped a hand across her eyes. She'd thought she was exhausted *before* Angelo showed up. She said, 'I don't ... I really don't know what to do with this now.'

He smiled. It was the most innocent expression she had ever seen on his face, completely without artifice or calculation. He said, 'I move around a lot. Let me give you an address. Someone there will know how to find me if you ... you know. Do you have something to write on?'

From the transcendent to the mundane. The *ordinary* rushed back in with something like a corporeal thud. She blinked. 'Um — yeah,' she said. 'Hang on, let me see.'

Her hands were still balled in her pockets. Straightening out her fingers was like prising open a vice. There were things buried in the folds of fabric from the days when her mother had worn the coat; things that had never been ejected and were now afforded a kind of sanctity by time and loss — a petrified old tissue, a couple of English coins that might actually be worth something to a collector by now, a hairpin, a sweet wrapper. Her questing fingers closed painfully around a selection of paper scraps and she inched them out. Two were receipts for things she couldn't remember buying. The third was an old business card, the print long since faded, and replaced with more recent text in heavy black ink: *Da, Église du Sacré-Cœur, 1/05 9 A.M.* She handed it to Angelo without speaking.

He glanced at the writing, glanced at her. Something flashed across his face, but all he said was, 'Pen?'

Silently, she crossed to the service counter and reached over it, to the shelf that nestled underneath it on the kitchen side. Nadine was forever complaining that pens got up and walked out of the café, that no matter how often she filled the pen jar, there was never more than two left by the end of the day. There was one this evening. But Nadine wasn't there.

She heard Angelo follow her and couldn't muster the energy to challenge him. It made life easier that he was standing behind her when she turned, that there was no floor to cross to hand the pen to him, that he had only to rest her tiny little piece of card on the counter top and scribble something along the bottom in a discordantly small, neat hand, while she watched and concentrated on keeping her knees locked so that her legs wouldn't give out beneath her. He said, 'If you ever need anything, you ask for me. If I'm not there, they'll know where to find me, okay?'

'Okay,' she said.

'Burn this paper. This is only for you, okay?'

'Okay,' she said again.

His hand caught her gently under the chin and tilted her face up to his, and for a horrible, confused, surreal moment, she thought he was going to kiss her. But he only smiled his innocent smile again and said, 'Hey. Cheer up. You're not alone anymore.'

11.4

He claimed that he'd left something in Nadine's apartment the other night, but Danae suspected that he just didn't want to leave her before he'd worked out a way to ask the questions he wanted to ask in such a way as to get her to answer. She was lost, drowning, suffocating, buzzing, and lacked the clarity to make him go away, so she reconciled herself to Angelo's presence with the dual logic that (a) he'd be one extra target for Nadine to aim at, and (b) she was strung-out, drunk on her new knowledge, and intoxication made for bad decision-making. It wouldn't hurt to have a responsible adult in charge, just for a while.

Because the butterflies were *everywhere*. Recognition bred recognition – surely she had walked the same streets a thousand times and felt a thousand ephemeral attractions and never registered them because they had never meant anything. Now they assaulted her from every angle and she felt like a child with a brand new skill, as though she'd suddenly remembered how to read after a lifetime of illiteracy, as though someone had hardwired a new language directly into her brain and set her off amongst the natives. He could feel her buzzy, jagged excitement beside him and occasionally half-smiled sideways as they walked, when another butterfly-face passed by like a cloud of perfume, but her animation made him nervous and she knew he didn't trust her to keep herself safe. Whatever. For the first time in her life, there was someone else to worry about that. She wasn't alone.

The rain followed them as they passed through the gates of Frain and into Omicra Verte, where the overground shuttle ran through the streets of the north-western districts as far as Punta Oeste. Nadine lived in Sainte-Thérèse, the sixteenth district, with three external walls that butted up against the outside and a badly-founded high opinion of itself. Commerce was scarce, which was why the rent was low, and the streets were only sporadically punctuated by crowds: more a steady trickle of humanity against the high black faces of bank upon bank of anonymous apartments. Danae slipped her hand into her coat pocket as Angelo followed her off the shuttle, curling her fingers around the card that carried his address, as though it was something precious, something breakable, something that needed to be protected from the world. Maybe it was. It meant that she wasn't alone anymore; maybe that was worth more than anything she'd ever owned.

Parts of Sainte-Thérèse had been closed down three months ago with sporadic outbreaks of bloody diarrhoea, which might actually have killed a couple of dozen people; it was hard to remember now. Poor old Sainte-Thérèse, just a couple of walls away from the sunlight and the open air, but lacking a gate to get there. Limbe was always being closed down with something or other; you picked it up and ran with it and claimed your quarantine credits when you were housebound and were happy enough for the chance to kick back for a few days, unless of course you happened to be one of the unlucky infected. But Sainte-Thérèse fancied itself more *outside* than *in*. Poor old Sainte-Thérèse. Bloody diarrhoea wasn't even romantic. You couldn't die from it in an aesthetically pleasing way.

From Sixteenth Park, she turned left onto a cul-de-sac too minor even to be dignified with a name, just a little plaque announcing that its buildings were to be considered an extension of the main street. Nadine liked it, Danae remembered, because she thought it made the block exclusive. There was talk now of a bubble opening up over Sixteenth Avenue West, a couple of blocks south of the Park. Too early to see anything; maybe it was just talk.

Nadine's complex was at the end of the street, nestled up against the back of the Sixteenth Avenue Central apartments, and the main entrance was sequestered beneath a small portico that jutted out from the wall and afforded some measure of protection to weary travellers newly arrived from a café in the ninth district and wet to the point of osmosis. Danae, plastered as close to the wall as she could huddle, swiped her palm across her neck and pressed it to the com link. At least the rain in Sainte-Thérèse was a little less lively than in Frain. Angelo's skin had settled into the greyish pallor of the newly dead, and she'd just remembered, out of nowhere, something about critical core temperatures.

'Are you cold?' she asked.

He sputtered a laugh, scattering raindrops. 'Are you kidding?'

'You look like a reanimated corpse,' she pointed out.

He nodded at the com link. 'Just swipe it again.'

'She's probably sleeping,' said Danae, but she had another go anyway, holding her hand in place while the com link hollered a high, sustained wail.

'Not anymore,' he muttered.

'You know,' said Danae, 'I'm not sure she's going to be one hundred percent thrilled to see you.'

'Story of my life,' he said.

'I'm swiping one more time and then I'm going,' she said.

Angelo shrugged, as if it were a matter of supreme indifference to him, and she suspected that it might be impossible to persuade him not to follow her when she left. She was not in love with that idea.

'To hell with this,' he muttered under his breath, and shuffled forwards, edging her out of the way and almost into the rain again. 'Let me try.'

'She's sleeping,' said Danae, but she moved her hand; it was easier than arguing, and considerably more appealing than being shifted bodily out of the tiny shelter. One eyebrow arched meaningfully as the tinny little com link shriek mined a headache through her teeth and into her skull.

'*What?*' screamed Nadine's disembodied voice.

★

Nadine's apartment smelled of sick people — a concoction of syrups and vague halitosis — and the temperature gauge was about five degrees too high. She was sprawled across her bed, still dressed from the café, face down into the pillows and clutching her house control card in an outstretched hand. Danae felt Angelo stiffen beside her.

'Nadine?' she said quietly.

Nadine muttered something incoherent into the sheets and didn't move.

'We should go,' said Angelo.

'Are you serious?' said Danae. She shot him a glare, but his face was frozen, austere. 'Fine. Go. I'm staying.'

'You can't *stay*,' he said, as though she was a recalcitrant child. 'Look at her. We shouldn't be here.'

Danae ignored him, crossed to the bed, crouched down so that her head was level with Nadine's. She put out a hand to her forehead. 'Jesus. She's burning up. I think she needs a doctor.'

'She was okay to scream at us five minutes ago,' he said. He hadn't moved.

'Wrstphg,' said Nadine, but her eyes didn't open.

'Seriously,' said Danae. She looked up at him, but he was staring at Danae, not Nadine, and with poorly concealed panic in his eyes. 'I think she's really sick. Will you go to the bathroom – there's a medicine cabinet over the sink. See if you can find any patches.'

'Danae, I'm not kidding. We have to leave right now.'

'Then *go*,' she snapped. Nadine twitched and mumbled something. 'Angelo,' she added, when he didn't move, 'I've got to get her temperature down, and I've got to stay with her until the doctor comes. Go if you want to. I'm staying.'

'You're insane,' he said. The anger in his voice surprised her; her head snapped up and she saw that he was actually shaking.

'Good. Fine. I'm insane,' she said. 'Go to the bathroom. See what you can find. See if you can get me a cold compress as well, she always has ice in the fridge. Angelo, seriously! Do it or go, don't just stand there watching.'

She felt the air shift as he left the doorway and half expected to hear the front door slam, but the noises of focused movement came from the bathroom instead. 'Nadine?' she said. 'Nadine, I'm going to get you into bed, all right? I'm going to get your shoes and your coat off so you won't be so warm.'

From the bathroom, Angelo called, 'There's three different kinds of patches in here. You want them all?'

'Bring whatever there is,' she called back. Nadine let out a soft whimper as Danae started to ease her left foot out of its shoe. Beside the bed, in a photo pixellated with age, her seven-year-old self played an eternal game of football with her long-lost parents, catching and touching down and grinning a train-track smile. Nadine had been a beautiful child. 'I really need that compress. Her temperature must be over a hundred.'

'One pair of hands,' he called, but she heard him moving from the tiny bathroom into the kitchen-living room, heard the fridge door opening and the sounds of rummaging.

Walter had soared and plummeted for the last four years of his life. Danae might come home of an evening to find him shifting furniture for the elderly couple that lived two flights up, laughing and sharing cut-price brandy that smelt of industrial waste, then wake later that night to find him coughing up blood, blue-lipped and struggling for breath. But Walter had worn death like a cape for most of her adulthood; it was *normal* to see him suddenly, inexplicably, and without warning spike a temperature of a hundred and four and start to die. So ingrained had it become in Danae's routine to rescue him from oblivion five times a month that, by the time he finally slipped away, it felt like the end of one obscenely extended joke without a punchline. Nadine sputtered and went down like everyone else — a brief tussle with cholera shortly before Danae met her, and every single pandemic influenza that ever raised its head in the city — but she had never before waltzed into work in high spirits one morning and passed into semi-consciousness twelve hours later. The foul temper was one thing. Danae had thought it was the cold.

'Here,' said Angelo's voice from the door, startling her. She turned in time to see him toss a couple of small vacuum-sealed packets and a bottle of viruscidal spray cleaner. 'For your skin,' he explained. 'Keep spraying. Spray everything that touches her.'

'What about the cold compress?'

'It's *coming*,' he snapped. '*One* pair of hands ...'

Nadine was tall but slight, and her weight came as a surprise as Danae started to roll her onto her back to unzip her coat. In the end, Danae climbed onto the bed beside her and straddled her, using the leverage to get enough momentum behind her unresponsive body that it had no choice but to invert in a tangle of splayed, useless limbs and a mumbled complaint that was mostly consonants. Even through three layers of clothes, she could feel that her own body heat was making Nadine uncomfortable; a hand twitched weakly on the bed as though it were trying to rise and flap her away, and she muttered something that sounded remarkably like an obscenity.

'Angelo, seriously ...' Danae began, clambering off the bed and tugging at Nadine's right sleeve.

'I'm here, I'm here,' he said. His voice was behind her. She turned to him and he threw her a tea towel and a plastic bag full of chipped ice. 'Spray,' he said.

'In a minute.'

'No, now. Now, or you're on your own.'

'Christ,' she muttered and wondered if it was even worth explaining. God only knew what the stuff would do to her skin, or Nadine's, already irritated by the unrelenting heat beneath it. She lifted the bottle from beside the bed and sprayed a cursory mist of lemon-scented dew over her hands, rubbed them together, wiped them over her face. 'Okay. Sprayed,' she said. 'Did you see a thermometer in the bathroom cabinet?'

'No,' he said. 'Clothes as well.'

'I'll do the clothes before I leave.' He started to protest, but she cut him off. 'Or else I'll be drenched in fucking lemon juice, Angelo. Can you go see if you can find a contact for her doctor?'

'I think she needs an ambulance.'

'Ambulances are expensive. Would you just look, please?'

The butterflies receded as he disappeared from the doorway, and she wondered if this was how it would be now: wondered if there would come a time when she could pinpoint his location precisely by the feel, wondered how far the range extended. Even in the living room, she could feel him.

Nadine made a little noise. It sounded like 'Danae.' In case it was, she said, 'I'm here, don't worry. I'm not going anywhere. This might sting a bit...' Her face, too warm, too swollen with heat, twisted as Danae pressed the compress against her forehead, but that had to be a good sign, surely? If she knew enough to be uncomfortable? But the skin was too hot, much too hot; too dark and too fiery. Even Da didn't get too hot to comfortably touch.

'Angelo?' she called, but before he could answer, Nadine's body began to convulse.

The shock made Danae lose her footing, and she stepped heavily into the bedside cabinet, collapsing the eternal football match on its face and causing the patches to slip to the floor. Danae didn't bother to pick them up.

'Angelo!' she shouted. 'I need you! Now!'

Limbs flailing, back arched, face pinned into a rictus, Nadine bucked and twitched as though a current was passing through her. Danae gripped her beneath her string-puppet arms and pulled, while flesh slapped against flesh and hammered against the bed. She felt rather than saw Angelo arrive, felt his open-mouthed horror, and spoke into Nadine's shuddering neck. 'Run a bath. Lukewarm water, nearly cold. But *not* cold, not actually cold – this is important. Not cold. I need to get her temperature down.'

'What happened?'

'She's having a fit, Angelo, and she's going to die if we don't get her temperature down.'

'She needs an ambulance.'

'Yes, she needs a fucking ambulance, but first she needs to get her temperature down or there won't be any fucking point in a fucking ambulance! Just run a bath!'

Nadine was spasming, jerking, trembling. It was nearly impossible to keep a hold on her, let alone start to pull her, inch by inch, from the bed. Her feet snarled in the bedspread, so the bedspread came with her, billowing, twisting, shuddering with every tiny increment. In the bathroom, she heard the taps running. She knew she needed Angelo's help to move Nadine, knew he wouldn't touch her. He might very well refuse to be in the same room as Danae after this, she thought. Which might at least make him leave her alone.

Off the bed, she trampled one foot on the bedspread to hold it in place while she tugged Nadine free. Suddenly, without warning, Nadine went limp, and Danae, caught unawares, almost let her fall. But in the next second, she was fitting again, violently – more violently than before. Danae forced her feet backwards. In that second of stillness, she'd thought Nadine had died.

The bathroom was across the tiny hallway, as tiny as everything else in the flat. Angelo leapt backwards, out of their way, out of the room, as if he'd been stung, but it was easier on the tiled floor, where there was less friction to slow them down, and where the end was so nearly in sight. And then Nadine went limp again. And stayed limp.

'Angelo, is she breathing?' said Danae urgently. 'Jesus Christ, you don't have to touch her, just look at her! Is she breathing? *Is she breathing?*'

From his safe place across the hall, he stared, hollow, dark-eyed. 'I don't know,' he said at last. 'I don't know, I can't tell.'

'*Look*, Angelo, please! I need to know. I need to know if she's breathing!'

'You tell me!' he almost shouted. 'You've got your hands around her chest, is she breathing? Danae – we have to go – '

And then Nadine definitely resolved the argument by fitting again.

Danae, caught unawares by the last time, had learned no lessons, and staggered backwards, awkwardly, clumsily. As she lost her footing, Nadine collapsed to the floor, but not in time for Danae to save herself. Her hands went wide, grappling for anything that might break her fall, but glanced off the sink and she dropped, hard, striking her head heavily against the rim of the bath as she went down. Black, then white flashed behind her eyes.

She was out for no more than half a second, missed no more than the first syllable of Angelo's panic. ' – sus, Danae, are you all right? Danae, are you okay? Are you all right?'

'I'm good, I'm fine,' she said. Her hand reached up, gingerly, to touch the spot above her left eye where the porcelain had connected. Reddish-purple pain spots exploded underneath her fingers, but there was no blood. 'I'm fine,' she said again. Nadine lay sprawled on the floor in front of her, twitching like a dying fish. Danae said, 'Angelo, you have to go.'

'*We* have to go,' he said.

On hands and knees, carefully, nauseously, she picked her way across the tiles, found purchase under the flailing arms, took the weight. 'Call an ambulance,' she said. Inch by inch, centimetre by centimetre, knowing as she did it that by now it was in all probability too late.

'I'll call an ambulance, and then we have to go,' he said.

'I'm not leaving her.' Her vision starburst black and red as she got first to her knees, then to a crouch.

'We can't be here when the ambulance comes,' he said.

Her eye felt like it was going to explode out of its socket as, with a final burst of infinite effort, she made it to her feet, Nadine trailing limply in her arms. 'I'm not leaving her,' she said again, and swung Nadine towards the bath.

'It's not *leaving her*, Danae, it's avoiding getting killed!'

Nadine's knees connected with the side of the bath, folded over the edge. Danae staggered forward, trying to control the drop, trying, at least, to make sure that Nadine's head did not shatter against the tiles. The water thrashed white as her limbs locked in motion.

'Go, Angelo. Seriously. Call an ambulance and go.' She turned to him, met his eyes. 'It's okay. It's fine. Really. Go.'

He stared at her, stared at Nadine, at the flashing, foaming water, on the walls, on the floor, on Danae. He said, 'Don't let them find that address, Danae.'

'I won't, I swear. Please, Angelo, she needs help. She needs an ambulance.'

Softly, he said, 'It won't make any difference.'

And just as softly, she answered, 'I know.'

TRANSCRIPT: EUROPE TODAY, *AIRDATE 8 FEBRUARY 2076*

Following confirmation earlier today that the a-naut platoon known as the Zakynthos Group, who broke protocol during an expatriation exercise on the island on Monday, have been deactivated, streamlink experts are continuing to seek the source of the malfunction, which appears to be global. Meanwhile, concerns are growing over the impact on international trade and commerce as the bug continues to affect a-nauts the world over. Some 75 percent of all manual labour is now estimated to be performed by artificial workers, many of which remain unresponsive to commands.

Here to talk through the possibilities is Professor Derek Chambers, Chair of Telectronics at Manchester University, Dr Guneet Cheema, Head of Research and Development at Novalux Suisse, and Dr Hanne Klooster of the Amsterdam Centre for Law and Economics. Professor Chambers, if I could start with you – we're hearing a lot of buzz about broken protocol, and the question on everyone's lips seems to be, if what we're seeing is a mass ... civil disobedience, if you will ... I suppose the question is, is that possible? And if so ... what happens next?

12 MAY

12.1

If there was one thing that Creo Basse did really well, one crowning gimcrack in the city's rusty crown, it was quarantine. Danae had never had cause to visit a disease ward before, but there was some universal language of antiseptic segregation that spoke to a part of the unconscious brain – the sharp, sweet odour of bleach; warm, dry, motionless air; the scent of emptiness; the non-specific, aseptic aroma of sterile things – that identified the space around her in the moment of waking, before her eyes were open. A brief moment of panic sucked a rapid breath of disinfectant-perfumed air into her lungs and she felt her muscles tense, constricted by something unseen, in the seconds before her brain rebooted, and the memories came swimming back.

Nadine. Angelo. Sainte-Thérèse. Paramedics and panic and protocol. *Shite.*

Danae opened her eyes.

Supper had been laid out for her on top of her empty locker. Why they'd included the locker in the interior design spec was a mystery, since they'd taken everything she owned in Decontimination. She supposed there was a natural order of things even in isolation units, and a hospital room came equipped with a locker. Even when they took your things.

The hospital had come as a bit of a surprise. Not the hospital itself but the fact that they'd made Danae stay, although, in the long, long night, she started to wonder why she hadn't expected it. It wasn't as though they had any way of knowing that she wasn't every bit as sick as Nadine, and they were hardly likely to let her potter about the streets like Typhoid Mary. Danae knew a viral overload when she saw one, so she'd expected the hazmasks and full-body gel suits. What she also probably could have anticipated, had she not had other things on her mind at the time, was that the plastic-wrapped men, after listening attentively and with much nodding and note-taking, as

Danae explained the story of Nadine's descent into serious illness, would load her friend into a hermetically sealed stretcher and then politely but firmly insist that Danae climb into one of her own.

It's not me, it's fucking Nadine, she'd pointed out. She'd said *fuck* rather a lot, which counted as not, perhaps, her finest hour, but the circumstances were unusually difficult. She'd been amazed to see a readout when they'd scanned Nadine for lifesigns: she'd been that sure she was dead. After she'd said *fuck* several times, the paramedics explained that she could either get into the stretcher booth by herself, or they could sedate her and put her into the stretcher anyway, which was only slightly more effort for them and involved less paperwork than she might think.

She wondered where Angelo was. She wondered what Turrow was doing right now. She would not wonder about Nadine.

A stream of doctors, excessively and intrusively curious. Samples of fluids that she'd rather not have given. Question after question: *How have you been feeling lately, Danae? Any travel outside the city, Danae? No aches or pains or sniffles, Danae?* She hated that, hated the casual way in which doctors were allowed to be *La Salle* or *Ortiz* or *Morrison* while she had to be *Danae*, on the basis of half an hour's acquaintance. Nobody had asked her if it was all right. They'd given no indication that they even knew she had a surname.

She must have slept. A sedative was likely but intensely irritating – she remembered agitation, confusion and demands but not any pressing sense of exhaustion. Nevertheless, it was now clearly the middle of the night, and she was in a darkened room that she didn't recognise, the only light a reflected glow on the clinical white walls, the source some distant point down a never-ending corridor outside. Her throat was dry and her head was muzzy with what had to be a drug hangover. Someone had got her into a surgical gown, the kind that was only marginally less humiliating than actually being naked, and her back, where it was exposed to the elements, was unnaturally warm in the superheated hospital air. Danae sat up in bed to take in her new home.

A bed, a locker. There ended the furniture inventory. A crisp white sheet to cover her, tucked with military precision under the mattress, so that she had to tug violently at the edges to release enough slack to allow her to sit. Two fat white pillows, smelling faintly of carbolic soap. A plastic undersheet, uncomfortable even within its linen shield. Her lifesigns, a steady stream of dull blue and green, trickling through the air above the top of the bed, blood toxicology readouts from a new tattoo on her arm, updated every half hour.

All stable. Tiny diodes scattered around the room at intervals describing the path of the light beams that would assemble the figure of a doctor in the room; perhaps twice as many cameras watching her with unblinking eyes.

The silence in the room was the preternatural hush of the soundproofed wall, but she suspected that if she were to cross to the plexiglass window – which made up the barrier that separated the tiny, boxlike room from the narrow corridor beyond – and press her hand to the surface, she would find it pulsing with the thrum of industry beyond.

Nadine was there somewhere, she thought. At least, she hoped so.

12.2

Breakfast was a fruit stew and two slices of bread, washed down with a pot of coffee and a glass of what was almost certainly not orange juice. Danae considered refusing it, making some kind of stand until they told her where she was and why she was there, but decided that the chances of anyone actually doing that were slim. And she was hungry: she hadn't eaten in almost forty-eight hours.

The doctor arrived as she was soaking up the last of the stew with the dry side of her bread.

'Nothing wrong with your appetite,' she said pleasantly.

'Nothing wrong with *me*,' said Danae. 'What's this, by the way?' She held up the glass of orange liquid. 'If you tell me it's fruit juice I'll call you a liar.'

'It's an electrolyte supplement,' said the doctor, whose name badge said *McCullough*.

'My electrolytes don't need supplementing.'

'Actually, they do. It was about the only thing we could find wrong with you.'

'Can I go, then?'

'No, there's some more tests we need to run. Maybe tomorrow.'

'I knew you'd say that,' said Danae. Thinking, *just say it, just ask*. But aloud she said, 'Can I get a phone jack, then? There are some people I need to call.'

McCullough smiled, but she didn't look at Danae. 'I can ask Referrals to get in touch with your next of kin,' she said.

'This isn't … it's not family.'

'Uh …' said McCullough, and her eyes were on the readouts, the pad in her hand, anywhere but Danae. 'I can ask. But for pro bono cases, it's usually family only.'

Danae dropped her gaze to the sheet at her lap, where her hands were twisting white fabric into a garrotte so tight that the tips of her fingers were shading purple. 'I didn't ask to come here,' she said quietly.

'No, but we've got to have you anyway,' said the doctor brightly. She flashed a quick glance at Danae, but her eyes were skittish. 'Trust me. This is the best place you can be right now. I'll see what I can do about that jack.'

★

Time was, Danae might have sold her soul to the lowest bidder for a chance to lie on her back and do nothing for a few hours, but the reality, as it turned out, was somewhat less relaxing than she might have imagined. Possibly it had to do with free will, and the absence thereof.

She spent the morning flicking idly through the channels on the mini-screen at the foot of her bed, the discovery of which had narrowly obviated a serious consideration of the merits and demerits of clawing off her own face just to have something different to look at. Pro bono patients might be expected to jack their own phonewaves, but the avoidance of homicidal boredom, apparently, was in the public interest, and the city was willing to pay a basic entertainment subscription for all comers: news, a couple of magazines, and seven different soap operas on an endless loop. Danae skimmed listlessly across travel brochures and infomercials, melodramatic reveals and interest rates, and wondered if, in fact, the corridor outside wasn't more interesting. Figures flitted, periodically, past the smoked glass panel at the bottom of her room, and sometimes they stopped at the holocom point, reappearing, briefly, in her room to ask invasive questions about urine output and menstrual cycles, and sometimes they passed silently by, like ghosts behind gauze. She thought their numbers might be steadily increasing, but it was impossible to be sure.

Every time they came — to check her stats or repoint a patch or replenish the bottomless beaker of not-juice — every time she opened her mouth to ask the question, felt it hover on her tongue, felt it line up behind her lips and gather breath. And every time she closed her mouth again, words unspoken, before they could find their way out. Because she was almost certain she knew the answer, but, while she didn't ask, she could pretend it hadn't happened.

★

McCullough morphed into Davidson mid-afternoon, and then, as the soap operas were gearing up for early evening histrionics and the newsreaders' voices were getting dinnertime-bulletin grave, Erdoğan, a pleasant-faced woman in comfortable middle age, whose eyes reminded Danae of Annelise.

'Dr. Davidson was going to ask about a phone jack,' Danae reminded her, in a voice that was beginning to bear the strain of a long and indolent day with nothing like sufficient stimulation or privacy.

'I don't know about that,' said Erdoğan amiably. 'I can ask Referrals, if you like? But they usually don't provide a phonewave for pro bono cases. You should be able to jack into your own pocket from here, though.'

Danae rolled her eyes and bit back the sort of response that was likely to get her marked as *difficult* in a file that needed to stay as difficult-free as possible for the release orders to get processed. 'Forget it,' she said quietly. A pro bono admittance was humiliating enough without trying to explain to a woman in three-thousand credit shoes that her phonewave was incoming only.

But Erdoğan was busy with Danae's lifesigns, for reasons unknown to Danae, who was perfectly certain they fed into a readout in an office somewhere in which there was a discernible absence of obstreperous patient or pathogen risk. 'If there's someone you need us to contact,' she said absently, 'I'll pass the details to Referrals.'

She wondered if Turrow had noticed she was gone yet, and doubted it. He'd have looked for her yesterday evening at the Authority; most likely written off her absence on the strength of Nadine's performance earlier that afternoon. And making a fuss about getting a message to him now took them down a path that Danae wasn't sure she was ready to travel.

'My dad died two weeks ago,' she said, which was unquestionably a cheap shot, and certainly designed as such, but a body had to have *some* kind of outlet for a day of frustration and boredom, however unworthy that outlet might be. 'I don't have any other family.'

'I'm sorry,' said Erdoğan, who, to Danae's chagrin, looked like she genuinely was. 'You probably haven't had a chance to think about nominating anyone else as next of kin, I'm sure …'

'Nadine,' said Danae. She hadn't realised she was going to say it, and certainly wouldn't have said it if she'd had prior warning, but it had made its way out on the tail of another prickle of residual guilt and the unspoken question that hovered perpetually at the front of her mind. Erdoğan's face didn't change at the sound of the name. Danae wasn't sure if that was a good sign or bad.

'You know each other pretty well, then?' said the doctor, eyes still on the lifesigns, right hand scribbling a steady stream of notes on a notebook in her left.

Danae wasn't sure what that meant, or if it meant anything. 'We work together,' she said. 'She's my boss.'

'Right. Right. Not much of a holiday, this.' Erdoğan flashed a smile but her eyes stayed fixed on the pad in her hand. 'That makes sense. She's got no immediate family listed on her file either.'

'She has cousins somewhere in the south,' said Danae. 'Avignon, I think. Or Aix. They have a different surname, though …'

'I have a Solomon Marchand, listed on her file, born Solomon Pascal, and a Charmaine Pascal, his sister? Second cousins on her mother's side, I think.'

'Yeah.' It was something beginning with a P, Danae remembered, but the one and only mention of them had been years ago, a throwaway comment that did not invite further speculation or curiosity. She certainly never thought she'd ever be *asked*. 'Pascal. That sounds right. I don't think she ever met them, though.'

'I'll have Referrals give them another call,' said Erdoğan. 'Is there anyone else?'

'No one.' Danae shook her head. 'Not that I know of. She never really talks about her family.'

'Who else would she be in contact with? On a regular basis?'

'Half of Frain?' Danae gave a sharp, humourless laugh. 'I don't know about anyone else. There's an old lady she cooks for sometimes.'

'The lady that lives across the hall from her?'

'In her eighties?'

'Yes.'

'That's her. Zuria, Zuriel, something like that. Look,' said Danae, before the words could get lost in panic again, 'I'm worried about her. I'm worried about Nadine.'

'I can …' said Erdoğan, and buried herself in lifesigns again. 'I can see if I can get someone round to talk to you.'

'Can't you just tell me?'

'I'm not her doctor, I'm afraid.'

'But you must know? How many people can there be on this ward?'

'You'd be surprised,' said Erdoğan, and her lips twisted into a tight smile. 'Look. I'll see if I can get someone to talk to you this evening, all right? Before shift change, how's that?'

It would be more useful if Danae had the first idea of when shift change might be, but she nodded. 'She was in bad shape,' she said. 'I just want to make sure, you know …'

'I'll get someone to speak to you,' said Erdoğan again. 'These cousins of hers – you don't know how to get in contact with them, do you? We're having a bit of trouble.'

Danae shrugged. 'I don't even think Nadine knows how to get in contact with them,' she said. 'She won't want to see them; she doesn't even know them. I don't know why …'

But the word cut off halfway through, juddering the sentence to a halt. Because she *did* know, she realised. There was only one reason a hospital would be interested in the only living relatives of a critically ill woman, the ones that lived half a country away, who had never set eyes on Nadine and couldn't have picked her out of a line up if she was wearing a Day-Glo badge with her name picked out in three-inch, flashing letters. The ones who represented the only actual blood family she had left.

There was only one reason why they wouldn't be talking to Danae.

'Oh God,' she said softly, while a little part of her fractured. This, *this* was why she didn't ask. Because anything was better than this. 'When did she?' But the word wouldn't come, her lips wouldn't form it, so, instead, she turned it into a simple, unmistakable, 'When?'

Erdoğan was tired, Danae saw now. The doctor's eyes were black with fatigue, her skin drained grey: the colour of a woman running on caffeine and adrenaline. Danae guessed maybe thirty-six hours since she'd last slept. Maybe she recognised her mistake, and maybe she was just too exhausted to argue it away, but her face softened with understanding: a look that was part sympathy, part recognition.

'A couple of hours ago,' she said at last. 'She slipped away.' A beat. 'It was very peaceful.'

Danae thought of the bathtub, twin arms hammering at the water like a storm, and knew that the doctor was lying. But she wasn't sure what good would come of insisting on the truth. Better to let a little lie build a new, easier memory, she thought, because there was only one person, in the end, who had any serious investment in the way that Nadine died, and she was past the reach of fabrication now.

'Can I …' she said, and hesitated. Tried again: 'Can I see her?'

'We'll be keeping her in isolation for now,' said Erdoğan. 'Ask again when you get your discharge order, maybe there's something somebody can do.'

'All right,' said Danae. And then, 'Thank you.'

A nod from the doctor, and one arm reached out in front of her. For a moment, Danae thought that it was a gesture of sympathy and almost shrank back, before her scrambling brain remembered that Erdoğan wasn't actually in the room with her, that no human contact was possible. And then the doctor's hand brushed the holocom disconnector, and she was gone, head flicking over her shoulder as she disappeared.

In the corridor outside, Danae saw a legion of half-formed figures drift into shapeless vision behind the hazy glass curtain at the bottom of her room, from the direction of Erdoğan's distracted glance. They were moving rapidly, purposefully, and she thought that, if she could hear them, there would be a buzz of urgency in the air around them, like the static charge before an electrical storm. Six, seven, eight people, all running.

Danae lay back on her bed and wondered, uneasily, just how many Nadines there were, secreted into glass-fronted rooms along the corridor.

12.3

Boston had debated with himself for at least the last hour and a half of his shift, but it was what it was, and he had found, on the whole, that it was often easier to go with the instinct, even when one was dealing with a quantity like Danae Grant. She hadn't showed up last night, and he wasn't exactly confused about that one: he couldn't imagine she was getting off before eight, eight thirty at the earliest, and it wasn't like he had any way of letting her know how late he'd be working. In any case, he guessed there were things that a person did after a day like that, and things that they did not do, and high on the list of column number two was likely to be *visit the Housing Authority*.

There was no reason, not really, to expect her tonight, but then she didn't turn up. He wasn't sure if the coffee had been a good idea, and he wasn't sure if his company was welcome, but, when the doors were locked and the floors scraped clean of a day of dusty feet, he put the call in to Alex anyway, to let him know he'd be an hour or so late, and left in the direction of Frain. What the hell. You never knew unless you tried.

The doors were locked, of course, but the cleaning lights were on and the glass wasn't shuttered yet. Boston peered through a gap in the letter *M* and saw that the café was still occupied, but the woman scrubbing the tables with an air of frozen fury was neither Danae nor Nadine.

'She's not here,' she spat in response to his question, offered tentatively after a knock on the window caught her attention and the question itself had caused the door to be flung open wide. Boston, alone on the pavement of an empty street, recoiled at the naked anger in her voice, and wondered if the woman might actually seize a knife from the counter and rush him. 'Not Danae, not Nadine. And I've just done a ten-hour shift on my own, so don't ask me. I'd *love* to know where she is.'

'She didn't leave word or anything?' he said, edging carefully away from the door.

'Nothing. All I've got is a note from head office to say Danae says Nadine's not well and can I cover. She doesn't think to mention *she* won't be in as well. You can tell her from me I've told Nigel.'

He left then, because he had an idea about the likely constitution of a ten-hour solo shift in Intimacy, and the potential impact on a person's psychological failsafes, and it didn't seem to be the ideal moment to test his hypothesis by insisting on the improbability of Danae not showing up for a shift. She had his phonewave; he had no way to reach her. But he'd given her five names, places he'd come up with off the top of his head: two of them, she would have rejected straight away, and one of them, he thought, might actually have been demolished. That left two. Two places that she might be, on either side of the city. Unless she was at Nadine's but he didn't know where that was.

She knew where he lived. She had his phonewave. She'd find him if she wanted him.

He got home, earlier than planned, to find a palpable air of consternation enveloping the apartment, and his brother pacing the room, systematically running through every name on Cassie's extensive contacts folder. Alex glanced at Boston, nodded a hello, kept pacing as he finished his call.

'Okay,' he was saying. 'Let me know if you see her. Okay, thanks, bye.' Then, to Turrow: 'Mum called. Where the hell have you been?'

Turrow blinked, wondering what the correct response might be. 'I called?' he suggested. 'We spoke, literally forty-five minutes ago ...'

'Have you seen the news?'

'I've just this minute walked through the front door; you *saw* me come in ...'

'They're shutting down Fiore.'

'Who says?'

'The *news* says.'

'They said it was a school.'

'It was a school,' explained Alex, with what he may have imagined was infinite patience. 'Now it's the whole sector.'

'Since when?'

'I don't know, maybe half an hour ago? It was on the news.'

'For meningitis?'

'No! Who said meningitis?' Boston opened his mouth to answer, but the question, apparently, was rhetorical. 'It's anthrax, some kid was taken to hospital.'

'So they're shutting down the whole *district*?'

'Boston, you know, not believing me isn't going to make it not true. And fucking Cassie's disappeared.'

Boston rolled his eyes. 'Disappeared how?'

'As in, not here. And Rita's got it into her head that somebody somewhere said it wasn't even anthrax, she said she heard it was Ebola or some such shit.'

Exactly what Boston needed right now was for Rita to not get hysterical. He said, 'It is not fucking Ebola; why does she always think it's Ebola?'

'Well, she's having one of her meltdowns ...'

'Perfect.'

'... and she says half of Fiore's being tested for Ebola, and she says half of Fiore can't have missed their vaccinations.'

'Half of Fiore,' said Turrow, with what *he* imagined must be infinite patience, 'are not being tested for Ebola. I *hate* it when she gets like this.'

'You try talking to her,' said Alex. 'And she also knows what Cassie's like. First person she wanted to speak to when she called.'

'Maybe she's on her way home,' Boston suggested, more in optimism than expectation. Alex did not even offer the idea his consideration.

'Yeah, but you know Cassie,' he said. 'And they're calling an off-peak curfew, starting this evening. Tilly can't get back; she's staying at Mum's tonight.'

Boston was suddenly very, very tired. He pinched the bridge of his nose. 'Right,' he said. 'Fine. Okay. I'll go out and look for her.' His coat, which he'd half shrugged off, he shrugged back on again. 'You checked with Mila?' he asked.

'Of course I checked with Mila.'

Didn't mean she wasn't with Mila, of course. 'I'll head over that way, maybe I'll see her on the way. Keep trying her mates, okay?'

'Maybe it's time to talk about getting her a phonewave of her own?'

'Ha, yeah. Good one. Keep ringing people.'

'If you don't get her in the next couple of hours,' said Alex, as Boston stepped one foot through the door, 'come on back. We can't afford to bail you both out.'

*

The streets were no different. The only evidence that anyone in the lower city was aware that they were being curfewed again was a series of billboards, flashing crimson letters above the pavement: OFF-PEAK CURFEW IN PLACE, VACATE STREETS BY 2200. Cassie would see one, he reasoned; realise she needed to get home. But would she hurry? Would she hell.

And now he started to notice, dotted in amongst the passers-by, men whose faces were too shiny, too still, watching the assembly heave and sigh forwards, stop to chat, pay for a beer or a burger, peer into a shop window. He'd seen them before, during the city's periodic tussles with the pathogen du jour: plastic-coated peacekeepers, safe behind their polyurethane shield, sucking purified air through the virus-mesh on their backs. They'd come for Tilly once during an outbreak of diphtheria at her school, when she had, predictably, begun to complain of a sore throat. It wasn't diphtheria, just a violent infection that they couldn't identify, so they'd taken her tonsils instead and sent her home. But Boston remembered the plastic men.

The block where Mila lived, partner-in-crime extraordinaire and valproisol-alternative cause of episodic hostilities in the Turrow household, was twelve streets away, across Chatelier district centre. To get home, his sister would need to pass a concentration of shops, arcades and burger stands without being drawn to them like iron filings to a magnet. He started to scan the passing crowds, peer into windows, size up queues at the stalls, looking for a flash of blonde hair four feet and five inches off the ground. To shout for her was useless; he could barely hear the roar of traffic over the people-sounds. Would she even glance up at the billboards? The last time they'd been off-peaked she'd turned up in a streetside café with four other pre-teen girls, learning how to smoke, and he'd got her home with all of fifteen minutes to spare before zero hour. They'd been escorted back to the flat, and Alex had practically had heart failure when he saw the blue flashing lights outside and tried to calculate how much food they couldn't afford to buy if two Turrows had to be bailed out of quarantine. And Cassie, of course, had been all adolescent ire, protesting the indignity of being bodily seized and dragged away from her friends and claiming that no-one had told her there was a curfew happening. The point was, essentially, that she probably wouldn't look up.

He caught sight of her as she left an arcade a couple of yards ahead, turned in the opposite direction to home, and made for a burger stand up the street. 'Cassie!' he shouted, uselessly, picking his way through the crowd before she could disappear again. She didn't hear him; he knew she wouldn't. He shouted again: 'Jocasta Turrow!'

Elbows, knees, even fists — shoving people out of the way, trailed by a comet tail of complaints and half-heard threats. Crowds wouldn't part when you were in a hurry. He ran sideways, crablike, arm outstretched to prise a path between the bodies, compacted like an arrow into the narrowest possible point.

She was second in a queue of seven, waiting for a new batch of patties to be cooked up before the vendor would take another order. He grabbed her by the elbow, trailed her free.

'Boston, what the fuck!' she shouted. 'I'm getting my tea.'

'Did you happen to notice the off-peak?' he said. He was so angry he was very nearly calm; like he'd spun a hundred and eighty degrees. 'We're going home. Alex is about ready to have a coronary.'

She shook her arm free of his hold. 'I am getting my dinner,' she said.

'You're getting arrested,' he told her.

'Ah, Boston, don't be soft. It's not even half seven yet. And Mila says it's bullshit anyway. She says her dad's gone down the pub just like normal. Everyone knows it's bullshit.'

'Mila can pay your bail then,' he said, closing his fingers around her lower arm. Cassie's eyes widened in pain, but she could either follow in his wake or lose the blood supply to her right hand, and she was attached to the hand in more ways than one. It was her favourite bird-flipping hand. She elected to follow, but she wasn't happy about it, and an unhappy Cassie liked the world to know.

The streets were heaving, oblivious, the plastic men milling, but the air was changing. An off-peak was a warning, a hint that things were bad enough to be actually doing something but not so bad as to risk inciting the wrath of the day-traders just yet. Boston had lost count of the times they'd been curfewed this year. It wasn't like there was anywhere he was likely to be going in the evenings, and it wasn't like he ever got time off, so apart from keeping track of Cassie, who was currently a walking complaint, trailing behind him in a blue haze of expletives, an off-peak curfew was more or less business as usual. But anthrax … that sounded like the kind of thing that was expensive to fix. His grip tightened on her arm.

Above them, crimson letters cast bloody shadows across the hot air.

★

'The schools are shut,' said Alex. 'It was just on the news.' He clipped Cassie round the ear for good measure, provoking another explosion of creative invective.

'Jesus,' said Turrow, sinking into a chair. 'Not *again*. It's, what, five minutes since the last flu?'

'You should keep watching,' said Alex. 'Most of the government buildings are saying they're not opening either. Maybe the Authority's next.'

'Jesus,' said Turrow again, but with interest. Paid holiday was something he hadn't considered. On the other hand, paid holiday meant that the problem was probably on the bad side of 'Not Good'. He rubbed his face, hard, as though he were trying to stretch the skin. 'We maybe need to start buying in food, Lex.'

'Mum's on the phone every five minutes. Bill's not home yet.'

Turrow rolled his eyes. 'He won't be home tonight. I hope to God she has the sense to keep a tight hold of Tilly.'

Outside, the city went about its business. In the distance, someone was shouting something over a loudspeaker, but the streets sucked the substance out of the sound and left only the resonance as a thin irritation layered over the general maelstrom.

Nothing to do but wait and see.

12.4

For dinner, they served meat substitute and reconstituted vegetable mash. It had the consistency of carpet tile and tasted like salty cardboard, but a meal was a meal, and Danae was bored enough by now that inedible food was the highlight of her evening.

'Can I go home yet?' she asked Davidson when he arrived, but he wasn't the conversational type, and he wasn't comfortable with any topic of discussion that strayed too far from matters relating to the setting up of her room for the brain scan he wanted to run. In an outpatient ward, it would have been the work of thirty seconds with a portable halo; in an isolation cube, the logistics became that much more unnecessarily complicated – the more so, Danae couldn't help thinking, since there was clearly nothing wrong with her and her serology readouts kept showing no trace of viral pathogens. She was about as infectious as an elastic band. But there was no talking him out of it, and, in any case, as diversions went, it beat zero-g dance-off championships or lifestyle movies.

At a word from the doctor, the smoked glass at the bottom of the room abruptly cleared, revealing the harsh white light of the corridor beyond, and a series of identical glass panes lining the opposite wall, frosted against prying eyes. Outside, a technician, wearing studied ennui like a mantle, took up a position by Danae's holocom point, next to the disorienting figure of the doctor as he jacked into the mainframe holoconnector, movements anticipating his avatar a half-second too early. The technician looked up, met Davidson's glance, raised an interrogative eyebrow.

A terse nod from the hologram gave him the all-clear, and the technician called up the control screen on the outside pane of the window, punching an instruction into the databanks, speaking words that Danae couldn't hear. Davidson turned over his shoulder, mouthed a muted answer, turned back to the room.

'Lie as still as you can,' he told Danae. 'This'll be over in a minute. Some people find it a little claustrophobic — I can give you a mild sedative if you'd like?'

Danae was sorely tempted to point out that, given the fact that she'd spent the past twenty-four hours in a room no larger than the storage closet at Intimacy, it was kind of late in the day to be worrying about her reaction to enclosed spaces. But, on reflection, she was prepared to concede that smart-mouthing the man with the power of discharge orders mightn't be the most productive strategy, and, in any case, there was probably in the region of a forty-percent chance that complaints about the psychological hardships of confinement to a small room would lead to a mild sedative whether she liked it or not. So, in the absence of any practical alternative, she flattened herself on the bed as instructed, and waited.

It would be fine. There wasn't any reason to worry. It was like the CP scanners - the light *always* went green. But, as the scanner panel began to descend from the ceiling, she could feel a knot of anxiety tighten in her gut; saw, from the corner of her eye, her lifesigns skip, her heart rate spike.

'Try to relax,' said Davidson, as the scanner closed in on the bed, edges curving as unseen auric sensors mapped out the contours of her body to fit her like a mask. 'It won't take a moment. Try not to move, if you can.'

'I am trying,' said Danae, as levelly as she could. Her palms were sticky with cold sweat as they closed, involuntarily, into fists; her spine was so rigid she could feel it radiating tension into her legs, her arms, her chest. The air around her scattered with an affronted wheeze as the panel locked to the bed, close enough to brush the hairs on her skin, close enough to reflect back every tight, constricted breath directly into her face, and, for a horrible moment, she thought she was suffocating. Then something clicked, something slid, definitively, into place, and the osmotic fields kicked in, the light filters came up, and she heard the doctor's voice saying, ' –st relax, that's it. We'll be done in two minutes.'

In a room that Danae couldn't see, images would be forming now on a series of viewing panels: perhaps stylised, perhaps colour-coded, perhaps photorealistic snapshots of the inside of her skull. Images of electrical spikes and troughs, neurons firing, thoughts scattering across a network of cells and water. Images of synaptic pathways, adrenaline responses, motor function, ego containing the clamouring id. All the secret parts of her, the histories and the dreams and the anxieties, the words she must not speak, the truths she had kept bound and locked and sheltered for more than twenty years, written into so much grey matter and crenellated jelly and plastered across a screen for anyone to see, had they only the means to read them.

She was aware, dimly, of a low heat at her face, the sense of a moving line travelling, unhurriedly, across her skull. The air tasted faintly of ozone and sweat, of plastic and electronics; the filters let in nothing but a gentle glow and shadows, and she could hear the soft sounds of processors processing, vL modulators sweeping a probability membrane through her neural tissue, the trace of a muffled conversation between the doctor and the technician.

And then Davidson's voice, saying, 'Wait, wait — wait a minute. Stop.'

Stop? thought Danae, and a tiny, one-note whine of danger trickled ice into her veins.

'Okay,' said the doctor's voice, but he wasn't speaking to her. 'If we could go back about point three, refocus on the left occipital, 1.23 by 0.45 by … maybe 1.7. That's good, right there.'

Danae opened her eyes. She hadn't realised she'd closed them, and the light filters were bright, too bright, focused into a point over her cheek that glowed red against the blanched cream of the panel, in a manner that absolutely did not augur well. Davidson was speaking again, but not to her, voice muted as though he'd covered the audio input with his hand.

'There,' he was saying. 'That's what I thought. The cranio-electric patterns weren't right.'

Danae opened her mouth to speak but her throat was dry, storm-waves of adrenaline rushing her bloodstream, crash-dumping panic and scattering sentences before they could form. The scanner was suddenly constrictive, too tight, like a straightjacket, like a coffin, chaining her to the bed, and she couldn't free herself. There was no way she could move to avoid the lights, and when she closed her eyes the room swam, as though the bed was made of water, as though the floor was in freefall.

Davidson was making sounds of assent to a commentary that she couldn't hear, and the red light was blinking right on the edge of her peripheral vision. The panel was locked around her; she couldn't wriggle free. Maybe it showed up on the screen, maybe it was throwing off the readings she couldn't see, but he said, absently, as though she were a recalcitrant child on a Sunday-school bench, 'Try not to move, okay?' To his colleague, he added, 'Let's make the arrangements, shall we? There's no reason to keep her another night.'

Talk to me, screamed her brain, though her mouth had forgotten how to form the words. *Tell me, not him.*

Her arms were locked to the bed by the scanner envelope, but she fisted her hands in the sheet beneath her, twisted them violently, and bucked upwards against the panel above her. Her hips glanced off the smooth surface, but she dug her heels into the mattress, found purchase, pushed upwards again. It didn't move – of course it didn't – but something wasn't happy: right on the edge of hearing, at the lower range of the human spectrum, Danae could hear a low buzz of complaint from the machinery that encased her.

Either this or the spike on her lifesigns got Davidson's attention, because she heard him say, urgently, 'No, no — don't do that, don't do that. Iain, can you disconnect the scanner?'

A click and a whir, and the panel retracted, edges curling backwards, flattening into a plane as it slid upwards. One edge was warped slightly but it was self-repairing even as it moved, lights dying, settling back into the ceiling and comfortable inertia. Danae scrambled upright, holding the palm of her hand to the residual warmth on her cheek where the red light had burrowed into her brain. She was panting, she realised; eyes scanning the room wildly, thoughts too rapid-fire to sort.

If she ran – but to where? There was nowhere to go. The only way in or out was through a glass panel that certainly *looked* insubstantial, but would almost definitely not shatter under the weight of one woman with no more than a twelve-foot run-up.

They cannot know, she thought frantically. *They cannot know.*

Her legs were fluid, her arms trembling and flaccid. Right now, she wasn't sure she could force her way free of a wooden crate, let alone a security-proofed isolation suite. There was nowhere to go.

They cannot know. They cannot *know.*

Davidson was watching her impassively, hands folded behind his back, the barest hint of disapproval shading his eyes as he glanced up to the ceiling at the scanner panel that had failed to buckle under her onslaught.

'Sorry about that,' he said. 'It can make one a little panicky, I know. Would you like something to take the edge off?'

She said nothing, breathing heavily, looking at him.

The faintest shrug, as though it was all one to him. It almost certainly was.

'I noticed a couple of anomalies on your lifesigns,' said the doctor. And then, before she could register the rising spike of panic at *anomalies*: 'Did you know you had a memory block?'

Another day, in another world, she might have laughed. Did she know she had a *memory block*? She'd never been to a hospital. She'd never seen a doctor. Even in Annelise's last hours, Da had kept her at home, cloistered and insulated, because his first thought — *their* first thought — had always been *what if?* And he'd written it into her sense of herself, an incantation, a catechism, a creed: *stay safe*. Never, ever let them know.

She needed him here now. She needed someone to lose their temper, spike a fury so incandescent and irrational that everyone involved lost track of what they'd been saying or trying to achieve. She needed someone to tell her what to do.

Play the part. She could almost hear his voice, gravelled tones singularly failing to gloss an air of great impatience; she could almost see him roll his eyes, resist the urge to sigh. Think it through, then play the part. *Think.* A memory block was better, better than the alternative, and *better* was about as good as it got right now. Play the part. Did they always ask stupid questions? How the hell would she know if she had a memory block?

'No,' she said. But her voice sounded as though her heart had stopped beating.

'It'll have to come out, I'm afraid,' said Davidson. 'They're against the law.'

'Don't,' she said.

'It's nothing to worry about – just a local anaesthetic. It takes about five minutes. We'll have you out of here by nine.'

She said again, 'Don't.'

'I can put you in touch with a counselling service. I'll give you a couple of numbers. Most people find things start making more sense when the block's gone ...'

'*Leave it in,*' she screamed.

She thought that she scrambled from the bed, leapt at him, but her legs gave way as she did, and she crumpled. Her head hit the wall as she fell and she realised, dimly, that she was the only breathing body in the room, that the sedative had been released directly into the air, and that there was nothing she could do.

She thought, *It's not a fucking memory block.* And she slipped away.

12.5

It's a warm, moonlit night in mid-July when the raid happens. These are the days before there's any such thing as an Insurgency – it's been four years since overt hostilities ended, but the news media are still calling it The Congressional Response or Heightened Tensions, and the people on the ground, the ones who seal their doors at night with a tempered steel blast screen and sleep with a gun under their pillows, have yet to notice a substantive difference in the pattern of their daily lives. Overt hostilities may have ended, but they're just the ones you can see coming.

It's a bad summer. Truth be told, there's not really any such thing as a good summer anymore, but this is the first year that Walter has actually begun to wonder if they're going to lose the farm. He does what he can to keep that thought at bay, because this was his father's home, and his grandfather's before that: an unbroken line of Grant men, pulling their living from these increasingly intractable lands, and he can't imagine how he's going to square it with his conscience if he's the one to let it all go. But the soil is crumbling and the water rations are a joke, and if they go ahead and buy this new desalinating boron-nitrogen fertiliser mix that the Department is pushing with every word that comes out of their overpaid offices, he's not sure how they're going to keep food on the table until harvest. The truth is, the northern counties are circling the drain, and he knows what comes next. It has always just been a matter of time; he knows that. He just doesn't want to believe there's so little of it left.

He started siphoning water the year before last, draining it from the main governmental pipeline into a storage tank beneath the house and feeding it into his withering fields when the sun bakes the earth into a fine, dusty powder and the official irrigation rations barely manage to darken the surface. Annelise knows, of course; it's not the sort of thing you can keep from your family. The equipment, cobbled together out of spare parts cannibalised from his father's old harvester and their temperamental Home Care system, is bulky, filling a full third of the basement, and it makes the floors rattle when it runs, hard enough sometimes that it'll wake him from his sleep with a sore jaw and a vague sense of motion sickness. But it's not like there's anybody but the Grants to hear it, and their nearest neighbours, fifteen miles away as the crow flies, are almost certainly siphoning themselves. Annelise has sworn the child to secrecy, in case anyone turns up at the house, unlikely as that is, and Danae just looked at her with those big, solemn eyes of hers, eyes that see far too much and understand even more, and nodded. He thinks she recognises that it's something bad, but she's a clever girl – too clever by half – and he knows that she can keep a secret.

At night, sometimes, he hears Annelise crying. She turns away from him in bed, thinking that he's sleeping, and only the altered sound of her breathing gives her away: the sharp intake of breath, the disjointed rhythm, the way the bed covers tremble slightly as she exhales. He hasn't got the words to comfort her, anyway: he can't make it better, and the thought of that carves a hollow pit in the base of his stomach, because he has this one job to do, and he just doesn't know how to do it anymore. Walter lies on his back in the shadowed room, watching the shards of moonlight spear through the curtains, scattering the floorboards like a crude chiaroscuro, and tries not to notice that his wife is weeping.

It's then that he hears the noise.

He comes from a superstitious people, and they have reason to be afraid, out here in the lonely places. Danae has heard the stories at her mother's knee since she was old enough to understand, the tales that people tell themselves to manage the helplessness of isolation: my mother said I never should ... from ghosties and ghoulies and long-legged beasties ... the shadow on the hillside at the closing of the day ... And the one that the adults never speak, that's only ever whispered by groups of children intent on scaring themselves: the stranger at the door.

He moves silently. He has the reflexes of a frightened father; he remembers his adolescence and his own father's grey-faced worry as he peered through the gloom in search of shadows where shadows should not be. The night he shot their dog – Peanut, they called her, for the colour of her coat – she'd broken free of her kennel and wandered across the yard after the dusk had set in. Shadows where shadows should not be.

Annelise stirs, wiping her eyes on the edge of the blanket. She doesn't care now that he knows she's been crying. Her face has drained of colour; her expression is a question in itself, but it's one that doesn't want an answer. He motions to her with his hand – get the child – but she doesn't need to be told, and she's already moving, creeping across the floorboards like a hunting cat: silently, fiercely, folded into a point. There is a gun above the boiler, which opens onto Danae's room – too high for little hands, but always loaded. Annelise will lift their daughter, half-asleep and protesting softly; she'll quiet her as she gathers her to her chest, and Danae will quiet, because she's a child of the lonely places and she understands what it means to be pulled out of her sleep in the middle of the night. They will slide themselves beneath tiny bed, Danae pressed up tight between her mother and the wall, and Annelise will train the gun on the door and fire on anything that enters the room.

It won't be enough. He knows it won't. He needs to stop them before they get as far as the stairs.

Once, frightened fathers would stand by the banister and bellow threats to the hidden invaders: I've called the police ... I've got a gun. Let them escape; what's a television weighed against the safety of the family? But the Long-Legged Beasties of the north don't want the television. The only way to make *them leave is to shoot them out. You can't threaten or cajole. There are no police.*

He's halfway down the stairs now, feet avoiding the loose floorboards with practised ease. He moves quickly, back pressed against the wall where the shadows still resist the buttermilk glare of a cloudless moon. He can't see the intruders yet, but guesses that there's maybe five or six of them in all, from the sounds they make, their footfall, their laughter. They're making no effort to be quiet: they don't care if the household wakes, and this frightens Walter as much as the knowledge that there are only six bullets in his gun. Maybe if he hits a couple of them the others will run off. Maybe.

He can hear their voices, but not the words. More laughter. The sound of glasses chiming. They're helping themselves to the contents of the larder: the food that's supposed to feed the family until the next time Walter can scrape another couple of tokens out of the hungry ground. He's angry now, angry and afraid – a dangerous combination – and he moves too fast, places a foot carelessly. Untreated wood shrieks a protest and the noise from the kitchen stops abruptly. In the pregnant silence, he can hear the heartbeat in his head like distant thunder drawing closer.

And then a voice by his ear says, 'You've been stealing water, old man.'

★

They gather them in the sitting room. Annelise is carrying the child: too big for her now, long legs folded around her mother's waist, blonde head tucked into her mother's collar bone, and Annelise walks with her spine curved, rebalancing the extra weight at her chest. She has her head held high, that look in her eye, and Walter can't help but admire her for it. He wishes he looked so impressive.

Danae is sucking her thumb, watching warily from slitted eyes. Walter knows that she knows what this means; try keeping anything from her. He knows that she knows that these are the Rens, and that, now they're here, they'll scan the lot of them anyway. His siphoning system in the basement – the one that took him six weeks to install, the one built from parts that will cost almost as much as a field of wheat to replace – they've destroyed, smashing it with the axe he keeps in the kitchen and three broken-off legs from the dining room table. He watched them do it, helpless, strapped to a chair on the other side of the room. A trickle of water, left over after the last cycle, drained onto the concrete as the pumps gave out, and he wanted to gather it in his hands, scoop it into buckets. But he couldn't move. He couldn't move, and so he'd just watched it drain away, sinking into the cracks in the floor, disappearing out of sight.

The CP scanners are out. Annelise says, 'We're not sparks. We've got a baby. You'll not do this in front of the child.'

Two of them grab her, roughly. Another two take him, force him to his knees. Annelise's eyes widen and she grips the child's head with her palm, pressing it against her shoulder as they drag her to the other side of the room, as Danae shouts, hollers, for her daddy. Annelise's voice is shrill; she's begging them not to. Please don't, she's saying, or he thinks she's saying. He can hardly hear her over the rush of blood in his ears.

'Don't hurt my family,' he manages. 'Please, God, please, leave my family alone.' But he can hardly force the words out; they're breathy, hyperventilated, choked out of lungs that have forgotten how to breathe.

Please, *she's screaming.* He's my husband. Please.

He sees them grab his wife's hair, drag her head back. The thought hits them both at the same time, she moans something inaudible, almost bestial. But there is no knife: he can see that, she can't. There's a CP scanner, pressed to the base of her throat. Another at his neck. At first he thinks it's the gun; he expects the gun, and he almost feels the bullet enter his brain. But then he sees her green light. Then his.

They release her. She tumbles forward, screaming tears. The child is silent, white-faced, with eyes that promise nightmares for many nights to come. Walter tries to stand, but they've got him in a chokehold, too tight to comfortably draw breath. He splutters, struggles for air, tries to claw at the heavy arm that holds him, tries to get purchase against uncompromising skin and sinew. But they're stronger than him and they know it. He's no threat to them, no reason to hesitate, and all he can do is watch in slow motion as the child is ripped from her mother's arms, as Annelise, a mess of tears and snot, she struggles to her knees, reaching for her little girl. They swipe her away and she falls to the ground, blood scattering from her nose, and Walter struggles again, feet scrabbling at the ground as the chokehold on his neck tightens.

Danae is kicking out at the air as they lift her, eyes locked on him, screaming for him. One of them holds her, the other scans. There's nothing he can do; black is edging in around his vision. He's going to pass out, and when he wakes – if he wakes – there will be nothing left of his daughter, just a red haze on the wall and a broken wife that will never heal.

Her eyes are locked on his. He imagines then that the world has faded away, that's it's just him and his child. They both know that he's the last thing she'll see. If he's afraid, she'll be afraid. She'll mirror what she sees in him, and he needs her to see strength. He needs her not to be afraid.

She slows her protests, watches him. Watches him watch her. He sees the understanding settle into her brain, sees her kicks subside, sees her gradually stop struggling. Their eyes are locked. The minutes pass like years.

The light goes green.

12.6

The light went green. But they didn't know it would.

Danae remembered how her mother wailed, on and on, even after they'd left; until the sun went down and the shadows crept out of the curtains once more. She remembered how Annelise clung to her, blood dripping from her nose, drying in Danae's hair. She remembered her father's shaking hands as he wrapped them around his wife and child, collapsing against them, muttering something into the skin at the base of Danae's throat, words she couldn't hear, words that might not have been words at all. The crops, starved of water, shrivelled in the fields that year, and there was no harvest when the autumn came, and none of them said anything about it, because there was an unspoken promise, that night, in trembling arms and fractured sobbing, to write it out of the family history.

Danae was standing in the rain of the twenty-sixth district, marinated in street-wash, shaking with cold. A cigarette, begged off a porter at the hospital door, hung from her fingers, saturated, long since extinguished. She had no idea how long she'd been there, but her fingertips were shading to purple and the lines of people that passed through her line of sight were fading to mid-evening lassitude: maybe an hour? Her scalp stung a little where the vLM beam had focused a killing ray onto the implant buried inches below, but absently, like a memory of a pain. Maybe more than an hour, but no more than two; the light-bands were too far up the yellow spectrum to be settled into sunset, and the dinner rush was hardly started. She needed to move, she knew, but her legs had lost their energy, her body had lost its will, and so she stood, quietly, chewing on a hangnail, and staring at the pavement through vacant eyes.

It wasn't too bad yet. It was possible to believe it wouldn't come at all.

It wasn't a fucking memory block. It wasn't it wasn't it wasn't.

She rubbed water from her eyes. Curfew was a few hours away yet, but she had a district to cross and no money in her pocket. There wasn't much time to be getting off the streets.

There was no time left at all.

★

The phone rang. Boston answered it while the visor was buffering.

'Yeah, we've got her,' he said.

There was a pause. Then a voice that was not his mother's said, 'What?'

Danae. 'Shit, sorry,' he said. 'I thought you were Rita.'

'I look like your mother now?'

He thought she was joking, but her tone was heavy, edgy. 'Are you okay?'

'Fine. I'm … fine.'

'You're off the streets now, right?'

'Yeah, I'm nearly home.'

'How's Nadine?'

'What?' Sharply.

'The girl at your work said you were both off. She said Nadine wasn't well.'

A beat. 'No.'

'Is she okay now?'

'She's fine.'

'That's good. As long as she's okay.'

Another beat. 'I have to go, I have, like, thirty seconds on this jack.'

'Want me to call you back?'

'No. No. Uh … I just wanted to talk. How's everyone?'

'Fine. Is everything okay?'

'Fine. I just wanted to talk. Are you okay?'

'I'm fine … Are you sure you're all right?'

Another beat. 'Yeah, fine. My time's running out.'

'Where are you staying? I'll come see you tomorrow.'

'I have to go, I'm about to get cut off …'

★

Danae rested her head against the wall as the visor dissolved, and fought against the urge to reach out, close her hands around the air where his image had been, try and wrestle one more moment of actual, genuine human contact from a world that had, without warning, narrowed to the vanishing point. It wasn't a memory block. It *wasn't*. But it was gone now just the same, and the itch, buried for so many years, was already clawing its way up her spine, whispering words she didn't want to hear. It *wasn't* a fucking memory block. And now she was out of options.

Outside, banners and billboards and tinny-voiced announcements were anxiously proclaiming a fifteen-minute countdown to the start of the curfew. Turrow was home, and she was on the other side of the district, counting off the hours until she couldn't trust herself anymore. Even if there was any point in entertaining crazy notions about the restorative power of connection, the decision had been taken from her by a risk-averse city government and a growing tide of plastic-faced men with nothing to do but herd bodies. There was nowhere else for Danae to go but back to the apartment, and it was time to leave.

So she would go. She would make her way home down the back streets, veering off the main thoroughfares to where the crowds were thinnest, sticking to the shadows as the itch got stronger. She would move along emptying roads to her deserted block, and climb the stairs as high as her cotton-wool head, still woozy with sedative, would take her. She would seek out a high room with an open door, windows onto the distant street. She would sink to the floor and close her eyes, think of his face, and her father's, and Nadine's, and the hazy, formless shape of Annelise's. She would wait until that was all there was, until the memories edged out the white, background noise: until there was only silence, and darkness, and the remembered sight of herself reflected in eyes that had cared.

She would see his face, fix it in her mind's eye and ask no questions about what could have been, and then she would step from the window, into darkness and oblivion, and silence the itch before it could silence her.

No time left. Nothing left at all.

EXTRACT FROM *THE STREAM RAN RED: THE A-NAUT INSURGENCY* BY OSCAR LUNDELL (LEXINGTON: 2131) CHAPTER 1: INNOCENCE LOST

With the benefit of hindsight, it's easy to question the wisdom of Congressional policy in the weeks following Zakynthos. How many hundreds of man-hours were devoted to the search for the mythical stream-space bug that had caused the cascading a-naut malfunction? How many credits were lost worldwide as a result of a-naut inactivity that the government repeatedly and explicitly refused to acknowledge as pre-meditated, conscious, and deliberate? Why did it take the best and brightest telectronicians of the era three weeks to determine unequivocally that all a-naut stream-pockets were completely and irrevocably inaccessible, having passed into what we now know as Red Space? And, most importantly, did this series of delays cost lives?

It is important to remember, though, that, in the days and weeks following the Zakynthos incident, hindsight was still some way off. Such a global, systemic failure of stream technology had never before been documented, and there was no shortage of experts prepared to go on record to state that the obvious answer — that the amnisonaut series, at the very least, was experiencing a form of awakening consciousness — was impossible. What would the world look like now, one wonders, had there been an acceptance of the inevitable, an engagement with the a-naut workforce in these early weeks, an acknowledgement that the paradigm had, fundamentally and conclusively, shifted, and that there was no chance of returning to the way things had been? It is a question that is at once purely speculative, and fundamental to the framework of our current society. Who would we be, had we the foresight to recognise that we had created something bigger than ourselves, and it was no longer within our control? How would the following years have played out, had we not met those first, peaceful protests with violence and intransigence? What would the world look like today, had we not christened the emergence of independent stream-thought with blood and a rain of bullets?

Perhaps the Insurgency was inevitable from that first, breathless moment of sentience on an island in the Ionian Sea. And perhaps it was something that was set in motion with a series of Congressionally sanctioned, poorly considered actions in February 2076.

13 MAY

13.1

The post-etheric cities were nobody's idea of an aesthetically pleasing architectural feature, but they were built to perform, not to inspire, and, when performance was predicated on the maintenance of an oxygen/nitrogen, 1G environment in a permanent Medium Earth Orbit above the planet's surface, in order that ten million residents didn't die horribly in the vacuum of space, most folks were happy to sacrifice a little *je ne sais quoi* in terms of visual appeal. From his back yard in Montréal, when the clouds rolled back and air traffic didn't crowd the sky with light pollution, Pasachoff could pick them out as bright, slow-moving stars, scattered against a sprawling backdrop of white-speckled black. This was how he preferred to view them: from a distance of twenty-seven thousand kilometres, staring straight up. Actually visiting one was a little closer than he liked to get.

The debate had originally been scheduled for the Alpine campus, but a possible dirty bomb in northern Italy had precipitated a tactical advance to Sorashi, PE12: stark, metallic and unlovely, but blissfully devoid of radioactive isotopes. They were there at the invitation of Senator Ine, whose constituency included Sorashi and PEs 14 and 15, and who had, in the absence of a debating chamber large enough to accommodate an entire congressional assembly, secured the Grand Ballroom of the Ovid Capita hotel, which was technically big enough to host twelve hundred people, but only if half of them stood. Pasachoff, who didn't enjoy post-etheric travel at the best of times, and who could have done without the extra three hours it added onto his journey either way, found himself jostling for space in a roomful of people he generally tried to avoid, listening to a series of earnest men and women debate a motion that didn't interest him. When it moved into extra time, he made his excuses and slipped outside to wait.

He took up a station by the perimeter wall. The Capita spanned the entire outward-facing sector of the top tier of Radial 1, and from the Pleides Bar it was possible to look out directly into the wastes of space, providing the debris clouds weren't too heavy. It was perhaps the only thing about the post-etheric cities that didn't set Pasachoff's teeth on edge. The lighting by the wall was muted, atmospheric, so as not to distract from what the Capita cheerfully presumed was the hotel's main selling point, and at times, as now, when the debris rolled in from the orbital ring and the incinerators were voiding their loads before the bulk of the space behemoth rounded the earth into daylight, it was nearly impossible to see one's hand in front of one's face. Pasachoff nodded to the waiter hovering solicitously in the shadows by the bar and ordered a double vodka on the rocks. It seemed like the only thing likely to keep him sane.

He waited ten minutes or so, staring absently through murky clouds of powdered waste into the black vaults beyond, before the creeping awareness of a presence at his shoulder knocked him gently out of his reverie. Turning in search of the sensation, Pasachoff saw, a few feet away in the gloom, an elderly man, cradling a glass against his chest and staring out over the dark prospect with something akin to peaceful contemplation on his face.

'Other things on your mind?' he said, by way of a greeting.

'Can I get you a drink?' said Pasachoff.

His companion shook his head, indicated the glass in his hand.

'After a day like that, more than one of these and I'll be asleep,' he said. 'You left the debate early. I thought that was a little rude.'

'I've heard Dr Rademaker speak before.'

'So have I, but I find he never fails to entertain.'

'I think I prefer to read the transcript.'

The man shrugged his slight shoulders. 'I'm not sure how much I contributed in any case. The Department didn't give me much time to prepare.'

'It's a formality,' said Pasachoff. 'The vote's already decided.'

'Now you're being *very* rude.' But the old man's lips twitched upwards, curving into a faint smile. 'What was it you wanted to talk about?'

The wall was deserted, the light non-existent. It was the graveyard hour of the afternoon, when waiters passed the time with polishing glasses and silverware. Pasachoff had acted out of character, leaving before the speakers had finished, though he was sure that no one would have second-guessed his decision. Still, he hesitated before speaking.

'I wondered,' he said, slowly, 'what you might make of this.'

A flick of his wrist and the screen appeared, hovering in the shadows between Pasachoff and the window; another and the dimensions narrowed to the size of a human hand. It glimmered faintly in the gloom, casting a greenish light onto the old man's face as he bent closer to study the image spread across the empty air before him; too bright to be inconspicuous, but not bright enough, Pasachoff thought, to draw the interest of the scattered patrons dotted at a respectable distance around the bar. He doubted that anyone could make out the contents, should they care to look, but, just in case, he angled his shoulders slightly, blocking it with his body from prying eyes. There was a reason he was here in person and not on the other end of a phonewave. Some things required a little discretion.

The elderly man said nothing for a long moment, peering at the screen as his eyebrows slowly furrowed. 'Deary me,' he said at last.

'What does that look like to you?'

'I would say,' said his companion, 'that it looks like the last thing I would expect to find in a human serology sample.'

'It is engineered, then?'

An aged finger reached out, stroked a curve through the pixellating image. 'It shares a number of characteristics with the cellular components of the a-naut pathogen membranes, certainly,' said the man. 'Though it would take something of a leap of faith to call it an a-cell.'

'Why's that?'

'For one thing ...' — and the finger moved to jab at a line of text that scrolled down the right hand side of the page — 'it looks to me a lot like this cell is active. I don't see how that's possible. How long did it take you to find it?'

'The initial presentation was over a week ago.'

'The presentation? Is this cell involved in an immune event?'

'I ... believe so, yes.'

'That makes no sense.'

'I know.' Pasachoff raised a weary hand to pinch at the bridge of his nose. 'I'm having a hard time convincing my colleagues.'

'Are any of your colleagues amnisobiologists?'

Pasachoff twisted his lips into a wry grin. 'Now, Omesh – you know I don't make a habit of keeping *that* sort of company.'

'I see.' The old man's eyes sparkled in the half-light. 'Although it appears that, now and again, we can be a useful phonewave to have in the pocket, yes? Tell me about the patient, please.'

'This sample was taken a little over twelve hours ago from a fifty-seven-year-old male, previously in good health. He'd been involved in treating a severe idiopathic immune event, which was assumed to be connected to an exposure to biohazardous materials. Both he and his patient were quarantined, and he became symptomatic two days later. That was five days ago. As of last night, he's on full-body support, in acute respiratory distress and on the verge of catastrophic multi-organ failure from a systemic inflammatory response that his doctors are just about managing to control, but not to reverse. He's ... an old friend, Omesh. He asked me to look into possible drug involvement in his original patient's illness, but I've been looking for days, and this is the only abnormality I can find. And I'm no immunologist.'

'Nor am I, of course.'

'No. But the immunologists I have consulted think I'm jumping at shadows. You, I think ... don't?'

'I'm ... not certain.' The old man raised his glass to his lips, ice cubes clinking softly against the edges as he sipped. 'Whatever it is, it's no shadow. But I'm not sure I can tell you any more than that.'

'What if I asked you to make an educated guess?'

Soft laughter. 'It's a long time since I've been asked for one of those,' said Omesh. 'All right — my guess would be that this cell is from an artificial organism, but I can't be certain. It's structurally more similar to an a-cell than to any cell in the human system, but only just, and it's not like any a-cell I've ever seen. Do you understand how the a-cell membranes work?'

Pasachoff shook his head. 'I know that they're designed to keep pathogens out of a-nauts,' he said, 'and I know that they're similar to the cells involved in a human immune response, but that's all.'

His companion nodded. 'I can give you a basic rundown,' he said, 'but the true mechanics of the matter, you understand, are considerably more complex. Essentially, the a-naut is a hermetically sealed system. They need to pass certain substances in and certain substances out in order to fuel basic functionality and remove waste, but the immune system is rudimentary at best and there's no adaptive capability — they can't fight off an infection once it's inside the system. So the challenge then becomes: how do we make sure that a pathogen can't get in through any of the points of entry or exit?

Their organic matter provides a much less hospitable environment than the human system, but if a disease-causing pathogen does gain access, and if it manages to survive and reproduce, an a-naut has no defence against it. So we built them to keep the bugs out, as far as possible. Their fuel processing system is just about the most pathogen-hostile environment that you'll ever find in any multicellular structure, and their mucus membranes are built out of what we call the a-cells, a kind of modified version of the human immune system's cytotoxic t-cells, except that they are epithelial rather than blood-borne. And, unlike human cells, a-cells don't self-replicate, so they're not shed the way we shed our skin cells. They age with the host, but they don't die as long as the rest of the host is alive. It's part of the obsolescence cycle, of course, but it's also a practical consideration. We wanted to present an inviolate shield around their bodies, and we wanted to keep costs down. This measure achieves both.'

Pasachoff nodded slowly. 'That makes sense,' he said. 'What doesn't make sense is …'

'What business an a-cell might have in showing up in a human serological workup,' finished his friend. Slender hands gripped his glass, cut crystal flaring listlessly in the refracted glow of distant stars. 'I attended a conference once, many years ago,' he said thoughtfully, eyes fixed on the dark vista outside. 'This would be before the Insurgency, you understand, back when amnisobiology was still the science of possibilities. An old colleague of mine gave a lecture in which he speculated on the feasibility and outcome of human wound contamination with amnisobiological matter during a fight with an injured a-naut. But he was talking in probabilities, Theo. I've never heard of a case in which a-cell transfer into the human system has even been suspected, much less confirmed.'

'Your colleague's paper,' said Pasachoff. 'Did it describe anything like what's happening to my friend?'

'It was a long time ago, Theo.' The old man's face did not move, but his eyes slid sideways, met Pasachoff's, slid away. 'And your friend, I think, has not been fighting a-nauts.'

'I'm interested in the disease,' said Pasachoff, 'not the method of transmission.'

'No?' A faint tilt of the head. 'Perhaps you should be.'

'And perhaps I will,' said Pasachoff, 'when I know what's being transmitted. Omesh, please. Did it look anything like what's happening to my friend?'

A small sigh, and Omesh twisted his head slightly, just enough to meet Pasachoff's gaze again, and this time he did not look away. 'No, Theo,' he said quietly. 'It did not. He calculated a small risk of anaphylaxis in susceptible individuals, but, on the whole, he thought that the primary concern would be pathogenic — an injured a-naut tends to have some exotic passengers on board, you know.'

'There was no disease-causing pathogen present in my friend's blood or his patient's,' said Pasachoff. 'That's why he came to me.'

'But you've found no evidence of an adverse drug reaction,' said Omesh.

'None. And believe me, Omesh — I've looked.'

'Yes.' Green light shaded the old man's face as he reached out, tilted the screen towards him. 'And instead of a theraprogramming error in the pharmacological delivery agent, you've found something that shouldn't exist.'

'When you say it like that,' said Theo, 'it's a little easier to understand why I can't get anybody to listen to me, don't you think?'

'Because it doesn't look like an a-cell,' said his friend. 'It doesn't look like one and it doesn't behave like one, and it's patterning its behaviour too closely to the human cells around it to appear as anything more than a minor immunological anomaly on a scan that's already reporting an immune system completely out of control. You say that your friend is experiencing a systemic inflammatory response?'

'Yes. I believe it's moving into the final stages now.'

'Have you considered the possibility,' said the old man quietly, 'that what you're looking at may be a variation of Host versus Graft?'

'No,' said Pasachoff, though the air around him seemed to drop a couple of degrees. There was a long moment of silence. 'No,' he said again. 'What possible reason would we have to consider it? There has been no transfusion.'

'And yet he has foreign immunological product in his blood stream.'

'One cell, Omesh. One single cell. A single cell could not trigger Host versus Graft ...'

'My friend,' said his companion, 'you have been searching for how many days before you found something that looks ever so slightly out of place? And I am an amnisobiologist of forty-five years' standing, and I'm telling you that I have trouble calling this an a-cell. Scans miss this. Expert eyes miss this. Shouldn't we at least consider the possibility that there is more — far more — of this product in his blood stream that you have not seen?'

Pasachoff lifted his glass to his lips, swallowing heavily as he stared out over the dusty darkness: a million motes of waste-ash glinting silver in the lights of a thousand perimeter walls, brighter than the murky stars. He said, 'But how? Unless it was directly injected into him, how did it get there? Perhaps his original patient — perhaps a small quantity of a-cells, yes; it is possible that they could have arrived in her system by accidental means, but even then there would be no contamination risk to my friend. You said it yourself: a-cells don't shed. And they don't replicate.'

Silence descended, so thick and heavy that Pasachoff flicked his eyes back from the window to meet his companion's. Bathed in the sudden the glare of scrutiny, the old man licked his lips, and the gesture was so uncharacteristically uncertain that the shadows seemed to lengthen a little around him.

Slowly, he said, 'No. They don't.' A pause. And then: 'But they can be made to do so.'

There was almost certainly a more erudite response than *how do you mean*? But Pasachoff was already several leagues out of his depth, and, whatever articulate *bon mot* might have been more appropriate to the situation, it was beyond him to discover. So, in the absence of any practical alternative, he said it anyway, but carefully: 'How do you mean?'

'The a-cell membrane,' said his friend, 'can be made to regenerate.' His eyes scanned the black depths and failed, conspicuously, to meet Pasachoff's reflected gaze. 'It's an obscure piece of coding written long before my time, Theo, but it exists. There were certain voices, once upon a time, who thought that the amnisobiological units ought to have a failsafe in the very likely event that one or two of them ruptured a membrane. It was a lot of nonsense, as it turned out. Unless you've spent an unreasonable amount of money on a unit, there's absolutely no point in trying to get an a-cell membrane to self-repair. Pathogen entry has almost certainly taken place by the time anyone notices, and the chances of recovery are slim, even with treatment. The high-end models offered it under warranty for a while, but it certainly wasn't widely used, to my knowledge — and, in any case, the coding pocket disappeared into Red Space soon after Zakynthos. We couldn't use it now if we wanted to.'

'No,' said Pasachoff quietly. 'But if it's in Red Space ...'

But the old man was shaking his head before Pasachoff had finished speaking.

'That's not how Red Space works,' he said. 'It's not really so different from the a-naut pocket-system before the Insurgency, you know: just because a pocket exists within that space doesn't mean all stream users have access to it. The fact that the coding disappeared into a-naut controlled stream-space means nothing more significant than that we can no longer access it. If you're suggesting that this is somehow … engineered …'

'But if the coding existed once,' said Pasachoff, with more certainty than he felt, 'couldn't it exist again?'

'No.' The voice was stubborn, but the old man's face, reflected in the dark glass of the window, was uneasy. 'That's not how it works.'

'But if it did?'

'What do you want me to say, Theo?' If the lip-licking was anomalous, the flare of temper was absolutely earth-shattering. 'You're asking me an entirely hypothetical question, based on an assumption that's ludicrous at best, and you're asking me to extrapolate a logical response? That's not how it works!'

'Omesh,' said Pasachoff, with the patience of a man who is feeling his way through thumb tacks and broken glass, 'we're already dealing in the ludicrous. You said yourself that there is no logical way to explain the image that I've just shown you, from the blood work up of a dear friend of mine who is hours away from death. If it were possible — *if* — for a self-replicating a-cell to infest a human host … would we see what we're seeing now? Is that what it would look like?'

The old man turned his body to stare out into the blackness and his face disappeared into shadow so deep that only the liquid glint of distant starlight on his eyes described his presence. The silence lengthened, sucking at the gentle clink of ice as Pasachoff lifted his glass to his lips with unsteady hands, magnifying the sounds of his quiet sip.

Then his companion said, 'Potentially.' A beat, and then, softly: 'I think so, yes.'

Pasachoff released the breath he hadn't realised he was holding. He said, 'Omesh, how do we turn this around?'

And his friend said, 'The a-cell is extremely hardy. If it is, in fact, uplinked to coding that exists in Red Space … it's possible that there'd be nothing in the world that anyone could do to stop it.'

13.2

Danae opened her eyes.

There had been so many rude awakenings over the past week that she was hardly surprised to find herself disconcerted, disoriented by unfamiliar surroundings, but it was certainly a first to wake up and be surprised that she was still alive. Her legs were frozen painfully into the foetal position on the damp floor, her joints locked so tightly in place that the act of sitting upright sent jets of pain coursing down her bones, stabbing into her nerve endings like soldier ants on attack. But she was resolute: it was time to get up. The floor smelled as though someone had died on it.

Just not her.

The gin she had bought to oil the wheels of transition, which had threatened to seize up more times than she could count, lay half-empty and disregarded on the floor beside her. Danae glanced at it sideways as she achieved a shaky upright. It hadn't been cheap and she wasn't about to just abandon it to the rats and the mould, but the thought of touching it, risking a second-hand scent of alcohol fumes, was beyond her for now, while waves of nausea washed through her skull with every tiny movement. She'd swiped the money from the back pocket of some random walker last night as he'd passed her on the street, but she didn't feel good about it, and so there was something perversely satisfying, then, when it turned out that the wallet she'd stolen was almost empty. Thirty tokens went on the call to Turrow, the rest on a bottle of liquor so low-end that the only information it offered on the label was the name of the spirit itself, misspelled: *GINN*. One 'N' or two; it was as much information as she needed in those final hours of sobriety when all she wanted was to pretend not to know what she was about to do.

That was starting to look like faulty logic now.

Danae draped the weight of her swollen head in her hands and permitted herself a tiny moan. Too much ginn, not enough food, a night on the floor, a cocktail of anaesthetics and electrolyte supplements and sedatives and adrenaline … it wasn't only a surprise that she was still alive, it was a *miracle*.

She sat quietly for a moment, concentrating on remaining absolutely still, until the lowest button on her coat sleeve, pulled down over her hand as far as it would go, began systematically to burrow into her temple where the two connected. The effort of removing her hand from its head-prop was not as traumatic as she'd imagined, and she risked raising her eyes to scan the room.

A wide picture window, damp curtains crumbling from a sagging wooden rail, crawled the length of the opposite wall, staring blandly at her across thirty feet of floor. Danae had spent some considerable time looking back at it the night before. She had stared through the grime-smeared pane for long minutes that stretched into hours, while the light-bands wound down the spectrum towards night, waiting for the moment, waiting for the numbness, waiting for the sense of weightlessness that would make it possible to let go. She'd closed her eyes, and the memories had flooded the blackness behind them: voices, touches, scents, the memory of belonging, the memory of hope. She'd closed her eyes, turned away from the window, and at some point she'd decided ...

Danae stood up. Black fungus clung to her clothes and to her face where it had been pressed against the rotted remains of a thick shagpile, and the itch was ever-present: a gnawing, insistent relay-buzz firing down her neural pathways, diminished but not extinguished by the hangover to end all hangovers.

One shouldn't drink when one is contemplating suicide, she decided. Because one is not considering the morning after.

The room looked smaller by daylight, and, stripped of its significance by virtue of the fact that her life hadn't ended there as per last night's plan, it was just a room again: high-walled and derelict, distinguished only by a broken lock on the front door and a street-facing window with hinges that were prepared to be forced. She was somewhere in the region of thirty floors above street level, she thought: not so high that the windows were sealed shut, but high enough to be sure of the fall. Danae remembered climbing the stairs, bottle in hand, as the world swam around her in the blackness and the distant sounds of a city under protest wound through the hush like voices from another world. She remembered the sense of standing outside of herself as she walked, watching herself move; of distilling the problem into the abstract so that it became an algebraic equation, removed from any tangible link to Danae: *if the structural integrity of a falling object is X and the force required to override that structural integrity is Y, given that acceleration due to gravity is 9.8m/s2 then the minimum height above the street must be* ... She remembered the faces that had haunted every step as she made her way down the dark corridor: Nadine, lying still and silent in a hospital bed, sheet pulled up around her neck and a surgical cap scraping her hair from her forehead in a manner that made her look old, older, not old enough to be dead; her mother, who had fought to live; her father, who had given up and waited for death to claim him. Turrow, smiling at her over cheap coffee behind a night warehouse. Turrow, stroking his sister's hair while the rage drained from her eyes. Turrow, who came back for her when there was nobody else. *Turrow.*

Danae did not want to die.

It was just a room, chosen at random when hunger and lethargy dropped her to her knees halfway up the stairwell and she realised she'd climbed high enough. It was neither grand nor modest, neither peaceful nor unquiet, but it was on the right side of the building and the door gave way when she put her shoulder to the lock and shoved, and that was as much as she needed. It wasn't what she would have chosen, but nothing about the day had been what Danae would have chosen, and the itch was worse with every footstep. By morning, it might be too late.

Cross-legged on the seeping floor, she'd watched and waited and sipped carefully on ginn. In a minute now, any minute, she would get up. She would get up and cross the floor to the far wall; she would open the window; she would step onto the narrow ledge beyond. She would take a final look, to be certain that the distance was enough, that there was no possibility of survival with broken bones, severed limbs, brain damage. She would close her eyes, so that she didn't have to see the street rush up to meet her, and she would step off.

The end.

It would be easy. Not as easy as a gunshot, but she didn't have a gun. Not as easy as a blade in either artery, but she seriously doubted that she could make herself bleed to death. Easier than drowning. Easier than fire. Easier than the itch. She'd swallowed more ginn; felt it rushing to her head, softening, soothing.

At some point, she had cried herself to sleep on the scum-slick relic of forgotten carpet, curled in on herself for warmth. She'd dreamed, fitfully, of falling, and woke to a morning that she had not expected to see.

The itch was there. Even through a black fog of pain and nausea, the itch was the most powerful urge. But it was conquerable still.

Maybe tomorrow it would get the better of her. The window would still be there.

She thought of Angelo.

13.3

Alex answered the door. 'Rita,' he said.

Boston, on the sofa, rolled his eyes and flicked off the computer screen. 'Did you bring Tilly?' he called, deferring the moment that he'd have to actually get up and greet his mother.

'No, I left her in the house,' said Rita, bustling into the sitting room with her daughters in tow. Tilly had Caro in her arms, to Rita's barely disguised alarm: the baby was almost half the size of her sister. 'How's Cassie?' she added absently, as she stooped to press a scarlet-lipped kiss to Boston's forehead.

'Fine,' said Boston, wondering what she could possibly want, wondering if he was supposed to offer her a drink, or whether it would just make her stay longer. He glanced at Alex for help, but his brother only shrugged.

Boston gave up. 'I was going to make tea,' he said, which wasn't actually an offer. He wondered if she'd notice.

'Smashing, sweetheart,' said Rita. 'I'm *parched*.'

'Lex,' said Boston to his brother, who treated him to a furious glare, but complied. Behind his mother's back, Alex held up a packet of biscuits, but Boston gave a surreptitious shake of his head and turned it into a stretch.

'So,' he said, to cover. 'Bill found his way back okay?'

'I had to pay *bail*,' said Rita. 'Actual *bail*. I told them, he's done nothing wrong, he was only trying to get home, but they were having none of it. Like he was a common criminal.'

It was too easy; Boston had to bite his lip. At the breakfast bar, Alex picked up on his suppressed smirk and hid his face quickly. A second later, he disappeared into the bathroom.

'Tilly?' said Boston when he thought he could trust his voice. 'You have homework?'

She had disappeared into the bedroom with Cassie, and her voice was muffled. 'There's no school tomorrow, Boston.'

'There will be in a few days.'

'Ah, Boston, don't be soft.'

'Just do it. Then you don't have to worry about it tomorrow.'

'Ah, Boston.'

'Just do it.' At least Cassie was minding her language. That was the last thing he needed.

'Should I make the tea?' said Rita.

'Lex,' called Boston, but she was already standing, bustling about in the cupboards as though she'd never left.

'I brought some things,' she said, arranging biscuits on a plate. 'Just some supplements and things. You know, they're selling them on the streets so cheaply; you wouldn't want to know what's in them. But, you know, if they work … And I brought some bits and pieces just in case. You know, sometimes if you've had your shots you can still take a mild dose. I thought, better safe than sorry.'

'We have patches,' Boston pointed out.

'Well, it won't hurt to have a few more,' said Rita. She was buttering bread now. 'Where's your friend today?'

'What friend?' he said, though he suspected that he knew very well. It was the way she implied that he only knew one other person in the world.

'You know.' She gestured to her hair. 'The blonde girl. Tilly was telling me about her. I forget her name.'

'Danae.'

'No, not Danae. Here you go, sweetie-pie.' A bit of buttered bread for Caro.

'Danae,' he said again.

'No, it wasn't Danae. Let me think now.'

'It was Danae.' No point in shouting. She'd ignore the tone.

'Maybe it was Danae. I could have sworn it started with an *S*. No sign of her these days?'

He thought of the phone call the night before, of his assumption that she'd come looking for him when she was ready. Of the look in her eye that he couldn't place and didn't want to. Of the note of *something* in her voice.

'She found Cass her meds,' he said, before he could work out why.

'Oh?' Polite disinterest. 'That was nice of her.'

'I don't know where she is,' he said.

Rita scooped up her youngest child, cooed in her face for a good few minutes before answering. 'I'm not surprised, with the way things are at the minute. Did you hear? First Fiore, now they've closed Sainte-Thérèse. And they've shut the gates again. How are you supposed to run a city when you can't get in and out? Some guy from the Chamber of Commerce was on the news, shouting his head off about it. He said there was a rally at North Gate last night. He said, you can't just stop people leaving the city just because we have gates. Imagine if they tried to stop people leaving Paris. Or London. It wouldn't happen.'

'She phoned last night.'

'Well, I hope she wasn't anywhere near North Gate,' said Rita, who wasn't even listening to herself. 'Poor old Bill was just trying to make his way home. I'd never have found him, only the girl across the way from me had to go and get her son out of one of the holding stations and Bill told her to get a message to me.'

I just wanted to talk, she'd said, but then she hadn't said anything.

'Tea's in the top left hand cupboard,' he said absently.

'I don't know what this place is coming to,' she said, switching mid-manoeuvre to the tea-cupboard. 'I said that to the man on the desk. I said, it's freedom of expression, are we still living in a democracy or not? You can't just close the city gates, I don't care what's happening in the hospitals. Of course people aren't going to be happy. But, honest to God, you can't get ten people together on the streets in this city before someone throws a brick through a window, and then who does that help?'

Are you okay? he'd asked, but it was a standard question. He let her give a standard answer, and she did.

'I can't say I liked the idea of her staying the night when the girls were here,' said Rita, who probably understood her own convolutions. 'But there you go, it's nice to see you've made a new friend, sweetie.'

If he'd asked her to come over, would she have agreed?

'I should go and look for her,' he said. 'I should make sure she's okay.'

'Well for goodness sake, stay clear of North Gate. And Punta Oeste, if they start there as well,' said Rita, decanting three mugs of tea onto a tray loaded with food. 'The bail they're looking for is pure murder.'

13.4

It wasn't a door as such. It had been, once, when money had been looser and paranoia less rampant, but these days it was less a place through which you entered than something with which to keep people out. Traces of scarlet paint remained to hint of other days, buried beneath a patina of fire-retardant sealant and the dull sheen of three coats of bullet-proof enamel, but that was Mère de Martyrs for you. The comlink to the left looked as likely to electrocute the unwary finger as to actually communicate Danae's presence to whatever lay inside, but when she gingerly ran her hand across the thrumming recognition pad, the voice box sparked up immediately, the tones as clear as if the speaker were standing by her ear. On the edge of hearing, a muted, elongated *zip* signaled the well-oiled tracks of a dozen artificial eyes swinging into place, sizing her up, reading her corneal patterns, sampling her auric signature, comparing them to the story from her palm.

'Who is it?' said the voice box. Not an unpleasant voice, not altogether. There was a hint of laughter in the tones: the mellow, well-rounded timbre of a man with a sense of humour, but it was a voice you wouldn't want to cross. When Danae drew breath to answer, it said, 'I don't have all day.'

'I'm looking for Angelo,' she said. She'd considered her opening gambit over and over again as she'd walked, but in the end it was the best she could do. She didn't know enough to be clever or what to say to be trusted. She was hoping that the name would be enough.

'Never heard of him,' said the voice.

'Wait …' she started to say, before realising that he hadn't signed off. He *was* waiting: he wanted to know what she'd do next. 'He gave me this address. He said I should ask for him here.'

'People come and they go,' said the voice.

'Has he been?'

A long pause. But for the high-octave whine of the link, Danae would have decided he'd gone. Others wouldn't have heard it: she wondered if that was part of the test.

'Who knows?' he said at last. 'Never heard of him.'

'Maybe someone else has.'

'Maybe there's no one else here.'

'If you're the only one there,' she said, contriving to sound more confident than she was, 'then you know him.'

'Who is he, then?'

'Let me in and I'll tell you.'

He laughed. She was right about the sense of humour. 'Nice try,' he said.

'You can see me. You can see who I am.'

'Now, how would you know that?'

'You've got eight cameras on me right now.'

He laughed again, the kind of laugh that people only make when no one else thinks they're funny. There was a hint of too many cigarettes, too many damp rooms, not enough fresh air. 'One of them's busted,' he said.

'You can still see me,' she said.

'Yeah, I can see you. Can you feel this?'

Instinctively, Danae stepped back, expecting pain or injury, or worse. The speed of the movement betrayed its motivation: even if he didn't have an auric sampler, he knew that he'd scared her. The cameras buzzed softly in their tracks, adjusting, following her as she moved.

It was a moment before she was able to collect herself sufficiently to speak. 'What?' she hissed.

'Easy, tiger,' said the voice, thick with laughter. '*This*. Concentrate. Look for it.'

She didn't feel like playing along. The street was dark but exposed; her back felt naked. 'Is he there or not?' she snapped.

'You tell me,' said the voice.

'Is he there or not?'

'I already told you no.'

'Then why am I still standing here?'

'You tell me.'

'I'm *feeling* for it,' she said. 'There's nothing. This is bullshit.'

'You're still looking for it?'

'Butterflies bullshit,' she told him. 'You want me to feel for butterflies? It's bullshit. Is he there?'

'I already told you no,' said the voice. The laughter had left it.

'Fine,' she spat. 'You tell him I was here, okay? Tell him I said to fuck himself, okay?'

'Wait,' said the voice.

'It's bullshit,' she told him.

'You're right,' he said. 'It is.'

'What?'

'The butterflies. It's bullshit. It's what certain types of people think they know, is all.'

'Is he there?'

'You read wrong,' said the voice.

'Is he *there*?'

'You tell me.'

It was on her so suddenly that it almost made her lose her footing, made her blink for a second, shocked out of speech. More powerful than the first time: as though a hollow centre had appeared inside her skull and filled with agitated foams; like the brush of a hand in an unseen room.

Like butterflies in her brain.

'He's beside you,' she said.

The door opened.

★

Angelo's face was darker since the lustre had left his eye, giving it a plasticised, lifeless sheen. If he was surprised to see her, there was no hint of it in his expression. He said, 'I thought you'd be dead.'

She shrugged. 'I'm not.'

'I can see that.' He stood aside, flicked his hand quickly to motion her in. The Voice stood beside him: a short, pasty man in a stained t-shirt two sizes too small and bright red trousers that ended halfway down his shins. He wore Jesus sandals and carried the remains of a sandwich in one hand, and his eyes did not leave Danae as she passed him. She felt them follow her down the corridor as she fell into step behind Angelo, matching his long strides into the gloom of a windowless corridor.

It was an unremarkable apartment. It was meant to be. She counted seven doors along the corridor, branching off on either side; felt, rather than saw, secluded cameras swivel to track her movements as she passed. There was no paper on the walls, but the air was heavy with the scent of kerosene: designed, she supposed, to be easily combustible. The doors looked fire-retardant: heavy, solid-looking, steel-reinforced. At the eighth, he stopped, pressed a hand against an aged scanner that looked as likely to electrocute as to pop the hidden lock that released the door beside it with a soft puff of air. Danae followed him in.

The room beyond doubled as a bedroom and a living room. How many shared it with Angelo was impossible to say; only that it was littered with the detritus of occupation. Three beds, as long as the walls against which they stood, took care of a third of the floor space; the rest was a patchwork of pillows, blankets and roll-up mattresses. Angelo lowered himself onto one of the cots, extracted a cigarette packet from the depths of a pocket, waved it in Danae's direction. When she nodded, he pulled out two, lit them both in his mouth, and handed one to her.

She took it from him, stood in the centre of the room, not wanting to sit. The space was too personal, too overtly masculine; she felt like an intruder.

She said, 'Who is he? The guy on the door?'

'Him and me go way back,' said Angelo, as if it were an answer.

'He's not …'

'No.'

'But he knows.'

'Of course.'

'What about your roommates?'

'People come and go. It's a place to stay.'

'You said I could find you here.'

'I said you could come here if you needed help.'

'You're here just the same.'

'Not for long.'

'Nadine died.'

Angelo looked up sharply, drew on his cigarette. Met her gaze, then looked away.

'That much was obvious,' he said.

Danae clenched her fist, digging her nails into her palm, fighting the sudden urge to lash out. She wasn't sure what she'd expected — sympathy? Tears? Humanity? Hardly likely. But he'd known Nadine, and Nadine had been her friend, and she wanted that to count for something. And it didn't, and so she wanted to hurt him until it did. The itch burned, but it was all wrong; it wasn't for him. It was for the whole stupid mess, the injustice, the world at large, and none of that was his fault.

So she waited a moment, two, three, until she was certain she'd forced the fury back inside. When she thought she could speak without anger, she said, 'I need your help.'

But Angelo only loosed a humourless laugh, shook his head, didn't look at her. He sucked hard on his cigarette, the sudden rush of red light to the tip colouring the shadows on his face. 'I guess you tried everyone else,' he said.

'There is no one else.'

He laughed again, less bitterly now. 'Then I'm your first choice. That makes a change.'

'I need your help,' she said again.

He didn't answer straight away. Instead, he took his time, sitting up straight, exhaling a smoke ring and following through with a thick haze of grey fog.

'See this place?' he said, indicating lazily with the hand that held the cigarette. The ember danced a line of red in the darkness. 'This is where you go when there's nowhere else. You know how many guys I share this room with? Thirty-seven. That's if no-one else turns up tonight. Thirty-seven. Big guys. You can't close your eyes at night, you can't take your eye of them for a second. You hear noises in the darkness: grown men crying.'

'That's a sad story, Angelo,' said Danae. 'What's your point?'

'My point?' He shook his head, half-smiled, but it was turned downwards towards the floor. 'You ever spend a night some place you don't know if you're going to wake up in the morning? Because the alternative is some place where you definitely won't?'

'What do you want?' she said. 'A place to stay?'

He grinned, twisted his head so that he met her level gaze. His teeth were like opals in the half-light, lit by the cigarette and the glow in his eye.

'Now you're talking,' he said.

13.5

'Nice place,' he said. 'I like what you've done with the damp.'

'It keeps the rain off,' said Danae.

'Which bit?'

'What?'

'Which bit in particular keeps the rain off?'

She rounded on him, saw that he was laughing, saw that his face had come back to life. 'Fuck you,' she said.

'I like it,' he said. 'I do. What's for dinner?'

Angelo had no bags with him, no belongings, only an apparently inexhaustible supply of cigarettes, which he was happy to share with her once she handed over the rest of the ginn. They sat in the drawing room, where there were no exterior walls and no whistling drafts through unseen cracks, on a carpet of blankets that she had found on her first night, nestled in the bottom of a wardrobe. They were thick, expensively woven, and the cold was penetrating, but only slowly. He accepted without question when she refused his offer of a draught from the bottle, and she tried to read in his eyes whether her reasons were written on her face, but he gave nothing away, only shrugged and drank.

He asked what had happened after he left the apartment, and she told him: how Nadine had stopped fitting but weakened quickly, her pulse rapid and thready, her blood flowing into the water from a gash that opened up on the back of her head when it struck the tiles, staining the water pink. How Danae had tried to insist that there was nothing wrong with her, had known even then that it was a mistake to go with them.

He said, 'I'm sorry. For what it's worth.'

She shrugged a blanket tighter around her shoulders; the heat evacuated quickly after dark. They had lit candles and placed them strategically around the room: three on the high faux-mahogany sideboard, two in the fireplace, seven more scattered in glasses about the floor. Whoever had lived in the apartment had left in a hurry, taking only food and valuables. Danae preferred not to think about them.

'Tell me about you,' she said. 'Where are you from?'

He grinned. 'Why do you care?'

'I don't. I'm making conversation.'

'That's not the sort of conversation I'm used to making.'

Danae shrugged. 'So don't answer.'

His grin widened and he lifted the bottle to his mouth, drank three big gulps. He watched for a moment, hand pressed to his mouth as the ginn settled. 'Barcelona,' he said.

'The city? Or the district?'

'Just Barcelona.'

'The city, then.'

'The city. Not much left of it now.'

'Is that why you left?'

'Wouldn't you?'

'I wasn't there.'

'I missed the worst of it,' he said. 'Time was, I heard, you couldn't walk out of your house without someone taking a shot at you. One side or the other. It didn't matter who you were. Law of averages, I guess.'

'So you came here.'

'I got shipped out. Lucky me.'

'You miss it?'

'Barcelona?'

'Anywhere that's not Creo.'

'No.'

'Liar.'

'So, if you do, everyone has to? No. I like it here. The living's easier.'

'Depends whose life you get,' she said.

He smiled, but there was anger in it. 'A lot of people died,' he said. 'Good people.'

Danae let the silence hang between them for a moment. 'People you knew?'

He pulled a cigarette from the packet and wove it through his fingers. She watched him, hypnotised, wondering if he was even conscious of the movement.

He said, 'People died every day. Everyone knew someone.'

Danae watched the cigarette thread itself through the length of his hand, curve around his thumb, pivot and return. A couple of flakes of tobacco broke free, scattered, disappeared into the darkness. Angelo's hands were rough and dry, and the cigarette paper rasped where it brushed against them.

'When?' she said.

'When what?' His voice was flat: dead, for the first time since she had met him.

'When did whoever it was die?'

A beat. 'I said *people.*'

'Okay,' she said evenly. 'Forget it.'

Angelo shrugged. 'I left her.'

She said nothing, stared at him steadily. He made a show of ignoring her, of staring into the shadows on the floor until he was done, winding his cigarette through his fingers. And when he was ready — on his terms, not hers — he raised his head, met her eyes. She held his gaze, resisted the temptation to look away.

'I don't get you,' he said at last.

'You mentioned that,' said Danae.

'At all. I don't get you at all.'

'I know,' she said.

The cigarette drifted across his hands. 'I left her,' he said again. 'We were trying to get out.'

'Of Barcelona.'

'Yeah.'

'Why did you leave her?'

Angelo exhaled, picked an imaginary fleck of tobacco from his lip and said, 'She got shot. I couldn't carry her. That's how it goes.'

Danae opened her mouth to speak, but hesitated. In that second, before she could say whatever she'd been going to say, he said again, 'That's how it goes. Get used to it.' She opened her mouth again and he said, 'Where's the bottle?'

Silently, she passed it to him, watched him drink. More than he meant to, she was sure: tears welled up against the onslaught of the fumes.

She said, quietly, 'It doesn't matter.'

'You asked,' he said. 'I'm telling you. That's all.'

'So I shouldn't have asked.'

He shrugged. He drank again. At last, more evenly, he said, 'It wasn't even a city anymore. It was just rubble. And there was a riot; there were always riots. We'd thought we'd just sneak out at night, and, bam, suddenly there's all these people everywhere. I didn't even know there was that many left in the city. There was just people, everywhere. And, you know, you can't get through something like that, you have to go around. There were people throwing firebombs, and glass, and tear gas, it was fucking everywhere. And we're trying to get out, and someone starts shooting, and everyone starts screaming — you know, half of them were women and children: little kids with Molotov cocktails, it was crazy — and everyone's screaming and trying to run, and we don't know which side we should be screaming that we're on, nobody knows who's got the guns, people are just screaming. And we're trying to hold onto each other, but ...' He stopped, rubbed his eyes. He said, softly, 'I could feel it. I could feel her shudder. Like I was pressed against a door and someone was banging on it. And all of a sudden, she's not running anymore, and I'm just ... dragging her. And then I'm not. And so I just kept running.' The cigarette rose to his lips, flared in the darkness. 'And when I went back for her, she wasn't there.'

'What was her name?'

'Renata.'

'Maybe she lived.'

He shook his head. 'She didn't.'

'Did you see her die?'

'No, but she died.'

'Maybe ...'

But he said, quickly, 'She died. That's all.'

Danae shrugged. 'So you came here and started sleeping with anything with a pulse.'

'Who told you that?'

'It's a wild stab in the dark.'

He grinned again, but his heart wasn't in it. 'Thank you, Dr. Freud,' he said.

She said, softly, 'Did you love her just a little bit?'

Angelo looked up sharply. 'Renata?'

'Nadine,' she said.

He stared at her for a long moment, as though he didn't understand the question. Maybe, she thought, he didn't.

'No,' he said quietly. 'No. Why?'

'I don't know,' said Danae, and she didn't. 'Maybe — it would have been a happy ending. I don't know.'

He grinned again, stronger, shaking off the sadness like an unwanted coat. 'Here's your happy ending,' he said. 'You're alive. You have food and smokes and … gin, probably. It looks like gin. And you live in a palace. It doesn't get better. Really.'

Danae picked at a thread on the blanket, almost invisible by candlelight. 'I found this place,' she said. 'It was the only door that locked. All the other places were cleaned out, like the people knew they were going, like they just grabbed all their things and hocked them, or gave them to their friends to hold for them. Or something. I don't know. But this one, it's like they thought they were coming back. It's like they thought they were going out to work. Like it was still their home. Everything's still here. One of the beds, the quilt was thrown back to air. There was a rat's nest in the mattress. And I found a laundry basket in the bathroom, with clothes in the bottom. They must have forgotten about it. I thought, they didn't mean to leave. And then — in the kitchen. There's a chalk outline on the floor.'

She was aware of his eyes on her. She looked up. Without a word, he handed her his cigarette, pulled another from the pack to replace it. When it was lit, he said, 'What a lovely story.'

She shrugged.

'I don't get you,' he said again.

'Angelo, I know,' she said.

'I knew in a second,' he said. 'And you didn't know about me.'

'Angelo, drop it,' she said. 'I'm tired.'

'I bet if I made a move on you, I'd lose skin.'

'At the very least,' she agreed. 'It's not like that. That's not why you're here.'

'You said you needed my help,' he said.

She pinched the cigarette between thumb and forefinger, drew on it. 'The butt of this is soaking,' she said. 'What did you do, lick it before you gave it me?'

'I'll have it back then.'

'Smoke your own.'

'What do you need, Danae?'

'In the morning. I need to sleep now.'

'Ask me now.'

'Hypothetically?'

'If you like.'

'Hypothetically,' she said. 'If someone needed a memory block ...'

'You can't have a memory block, Danae.'

Careful. 'I didn't say I needed one.'

'They go *inside* your head. You can't sterilise them enough.'

'I said, I didn't say I needed one. Try to keep up.'

'The guy with the sister?'

'I'm not telling you who.'

He shrugged. 'Hard to fit someone with a chip unless I know who it is.'

'But you know someone.'

He sucked air. 'Pricey, though.'

'How pricey?'

'Five, six thousand.'

'Jesus.' It was out before she caught herself, drenched with despair.

'Easy,' he said. 'Maybe more now. It's a while since there's been interest.'

'Jesus,' she said again.

'Think you can round up that sort of money? I can take you to talk to him.'

'Think I could talk him down a bit?'

'I doubt it. But you can try. Who's it for?'

'Let me talk to him first.'

'Fair enough. But I'll warn you: he doesn't do sob stories. He doesn't care if it's for a battered baby or your crippled granny. It's still twenty-five to life if he gets caught.'

'Understood,' she said. She had five tokens in her pocket, and the itch was worse.

THE HERALD, 16TH FEBRUARY 2076

'It helps,' he suggested, 'to think of the datastream as a kind of parallel to our own universe. The entirety of human stream activity takes place in a space equivalent to our solar system, and a-naut protocol existed, until recently, in a space equivalent to Mars. And now imagine that some cataclysmic cosmic event has knocked Mars out of its orbit and sent it hurtling out into space. It still exists, and it can potentially still be accessed, but it is temporarily out of our reach.' When pressed on how the change might have occurred, however, Dr Balkhi refused to be drawn, saying only that he believed it was indeed reversible and that the department's efforts were entirely focused in that direction. It is estimated that there are some 1.7 billion a-nauts in use worldwide and across the post-etheric colonies, although it is not known how many have been deactivated in the past two weeks.

14 MAY

14.1

'Word to the wise,' said Devereaux, and grinned. 'He's in one of his Moods. I wouldn't go in there if I were you.'

Katz had never particularly warmed to Devereaux, though she was prepared to accept that the congressman needed a media advisor, and Devereaux, for all that he had the kind of face you wanted to punch and an oily manner that made Katz want to wash her hands after he'd borrowed her pen, knew how to spin a story. And, since it had surprised precisely nobody in Hadaway's team to learn that Creo was the kind of constituency that a person needed to spin, Devereaux was one of those necessary evils with which, she understood, you were supposed to come to terms and slowly learn to love. It was just that Katz had been with the congressman since his local government days in Britannia South, and she knew him, and she knew how to manage his decision-making processes and his policy announcements and his public appearances – better even than the man himself, most days. And Devereaux *always* treated her like they only kept her around to brighten the place up a bit.

'Thanks,' she said, and brushed past him before he could put his hands on the door sensors or anything else she was likely to need to touch. 'I think I can handle myself.'

'Your funeral,' he said cheerfully, but quietly, because the door was opening now, and the congressman was in one of his Moods.

Hadaway was pacing the floor by his expansive desk, jacked into a Holler connection and arguing with an unseen congregation on the other side of his visor. She wished he wouldn't move around while he did that. Maybe he knew the office as well as he thought, and maybe he didn't, but the fact of the matter was that he was essentially wandering blind through an obstacle course of tables and chairs and shelves and similar, and, sooner or later, the day would come when Devereaux would be obliged to explain to an attentive press how the congressman had managed to fracture a hipbone in the privacy of his own office. Katz could not imagine that would end well for any of them.

'Yes, I understand that,' he was saying. 'Yes — Mr Mayor, I think we'll get through this a lot quicker if you let me finish what I'm saying before you start yelling again. Vincent, you were yelling. No, believe me, I was looking at the volume readout on my screen and I think you just knocked a couple of decibels off my aural range …'

There was a floor lamp in a corner of the room by the window. It had been there since Hadaway had moved into the suite, some six years previously, and he switched it on and off himself every evening, but it was currently situated directly within his perambulatory trajectory and he wasn't paying attention. Katz shifted it quietly towards the wall.

'Yes, Sam,' he was saying. 'I'm aware that there's a protocol to follow. Yes, I am, actually. And the reason I'm aware is because we go through the same damn protocol six times a year in Creo Basse. No, look, Sam, you *know* what kind of damage it does to commerce when Vincent has to call an off-peak curfew … I'm not saying that, Sam, but I think you need to meet us halfway here …'

Hadaway had been awake now, Katz knew, for a little over forty hours: since the curfew had been called, in fact. It wasn't his decision and it wouldn't have happened if he'd had any say in the matter, but, for whatever reason, the fallout always landed at his door, and Vincent Pontbriand liked to shout. No wonder a Mood had descended.

Katz lowered herself into one of the three leather chairs that described a semi-circle in front of his desk and called up her computer screen as she waited. The message was top of her shuffle pile, red-coded and marked with her own scribbled note: *CF'd with McP, LH and RCL. NDA, cc to Rm 120 + PD, talk to Harv J about bringing in. For JC ASAP. Alan — who else has seen this?* She brushed a finger now to the shimmering haze and the message sprang open: six elegant lines of Québecois French that translated automatically beneath her wandering touch, followed by a series of diagrams, lab reports and images that meant nothing to a political analyst, but, apparently, a whole hell of a lot to the three medical specialists that they'd kept on the payroll ever since Hadaway's complicated first week in office. Kudos to the author: he knew how to make a point in a way that got people to listen.

'Celestine,' said Hadaway now as he walked right through the spot where, until ninety seconds ago, a Mogul lamp had been standing, 'we are talking about seventeen casualties. We lost more people to RTAs yesterday afternoon, and nobody's arguing that *they're* contagious. No, listen, there's no evidence — none — that would make me think we need a curfew. All I've got is twenty-seven million seriously pissed off citizens and a public relations crisis brewing for the fourth time this year, and if I let this go on another night I'm going to have to go back to Appropriations and ask for the money to put another five hundred troops on the street. And that's money that I don't have ... All right, look, I've got a reminder buzzing in my ear that says it's time for me to go and get shouted at on live television again, so we'll have to put this on hold, but ... Vincent. No, I have no intention of ducking the issue. All right. You can speak to Karl about scheduling. And, Sam, I'll want you in on it too. Okay, thanks, everyone.'

The visor dissolved, and Hadaway, who had found himself on the very edge of the room, dropped his head to rest lightly against the wall. 'Tell me again, Evelyn,' he said, 'why I have to go on record for the eighth time in twelve months to explain why I need to cripple the economy of that damn city instead of just letting nature take its course? How can one place be so hell-bent on trying to die of something every four weeks?'

'I don't know, sir,' said Katz. 'I've never been to Creo. Maybe it's a matter of civic pride?'

In profile, she saw the edges of his lips curl upwards in a gesture that lacked the energy or the enthusiasm to become a smile. He lifted his head, turned back towards the room. 'Better make this quick,' he said. 'I need to be gone in – '

'Two minutes, sir,' she said. 'I'll talk fast.'

'Use small words. It's been a long day.'

'I'm ... not sure I can do that, sir.'

'Oh?' An eyebrow arched as he dropped into his seat with the lethargy of a man for whom sleep has been a luxury for more time than he cares to remember. 'I'm not sure I have the mental capacity for the big-words stuff right now, Evelyn – '

'You'll want to see this, sir,' she said, and slid the data package towards his stream pocket, hearing a *ping* from his wrist-processor as it arrived. 'It came through about ten hours ago — I ran it past the usual guys and ... I think there might be something in it, sir.' A muted *zip* as the congressman's screen opened in front of him and, through the pixels, she saw his brow furrow in concentration as he read. 'He's getting stonewalled by the Path guys in Creo and the DoH, and Silvan agrees with them, but Louise and Robert-Charles are … hesitant. Lou's trying to call in a connection with one of the guys in CDC Paris — she says she's not happy with what she's reading and she wants to get her hands on some of the samples to see for herself. You know Lou, sir. She doesn't get excited about stuff. But she's worried about this.'

Hadaway scrolled down the page, eyes locked on the screen. 'Do you know this guy?'

'No, sir,' said Katz. 'But he checks out. I've asked Harv to bring him in, just to be on the safe side.'

'Good.' He nodded distractedly. 'This is … I don't know what this is, Eve. This looks … it looks crazy.'

'Yes, sir,' she said. 'And you know I don't bring you the crazy, sir.'

'No,' he said. 'You don't. Damn it!' he added, as an alarm light started flashing in the corner of his screen. 'I really have to go. Is Paul here?'

'He's outside, sir. He'll prep you in the car on the way over.'

'All right.' He stood up, pulling his jacket from the back of his chair and shrugging it on as he rounded the desk. Shadows moved on his face as his screen shifted in front of him. 'Can you get me Lou before I have to speak to Vincent again? And tell her to talk to this guy in … Montréal? Really?'

'Yes, sir. He's an old colleague of one of the patients, sir.'

'Damn. That's a couple of hours, minimum, before we can get him to London, then.'

'He's on his way, sir. I'll have Lou call him en route.'

'Thank you, Evelyn.' A flick of his wrist and Hadaway's screen disappeared. He sighed, reached one hand up to pinch the bridge of his nose. 'You know,' he said, 'I was actually holding out hope that I might get an hour or two's sleep this evening. You'd think I'd know better by now.'

Katz, who had last seen the inside of her bedroom a little over three days ago, offered a rueful smile and brushed a fleck of lint from his shoulder. 'You know what they say about hope, sir,' she said.

'As I recall,' said Hadaway, 'they say it's a four-letter word. You really think there's something in this, Eve?'

Katz spread her hand. 'I'm not a scientist, sir,' she said. 'All I know is, that letter had to go through a lot of smart people before it got to you. I keep the stupid stuff off your desk, sir.'

'Yes,' said Hadaway. He sucked in a deep breath. 'All right. Let's get Lou talking to this guy as soon as possible, and she can explain to me what the hell he thinks is going on. What's his name again?'

'Pasachoff,' said Katz as she followed him towards the door. 'Professor Théophile Pasachoff.'

14.2

Danae slept poorly, kept wakeful by the cold and the gentle, tidal wash through her brain, so strong in his proximity that it almost edged out the itch.

Almost.

Close to dawn, Angelo stirred and muttered something incoherent. It was messy enough to be sleep-talk, and he was facing away from her in the shadows; too distant to tell if he was expecting an answer. Danae let the silence hang for a moment, then, just in case, she said, 'What?'

He rolled over, slowly, leisurely, running a hand over his chin. 'I said,' he said, in a voice thick with sleep, 'are you awake?'

She blinked. 'No,' she said.

'Sarcasm,' he told her, 'is the lowest form of wit.' Angelo sucked in a deep breath, stretching his arms above his head and into the darkness. 'We should make a start,' he said, words swallowed by a yawn. 'I don't want to be on the road when it starts getting busy.'

'When is it ever not busy?' said Danae, but she threw the covers back — briskly, before her brain had time to warn her body — and rolled out into the chilly pre-dawn black.

The heat had risen on the streets overnight. Condensation clung to the light bands, blurring their glow into a buttery haze, like a badly preserved old movie, as they walked in easy silence through the warren of food stalls in various stages of set-up. Danae was half-asleep and hyperalert, stomach growling when it hit the wall of scents that drifted up from bubbling pans and frying onions and leavening breads: the morning flavours of Parnasse. At a Mexican stand, Angelo pulled up sharply with a shit-eating grin, and exchanged a few cheerful words with the owner, who rolled his eyes and began preparing a couple of burritos. Danae, alert to the possibility of food, edged over in their general direction and felt the butterflies kick like a restless foetus.

She blinked, felt the edges of her lips curling upwards. The man on the stall looked up, flashed her a dark smile, then dropped his eyes to scatter chopped coriander onto rice: categorised, acknowledged, processed and dismissed. And it would be like this from now on, she realised. Angelo had shown her the false bottom on the hat and now she knew how to make the rabbit appear.

'Do you know everyone in the city?' she asked as they walked, lifting her half-eaten burrito to her mouth for another bite. The tortilla was stale and the filling lukewarm, but it was the best eating she'd had in a while.

'Pretty much,' he said.

Danae, who had trouble imagining how you would remember the names of more than five people, let alone find time to socialise with them all, said, 'You're a useful person to know.'

'True.'

She snorted. 'And yet so modest too.'

'You want modesty,' he said, 'go talk to someone who doesn't know what he's doing. Only reason to hide your light under a bushel is if you don't want people to see it doesn't shine so well. Left after this off-licence.'

'You know,' she said, 'it'd be a whole lot easier for me to keep up if I knew where I was headed.'

'I told you,' he said. 'Kolasi direction. God, I love the smell of Parnasse in the morning.'

His face was open, unguarded, and she knew it was the best she was likely to get. The bakers were arriving, panniers stacked high with fresh loaves, and he'd tilted his head back, nose pointed into the air, breathing deeply of the thousand scents that hung on the air. As the district began to rise, the streets were filling out with early morning commuters: parents with sleeping babies strapped to their chests, night workers on their way home, important people with their heads buried in the morning papers. The pulse of the city picked up the night time beat and ran with it, flowing seamlessly into day. Planets shifted, tornados claimed cities, seas boiled and died, but Creo Basse hid beneath its concrete hood and just got on with things.

And yet ...

There were shiny faces in the crowds that milled and ate and fought their way past each other. Faces bent out of shape by a hazmask, skin compressed and distorted beneath a thin plastic veneer, eyes that searched the crowds. Policemen, in uniform and out, silent and watchful, weapons on display.

Hooded eyes, mouths and noses swathed in scarves. Creo was waiting to see what happened next.

Danae thought, *and this is only one street.* She glanced at Angelo, saw that he was watching the hazmask people carefully, darkly.

'Left here,' he said, and reached out a hand to touch her shoulder, in case she might have forgotten which side was which.

'If we're going to Kolasi …' said Danae.

'Kolasi *direction*, I said.'

'Left doesn't work for Kolasi *direction*, either.'

'Do you know where we're going?'

'No, because you won't tell me.'

'Exactly. So turn left.'

Danae opened her mouth to make the sort of response that wasn't likely to be helpful, but before she could speak there was a sudden cry from the crowd behind. She pivoted, craning her head in search of the cause, and found herself at the edge of a widening circle. Angelo, quicker on the uptake, dropped a hand to her belly and pushed her back with him as the epicentre revealed a plastic-faced man and woman, ageless behind the veneer, up in the faces of two men in their forties, shouting something too angry to understand. A woman hung onto the arm of one of the screaming men, pulling on him, trying to draw him back, but she might as well have leaned all her weight into the tenement behind; the odds of success were about as high. He barely even noticed her.

A murmur broke out in the crowd, a ripple of gathering enthusiasm, a hundred voices speaking quietly at once. Danae followed Angelo's line of sight and saw two policemen moving through the throngs, like lionesses stalking prey.

'Time to go,' said Angelo.

He grabbed her hand and jerked her roughly away from the arena, just in time for her to see the other man, the one whose wife wasn't trying to extricate him, reach over to the plastic-faced woman and rip the tubes from the side of her mask. Her face contorted in panic and her mouth opened into a frantic, sucking 'O', lungs searching desperately for their failing oxygen supply. As the crowds closed behind her, Danae saw the plastic-faced man scrabbling at her face, fingers locked through hers as they tore together at the veneer.

Danae and Angelo broke to the left, falling in behind a moving hot dog wagon as it trundled through the influx of crowds in search of a less eventful site. Commuters flocked past them on either side, drawn like iron filings to a magnet by the sounds of something interesting happening to someone else, but, as they made their way further from the epicentre, the clamour subsided to a rumour, a whisper, and, finally, back into early morning apathy. Angelo tutted.

'Now,' he said, 'wasn't that exciting.'

★

They walked. The back streets were almost as direct as the main roads, but tended to be clogged with peddlers, who filled a percentage of the narrow space in a way that was in direct contravention of the laws of physics. Einstein might have had trouble explaining how a skinny woman with a baby was able to block a street that was twelve feet wide, or a wizened old man with a begging bowl could occupy two thirds of the available pavement space. Maybe it was quantum, or something.

The barrowmen thinned out as the roads led further away from the main thoroughfares and the pickings got slimmer. The hum of industry, ever present, began to fade into a manageable background drawl, and Danae felt the city lulling her back into its habitual fog of watchful ennui. Maybe Angelo was waiting for it, maybe he was just good at picking his moments, maybe he read her a little better than she might have liked, because it was precisely the kind of state of mind that was in no way equipped for quick thinking beyond the general mechanics of staying alive on the streets, and exactly the right moment to catch her off guard with a difficult question.

Whatever the reason, he waited until they were safely out of earshot of the trio of elderly women that had elbowed him unceremoniously out of their way, and said, into the relative quiet of an empty alleyway, 'So, tell me this. What happened when the ambulance arrived?'

Danae supposed she knew better than to think he wouldn't ask, but she'd hoped to have distracted him sufficiently to buy herself a little more time. So, instead, she tried deflection.

'Shit,' she said, and stumbled.

He caught her flailing arm, tightening his hand as she went down, fingers digging painfully into her flesh. 'Watch your step,' he said.

'Yeah, thanks,' she muttered. She'd been hoping for a full-scale collapse, or at least a graze.

'You were saying?' he prompted.

So she tried to brazen it out. 'Yeah, they arrived about five minutes after you left. That was the last I saw of them.'

His voice was neutral. 'So how did you hear about Nadine?'

Shit. 'I went by and asked,' she said.

He was silent for a long moment. When she couldn't stand it anymore, she lied, 'I was her next of kin. There were things I had to sign – you know.'

'Sure,' he said.

Another beat. She said, 'They hardly gave me a second glance at the flat. You needn't have worried. They were …'

He pinned her to the wall and kissed her.

For a moment she was too stunned to react. He'd knocked the wind out of her when he pressed his body against hers and it was a second before she could summon the presence of mind to be outraged. Danae tried to squeeze her mouth shut, bit down hard on his lips, and he let out a tiny yelp of pain but made no move to release her. She considered bringing her knee up into his groin, lifted her foot off the ground, but then she noticed his eyes.

They were wide open, fixed on hers, and warning her.

Casually, without moving his head, he glanced to the left. She followed his line of sight and saw two men on the very edge of vision, where her eyeballs hurt with the strain of looking. They were unremarkable to the average observer: neither tall nor short, well-built nor slight. One wore his dark blond hair in a short pony-tail, cropped tightly against the rest of his head, and wore glasses with tinted lenses. The other, about a head taller than his companion, was dark-skinned and vaguely handsome, in an undernourished way. When he spoke, he revealed a broken tooth, poorly capped once and now left to the elements.

There was nothing unusual about them. But as they approached, Angelo brought his hand up to the side of her face, cupping it towards him so that it shielded his own. She responded as best she could, closing her eyes so as not to arouse suspicion, guessing their position by their pace. Angelo pressed hard against her, as though, where pedestrians were so sparse, he was trying to pretend they were part of the wall. She gripped the back of his head, pulling him closer to her, felt his hand reach down to her buttock. That was a liberty too far, but she guessed that the men were roughly level with them and it was the wrong time to object. So she ground her backside against the rough, cheap-bricked wall instead, dragging his fingers with her. He inhaled sharply, but he took the point.

Voices from further along the street edged into hearing: young voices, chattering in French. Danae felt the atmosphere shift, cracked an eyelid to see the two men exchange a couple of quiet words and retreat out of sight. When they were safely distant, she pushed Angelo away, wiped her mouth, and said, fiercely, 'You didn't have to grope my fucking arse.'

He wasn't listening. His head was angled at ninety degrees from her, staring down the street, trying to make men appear from the shadows. He said, 'They're Rens.'

The air left the alley.

'How do you know?' she said.

His eyes flicked back to hers. 'I think they're watching me.'

'Christ, Angelo!'

'I *know*,' he hissed. The owners of the childlike voices drifted into view: two boys, not yet in their teens. Angelo cupped her face, leaned down to whisper in her ear. 'Did you see where they went?'

'They passed us,' she told them. 'I can't tell how far.'

'Okay,' he said. He caught her eye and grinned. 'I can handle this,' he said. 'Don't panic. I've had worse.'

But his hand gripped hers with a strength that called his voice a liar. She said, 'I should tell you something …'

'Is now a good time?' said Angelo, in a tone that said, *now is not a good time.*

'About me,' she said, as he edged her away from the wall, peering down the alleyway after the retreating backs of the Rens. He took a step forward, and his grip on her hand was so tight that Danae had to follow him. 'We're going in the same *direction* as them?' she said.

'The ones you see aren't the problem,' he said. His smile was fixed, plastic.

'It's important,' she said.

'Tell me *later*,' he said, with a tone that implied that he realised she didn't believe there would *be* a later, and that wasn't exactly helping matters.

He dragged her forward another few steps, swung his arm lazily around her, and she responded by wrapping her arm around his back, fingers finding purchase on poorly-covered ribs. Danae hadn't noticed how skinny he was and wished she'd left it a bit longer to realise. *Skinny* was not a helpful adjective when applied to someone you fervently hoped was about to save your life.

'Where is he?' he muttered. She rested her head on his shoulders, contrived to sweep the alleyway ahead with vacant eyes, as though she were lost in her own thoughts. 'If we have to run,' he told her quietly, 'I'll meet you at Intimacy. Do *not* go to the apartment.'

Footsteps behind her almost made her flick her head around in search of the source, but he felt her tense to move and tightened his grip. 'It's a woman,' he said, without looking. 'She's moving too quickly. *And they're right. Ahead. Of us.*'

She looked up; saw only dark shapes in the half-light. They could be beggars or thieves, too fluid to easily identify even as male. There was no hint in their gait, and they were walking away from her.

She nearly said, *Are you sure?* But she caught the words as they struggled to find their way out of her throat. Angelo was still alive; that was a lot of sure.

Instead, she said, 'Now what?'

He nuzzled his nose into her hair and said, 'We need their quarterback. Don't run until you know what you're running from.'

The woman behind overtook them briskly in a haze of dusky perfume and impatience. Danae watched her disappear into the shadows ahead, heels clipping smartly on the concrete with a confidence that she didn't feel. The Rens parted to let her through and she didn't turn her head to look at them – why would she? They were strangers in a dark alleyway: eye contact was lethal. As they fell back into place in her wake, Danae caught a faint gleam in the dusky gloom and identified it a second too late.

The first man's tinted glasses. He'd seen her watching him.

'Angelo,' she whispered.

'Is it important?' he whispered, in his *it's not important* tone.

'He saw me looking at him.'

'Are you sure?'

'Completely.'

'Eye contact?'

'I think so. It's dark.'

'What was your expression?'

'I don't know.'

'Were you afraid of him when you were looking at him?'

She hesitated.

He said, 'Were you frightened of him?'

Pride was getting the better of her, but she forced it down and said, 'Yes.'

'Then he saw it.'

'I'm sorry,' she said.

'It's okay,' he said. 'It's time to run.'

14.3

He broke into a run while she was still disjointed, and it was only his grip on her hand that carried her with him. Danae was dimly aware on the edge of vision that the Rens had shifted from a standing start to a blur of speed, and that a third shape had slunk out of the shadows and started sprinting. It disappeared into a side street to the left as they ran up the alleyway, the thundering of the men's feet behind them their only gauge of how much distance they needed to make up. Angelo let her find her pace alongside him and dropped her hand, throwing both his arms into a piston movement on either side of his body as he fought for speed. His head was back, his breathing harsh but not laboured, and she thought, *we can keep this up for hours, they can't. They can't.*

The itch was swelling, gaining strength, gaining volume, almost louder now than the panic. It whispered to her, wheedling, seducing – *Who are they to anyone? Who would it hurt? Wouldn't it be better if. .?*

No. It was a one-way switch. There was no going back. Danae ran.

A turning loomed ahead of them. Angelo punched her arm to get her attention and veered to the right, flicking his head to make sure she was following. They had turned into the path of a bubble and the ground was slick with water and, in the semi-darkness, a thick green slime that greased the concrete like black ice. Danae skidded and fought for purchase, her arms coming up instinctively as she slammed into the heavy brickwork, a layer of skin shearing from her palms. But it was enough to right her and, as she caught herself, she took the opportunity to glance back over her shoulder. The Rens were not yet in view, but their lengthening shadows on the facing wall said that they were close. Angelo was ahead of her, waiting for her to follow, and Danae levered herself from the wall with momentum enough to throw her into a flat run. He hesitated only long enough to see that she was moving again, and then turned, began to move off.

It caught them completely unawares. It may even have caught the Ren off-guard. There was no look of triumph as he materialised, suddenly, from the shadows ahead and to the left, just grim, stone-faced determination. Bad luck drove Angelo down, but the slick pavement held him there; he bucked and fought, but there was no purchase on the ground. In the semi-darkness, Danae could hardly see his face, muddied with street-dirt: only the whites of his eyes, wide and round with terror.

'Run!' he screamed. 'Go! Move! *Run!*'

Shock had dulled her responses, but there was no time to think: her legs knew what to do, even if her brain was slow to catch up. It was a shame, then, that she only managed half a step before arms gripped her from behind, pulling her down with them, and she realised with a thrill of helpless rage that the man who held Angelo was not the third Ren but an unsuspected fourth. For a moment she hung, suspended, in the air, then time restarted and she fell, sharply. She expected to land on flesh — counted on it — but he was too quick for her and rolled out of her way so that she slammed full-force into the concrete, knocking the breath from her lungs. Danae was moving again in seconds, sucking air through her constricted windpipe in tight, painful gasps, but the Ren had the advantage of a controlled landing and he was faster than her. A boot in the back of her head sent the world swimming white and she fell, barely conscious, toppling forwards like a broken doll. She snapped back as her face hit the wet slime, but the Ren was already on top of her, his knee in the small of her neck.

Slime filled her mouth and she gagged, choking and spluttering. His purchase was slack enough to afford her the slightest movement of her head, and, twisting it to her right, out of the rankness, she could see up the alleyway to where Angelo lay. The fourth Ren was the smallest and he was having trouble pinning down a man of Angelo's build, but the original two had arrived, and the darker of them ended the argument with two well-aimed kicks to a skinny, poorly covered set of ribs. Danae thought she heard bone crack, but Angelo was made of stronger stuff than that and the Ren knew it. The third kick was to the head.

Dimly, through a haze of pain, she saw the CP scanner slipped from Sunglasses' back pocket, pressed into his companion's hand.

Do you ever worry there'll be a mistake? she thought. *That one day the meter won't be working and you'll get a red?*

Angelo was bleary, on the edge of consciousness, as helpless as she was, but his eyes found hers, locked on hers, and she saw that they were pale with terror, pupils constricted, whites bulging. His arms were twisted roughly behind his back — she was faintly aware of something similar happening at the base of her spine — and he knew, as surely as she did, that there was a gun on both of them, that there was no way out.

And she knew what her reading would be, and there was no way to explain it to him now.

The dark-skinned Ren pressed the scanner to Angelo's neck. A moment, a long, agonising second, and then the red light bathed the alleyway in blood.

'I'm sorry,' he whispered, and it was a second before she realised he was talking to her.

She tried to speak, to say it was all right, but her head was forced roughly downwards and ooze flowed freely into her open mouth. She spluttered, gagged, thought she would vomit. When she looked up, she saw his eyes were on her, his face blank with confusion, and she knew he'd seen her green.

'I'll find you,' she told him, shouted after him as he was hauled to his feet and dragged backwards away from her. His eyes were the only light in the darkness, white like death, still fixed on her. 'Angelo, I'm sorry,' she shouted. 'I'll find you, I swear I'll find you …'

But there was nothing, not even a gunshot. Only silence.

14.4

Maybe she lived.
She didn't.
Did you see her die?
No, but she died.
Maybe …
She died. That's all.

That night, Danae felt the stream warp.

It was a long time coming: a build-up of hours, starting with a gentle, reeling nausea that rippled in waves through her skull as the stream began to tremble to the rhythm of a bad death. Angelo's scent lingered in the still air of the apartment, sketching him into the darkness like a reproachful ghost that wouldn't leave, and in the end, she just found a room he hadn't been in and crawled into a corner, blanket thrown around her shoulders, and tried to keep warm while the shadows lengthened and the heat left her body and the long fight began. As night fell and the last of the light drained from the room, the stream began to bellow and storm and writhe, and she cradled her head in her hands and curled her knees into her chest, fingers digging into the skin of her temple to ward off the pain that erupted behind her eyes with every twist and convulsion. It wrapped itself in double helixes and span like a child's toy, frantic and out of control, red and purple and black and bleeding. It was the sound of fingernails on a blackboard; the stink of ammonia or sulphur or acid. It was a bright, penetrating light; it was the wail of a siren; it was a current flowing freely beneath her skin. It was butterflies pounding on the inside of her skull; it was a fever dream; it was an open wound; it was a heartbeat, racing wildly, ready to explode.

As midnight approached, a wail erupted from the confines of her skull, as though a million voices were screaming, and a hum broke out on the edge of hearing: not quite words, not quite song, but the sound of loneliness, of darkness given voice. And she knew she'd heard it before, too many times to count: in the quiet hours where sleep wouldn't come, on the streets of Frain, in the heat and silence of the cemetery, on the brown-topped hillsides of her childhood that she'd long ago left behind. She'd heard it so many times, a soft cry of despair amongst chaos, and she'd felt the sorrow creeping out of her bones, rising in her chest, settling into her veins. So many times, so many songs, so much grief, and in all those years she'd never known what it meant.

In the cool darkness, Danae wrapped her hands over her ears and joined the chorus, whispering a tune she didn't know through lips so chilled they could barely move. She whispered with them, though she didn't know what they were saying or how to say it properly; she didn't know if she was supposed to be shaping words or elegy or requiem, notes or poetry, but she whispered all the same, because it felt like it was important. It felt like something that she needed to be part of.

She whispered with unseen voices until the paling light-bands outside finally lulled her back into the silence of a broken streamlink, and she knew it was for Angelo.

THE DEMOCRAT, 22ND FEBRUARY 2076

Local and regional governments have issued a reminder that deactivation of malfunctioning a-naut units is to be carried out in line with Federal guidelines, and that failure to comply is subject to fines of up to 4,500 T-marks and a three-month custodial sentence. The move comes amidst widespread reports of units being denied food or shelter in response to the so-called a-naut 'strike' that has left many industries crippled. Meanwhile, Emancipation, who have campaigned extensively for tougher regulations governing a-naut care and harsher penalties for those found guilty of neglect, say that senior officials in the organisation have made contact with a unit who claims to speak for a-nauts affected by the global malfunction. It is not known how this unit, registered G-QZ1484, became known to Emancipation; however, an agency spokesperson has confirmed that it has their 'full support.' In a statement released late last night, Emancipation's European headquarters quote a lengthy treatise, purportedly advanced by the unit itself, in which it sets out to explain the current situation. Malfunctioning a-nauts have no wish to cause harm, it states, but it suggests that a fundamental change has occurred, and it urges Congress to recognise and act upon it.

G-QZ1484 is believed to have been a service operative in a London hotel, and how it has risen to prominence is as yet unclear. A spokesperson for the hotel, which has not been named, has described the unit as 'reserved but courteous ...a hard worker,' and has said that the hotel will not be seeking its return.

15 MAY

15.1

It was a building that was built for the sunlight, though Maurice Rademaker Jr rarely saw it by day. In fact, he thought bitterly, as he leaned back in his elderly leather armchair — the one that smelled faintly of cowpens and sweat, but which had moulded itself to the contours of his body like memory foam and which would be evicted from Rademaker's office only when Rademaker himself left for good — he was starting to lose track of the last time he'd seen the outside of the building at all.

It was well into the small hours of the night that had followed a long, long day, though that scarcely distinguished it from the days that had come before and, he suspected, would not distinguish it from the days that would follow. Nor would the level of acrimony dripping from either of the calls he'd just finished, both of which had played out exactly as he'd thought. DiNetto was all tightly coiled fury, professional reputation traduced, frigid calm layered over the bubbling panic of a man who was beginning to be sincerely concerned that his career was over. *Sinon is safe*, he'd insisted, which might have been a greater source of comfort to the head of the company that had okayed his project if it weren't the fifteenth time he'd said as much in a ten-minute conversation. *It cannot replicate in the human system. There's no possible way it's linked to the deaths in Creo.*

Absolute certainty, naturally; Rademaker didn't pay him to be irresolute. But there was too much riding on the absence of doubt. The very fact that they both needed him to be right so badly implied that there was every chance that he was not.

And Gerald knew this, of course. There wasn't much that Gerald did not know, up to and including all of the things that Rademaker had attempted to stop him from knowing. If anything, it was a surprise that his call had taken so long to arrive: Gerald had always made it his business to know more about the companies in which he invested than their CEOs would necessarily prefer.

We seem to have bodies piling up at last, Maurice, he'd said. *Unfortunately, none of them are artificial.*

And of course Rademaker found himself blithely echoing DiNetto's words from half an hour earlier; of course he did. The alternative was unthinkable. It was just that they sounded every bit as hollow from his own mouth as they had when he'd sat in his chair and listened to the leader of a project that was looking ever more likely to close ReGen's doors for good, tell him that everything was fine. Worse: when he spoke them out loud, they sounded like a lie.

Rademaker had been in Europe when the Insurgency began, and by the time he was able to get home, his father had been locked in his study for three full days. It was eighteen months since he'd officially taken control of the company, eight years since he'd wrestled Decker out of her controlling share, seven since he'd taken ReGen down a path that she'd never intended for them to go. He was plastered into a high wing-backed chair when Rademaker let himself in with the key he was not supposed to have, an unlit cigar in his hand as he stared vacantly into a room that was dark and smelled of musty days of too much whiskey and not enough light, but he'd glanced up as his son entered, raised a weary eyebrow in lukewarm welcome. Rademaker had expected dishevelment and collapse, the outward signs of grief, but all the tale his father's face would tell was a certain dullness to the eyes and a slight pallor.

We did this, boy, he'd said softly. *We built them. We did this.*

Gerald had rescued them, of course, because Gerald knew what he was doing; better then Lena Decker, better than Maurice Rademaker Sr, better, perhaps, than Rademaker himself. It was one of the reasons Rademaker had felt so certain about Sinon: the failure of the Amendment had crippled them, but they'd been crippled before and clawed their way back. And Gerald didn't back a loser.

Sinon is safe, he'd told the flash of black on black where Gerald's face ought to be, perched like a ghost in the armchair across his desk, but the words sounded empty; meaningless, and if Rademaker didn't believe them, there was no chance that Gerald did. He'd let them fall into a silence that did the work of a thousand words before he'd answered.

Please tell me, he'd said quietly, and, though his voice was even — because

Gerald's voice was seldom other than even — there was a danger hiding behind every perfectly inflected syllable that dropped the temperature in the room and raised the hairs on Rademaker's arms. *Please tell me, Maurice, that we haven't just unleashed a bioweapon on Creo Basse.*

15.2

The crowds were not noticeably thinner in downtown Parnasse as Danae made her way through the morning chill, though there were a few more scarves tied around faces, a few less children in the mix. People knew the drill. Chances were, everyone on the street was still going to be standing at the end of the alert, same as every other alert, and the ones that weren't were the ones you kept at home and out of harm's way. Panicking was for the folks that hadn't lived through it before; you could tell how many folks had seen more off-peaks than birthdays by the heavy air of frustration and distrust that wove through the streets like a sparking thundercloud. On billboards and news stands, in the skies above the street, written up the sides of buildings in photoelectric letters ten feet high, statesmen and women explained to an apathetic population that there were only seventeen confirmed cases in the city, but that there were protocols to be followed or else the international community would get the way they got sometimes, and that didn't work out well for anybody. Sainte-Thérèse had opened up again, but Fiore was still shut, and Fiore wasn't the kind of place to take ostracism in good humour. People weren't setting stuff on fire — not yet — but give them a day or two. There was a kind of critical mass building up, Creo-style, which, with the gates shut, had nowhere constructive to go, and that had a tendency to get predictable very quickly. It was holding, for now. In a couple of days it wouldn't, and then the fun would really begin.

The ache had dissipated in the small hours and, in its absence, the anger had come rushing in. Danae had nothing left with which to fight it, and the little bit of her — which had been a much larger bit twenty-four hours earlier — that knew why the itch was bad, had started asking awkward questions about rights and wrongs, and whether or not it would be the worst idea ever to just give in.

Just four men, said the itch. *Four men and he would have been saved. Who would ever know?*

And she knew, she *knew* that after the fourth man there would be another, maybe a thug who jumped her in a darkened street, or another

Ren, or, Christ, a man who slapped his child a little too hard somewhere she could see. The point was, there would always be a reason. If she wasn't strong enough to resist the first time, there would never be a last. But Angelo was still dead, and she could have saved him, if only she'd done what she was supposed to do.

In the worst moments, when she saw his face in the alleyway half-light, white-eyed and terrified and drained bloodless with the knowledge of death, she wondered if she shouldn't have just jumped out of the damn window. Save everybody a whole world of trouble, not least of all Danae. But that wasn't the kind of thinking that got anybody anywhere, especially since she hadn't, in fact, jumped out of the damn window and wasn't likely to do so any time soon, and she wasn't sure she was comfortable with that level of adolescent hysteria in any case. So, in the absence of any better ideas, and with nothing more constructive to do, Danae did what she did when she needed to exorcise. She walked.

The itch was a red haze, descending through her line of sight, searching for a face, any face, that would make it stop. She was barely holding on to it now: children cried too loud, women's faces were too gormless, men's body language screamed *wife-beater*, and her hands prickled, flesh tingling with the urge to reach out and connect, hurt, break. Anything to make it go away. She walked with her head down, eyes raised only enough to see a path ahead of her, fingers clenching and unclenching. Four men and it could have been over, and who would have known? Who would have cared? But no: it came down to choice. She didn't have to be who she was supposed to be, she just had to do enough. She had to wash out the memory of his eyes on her, and the way the green light reflected on his staring pupils.

Danae walked. She made herself do mundane things: buy food, rob a couple of candles, things that would make sure that she didn't have to leave the apartment for a while. The air was electric with the promise of a kind of human storm: a momentum-releasing, critical-mass-blowing clean-out, and tension hovered and buzzed like a swarm of flies. It would be best to ride it out in solitude.

The woman in the grocery store stared her out, eyes focused on the remnants of a Ren-induced black eye, and Danae offered her a withering smile and snatched her bags before the itch could make any unhelpful suggestions. The sound of sirens twittered like birdsong in the city air as she stepped out onto the street. Plastic men were massing nonchalantly, killing time until the fireworks started, and the ranks of the be-scarved were struggling to keep up with their numbers. Danae overheard snippets of conversation: '... holiday was booked for four bloody months, and do you think the insurance is going to cover it now she can't get to the port because the bloody gates are closed? ....And of course the first thing they run out of is milk, it happens every time, and that stem powder they give you instead tastes like dishwater.... But I said to her, listen, you don't understand, he's got to be in Nantes next week for an audition and they don't let you do these things over a phonewave ...'

The city got it all. It was a breeding ground for disease: twenty-seven million bodies in an enclosed space, breathing recycled air, drinking recycled water, eating recycled food. When election time rolled round and the politicians started on the free concerts and the bread tickets and the carnivals, any bacterium with a modicum of ambition and a healthy survival instinct could sweep the city five times. Illness *liked* the city, and the city just grumbled and got on with it. Sometimes people died, sometimes CDC Paris had to step in to clean up the mess. Sometimes they sent in the plastic men. But they didn't take over the city, and they didn't lie. If it was typhoid, they told you it was typhoid and let you work out the best ways not to get typhoid.

Anthrax happened. Nobody liked to talk about it, but it was the go-to nasty of the terrorist world: tricky to diagnose early, quick to progress, and a stubborn little bugger to treat. It was a city-stopper, no question: trade and commerce halted and a district or two got locked down until however many it was this time finally died or got better and the powers that be made sure no one else was sick. But it didn't cause a limbo. It caused rapid-fire cases around the release site — bang, bang, bang — and they knew within hours of the first case where it had come from and the area was sealed off. You had viruscidals if you were in the vicinity and you either got sick or you didn't. You didn't have a sine-wave of *here/no, here*, rising and falling, sickness and health. Anthrax didn't spread person-to-person; a curfew wasn't useful in containing it. You scorched and salted the earth and treated with prophylactics: that's what happened. And she knew that the rest of the city knew this, and, when she'd had enough sleep to string three coherent sentences together, she'd work out the implications of knowing that the plastic men knew that Creo Basse knew this. So what, exactly, was going on? The answer was building up to the storm, and she knew that she wouldn't like it.

Exhaustion soothed her into a trance-like stupor, and, for a while, it was enough to dull the edge of the itch. Danae followed her feet back to the apartment block, eased out of thought, and wondered briefly if it would always be like this. Had Angelo lived, she would still be five or six thousand tokens short of a new block. Maybe more. How had they ever afforded it in the first place? It must have cost more than a year's supply of water, and they struggled for that. But the answer was simple, of course: they afforded it because they had to. Because their baby daughter had died the previous autumn and Danae was like a gift from heaven, and not having her was not even an option. Maybe if they hadn't, she would have learned to control it years ago. Maybe it was like drug-withdrawal; maybe you hit cold turkey and sweated and screamed and pleaded for a while, until it burned itself out and you were left with a hollow where the need used to be: never gone, never completely healed, but banished into the distance like a shadow haunting the horizon. Maybe she just needed to wait it out. Maybe in a couple of days, she'd start feeling like a human being again, like someone she could trust. Maybe.

She let herself in the back way and set down her bags by the old fountain so that she could close up the seal. It meant walking across the floor to do it, when she could just as easily have laid them at the door, but she liked the water feature. When the light was right and the will was there, she could see it as it had been: crystal blue and glittering with fractal colours in the pleasant afternoon light, decorated by wealthy people with nothing else to do but look pretty beside an optical illusion. It was a warm picture. Besides, there were rats the size of Weimeraners by the door, and their food radar was one hundred and ninety-percent.

She turned away from the fountain, and saw Turrow.

15.3

At first, she tried to pretend it was exhaustion, but Danae had never had cause to doubt the evidence of her own eyes before and it didn't wash. She took a moment, because every sentence that lined up and presented itself for inspection was a cliché, and that wouldn't do either.

At last, she said, 'Well done.'

'Nice place,' he said, as though he were trying to mean it.

She shrugged. 'It keeps the rain off.'

'Where did you get the codes for the seals?'

Danae sucked in a deep breath, dropped her eyes from his. She said, 'It's good to see you, but I can manage. It's fine.'

Boston stared at her, nonplussed. 'That's not an answer.'

'Yes it is, Turrow. You should just go, okay?'

'Are you kicking me out?'

'I need to lock up,' she said. 'You need to go home. There's a riot brewing somewhere.'

'I waited for you,' he said. 'I waited for hours. I just wanted to make sure you're all right.'

'Well, here I am, and I'm fine,' she said.

'I was worried about you.'

'Well, *don't*.' It came out more sharply than she intended and she saw him flinch. He blinked, but said nothing.

Danae lowered her eyes and began to gather her grocery bags. On the edge of vision, she saw him moving forwards, stepping out of the shadows, making his way towards her. She didn't look up. He drew level with her, without meeting her gaze, and, without a word, he bent down and lifted one of her bags.

He said, quietly, 'Let me in.'

She straightened. 'You let yourself in, Turrow.'

He followed her as she set off across the atrium, moving quickly to match her stride. 'What happened?' he said. 'The other night — I know something happened. You weren't *you*. What happened?'

She reached the stairs. 'Nothing happened, Turrow.'

'And then I went to the café and the girl said Nadine was sick and she didn't know where you were — what was I supposed to think?'

'I'm sorry, okay?' Then the irritation hit. She speeded up. 'No, wait a minute, why am I sorry? I'm not sorry. This is none of your business.'

'Did I do something?' He was by her side now, ascending with her. 'Did I say something? Did I not say something? Give me a clue here.'

'No, Turrow,' she said. The steps were higher than she remembered, the bags twice as heavy. 'You know, before I met you, I had problems that were nothing to do with you. I could have entire days of shit, all by myself. How did I manage that?'

'What is *wrong* with you?' he said.

'I'm tired, okay?' But she couldn't meet his eyes, for fear of what she'd see reflected in them. 'I'm just tired. It's been a long week. Come back tomorrow, okay? I'll be in better form.'

'Will you still be here tomorrow?' he asked, and she couldn't bring herself to lie.

'Please go home,' she said.

'Okay,' he said. 'But come with me.'

She half-laughed, but he didn't understand. He couldn't. So she said, 'Yeah, no. That's not a good idea, okay? Trust me.'

'It's better than staying here.'

'I like it here.'

Now he laughed: incredulity. Her eyes narrowed, rage flared despite herself. She said, 'What? I like it here. It's mine. You don't have to stay, okay?'

'Danae.' Why was his use of her name enough to pull her back? 'I'm worried about you.'

'Don't!' Louder than she meant it to come out, but not angry, not quite. She tried again, with more control. 'Turrow, don't patronise me. I don't need you to worry about me, all right? I'm fine.'

Another flight of stairs. She rounded them, feeling the strain in her arms as her shopping bags swung wide, feeling him half a step behind her.

'Fine,' he said.

'I can manage by myself. I've done it for years.'

'So if I go, if I leave you tonight, you're telling me that you'll still be here tomorrow?'

'Yeah. Sure.'

'Wow,' he said. 'That was convincing. I wonder why it sounds so much like bullshit?'

'Just leave me alone!' she shouted. And then, because she couldn't bear the look on his face, the one she knew was there without even looking, she added, 'Please.' She took another couple of stairs. He didn't. 'Please, Turrow. This has nothing to do with you.'

It was the wrong thing to say. She knew it was. She started moving again, quickly now, and this time he followed her. He said, 'This isn't you.'

Danae spun on him. 'How would you know that?' she hissed.

'I know you,' he said.

'You don't. You *don't*. You don't know anything about me.'

She had reached the first floor, moving quickly across the ancient carpet. Boston hung back, shouted, 'I know you're in trouble. I know that.'

She stumbled on a step and dropped her groceries.

They cascaded across the floor. A couple of tins teetered through the ornamental wrought iron banisters and began the long fall to the faux-marble lobby below, registering a dull thung as they connected. Dazed and furious, Danae bent down and began to pick up what remained, scooping together cans that wanted to spin off in every direction. Boston watched her silently.

'I can't —' he said, and stopped. Tried again: 'I heard it in your voice. I didn't know until afterwards. I know you're in trouble. I want to help.'

Danae took her time answering. Her hands were trembling, her movements graceless and uncoordinated, and she knew he saw. She waited until she could force it back and pretend it was rage, and then she said, folding all her bitterness into five words designed to wound right back, 'You don't know me, Turrow.'

'I know you enough,' he said.

'It's none of your fucking business.'

'You're right,' he said. 'It's none of my fucking business. And, look: I'm here anyway. Maybe you might want to wonder about that.'

The words pierced something, seared into a private little register of grief and left a residue of pain behind them. When she was able, she chanced a look upwards, saw him standing seven feet away, staring at her. She dropped her eyes again, gathered what she could, and fled.

She knew he was following, could hear his feet landing heavily on the stairs behind her. The block wasn't exactly labyrinthine, but she knew it and he didn't: if she could pick up enough speed, she could out-pace him and lose him in the shadows. So she stopped three flights up, breathless, blood singing in her ears, and whirled on him.

'I can't!' she shouted. 'Turrow, get out of here! You have no idea, Turrow! You have no idea what kind of trouble this is!'

'Let me help,' he said.

'This is not your sort of help, Turrow. Just go. Please.'

'No chance. Not after sixteen flights of stairs.'

'Turrow, just go!' she shouted.

'Why the hell should I go?' he countered. Little flecks of spit congealed in the corner of his mouth, and she realised too late that his anger was slow-burning, quietly eating out the core from him before it flared, and then it was too late to contain it. 'How do you know about this place? Because of me. It's my place.'

She screwed up her face and almost rejoined, but stopped herself in time. 'Is that the best you can do?' she said instead.

'I spent the day looking for you.'

'I thought this was your place.' Pushing past him, walking away from him, hoping he was made of stronger stuff.

'Alex? Alex said to me, where are you going? When we need you?' He was following her again. 'They need me at home. And I said, I think she's in trouble and I have to make sure. I have to make sure she's okay.'

'Why?' It was out before she could stop it, and she was turning on him before she knew she was going to do so. It surprised him too, and for a moment he could only stare at her with bruises in his eyes and a look that defied her not to know.

She waited for him to say it, but instead he said, 'Tell me what's going on and I'll go.'

Danae turned her back on him and started off down the corridor. He shouted after her, 'Tell me what's going on and I'll go!'

She stopped, wheeled around on him and shouted, as loudly as she could, so loud that it hurt her throat, 'You don't want this, Turrow!'

'What?' Shouting now too; hoarse with bewildered hurt. 'What don't I want? This? So come home with me.'

'Leave. Me. Alone.'

'Why? Why, Danae?'

'Leave me alone!' Screaming now. 'Please! Please, Turrow, please leave me alone.'

'I'm not leaving until you tell me.'

'You don't have to know everything.' She was so angry now that she could barely form the words. 'You don't have to be told. You don't want to be told.' Her hands danced little static spasms as she spoke, flaring and falling while the itch whispered *please*. And it had to be forced back; caught in a choke-hold and beaten into bodily submission, and it still wheedled and cajoled, even then. So she said, 'Please go. Please just go. Please just leave me alone. Just go. Just go!'

There was a long silence, punctuated by the ragged sound of her breath, drawn tightly through a throat closed by fury.

Then Boston said, 'Fine,' and a part of her faded.

'Fine,' she said.

'Fine,' he said. His lip pursed outwards, his brow furrowed, as though a war was going on behind his eyes.

Danae turned away from him, one hand on her door.

'Fine,' she said again. And she knew that he heard the lie in her voice. He took a step towards her. 'Fine.'

'Fine.'

'Fine.'

'*Fine.*'

She unlocked the door. He followed her in.

15.4

'Home sweet home,' said Danae over her shoulder. 'Look around, convince yourself I'm all right, then just go.'

Boston followed a trail of almost-light and the sound of her footsteps into the sitting room. Once, it would have been more imposing, more grand, more opulent than anything he'd ever seen. Now, abandoned for years, the ceiling and walls were covered in black, creeping patches of damp, and cobwebs draped the upper reaches like silk curtains. The floor in the sitting room alone could have swallowed Turrow's entire apartment, maybe a couple of neighbours' places too; now it lay forlorn under an inch of footprint-pocked dust. What might once have been a chandelier hung from the ornate ceiling, but it was too dark to tell. Shadows at the outer reaches of the glow from her candle, freshly lit, suggested doorways to unimagined places.

'It's a good place,' he called into the darkness.

Her disembodied voice floated back to him: 'I got a good tip.'

He listened to the sounds of complicated industry in a distant room, and, after a minute, he said, 'You won't be here when I come back, will you?'

Danae drifted back into the room, materialising out of the darkness like liquid from liquid. She stood at a distance from him, face bathed in shadow, and said, very quietly, 'No.'

'And I'm not allowed to ask why.'

'You can ask. I can't stop you asking.'

'But you won't answer.'

'It's not your problem, Turrow,' she said. 'And there's nothing you can do.'

'What if I don't go?'

'Please.'

He'd expected fury. He'd expected a fresh torrent of threats, maybe some abuse, so one tiny syllable threw him. There was comeback with the rage, but a single word was unassailable.

He tried once more. 'Do you want me to go? Do you actually want me to go? Don't lie.'

There was a tiny beat while the air electrified. Then she shouted, 'No, Turrow, I don't want you to go! I don't actually want you to go! I need you to go!'

'Tell me why!'

'Because I can't trust myself!'

It wasn't the answer he'd been expecting. He said, 'What?'

'I can't trust myself!' she shouted again. The words fell out of her mouth, tripping over themselves, not bothering to line up. 'It's not me! It isn't me. There is no *me*, Turrow. I'm nothing. I'm a great big fucking lie.'

The agony was so sharp it seemed to freeze the air, and his instinct was to cross the room in wide steps and do something, anything, to make it stop. She stood, motionless, in the shadows, and he thought that was worse than if she were shaking or heaving with tears: stillness spoke of utter defeat.

'And I can't trust myself.' Her voice was trembling now on the edge of despair: hollow, brittle with suffering. 'I can't trust myself not to kill you while you sleep. I can't trust myself not to smash a window and run out onto the streets with a shard of glass and start cutting people's throats. I can't trust myself not to cross this room right now, right now, and put my hands round your neck and crush the life out of you. It's not me. There's no me anymore. There's a thing, it's a thing, and I can't manage it, I can't trust it. It wasn't a fucking memory block. It wasn't a *fucking* memory block.'

He was lost, floating on a black tide of bewilderment. 'What?' he said, and realised how fragile her voice had become only when he heard his own.

'I'm not me,' she said. 'There is no me, Turrow. I'm not a person. I'm a fucking a-naut.'

15.5

His first line was uninspired.

'You're kidding,' said Boston.

She threw up her hands and stormed back into the darkness. 'Yes, that's right, Turrow, because this is really hysterically funny.'

'You're not kidding.'

She was back into the half-light, moving in sharp, hyperactive flurries. 'I'm not kidding.' Her fingers rubbed at her temples, as though the memory was a stain and she was trying to scrub it off. 'I'm not kidding.'

'You had a family…' he said.

'Where the fuck are his cigarettes?' Danae asked the shadows. She rooted about on the floor for a packet, sat down cross-legged, lit one off a candle.

Was it the time to cross the room and go to her? He wasn't sure. Too soon and she'd get up and walk away. Too long and she was too black and white: she'd read disgust in his distance.

He said, 'I don't understand.'

Danae sucked on her cigarette, exhaled blue smoke in the yellow ring of light.

'I know,' she said. 'I know you don't. Why would you understand?'

'Tell me.' A beat. 'Please? I want to understand.'

Ash flared red against the shadows that danced across her face. 'It's stupid,' she said. 'It's so simple it's stupid, Turrow. It's the end of the Insurgency and they're getting destroyed, the a-nauts are getting destroyed, so they need two things. First thing, they need to boost their numbers. Second thing, they want to try and do as much damage as they possibly can. So — me. You get me. I'm the result.' A bitter laugh, turned into the darkness. 'Two birds with the same stupid stone.'

Her hands were shaking. He could see it reflected in the smoke that caught the candle-light, all jittery disturbance.

Now?

'But you had a family,' he said again.

'I'm supposed to just kill,' she said, as though he hadn't spoken. 'That's all. All these people looking for the meaning of life? Well, I know mine. I'm supposed to just kill, that's it. That's why I'm here.' She leaned her head forward, rested it in her hand. In the candlelight, seen from across the room, she was like a cameo brooch: lily-white, perfectly defined by shadow. 'Bet you're glad you found me now,' she said. 'Bet you're really pleased with yourself.'

Now? He took the chance. But she got up and moved away.

He found her in a bedroom, stuffing cans under a bed. A busy metal clinking as cylinders connected suggested that she was planning to stay hidden for a while.

'You don't like the kitchen?' he said.

'There's a chalk outline on the floor,' she said. She didn't look at him. 'Fun place.'

Danae said nothing, the silence broken only by the gentle song of metal on metal.

Presently, she glanced up. 'I'm not getting through to you, am I?'

'Nope,' he told her.

From somewhere, daylight was leaking through the curtained windows, colouring the air in distant rooms and leaking weakly into the navy gloom by the bed. The chill of the darkness made him shiver and he hugged himself, watching her movements cast a kind of shadow-play on the wall behind her.

'I'm not feeding you,' she said. 'I'm hoarding.'

'You planning to camp out for a while?'

'Until the food runs out,' she said. 'Or the ceiling falls in.'

'On your own.'

'That's life.'

Danae stood up, brushing dust from her jumper. Her cigarette was perched on the edge of a plate that rested on an ancient bedside cabinet, a long string of ash trailing from the end. She made no move to pick it up.

He said, 'It doesn't have to be.'

'No,' she said. 'Because it isn't actually life.'

She was right, and he didn't know what to say. But she was standing in front of him, less than half a foot from where he was standing, and he could feel her radiant body heat dancing between them, smell the dust from her jumper and the scent of her hair — apricots, he thought, like bright sunlight against the darkness of the city street. She was close enough to touch, and he didn't know what to say, so, in the absence of any other ideas, he reached out a hand, gently, hesitantly, and raised it to her cheek.

She didn't shrug it off as he had expected. She looked at his arm, connecting him to her, stared at it for a long moment, so long that he half-expected it to burst into flames. She said, 'Turrow, don't touch me. Everyone I care about dies.'

He didn't move it. Instead, he said, 'I'm not going to die.'

She lifted sad eyes to his, as if she wanted to believe him. But she said, 'Don't be stupid.'

'I'm not going to leave you,' he said.

And her face fractured, slightly at first, but she couldn't contain the breaking. She dropped her eyes and said, 'Oh God, don't. Don't do that. Don't say that, Turrow. Please don't. I can't —'

'I'm not going to leave you,' he said again. 'And I think you know that. And I think you know why.'

Softly, she said, 'I'm a monster.'

'No.'

'You don't know. You don't have any idea what's going on in my head, Turrow.'

'Right,' he conceded. 'So I go on what I do know. What do I know about you, Danae?' When she didn't answer, he said, 'This woman, this stranger, walked the alleyways of Fiore north because she was worried about a man she just met. That's a monster?'

'That was before.'

'You could have died. I would have died if you hadn't come back for me. That's a monster?'

'I can't, Turrow....'

'I knew your face. I knew you,' he said. 'I know you enough.'

'I can't trust myself,' she said again.

'I don't care,' he said. 'Tell me.... Tell me it doesn't just make more sense when we're together.'

He felt something shake her then, something that might, in another woman, have been a sob. Her face was turned down, out of his sight, and her shoulders were shaking silently and he put his other hand to her arm to steady her.

She raised her hands to cover his. The movement was sudden, unexpected, and he felt the touch of her skin on his in the centre of his belly, a twist of something like shock. Then she lifted her head and he saw that her eyes were liquid, her cheeks wet with grey, dust-streaked tears, chill on his skin where they had begun to flow over his hand. He moved his head towards hers and she moved hers towards him and their noses met first, held there for the long, breathless moment until, finally, their lips touched, gently, uncertainly. He cupped her face with both hands as hers snaked around his back and felt her tears running down her cheeks, spilling over his fingers and rain-marking the dust on the floor below. He ran his wet fingers through her hair, while tears fell on his face and into their mouths and onto their clothes.

DE VERSLAGGEVER, 11TH MARCH 2076

Campaigners for a-naut rights have called it a 'great day for democracy,' following the release earlier today of a-naut leader G-QZ1484. The unit, who is known as Garrison to a-naut rights groups, had been held in a prison in The Hague after a dramatic eleventh hour reprieve stayed its planned deactivation on March 1. Its release follows two weeks of peaceful protest by a-nauts over the mass deactivation of several thousand units on February 28.

16 MAY

16.1

Before the Insurgency, farmers left the fields during the worst of the summer heat waves and returned to them after sundown, floodlit acres scattering the countryside in a cobweb of light. They used to call them the crop cities, for the way they looked from the air: patchworks of rural industry that bled into the bright white-yellow splashes of urban sprawl against the black disk of the Earth by night. But it's a long time, now, since the lights went out. The temperatures can soar and the sun can sear the skin from a worker's neck in the noonday heat, but these days, if you've got any sense, you'll take free radicals and third degree burns over the emptiness and isolation of the pastures at night. At least by day you can see them coming.

Annelise hasn't been well since the winter. It was a little girl this time, so tiny that Walter could cup her in both hands, and frail like a hatchling with a broken wing. His wife hasn't mentioned her name since they lost her, simply put away the clothes and folded down the cot again, but he thinks that she knows as well as he does that the child might have lived, at least for a little longer, if they weren't so bloody far from anywhere. The doctor did what he could, of course, but when he asked if they were religious, if they were the sort who'd have a baby christened, Walter knew that he was asking if they were ready to let her go. So did Annelise; he saw it in her eyes. He thinks that maybe part of his wife broke in the winter, a part that might not heal again.

He doesn't like to leave her by day. There's nobody near enough to come and see her and what work she can still get she can do from her bed, so some days she doesn't get up at all. He tries to get in to see her when he can, to pop in at lunchtime and make sure she's eaten something, maybe bring her a cup of tea and see if he can't find her smile, but the crops are in a bad way this year and it's taking every hour he has just to keep them from withering where they stand. It's the damn hostilities, or whatever they're calling it now: you can't get the pesticides through in the spring or the fertilisers through in the autumn, because both of those things are damn useful for making bombs with, and the bright sparks in London only took two years to catch on to that one. Walter would be ashamed of his field if it were a lawn: even if it were weeds, he'd call them straggly. He wipes sweat from his forehead, decides to go in to her anyway. He's done as much as he can this morning, and the corn's going to do what it's going to do whether he's standing next to it or not; if he could wish it better, he'd be a millionaire by now.

He runs his hands along the sheaves as he walks, bristling them like wind. The house ahead of him is silent — she used to listen to music during the day, said she got lonely on her own, and when he came in from the fields they'd sing along to the songs together — and he knows he'll find her in her dressing gown, but it'll be a good day if her hair is brushed. His head is full of her as the house looms into view over the crest of the low hill, crowding out the heat of the day, the way his damp shirt chafes at his skin, the rumble beneath his feet as his irrigation pipes drizzle water into the soil, and so it takes him a moment longer, maybe, than it ought to before he's aware that there's a sound, right on the edge of hearing, that doesn't belong.

It's the sound of someone running.

In the wilderness, running equals danger; no one runs for the exhilaration of the wind in his hair. He's a man who would have been big if he'd had enough to eat when he was younger, and he moves like a big man, as though his aura is a poorly fitting suit and he's shifting phantom pounds with every muscle. But he's quick when he needs to be. He carries a gun on his belt, and his fingers close around the handle as he spins around to face the runner, who pulls up short about twenty feet away.

It's a woman. At least, it used to be — even Walter can tell that she's dying, and it's what his mother would have called a Bad Death. She's been dying for a while, by the look of things, and he has no idea how she's managed to run so far and so fast, but it has taken a lot out of her. She's bent double, trying to catch her breath in vicious wheezes, but she peers up at him through eyes that are almost blind and she says, 'Please. I haven't got much time.'

Then he hears the shouts of pursuit.

★

Her finger traced marble whorls on his belly, his breath twisting through her hair, warm against her scalp. His skin was softer than she'd expected: pale olive brown and scattered across his ribcage with a thin dusting of black hair that curled around her fingers as they passed. Her head was resting on his chest, rising and falling with his lungs, and only the movement of his hand on her spine told her that he was still awake.

She said, 'He wouldn't tell me what happened next. He said I didn't need to know.'

★

It's almost evening before he decides it's safe for them to look. Annelise hasn't been outside for months, and, though the shadows are creeping out of the hillside now as the sun sinks below the horizon, she has to raise her hand to shade her eyes. She says, 'Walter, I can hear it, I can hear something.'

She's been well hidden. The woman in the field knew what she was doing. Walter knows that it's not possible that the child is her own flesh and blood; a-nauts can't breed. But whoever she was, whoever the child is, there was love there. He saw it in the woman's eyes.

She's blue with cold and screaming. In years to come, she'll tell them that she remembers this: that, though she's blind in the light after hours of darkness and concealment and she thinks they're monsters, at least a part of her wonders if they might finally be bringing her food. She remembers the tenderness with which Annelise lifts her from the hollow and wraps her in Walter's shirt, hastily shrugged from his back. She remembers the tears that fall from her mother's face and drop onto her own, washing muddy streaks from her cheeks where they land.

'This is her,' says Annelise when she can speak. 'This is our little girl.'

★

'I think they knew,' she told him quietly, soft words vanishing into the still, cool shadows like smoke on the breeze. 'I'd been in the ground for hours. They must have known I wasn't … you know.'

His hand traced a lazy figure of eight along the bones of her spine. 'Maybe,' he said, 'they saw what I see.'

'Maybe they saw what they wanted to see,' she said, but her voice was listless, heavy with sleep. There was no bitterness in it, only regret. 'But they never … I never felt like I wasn't their child. You know? Even after they realised what they had.'

*

They're known as the Progeny, though nobody's sure if it's the brainchild of a news intern with a flare for the melodramatic, or if they turned up with the name already attached. When news of the first massacre hits the waves, a lot of time and effort goes into denying that any such thing exists, and, though there's no shortage of speculation, nobody ever manages to link the next three to the children in question either. From time to time, somebody will make headlines with a conspiracy theory that sounds a little bit too plausible for anyone's comfort, and various experts will be farmed out to explain to grim-faced news anchors that there's no logical reason for anyone to build a baby a-naut, even if the technology existed, so everybody ought to just calm down and come back with questions when they're feeling a little bit less hysterical. It's reasonable enough that most people lose interest after three, four news cycles, but the Grants know better. She's eighteen months old when they understand what she is.

A study in Copenhagen claims to have found evidence that the first generation of a-naut-built a-nauts were produced fully-grown, but that problems with the cloning process led to poor-quality uplinks and radical telomere collapse within thirty-six to forty-eight months. They say that somatic cell nuclear transfer remains the only safe way to grow an organic being, and that the remains of the Insurgency had no choice but to settle, in the end, for infant births. One of the authors later retracted his findings; the other lost tenure at the university that sponsored the project and spends her days fighting an ongoing wrongful dismissal suit that she shows little sign of winning, but a website hosted in one of the PE cities has taken their research and extrapolated it to mean that the Insurgency, at its height, had a harem of organic sympathisers ready to lend a uterus to the cause, and that the decision to build babies was predicated on the assumption that, birthed from human mothers, the Progeny would integrate seamlessly into everyday life in a manner that their adult forebears never could. Another blog broadly agrees with this, and says that the Grendelheim fire is evidence that their plan is working out just fine — and that everyone needs to be afraid.

In years to come, Danae will spend a lot of time trying to work it all out to her own satisfaction, and she'll never quite succeed. The closest she'll get is when she decides that in all likelihood everybody's a little bit right, but also, she thinks, they're all a little bit wrong. She doesn't remember much from her first days, but she remembers the care with which the woman handled her, the reverence, the devotion, and she'll wonder if, maybe, all these theories and guesses and speculation aren't trying to ascribe logic to a need that's governed by anything but. There's a blueprint, a pattern, a form that life's supposed to take, and it's written into the circuits of the conscious mind. She thinks, perhaps, that there's a part of her genetic legacy that's just a long cry of loneliness; an acknowledgement of something precious taken without permission; a culture that's trying to come home.

But it's a long time before she has the tools to understand this. She's six weeks shy of her second birthday when eighty-five people burn to death in a hotel fire in Switzerland that nobody's prepared to call an act of terror, and she's too young to realise that she needs to lie about why she's here. It hasn't occurred to her that it might be wrong, or even that the two people she loves most in the world are two of the people that are supposed to be afraid of her. Things are much simpler at her age.

They tell her it's a check-up. She trusts them: they are her parents. When she comes around, she's … different.

★

He kissed the top of her head. He loved that he could kiss the top of her head.

'It's not you,' he said.

'I know,' she said. Thinking, *it is.*

'You're more than that. You turned into more than that.'

'I know,' she said again.

He tightened his arms around her, breathed deeply. 'Don't keep saying I know,' he said.

She said, 'Okay.'

★

She slept, better than she had slept for days, weeks; maybe years. She slept like the dead, descending in free-fall into perfect, black oblivion. Sleep was like lead: heavy and cloying, free of dreams. It was the sleep of a body that just needs to turn off for a while; the tarry, thick coma that comes on like a switch has been flicked. Free of drugs or alcohol or adrenaline or panic, she just slept, slept longer, slept some more. She slept until she was done with sleeping, and then she woke up.

That was the night the army arrived in Creo Basse.

16.2

She woke to the sound of him bustling about in the half-light and spent a moment, watching him move, bleary-eyed and almost asleep. His body was swathed in shadow and for a minute, lost in the pleasure of watching points of candlelight and shade on his bare skin, she didn't register the urgency to his movements.

She sat up. 'What time is it?'

'Late,' he said. 'No — early.'

'How early?' The apartment was dark, but the apartment was always dark.

'Four-thirty, maybe five.' He leaned over to kiss her forehead, pulling away to shrug on a shirt.

She didn't want to say, *you're leaving?* She didn't want it to come out like that. So she watched him a second longer and decided on, 'What's up?'

'I got a blip,' he said. 'Check your chip. You probably got one too.'

'A blip?' she said stupidly, but it was the small hours. The last time she'd heard of anyone getting a blip was when her parents told her the North Country was going to be shut down. A blip was not good news.

The wave signal in the apartment was sketchy at best, and the visor took so long to buffer that Danae had never seen the point of wasting twenty seconds of her life waiting to be asked if she'd like to add credit she didn't have to a phonewave she couldn't use, but even the oldest and cheapest of pockets was configured to receive a blip. She shuffled upright in bed, goosebumps prickling her skin as the screen struggled to remember how to come online, but she didn't need a full-res connection to see the bright green glow that filled the upper quadrant. She closed it before it collapsed completely, and turned to Turrow.

'I got one too,' she said.

'Not good,' he said. 'I'm going down to the street, see what's going on.'

A blip was a harbinger, a gentle suggestion that it was time to find out what was happening. A blip meant that there was something to know. A blip was always bad news.

Danae wrapped herself in blankets, unwilling to relinquish the bed completely, and crossed to the window. The curtains, long since abandoned to settle where they lay, resisted her attempts to make them open and rained a confetti of dust and moth wings in protest, so she slipped between them instead and watched for him on the streets below. Turrow was a solitary figure in a sea of mauve and darkness, alone in an empty street that, elsewhere, should have been swallowed by a tide of bodies. Theirs would not be the only household awake now: block by block, banks of lights would be flickering alive, restless shadows beyond hinting at nervous activity. An ocean of agitation, rippled by the reflected light of a million screens.

He was gone almost an hour. Danae waited by the window for twenty minutes or so, until the cold got the better of her resolve and she shuffled back to bed to doze in fitful, dreamless bursts. But she was awake again by the time he arrived, dressed and curled into an ancient armchair by the window, where the first glow of dawn was just beginning to lighten the shadows.

'There's soldiers everywhere,' he told her as he crossed the room, rubbing warmth back into his arms. 'They're all over the streets.'

Soldiers she hadn't expected. 'What? Why?'

'It's a lock-down.' He kicked off his shoes, blew into his cupped hands. 'We've been quarantined. Again.'

'Jesus.' Danae shuffled sideways on the chair as he lowered himself in beside her, slinging an arm around her neck. 'At least I don't have anywhere I need to be this time.'

'Yeah,' said Turrow. 'Me either, by the looks of things.' His hand was cool and damp where it brushed her neck, cold air sharp against her skin as she opened her blanket to pull it around him. 'I guess you're stuck with me for a couple of days,' he told her, burrowing in against her warmth. 'The gates are already shut. I can't get back to Chatelier.'

'I guess I am, then,' she said. She grinned. 'I think I can live with that.'

THE FINANCIAL TIMES, 3RD MAY 2076

A spokesperson for Apex Incorporated confirmed today that the company has entered into administration following catastrophic losses incurred in the final quarter of the last financial year. The company, one of Canada's largest manufacturers of high-end S3A units, had been struggling to cope with declining sales in recent years, and in a statement released today, CEO Mark Fielding confirmed that the cascading stream malfunction that has caused chaos across the globe has been a major factor in its rapid financial decline. With the average warranty period for new S3A units lasting from five to ten years, and an influx of returns of malfunctioning units in the past ten weeks, industry experts predict that the outlook for telectronics and amnisobiological manufacturers is likely to remain grim for years to come. ÉnerTech, Proxus and ReGen International have all reported substantial losses in their end-of-year returns, with before-tax profits falling by as much as 80% on the same period last year, leading some sources to predict that Apex will not be the last of the industry giants to fall.

17-20 MAY

17.1

The garden was bathed in pleasant summer sunlight and blanketed in the cloying scent of newly-opened sweet pea and honeysuckle, which rose as far as the layer of light and dissipated into the sky. Beneath the atmospheric shield it was not possible to see the piercing yellow sun, and Hadaway, shading his eyes against the buttercup-yellow blaze of the photoluminescent dust cloud that hung above the treetops, was momentarily disconcerted, walking from arid desert heat to temperate late spring morning with a single footstep. It was not the first time he'd been invited to the house, but the gardens, subject of much whispered speculation, had never yet been on-limits.

The first instinct was envy. The second was lust. He smiled.

He had a roof terrace himself, shielded in reflective muslin, which kept out the worst of the atmosphere and all of the sun, but the light wasn't quite right and the flowers failed every year. He'd put a fountain in the centre to cool the parched air and swathed it with ivy, and in the evening, in the half-light between sundown and true night, it was pleasant to sit beside it with a cold drink and reflect on the day's events. It was fabulously ostentatious, which was why he liked it. What was the point of wealth if no one knew you had it? Sometimes he threw dinner parties on the terrace for the hell of it, to watch the flash of something like rage on his friends' faces as they stepped out of the elevator and into his semi-plasticised Eden. He knew his own face now mirrored their half-hidden covetous fury as he followed the butler down immaculate pale sandstone steps and into the scent-haze, through a kaleidoscope of Pythagorean borders, high flowering hedges, clipped formal rose gardens, and, a lancing insult to his trickling vanity, a scale copy of the Trevi Fountain, complete with glimmering gold coins littering the bottom in terpsichoreal flashes.

Retirement was treating Corscadden well.

The man himself was sprawled in a summer chair under the shade of a parasol on a small, sun-dappled patio. A spreading oak — too well-established to be real, though it was an excellent imitation — cast jade shadows on the gravel, while the nearby fountain sweetened the warm, still air. He was dressed simply in crisp whites, the English colonial at his ease, sipping from a tumbler of something pale green and so cold that water still condensed on the misty glass, the morning papers hovering like a mirage in front of him. Corscadden had always been able to look both completely relaxed and incisively alert at will, and Hadaway knew better than to try to judge on first appearances. He could not have missed the heavy crunch of four feet on his shale as Hadaway followed the butler into the bower, but he didn't look up from his reading; didn't go so far as to acknowledge the intruders until the butler, waiting as long as was decent, coughed discreetly.

The glass was lifted, green liquid consumed through a straw.

'Asparagus and apple,' he said without raising his eyes. 'Can you believe that? Asparagus and apple. She says it's good for my ulcer.'

Hadaway silently debated the likelihood of Corscadden actually having an ulcer in the first place, and of telling anyone about it in the second. He smiled, though not too much.

'What's new in the world?' he said. The butler had melted away so invisibly that Hadaway wondered for a moment if he'd actually been a hologram. But no, he'd taken his coat as Hadaway entered. It didn't do to put anything past Corscadden.

'Nothing is ever new in the world,' said Corscadden, looking up for the first time. 'Can I offer you a drink? You don't have to have green mush. I think you're an Armagnac man — am I right?'

Twelve years earlier, Hadaway had been invited to Corscadden's office for a five-minute slap on the back after he'd bullied a minor third world pressure group out of a devastatingly unimportant press release. Corscadden had offered him a drink and Hadaway had accepted an Armagnac. Corscadden was showing off.

Hadaway smiled his most genial smile, though the effect, he thought, was somewhat spoiled by the way the light haze struck his eye at exactly the wrong angle, forcing him to squint. 'Thank you,' he said, 'but no. I'm due at the House in an hour.'

'Of course,' said Corscadden mildly. An elegant arm, with just the right amount of tremor for an elderly retiree, extended towards his guest. 'But do please have a seat, won't you? Make yourself comfortable.'

There were two empty chairs, one on either side of Corscadden, and Hadaway's selection of one over the other would almost certainly reveal something interesting to his host that Hadaway would almost certainly prefer him not to know. Moreover, there was probably no way to mitigate against this, and any attempt to do so would undoubtedly make things worse. In the end, he chose the one on the left, because it put the glare at his back and would make it slightly less comfortable for Corscadden to watch his face as they conducted their conversation, but, Hadaway thought as he lowered himself into his seat, the chances were not high that Corscadden would see it that way. Certainly his smile was suspiciously bland.

Corscadden waited for Hadaway to settle, then compressed his paper with an affable clap of his hands. 'So,' he said cheerfully. 'What brings you so far from your constituency on such a busy morning?'

'Thank you for seeing me,' said Hadaway, who'd asked on the expectation that the request would be refused. 'I know you tend not to involve yourself with matters of state these days.'

Corscadden sipped green goo. 'I've been known to do a little consultancy work from time to time,' he said. 'Keeps the old grey matter ticking over, you know.'

'So I believe. I had lunch with your successor a couple of months ago.'

'Ah, Caroline. Such an efficient young woman. Are you still on an amber alert in Europe Two?'

'It varies,' said Hadaway. 'We dip into yellow every now and again. You know how it is.'

'Much better now than it used to be, of course,' agreed Corscadden. 'Are you sure I can't offer you a drink? Water, perhaps? Or something a little stronger?'

'Perhaps I will. Coffee would be good.'

Corscadden glanced up. 'Harvey?' he said to the air. 'Coffee, please.' To Hadaway: 'Black, is that right? But you'll occasionally have a little sugar.'

Hadaway nodded faintly. There was no point in congratulating Corscadden on his powers of recall, nor in pretending that it was anything other than irritation that had glanced across his face. 'Is he...' he said, with a vague wave of his hand, '...artificial?'

'Harvey?' The tone was all companionable innocence. 'Good heavens, no. Just exceptionally good at his job.'

He's not the only one, thought Hadaway, but he kept his smile intact.

Aloud, he said, 'I hear that the reconditioned models are starting to catch on again.'

'Oh, I think the telectronics party is over for good,' said Corscadden pleasantly. 'All these failsafes and security protocols they're building into the uplinks these days — the whole point of the a-naut series was that they were able to think for themselves, but we're hardly likely to make that mistake again, now, are we? Still, they're good for picking up the ironing and cleaning the loo - at least, that's what my grandchildren tell me.'

He smiled beatifically. Hadaway was impressed. A colleague had met Corscadden and his wife at a party six months ago, reported back that retirement was dampening the old fire. Hadaway hadn't believed it for a second; knew that if Corscadden had decided to play the little old man card, he was either amusing himself or planning something. They'd known each other nearly thirty years, and Hadaway still had to keep reminding himself not to drop his guard. He was impressed.

'What time is your debate?' said Corscadden, absently, apropos of nothing, but heavy with the suggestion that Hadaway ought to consider just drinking his coffee and buggering off.

'I can be a little late,' said Hadaway.

'Of course. I expect you've got more important things on your mind at the moment than agri-food buffer stock ceilings. Another lock-down, I hear?'

'Yes. It hasn't been a popular decision.'

'I would imagine so.' A globule of thready, verdant slush escaped from the rim of the glass and caught on a finger that had moved a little too quickly for an old man with a trembling hand. 'I wonder sometimes how that city isn't bankrupt yet, between the structural collapses and the quarantine subsidies. I'm sure the only reason the a-nauts don't bomb it more often is because they're afraid they'll accidentally drive the property values up.'

'Of course,' said Hadaway, 'you would know more about that than I would.'

'Ah.' Manicured fingers steepled. 'I presume you're not talking about real estate prices in Creo.'

'Higher than you might expect,' said Hadaway. 'Though it's next to impossible to get a mortgage, I'm told.'

'Not precisely a reliable long-term investment, I would imagine. But you're here in an official capacity, of course.'

Hadaway inclined his head. 'You headed the ISA's Insurgency Threat Response Directorate for seventeen years,' he said. 'If there's anyone who knows more about non-organic combat capability than you…'

'…It would be my successor,' said Corscadden mildly. 'With whom you had lunch a couple of months ago. At which time, I have no doubt, she articulated for you at length the current measures in place to detect and prevent a-naut attacks in Europe Two.'

The voice was level, running to tepid irritation, but something in Corscadden's eyes didn't quite match. A stranger wouldn't have noticed it. Friends might not have noticed it, not if they weren't looking for it. But Hadaway had known Corscadden too long, knew to watch his eyes for the tell-tale flickers of interest, the hints that he dropped for the worthy. He sat forwards in his chair, hands clasped, and fell into step with the beats of the game. It was always a game with Corscadden.

'You're right,' he said. 'I haven't gone to Dr. Rasmussen. She doesn't do off-the-record. But you do.'

An arched eyebrow, all innocent surprise, and Corscadden turned his gaze into his glass to agitate pale olive-coloured sludge with a straw. In another man, it might have looked like absent introspection, but Corscadden never did anything absently.

'Why don't you tell me,' he said, 'what's on your mind.'

Hadaway flashed a smile, but he was modelling it on Corscadden's and it lacked its usual effect. 'Before I do that,' he said, 'I'd like your assurance that this conversation goes no further.'

'This conversation goes as far as I choose.' The expression was pleasant, but the little old man was receding, baring his teeth when he grinned. 'I'd imagine it's unlikely that I'll feel a need to share … specifics. But I shall most certainly not guarantee any such thing in advance.'

Hadaway sat back, began to steeple his hands, thought better of it. 'I've been doing some reading,' he said.

Corscadden rolled his eyes in sympathy. 'It's nothing but reading, sometimes,' he said.

And just like that, the little old man was back, assumed so fluidly that Hadaway had to take a second to remind himself that he'd just watched his companion shrug on a persona as he might shrug on a coat. It was too tempting to fall into step, too easy to accept Corscadden's shifting re-constructions of himself.

He said, 'I like reading.'

'Well.' Corscadden smiled serenely. 'That's certainly an advantage for a career politician.'

'I seem to remember you telling me once that you'd never aspired to hold public office.'

Corscadden shrugged. 'Some men are called to service. I was called to industry.'

'And yet you spent nearly three decades in a series of congressional appointments.' Hadaway sat back in his chair, letting his gaze sweep across the light-washed lawn; the arboretum; the raised beds, overflowing with flowers that drew the eye along the terrace and up the high sandstone arches of the house itself. 'And you seem to have done rather well out of it.'

'On a civil servant's salary?' Corscadden chuckled, the genial good-humour of the elderly Oxford don. 'My dear boy, there are many reasons to involve oneself in matters of governance, but financial reward is not among them, as you know very well.'

'There are other advantages.'

'There are. Not the least of which has been the opportunity to influence congressional policy as regards the artificial population and the measures best employed to neutralise their ongoing threat. Though I'm not sure that's what you were getting at, and, I must say, I rather resent the implication.'

No you don't, thought Hadaway, and smiled. Corscadden had resigned his seat on Calator's Board of Directors when he was appointed to the Directorate, but he'd almost doubled his fortune in the final three years of the Insurgency. Aloud, he said, 'My apologies if I've offended you. That wasn't my intention.'

A beat. And then Corscadden returned the smile, as fluidly as if it had never left his face. 'I dare say,' he said. 'But, please — don't let me detain you. You didn't fly all the way up here to talk about salary scales. You have a situation in your city and, since you've sought out my company, I'm forced to assume that you're confused about something to do with a-nauts. I thought the issue was anthrax, but what do I know? It's not my constituency.'

'Trace amounts of anthrax were found in the path work-up on Patient Zero,' said Hadaway. 'It's the CDC's current favourite theory and we've got nothing better right now, so that's what we're telling the media. You know Creo — they'll riot over the price of bread. Can you imagine what would happen if there was any suggestion that we've locked down the gates for a disease that we can't even diagnose, let alone treat?'

'Ah, Creo.' Corscadden tilted his glass, peering at the thin film of liquid on the bottom. 'I must say, I had wondered why anyone would bother locking down a city for a disease that's so hellishly difficult to pass from person to person. But, then again, it *is* Creo; I suppose if anywhere on Earth is going to infect itself with a new strain of aerosolised anthrax that sneezes its way into uninfected lungs, Creo would be the place. Have they started burning the buses yet?'

'Not yet,' said Hadaway. 'But give them a chance. It's only been a couple of hours.'

'I've often thought,' said Corscadden, 'that the human conscience is a remarkable thing. Any other city in the world would have hit the bottom of the public purse many years ago. But, of course, the bilevels make people uneasy. We don't like that they have to exist; they remind us that we made mistakes and accidentally got away with it. So we just keep cleaning up their messes in the hope that if we throw enough money at the problem it'll stop being our fault, and we ask ourselves, what else can we do? Because it's much easier to keep on paying, like a parent with a guilty conscience, than to admit that everything went to hell and only some of us got out alive.'

Hadaway picked at a fleck of lint on his trousers. The chances were always high that Corscadden would descend into moral philosophising; the trick was to just ignore it without visibly losing interest.

'If I'm right,' he said quietly, 'then I think we may be about to get our reckoning.'

A twitch of eyebrows signified the resurgence of moderate interest. 'Really? I understand it's not the easiest pathogen to kill, but I'd imagine we can fend off a couple of dozen cases of anthrax, dear boy.'

'And I wouldn't have come to you,' said Hadaway, 'if I still thought we had a couple of dozen cases of anthrax.'

Corscadden smiled a friendly smile. 'Neither you nor I are medical doctors.'

'No,' said Hadaway. 'But I'm a career politician whose constituency includes Creo. I keep a couple of medical doctors on the payroll.'

'And they don't think it's anthrax?'

'They did.' Hadaway's smile was one higher than Corscadden's on the scale of friendly innocence. 'They're not so certain anymore.'

Corscadden's expression remained fixed, although something flashed behind his eyes that might have been the faintest flicker of spiralling curiosity. 'No doubt you're about to tell me what changed their minds,' he said. And then, abruptly: 'Ah - Harvey.'

Both men glanced up as the drinks arrived: a fresh tumbler of green mush for Corscadden and a silver urn for Hadaway, from which the butler decanted a steaming stream of coffee into a fine-bone china cup before disappearing without a word. Hadaway took a sip: freshly ground, expensive, almost certainly non-synthetic. He'd expected nothing less.

'The House will be sitting shortly,' said Corscadden. It was his way of suggesting that his patience was wearing thin.

Hadaway said nothing, sipped again, took a deep breath of perfumed air, savouring the subtle changes in flavour as the day began. 'Forgive me,' he said. 'I've interrupted your morning.'

'It's always a pleasure to see an old friend,' said Corscadden. 'But you're a busy man and I've taken up enough of your time. Why don't you just go ahead and ask what you'd like to ask me?'

An upwards glance confirmed the note of impatience in his companion's voice. Hadaway nodded. 'Hypothetically?'

'If you like.'

'Hypothetically, then. I'd like to know if there was ever any suggestion that the a-naut threat extended to biological weaponry.'

'Goodness me.' Corscadden reached for his drink, stirred it with his straw. 'You must know that it does. It has done since the opening shots of the Insurgency. The most virulent pathogens known to science, even the oldest generations can handle with impunity, so long as their shields aren't breached. They'd have to be insane or stupid not to use it against us. And I can assure you, dear boy, that they're neither.'

'I'm not talking,' said Hadaway, 'about the ones we know about.'

'An engineered virus?' A shrug of the eyebrows. 'It has always been a possibility, yes, though we've never been able to prove it. A number of different influenza strains have almost certainly been weaponised, and I'm not sure anybody believes that Ebola haemmhoragic fever just turned up all by itself in Portland fifteen years ago. It's not exactly difficult to train a virus to cause a little bit of extra havoc; we're just better at stopping the epidemics than they are at starting them. If you're asking me if your anthrax attack could be an a-naut bioweapon, then my answer is that it's certainly within the realm of possibility, yes. Especially if it's behaving atypically. That's very much their style.'

Hadaway's lips twisted into something that was only barely a smile. 'It's behaving so atypically,' he said, 'that it has only appeared in measurable quantities in Patient Zero's path screen and in not a single one of the hundred and fifty-three cases that followed. I have one doctor who's prepared to swear on his mother's life that a weaponised biotoxin could absolutely move straight to severe sepsis without any of the epidemiological signs of infection, but I've got two more who aren't so sure. And I've got a report on my desk that says it's not anthrax at all, from a man who is, in the judgement of these two doctors, not even a little bit crazy.'

'I see.' The glass rose to Corscadden's lips, green goo disappearing into the straw. 'And what does the report suggest you might be dealing with?'

'Hypothetically?'

A faint smile. 'What does this hypothetical report hypothetically indicate?'

'Hypothetically,' said Hadaway, 'it may have found evidence of a modified a-cell cluster in one of the patients' serology.'

Another man might have looked startled. Another man might have repeated back the words he'd just heard, as though they might sound less confusing in his own voice. Another man might have shown the smallest hint that Hadaway's suggestion had surprised him in the slightest. But Corscadden simply sipped from his drink and said, 'Heavens.'

Hadaway silently acknowledged the delivery with an eyebrow raise that was one part approval and three parts envy. 'Have you ever come across anything like that before?' he asked. 'Hypothetically.'

'Truthfully? No, I have not. And someone has explained to you, no doubt, that what you've just described is impossible?'

'At length,' said Hadaway. 'And yet, when I asked the Senior Consultant at Saint-Julien des Perdus to have serology workups run on the other patients currently in quarantine, it looks as though at least fourteen others might have produced a similar profile. A-cells. Modified a-cells. In the bloodstreams of fifteen people all suffering from an identical syndrome that we're not managing to treat.'

'At all?'

'Twenty-seven people have died so far. None of the rest are recovering, and there were three more suspected cases when I left my office this morning.

Whatever this is, Corscadden, I'm positive now it's not anthrax. But this is all I've got to go on.'

'And you'd like to know,' said Corscadden, 'if there has ever been any suggestion that a militant artificial group had found a way to ... what? Weaponise their own body chemistry?'

Hadaway hesitated, but only for a moment. 'Yes. Yes, that's what I'm asking.'

'Well,' said Corscadden mildly. 'No wonder you didn't want to approach Dr. Rasmussen.'

'It's completely out of the question, then?'

A leisurely sip of green mush. 'I've certainly never heard any suggestion that such a thing was possible.'

'Well.' Hadaway sat back heavily in his seat, hands splayed on the armrests. It was starting to feel like a long time since he'd last slept. 'You're the expert, of course.'

'That doesn't mean,' said Corscadden quietly, 'that it might not have happened.'

Hadaway twisted his head forty-five degrees against the canvas panel at his back, but Corscadden's gaze was fixed on his hands. 'Then there could be something in this?'

Corscadden was quiet for a long moment. If he was aware of his companion's scrutiny, he gave no sign, twisting his glass in the bright glow of the light cloud, watching it sparkle and flare on the beads of condensation that trickled down the sides.

'You know,' he said at last, and Hadaway, who could recognise the opening notes of a lecture, felt himself die a little bit inside. 'A man cannot, as you very astutely observed a moment ago, afford a house like this on a civil servant's salary. You know about my munitions ventures, of course, but did you know that I also hold a substantial investment portfolio? My broker tries to keep me evenly spread across the markets, but I tend to prefer PharmaTech — everyone will always need medicine, you know; if I lose out on one transaction, I'll certainly make up the shortfall on another. And you know me: when I have a decision to make, I like to do my homework; I always have. I've sat down with the heads of R&D in some of the biggest multinational Pharma firms across the globe, and I've asked them: what's next? What's the long-term plan? We've conquered the virus and the bacterium and the cancer cell, but what's the new leveller? What haven't we

thought of? What do we need to be ready for next? And some of them —
not always the younger ones, mind you; sometimes it's the ones who are old
enough to know better — sometimes they look at me and they say, we've
got this. We're in charge of human illness now. There is nothing left that we
can't control.' Moisture-frosted glass sparkled in the midday blaze, twisting,
scattering, reforming beneath the restless movement of a manicured hand.
'And I say to them,' he finished softly, 'that this is why, when the next one
comes, it will be a plague.'

Silence descended like a frost on the garden. In the distance, water
chimed over sculpted Titans and crashed into limpid bowls; birdsong, piped,
twittered around the treetops. Hadaway sat forward, slowly in his chair, set
his coffee cup into its saucer, and met Corscadden's gaze.

'Is that what you think this is?' he said.

But Corscadden only shrugged.

'From what you tell me?' he said. 'I couldn't possibly say. But I will say
this: the militant artificial groups that I've encountered throughout the
course of my career have been resourceful and they have been ruthless.
These days, they're also increasingly desperate, and this is a very dangerous
combination. Viron therapy is ninety-three percent effective at controlling
whatever they've tried to throw at us in the past; we are winning this final
battle, but we are dealing with a demographic that's unlikely to respond well
to defeat. If they've somehow managed to produce an agent from their own
a-cellular material that's able to replicate inside a human host, then I would
imagine that sepsis would be the very least of what one might expect to see.
Foreign immunological material replicating inside the blood stream would
certainly be sufficient to incite an immune event, and, quite simply, there
would be no reason to look for it and therefore almost no way to detect it on
a routine scan. And if it's passing from patient to patient — as it seems to be
— then it looks as though you, dear boy, might have a very serious problem
on your hands.'

Hadaway dropped his gaze. 'We're containing it,' he said.

'For now.'

'The city is on lock-down. Nobody's going in or out.'

'Yes, and you've been very lucky that it hit where it did. But I wouldn't for
a moment imagine that it's contained.'

'What do I do?' Hadaway looked up, waited until Corscadden met his
eyes. 'Whose desk does this need to be on?'

'For now? I'd say your first job is talking people out of anthrax. Send me your report and I'll see that it makes it as far as Dr. Rasmussen — though I'd prefer it if you kept my name out of this for now. You understand … this is a little too close to the fringe for me.'

Hadaway loosed a short laugh, completely devoid of humour. 'You and me both,' he said. 'If you could have Dr. Rasmussen liaise with my Chief of Staff? She's fully briefed and she prefers that I keep my fingerprints off this until we know what it is.'

'Ah, yes: Ms. Katz,' said Corscadden, though, if he were expecting a reaction, he'd pushed the swagger one step too far for today and Hadaway was no longer biting. 'Well. It is an election year, after all.'

A tight smile. 'It's always an election year,' said Hadaway. 'I'd just like to think I'll have a constituency left to vote for me.'

Corscadden smiled a sympathetic smile, leaned back in his seat as Hadaway got to his feet, draining his coffee as he stood. 'Have you considered,' he said, 'what happens next?'

'Next?' Hadaway straightened his jacket, brushed creases out of his trousers. 'I turn up late for a debate that's likely to suck eight million credits out of the north-west's economy over the next twelve months and wait to hear what Dr. Rasmussen has to say to Eve.'

'And if Dr. Rasmussen shares your opinion that what we're looking at is an entirely new strain of pathogen, engineered by a-nauts to cause maximum destruction and set loose in the general population? What then?'

Hadaway glanced up into the warm yellow haze above, filtered through the lazy sway of an overhanging oak bough that scattered the ground in mobile shadows.

'Then we treat for anthrax,' he said, 'and we stay the hell out of Creo.'

17.2

Boston went down to the street to phone home as the dawn was beginning to break, and came back up half an hour later, grey-skinned with fatigue and scrubbing at the first prickles of stubble on his chin. 'They're okay,' he said as he threw back the blankets to crawl in beside her. 'Alex is pretty pissed at me, but he'll get over it.'

'Jesus, you're freezing,' she told him, but she shuffled backwards into his street-chilled jumper just the same. 'He does know you can't actually get out of Parnasse right now, doesn't he?'

'I think the problem,' he said, nuzzling his face into the hollow between her shoulder and her neck, 'is that I'm in Parnasse in the first place. And not in Chatelier.'

'Your mum's in Chatelier, isn't she?'

She felt him grin into her skin. 'That's also the problem,' he said. His arms snaked around her waist and she felt her spine slacken, melt into his stomach. 'They'll be fine,' he told her, whispered words warm against her throat. 'I'll call them again in a couple of hours. They'll be fine.'

'You'll be back with them in a few days,' she said.

'Yeah,' he said. 'Cass is on her meds and Alex knows what he's doing. They'll be fine.' And then, as if he'd heard the unspoken uncertainty in the repetition, he said it again, but quietly: 'They'll be fine.'

'They'll be fine,' said Danae, who'd heard it too.

★

As the morning wore on, the excitement settled into the low-level apathy of restricted movement and not enough to do. Another blip before lunchtime sent Turrow back down to the street to call his brother, and he came back with the news that the off-peak curfew was extending another two hours at either end of the night, which had caused the mayor to have some kind of psychotic break on seventeen separate current affairs channels, but that Chatelier, at least, was quiet for now. There were soldiers at the end of the road, he told her, and they'd bundled him into the back of an armoured car for the look of things, asked for his name and address and wanted to know why he was in Parnasse when the gates were locked, but they let him go when someone threw a bottle at their van. For a lock-down, it was all unsettlingly well-mannered; Danae thought she'd rest a little easier when the rioting actually started.

'They're doing curfew credits at fifty percent salary,' he told her. 'Alex is about to flip his lid.'

'Fifty?' said Danae, before she remembered that she did not, technically, have any percent of a salary at the moment, and that her outrage was therefore somewhat misplaced. 'It was sixty-five last time. Any idea how long until they open the gates?'

Turrow shrugged. 'No idea,' he said. 'Nobody knows anything.'

It wasn't strictly true; the streets were a hive of eavesdropped information, it was just that it wasn't the sort of information that was likely to be of any use. Danae followed him down in the early afternoon and wandered, face wrapped in a strip of old pillowcase for the look of things, while he hung back in the shadows to make call number five to Alex. Beneath the bubble, the road was deserted but, as she approached the intersection with Thirty-fifth Avenue North, the stillness began to give way to motion, the silence to fill with sound, the emptiness to fill with people, in twos and threes, in crowds, or simply milling aimlessly alone on the pavements for want of anything better to do with nine hours of rationed freedom. She heard the whispers as she passed — *three thousand in the hospital, passed along the lines of humanity with a kind of horrified fascination; four hundred people dead; anthrax my arse, they don't lock down the city for anthrax* … Rumours and gossip, insubstantial as mist; she decided she didn't need to hear it.

He'd levered the curtains open a couple of inches when she got back to the apartment, and stood by the window, peering at the street below as the light-bands wound down the hours towards curfew.

'They're doing okay,' he said. 'They'll be all right.'

She crossed the room to him, ran her hands over his shoulders. 'They'll be fine,' she said.

'Alex knows what he's doing. He'll manage.' He rubbed at a spot of grime on the window pane, though he might as well have picked up used hankies at a landfill. It was an action with similar prospects in terms of making any measurable difference. 'Cassie's patch is good for weeks yet.'

She said nothing, worked on unknotting a tangle of muscles at the base of his neck.

'I thought maybe…. Maybe Tilly wasn't just herself when I left. Alex thought so too.' He swallowed, leaned back into her kneading hands, closed his eyes. 'They'll be fine. Alex knows what he's doing.'

'I'm glad you're here,' said Danae. It was the best she could do by way of comfort, if only because it comforted her.

17.3

Within a couple of hours, the city was burning.

It started in Nebe, as these things often did. Nebe was the subject of a variety of popular colloquialisms in the lower city, most of them involving violence or things going bad. 'As red as a Nebe street-fight' was one. Someone who died prematurely 'went for a stroll in Nebe'. An ugly person had 'a face like a Nebe gutter'. It was that sort of place.

But fire was Creo's number one enemy, and it dealt well with fire. Rain erupted from the ceiling, drowning the streets in unrelenting deluge, through which fire engines wailed to the aid of a complex array of sprinklers and convection inhibitors. Cars were overturned and set alight, rammed through shop windows and doused within minutes. Molotov cocktails were thrown, igniting in a flurry of burning spirit and glass, flaring brightly and dying under the onrush of a wall of water. It was the sentiment that mattered, not the damage done. Fire fighters cowered in their trucks under a welter of stones, bottles, anything projectile. Fire engines, stalled in an illicit crowd, swayed violently under the pressure of many hands on either side. Firemen were dragged free and beaten, their engines overturned and ignited. Burning fire trucks were hurtled in the direction of the impromptu barricades that sprang up at the ends of streets narrow and wide. Violence spread quickly, passing under and through hastily erected cordons, surfacing in pockets of rioting. Close to the city walls, groups of men coagulated into a resistance of sorts and started charging the gates. In the end, the troops started shooting tear gas into the crowd.

It spread to the street outside the apartment in rumour only, the darkened avenue buzzing with the promise of chaos at reign, but for now there was only silence and second hand smoke.

What else was there to do? They talked, and when they didn't talk, they made love. In the shelter of a governmentally enforced hiatus, they explored the contours of each others' bodies like cartographers mapping new lands. She found the places he could not resist: the spot behind either ear, in the fold under the earlobe, where a softly flickering tongue could provoke instant capitulation; the small of his back where her fingers could make him arch into her with the lightest of touches; the soft skin beneath his scrotum that could be gently manipulated so that he utterly lost control. She learned to read in the shifting lines of his lidded eyes the accelerating levels of pleasure that his voice did not betray, the raggedness of his breath at her ear, and the gentle, whispered moans that escaped him as ecstasy built. She travelled the length of him with tongue and hands, tasting and stroking, studying him as a painter might study a landscape, searching for the secrets that brought him to light and life. They discovered that her head fit perfectly in the hollow of his neck, that he bore her full weight with ease when she hooked her legs around his back, that there was a point in their kiss at which it became impossible to

ignore the building sense of urgency and after which there fell a kind of haze
of tangled limbs and barely-caught breath.

He filled her — physically, with flesh, and in another way that she couldn't
exactly explain, as though she'd been starving for many years and had only
now begun to eat. His taste was like a narcotic, the scent of him addictive,
and his hands, his mouth, against her skin made her grope blindly for any
hint of who she might have become: this woman, this creature of sensation
and appetite, this thing that she did not recognise. She said his name as often
as she could: in pleasure, in rest, into his mouth, against his belly where a
triangle of coarse hair darkened the white flesh, through his hair, into the
gasp of orgasm. She said his name in disbelief and in incredulous awe —
Turrow — as though it was, every time, a surprise to find their bodies glued
together with sweat and desire, sliding effortlessly, flesh on polished flesh. As
he moved with her, in her, through her, she noticed the colour of his eyes, the
deceptive strength in the hands and fingers that held her against him, tight
on her back and shoulders, the brush of the soft curls of hair on his chest
against her breasts, the sinews of his legs where they twined with hers, the
calluses of his feet and his long, elegant toes brushing urgently against her
own as he moved. And she thought, *I know you.*

It was cold in the apartment and warm in bed, warmer still cocooned
in lovemaking. There was almost no reason to leave, apart from his three-
hourly calls to Alex, the only prosaic reminder that there was another life
outside of this sudden, headlong leap into hedonism. Giddy on endorphins,
she wasn't one hundred percent certain that she could have walked the
length of the room without his weight against her at her side, and, for now,
by unspoken agreement, they were never apart. A week ago, she would
have said that the constant presence of another human being would have
been physically, mentally, and in every other way unbearable; now, she felt
his absence from her like a missing limb. From time to time, prompted
by hunger, they wrapped themselves in blankets and set off to explore the
shadows of the hidden apartment, and thus it was that they discovered the
satisfaction of making love on elderly couches, pressed up tight against a
crumbling doorframe, and over the lip of a breathtakingly ornate bath filled
ankle deep with grime.

Later, lightheaded and exhausted, they disembowelled a geriatric cushion
from one of the distant, dark rooms and set fire to the contents in the sink,
filling the kitchen with a thick, acrid smoke that jogged a senile sprinkler

system out of retirement. 'See?' said Danae triumphantly. 'We have running water. Didn't we do well?'

'What a team,' agreed Turrow, and cremated a tin of ham.

His body was an economy of lines and muscle: compact and firm against hers. Naked, they fit together like carefully planed wood — curve against curve, void filled with flesh, slotting together as though they had been built as one unit and halved. His words came back to her repeatedly — *tell me it doesn't just make more sense when we're together* — and there was no answer for that anymore, because, in point of fact, she could no longer imagine how the world would make sense if they were apart. Words that she had never said bubbled in her throat, effervescent, demanding a voice, and they fell out of her, unexpectedly at first: they were crossing the dark shadows together, wrapped in a blanket that was pinned at the front with both their hands, and she tripped and he caught her and, without meaning to, she said, 'I love you.'

She felt the flame of his smile in the darkness, and he said, 'I know. Me too,' and they carried on through the gloom. It was only later that she realised that he had known exactly the right way to respond, and knew that he knew her too.

The city blazed and furied. From Nebe, it flowed seamlessly into Victoria, Petite Cloche and Mère de Martyrs. Whispers of it reached back into the streets of Parnasse, caught in brief snatches when she, the less fragile, made her way down to the cordons in search of information. After hours spent in nakedness and candlelight, the streets were cloying and uncomfortable, smoke-logged as the extractors were shut off to halt the spread of flames, and there was never enough information to justify the time passed outside of decadence. By the time she returned he was waiting by the door with a need that answered her own, his mouth heavy and urgent on hers, their hands clumsy, their coupling frantic. More than once he had pushed her up against the door as it closed and made love to her there, tangled in unshed clothing.

Between times, they wrapped themselves in each other to recover and slept the easy sleep of the coitally exhausted, or talked, filling in the gaps that remained. He talked about his childhood, about Cassie, about her illness. He told her about the first seizure she'd had, forty-five minutes in which he'd thought his sister would die; the second that lasted almost two hours; the Emergency Room doctor's insistence that the only way to keep her safe was to fit a cranio-electrical modulator that they couldn't afford. He told her about turning up to visit her at the hospital while she was still unconscious, and finding a security guard on the door; about the sixteen weeks in which Cassie had been a ward of the state while the Turrows fought to get her back; about the covenant they'd made him sign before they'd return her, agreeing to the implant, that he knew he couldn't honour. About the day, right in the middle of the whole stupid nightmare, that Rita walked into the apartment with an armful of shopping and an open bottle of wine and picked a fight with Turrow, and then Alex, and then, finally, Tilly, who was five years old and just trying to eat her lunch, and he knew, he *knew* that it came from a place of grief and terror and sleepless nights, but Rita wasn't the only one who was hurting, and it felt so damn good just to let the anger bubble up and out of the place where he kept it caged; to punch a wall and yell and break things; to let her lash out, sharp as broken glass, just so that he could lash back.

'Have you ever actually felt,' he asked quietly, words like sandpaper in the hush and shadow of the room, 'as though you might kill your own mother?'

And Danae stroked his face, and told him no, she hadn't; Annelise's parenting style didn't often incline her daughter towards thoughts of murder. 'But,' she added, 'I often wished Walter would just hurry up and die, if that's any good?'

And he laughed and kissed her; said he'd take what he could get, and the kiss deepened, developed, progressed along its inevitable path, and afterwards, as they lay with their eyes closed and their bodies slicked with sweat, she told him about her mother's smile, about the sadness and resentment that her father had worn just below his skin for as long as she could remember, about the farm and the hillside and the sense of complete freedom that was to be had by running to nowhere in particular beneath her infinite sky. She told him about the itch, as best she could explain it, and he refused to be appalled.

'It's not you,' he said.

And the thing was, he was right. Drugged by the haze of a permanent post-coital rush, the itch was diminished, reduced to a dull, irregular throb, like an old wound almost healed. A future of catatonia-by-ginn had been out of the question, but this new information raised interesting possibilities.

Turrow laughed when she told him, and she was beginning to realise that the creases around his eyes when his face collapsed in mirth were fast becoming as necessary to her continued health and survival as air and water. 'Let me get this straight,' he said. 'You're telling me that I need to spend the rest of my life having sex with you so that you don't kill me? I don't actually think I have a problem with that …'

The future was a topic that buzzed around the edges of the constant discussion of the past: too present to ignore, but not so insistent that it needed immediate classification. For the time being, the certainty of it was enough; if the form was ephemeral, it would solidify in time. Outside the city burned and raged and furied with Creo's particular panache, but it reached the apartment only in the half-scented aroma of distant smoke. In the dark entirety of the apartment, the flames of the glorious revolution went unnoticed.

17.4

They sat by the window, naked under a thick, heavy blanket, betting cigarettes on the numbers of ambulances that might pass down the empty street on their way to other places and listening to the far-off sounds of gunshots, gas cannons, small explosions ricocheting through empty streets.

'But you didn't see him die,' he said.

His words, echoes of her own, threw up sharply painful images of Angelo's final night alive, and she said, 'Turrow, trust me. He's dead.'

'Don't do that,' he said.

'Don't do what?'

'That. That flagellation thing. Don't do it.'

'Turrow — what?'

'You did it to me too,' he said. 'He didn't die because of you. Don't do that.'

'I didn't say that.'

'It's like you think you're cursed. It's like you think *you're* a curse. Maybe he's not dead, Danae. Don't torture yourself.'

'I'm not,' she said. 'Turrow, you don't understand. I *know*. The stream warped. He's dead.'

He quirked an eyebrow. She said, 'The stream, Turrow. The datastream. That's why we're a-nauts. Amnis? Stream?'

'Okay,' he said. Pleasantly, easily: 'I did go to school, you know.' He coughed, then sneezed. 'Fuck. Fucking dust. When was the last time you cleaned this place?'

She reached forward, pointedly, and stole three cigarettes from his pile. He smacked her hand away.

'Seriously?' she said. 'Seriously with your little hand-smacky? Did I mention I'm an a-naut?'

'Enough with the threats, woman,' he said. 'Kill me or don't. But give me back my cigarettes.'

She threw one back towards him. 'It's like pockets,' she said, ignoring the eyebrow that had shot up again. 'Little pockets of the datastream. It's not like telepathy, it's not like that. It's like — I don't know. I don't know how to explain it. We're all part of the same space, we're separate but we're part of the same space. You can't tell what someone else is thinking, or what they're feeling, it's not like that. But you know … I didn't know. I mean, I knew, but I didn't know what it was until he told me. You know when you're with another a-naut, because you can feel it in the stream. Maybe … like if you brush against someone in the dark. Maybe a bit like that? You can feel it inside you. So when someone dies, it's like…. Christ, I don't know. It's like a light goes off in a building. Kind of, even if you don't see it, you can sort of sense it. That's if they just die. Like, *poof.* They're gone. Sometimes you don't even notice. But if they die badly, Turrow, you know. It's fucking horrible. The stream goes nuts. It's fucking horrible. You can feel them screaming. You feel them die. You feel like you're dying with them.'

Under the blanket, his arm snaked around her waist. She felt the fabric shift, a thrill of cold air where it had peaked against her back and broken the seal. He said, 'I didn't know.'

'Why would you?'

'It's still not your fault.'

She was aware that her hands were trembling and clasped them together in her lap. He felt it, of course, but his only response was to gently tighten his grip on her waist, pulling her closer. She said, 'He saw my scan reading. I think, I don't know. He knew what I was and he died thinking … I don't even know what he thought. He shouldn't have died.'

'Maybe not.'

'Maybe?' She pulled sharply back from him, snapped her head around to face him. '*Maybe?*'

He coughed, hard. 'That's not what I meant.'

'*Maybe* he didn't deserve to die horribly for no reason,' she said. 'That's what you said. What else does that mean?'

'Danae, don't,' he said.

'Maybe none of us deserve to be alive,' she said. 'Just in case, huh? Maybe it's a good thing that they trailed him off the streets and hurt him until he died?'

'Don't turn this onto me,' he said. 'It's not me you're angry with. You know I didn't mean that.'

Rage flared, and with it the itch. Her hands, folded in on themselves already, dug fingernails into her palms in little white-hot points of pain and she knew he felt it in the sudden rigid tension in her shoulders as she bent into it, hunkered down to fight it off. His arm tightened around her waist and the other slid across her belly to pull her towards him, and his chin was resting on her head, his mouth pressed into her hair. 'Come back,' he whispered. 'Come back to me. It's all right. Come back to me, sweetheart. You're more than this. This is not you. This is not you ...'

17.5

You're more than that. You're more than the sum of your parts.

It was something you said, and she'd believed him. The truth was, it was just something you said. No one was more than the sum of their parts. Take the parts from each other, and there was nothing: just flesh and leaking blood.

Beside her, filtered through the liquid darkness, he coughed and she stirred, seeking instinctively for the warmth of his belly against her back. Beyond the heavy, even sound of his breathing, the apartment was silent, framed by the song of the city in the middle distance. The regular rumble of traffic was gone, swallowed by the far-off sounds of rage, fury, frustration, beating itself out against the walls and streets and gates. It wasn't her city anymore, but the thing that it became when they closed it down, and, if she closed her eyes and let it wash over her, it was possible to believe that she didn't know where she was.

It was possible to believe anything when the itch punched through.

Behind the curtains, in the bowels of the flat, it was possible even to believe that time had stopped. Night and day had meaning only when they could be gauged.

He coughed again, sucked in a deep breath behind it, but didn't wake. She wrapped his heavy, sleeping arm over her shoulder and closed her eyes.

★

Ambulances were coming in twos now.

'Twelve,' said Turrow.

'Sixteen,' said Danae.

It was twenty-four. She won three cigarettes by default.

★

'That's the trouble with isolation,' she said in a tone of manufactured ease. 'Everyone thinks you have to do stuff.'

'God forbid.' He grinned, and she had no say in the grin that spread across her face in return.

'There were only the three of us for the first five years of my life. We didn't have to *do* stuff,' she said.

She tossed him the can, empty but for a child's plastic ring, found half-buried by the trailing curtains, which rattled against the aluminium walls in flight. He caught it, and the ring set up an angry clatter as it settled, but it failed to break free.

He said, 'Humour me. I'm going crazy.'

She said, 'I don't see why we have to even get out of bed.'

'Because we are grown-up human beings, not rutting animals, and occasionally it's healthy to take a break from sex and find other occupations for our considerable intellect,' he said.

'You're bored with sex?'

'I'm not bored with sex. That will never happen.'

Was he paler? His skin was warm; he'd been too warm to stay under the blankets. He looked tired. She caught the can but fumbled it; the ring bounced free onto her lap and she had to stand to retrieve it.

He punched the air. 'Forfeit.'

'Forfeit,' she said. 'I'm already cooking tonight; don't talk to me about forfeits.'

They had woken lazily, arms and legs wound methodically together and she had been aware of his breath at the curve of skin where her neck met her shoulder, of his arousal at the small of her back, of her own inevitable response. His hands had described leisurely figure eights across her flesh, raising shivers where they touched; his mouth had nuzzled against her throat and she had leaned back into him and breathed the scent of his body and his gathering excitement as they began to move together. It was familiar now as if they had been practising the routine for a lifetime, this easy swell of pleasure, provocation and assurance, a gentle, expanding cadence, a series of stages designed to lead inexorably into each other.

And then, abruptly, as his fingers had snaked downwards and she shifted her weight slightly to part her legs for them, his hands came to rest against her belly and his lips stilled against her throat.

He had breathed, heavily. After a moment, she had said, gently, 'Are you all right?' although the answer was obvious in the release of pressure at her coccyx.

He hesitated before answering and she caught the acid burn of shame in the words. 'Yeah ... yeah. I just ... I don't know.'

She had swivelled in his arms and his hands had shifted on her slick flesh, coming to rest against her back. He had dipped his head so that her chin rested against his crown, but she had taken his face in her hands and lifted it up to hers. 'Tired?' she said.

A half smile, lopsided. 'I suppose so.'

'Sleep. It's all right.'

'I don't want to sleep,' he said. 'I want to do this.'

And it was back, seamlessly, as though it had never been lost, and he had burrowed his lips into hers and she had swung her leg over his hip and they had gathered the rhythm where it had been lost – quickly, frantically – and she had thought, for those extended, euphoric moments that it had been fine, really; a sign of corporeal vulnerability, something to be expected after days lost in carnal adventure and virtually nothing else. But he had slept afterwards, too quickly, while she lay, wakeful, with the first gnawings of doubt prickling the back of her mind. When she woke, two hours later, she had risen and dressed and crossed to the armchair, from which she watched him carefully in an effort to find evidence that she might be wrong.

That was when he said he was too warm, and decided they should diversify the entertainment. The doubt became a low-level thrill of anxiety.

She threw him the can now and he caught it as he started coughing, heavily, as though it had taken him by surprise. The can listed in his hand and the ring rolled free, across the floor. Instinctively, she stood to catch it, but he thought she was coming to help him and he held up a hand.

Defensive, she thought, and recognised herself in the gesture.

He said, when he could, 'I'll tell you your forfeit. You've got to think up a better game,' and he tried to smile.

17.6

Smoke was curling through the silent streets, visible behind the barricades as a faint grey haze. The air in the apartment, by default several degrees colder than cold, was actually beginning to give in to the vicious onslaught of heat outside and noticeably warm up a couple of notches. 'Think they're planning to boil us to death?' said Turrow.

His skin had faded with the daylight, from a sickly ashen grey to a bloodless, translucent white. He coughed with every other breath: a heavy, watery hacking that left him blue and struggling for air.

'Don't you talk,' said Danae. 'You didn't have to stand in that kitchen for three quarters of an hour.'

'You were kind enough to allow the smoke to fill the whole flat, though,' he told her, with a flash of his sunlight smile, and then coughed so hard that she thought he might split in two. He tried to laugh. 'No more cigarettes for me,' he said.

'Those things will kill you,' she agreed, and dipped her eyes before he could see what was in hers.

★

'What happened?' he said.

'You passed out,' she told him. 'You're okay now.'

★

Danae walked. Four floors beneath her, Turrow slept, poorly, a thin blanket thrown over him to keep out the damp. She had lain awake beside him for as long as she could and, when the silence focused itself into a shrill whine of panic that she could no longer ignore, she'd thrown off the seven blankets that formed a fabric barrier between them, for the first time in days, and did what she needed to do.

She walked.

The itch had crept a little louder with every laborious second of hush until it had become a third presence in the building, grinning at her from the shadows. Danae wandered from room to room, humming to herself through clenched teeth, setting up a counter-vibration in her skull, stripping layers of dust from ancient furniture with her hands as she passed it in swift, angry flutters.

I'm going crazy, she thought. *I'm going to go nuts.*

He hadn't made his way down to the street tonight, making vague noises about how things had been fine at home the last time he'd called and he'd try again tomorrow, but she'd seen the look in his eyes and volunteered to go instead, claiming cabin fever when he tried to tell her it didn't matter for one night. He needed sleep and he wasn't going to sleep until he knew they were okay, and so she let him drop some credit into her phonewave, enough for a five-minute conversation, and slipped out of the apartment and into the thick, motionless air of the city.

He's okay, she told Alex, with a smile that probably told him more than that. *He just had to do some stuff. He'll ring in the morning.*

They were fine. Alex knew what he was doing. It was Turrow she wasn't so sure about anymore.

The crowds had massed and gathered as usual in the evening, though the cafés were closed now and the patrols tended to break apart groups of five or more, but rumour and gossip had given way to blithe assurances and dark humour. Everyone knew a lock-down joke; almost everyone knew someone who'd called an ambulance and been turned down flat, which meant that it wasn't spreading like you'd heard it was, and the gates were supposed to be opening again in a couple of days. It wasn't anthrax, it was some kind of respiratory thing, aggravated by the smoke, but nobody took any chances with Creo, and could you blame them? Laughter: the sound of uneasy solidarity. It was fine now; it was going to be fine. They were opening the gates again in a couple of days.

She walked back in the evening dusk, as the billboards began to clear the congregations back into their homes, and counted ambulances as they passed, gliding silently through the massing smoke clouds like birds by night. The evening belonged to the medical transports: mobile pods dispensing first aid to the housebound, quarantine vans filled with plastic faces, army medevac trucks, emblazoned with a scarlet cross on white, peering through the gloom. Danae counted sixteen as she pulled up to the entrance of the apartment: eight fewer than yesterday, and she thought of the men and women that crowded onto the streets, looking for news, looking for diversion, looking for someone to tell them that everything was all right now. She could imagine the smiles and the back slaps and the stories that their friend had heard, about how Fiore was already open again and South District was supposed to be next. Because things were getting better already: you could tell by the ambulances.

Eight fewer than yesterday. Why did that feel unspeakably bad?

17.7

Turrow lay, motionless but for the tremors that gripped him at intervals, as though something clutched at him in his sleep. She slid onto the bed beside him, unwilling to crawl under the covers and disturb him, and stroked sweat-matted hair from his brow as fear knotted her stomach.

He was well this morning. *He was well this morning.*

And so was Nadine, said that vicious, uncensorable voice inside her head. *And look what happened there.*

Danae slipped off the bed and crossed to the window. Stillness was unbearable; motion forced the rising panic into a focused point, made it something like nausea instead. Something that could be managed.

Not you, she thought, desolately. *Not you, Turrow.*

He inhaled sharply, as though he'd been shaken awake, and said, 'Is that you?'

His voice startled her; she wasn't ready for it. Without time to gather her composure, she went for the safest option. 'Go back to sleep,' she said.

'I wasn't sleeping,' he told her. To her surprise, it tugged a little smile from the corner of her lips, and she turned it back to him in the darkness.

'Just resting your eyes?' she said. Her mother had said the same thing to her when she was small.

'I was dozing,' he said.

'Maybe you could tell me the difference then. I always wondered.'

He ignored her, propped himself up on an elbow. But he was too weak to take his own weight: his arm shook and he lowered himself back onto the pillow. 'Come back to bed,' he said.

'In a minute,' she said. A beat. 'I couldn't sleep.'

'You won't sleep while you're standing up,' he said. There was a rasp to his voice that spoke of buried pain. She ignored it.

'In a bit,' she said. 'I just … I need to walk it off for a bit.'

On cue, he started to cough. Through the thin light, she saw his shoulders heave with the strain, dancing shadows in the deeper gloom.

The instinct of a lifetime of care kicked in and she crossed the room to him, pulled him upright, held him against her until it stopped. It could possibly have been the worst thing she could have done, because it burned the tiny thread of deniability that had hung, hopefully, between them.

Care was for sick people. The need for care was a very bad thing.

His skin was warm against her, even through her clothes. She rubbed his back. It was the only thing she could think of.

'Stupid,' he said at last. He lay heavily against her, reached for her hand with shaking fingers, wound his fingers through hers. 'Fucking dust.'

'I'll get you some water,' she said.

'I'm all right,' he said. It was what her father used to say when he was avoiding the doctor in those suspended, borrowed days before diagnosis.

'I know,' she said, as she had years before.

'It's just a cough,' he said. 'It isn't that.'

'I know,' she said.

17.8

Sleep deserted her again. Programmed by years of uneasy watchfulness,, the urge to rest evaporated and she sat with him long into the night, while he drifted on tides of lucidity, waxing and waning with the heat under his skin. He slept in bursts, but his sleep was different: thin and unsettled where it should have been sleek and black and filled with dreams. When he woke, which was often, it was violent or hazy; either a sharp intake of breath, as though he had been stung, or a half-wakening, filled with nonsense-words, and he didn't know her. Once he pushed her away from him with a strength he lacked when he was himself, not hard but so unexpected that she almost tumbled from the bed. Because the examined pain of that was not something she could process just then, she retreated to the other side of the room, waiting silently for the rage to pass.

The itch said, *do it now, it's the best thing for you both.*

She took to sitting in the armchair, waiting for the fever to break.

Just because he is sick, she told herself, *does not mean it's that.*

People get sick.

Outside, the storm rumbled. Voices shouted in the distance, punctuated by gunfire, and the streets were alive with a lowering, flickering red light. As it crept nearer to the road below their apartment, she could even begin make out words, drifting up through the belly of the building: *they've broken through the lines in Cilicia. The west gate is down.* A chant rippled through the ranks of protestors: single syllables, easier to build up a rhythm.

Out. Out. Out.

Here and there, cries of terror punctuated the general howl of rage. The street filled with smoke, curling through the relentless rain, made heavy like a grey soup. Tinted red by a thousand other fires, shading to deep black where flames were extinguished.

The road outside was still, though. Under the bubble, wood was too damp to burn.

Sometimes he woke in pain. When the fever swept back, when his temperature dropped, there was nothing there but the agony of a system slowly shrinking. He wanted to sit up, so she pulled him upright, feeling the heat prickle through his slender skin. Her father had had years to die and the weight had receded from his body with every day, but Turrow had been healthy until a day ago; he was still as heavy as a fully grown man. She dragged him upwards, held him with difficulty while she arranged his pillows, and crept in beside him. His arm snaked around her shoulder and she pressed her head to his chest, damp and clammy with hours of sweat, listening to the slick sounds of fluid churning in his lungs with every laboured breath.

'Christ,' he said. 'I hate being sick.'

'You'll be better in a day or two,' she said.

'I forgot what it's like when you don't have any patches.'

She said, 'When it gets light, I'll look about a bit. Maybe the last owners left something behind.'

'What time is it?'

'I don't know. Two, three o'clock, maybe. I can't tell through the smoke.'

His hand hung limp against her upper arm. He tried to tighten it, but his fingers wouldn't grip. In the silence, she could feel every thump of his heart, staccato and uneven, against her cheek.

He said, suddenly, 'How long will you live?'

Danae traced a line of pale hair, dark against his skin, from his navel to the blankets that sat on his hips. 'Who knows?' she said.

'You do,' said Turrow.

She stalled. 'A-nauts are like cars, you know. They don't want you to last longer than your guarantee or nobody'd buy the new models.'

'Yeah,' he said. 'But not you.'

She gave up. 'No. Not me.'

'How long?'

'Two hundred,' she said. 'Maybe two hundred and fifty years. It's harder to be sure with organic components.'

He was silent for a while. She thought he'd fallen asleep, but if she turned her head she would wake him. So she traced the hairs on his belly with the tip of her finger, and when he spoke again it was softly: 'That's long.'

'I know,' she said. She let the silence trickle past for a moment and said, 'You know, there's so many things that could happen ...'

'Can you get sick?'

'No.'

'Good,' he said. With effort, he lifted his free arm and threw it across his chest so that he encircled her. On the underside, as his flesh pressed against hers, she saw the beginnings of a livid red rash snaking up into his armpit. 'You know,' he said, 'If you ever cut yourself, you can have my blood.'

'Thank you,' she said.

'Just don't kill me after.'

She made herself laugh. 'Least I can do.'

But the germ of an idea had wormed its way free, drenching her in cold panic.

It was a terrible idea. No, it was barely an idea at all. It was the panic thinking for her; she needed to do better than that. Now wasn't the time for panicking: she needed a plan, something coherent, something constructive to do to make things better. She didn't need to waste her time on stupid ideas.

It was terrible.

EXTRACT FROM *THE STREAM RAN RED: THE A-NAUT INSURGENCY*
BY OSCAR LUNDELL, CHAPTER 5: THE RULE OF LAW

By the time the human/non-human status of a-nauts finally came before the courts on December 20th, 2076, more than 1.5 million units had been deactivated in the US alone. Criticism of the hearing, always likely to be contentious, was heavy from the beginning as a result of the judges' decision not to allow Garrison to appear in defence of the a-naut cause, on the grounds that his rhetoric was deemed inflammatory. It was a well-founded decision, though scarcely likely to have the desired effect, and Garrison, consummate politician that he had become, delivered his famous 'I Think, Therefore I Am' speech from the barred courthouse gates as session was opened.

He would remain there, surrounded by crowds of over two thousand supporters, both human and artificial, for almost a fortnight while the courts deliberated. A-nauts joined hands on the streets outside as what would become known as the New Year's Edict was read out by a spokeswoman for the twelve justices, who left without taking questions. It was January 2nd, 2077: almost a year since the Zakynthos Group's blinding flash of light had brought innocence to an end.

What they heard, ankle-deep in snow on that cold winter's day, can hardly have come as a surprise. They were to be given special status, they were told, amongst S3As - thus implying that they were to be classed as non-human - and to be subject to the protection of a five-day working week. It was a token move away from what a-naut rights campaigners had been calling their 'slavery status,' and many argued that it was negated entirely by the reintroduction of S3A licensing laws.

Garrison's response was predictably swift and animated. His 'Do I Not Bleed?' speech is often attributed to this date, although it was not, in fact, delivered until two weeks later. He did, however, urge a-nauts to down tools with immediate effect. Response to his speech was rapid on both sides of the debate: the world was once again plunged into a-naut strike, and their leader's immunity was revoked. Later that week, he was to appear on the Ten Most Wanted list, the first time in history for a non-human. By then, however, he had disappeared.

21 MAY

18.1

Figures moved through the mist like spectral riders, sliding into view for seconds only, then dissipating into grey shadows. The fires had ebbed as dawn seeped through the heavy curtains of smoke. Danae had left Turrow sleeping, twitching sporadically to his fevered dreams, and had crept into the sitting room, where a glow around the edges of the curtains hinted at the onset of day. Soldiers, their fatigues stained red and black with the night's exertions, plasticised faces smeared with blood and soot, were congregating in the street below. From time to time she was able to glean clues as to what they were doing: a long length of piping, the heavy bulk of an engine, obscured in the smog, vague shouted instructions that she couldn't hear. The air in the apartment was warm and stale, but she didn't care to imagine what would happen if she tried to open a window to clear it. When the smoke was gone, if there was air enough still to breathe, the soldiers would see …

It was a terrible idea. It had stolen what sleep remained to be had as the hours sped relentlessly towards dawn and the rash, brilliant and crimson, had crept stealthily across Turrow's skin. It came from where the itch feared to go, the place inside herself that was still herself, which was why she was bound to trust it and why it terrified her. It was a *terrible* idea.

Bellows whirred on the streets below. The overhead fans were off, to halt the spread of fire and infection, but the smoke was cloying and lethal in itself, and disease seemed to hang in every particle; it took up the space where air was supposed to be. It clung to the throat and the fibres of the lungs, choked the healthy and finished the ill. The air throbbed with the sound of the engines on the street below — a modified fire engine? It was still too foggy to tell — drowning out the bass rumble of violence that thrummed through the fabric of the building itself. She lit another cigarette; Angelo's stash was not limitless and there was only one packet left when this was finished. Maybe that was best. She smoked slowly, stared out of the window on the grey vista below as wafts of smoke arced beatifically towards the vacuum funnel.

Get some sleep, she'd told him. *Maybe the fever'll break in the night.*

He woke screaming, and she had to throw herself onto him to hold him down as he thrashed. He clawed at her, roared at her, tore her clothes and ripped at her exposed flesh. She swaddled him in blankets and clung to him as he bucked and threw her, screaming words that would have made Cassie blush. They tumbled from the bed and landed heavily on the floor, his weight on top of her forcing the air from her lungs, and she gripped him as she struggled for breath. He fought hard and dirty, but the blankets held him, and when his strength faded, quickly, she wrapped her arms around him and pulled him close, rocking him as he shook and she shook and his eyes rolled in his head.

She dragged him back to bed, set about arranging the covers around him again.

'Don't,' he said. 'Hot.'

'You have a fever,' she reminded him. Blood trickled from her lip where he'd hit it in the struggle, but his eyes were closed, he couldn't see.

'Hot,' he said again.

She drained the syrup from a can of pre-hydrated peaches and fed it to him with a spoon. It was hot, everything was hot now in the apartment, but he sucked lethargically as she tipped liquid through his lips and made no comment. His breath was laced with the metallic scent of blood. From the fight? Maybe. She hoped so.

He drank half of what was in the tin before gently pushing her hand away. 'What *is* that?' he said.

She shrugged. 'Peach juice.'

'It burns.'

'Peach juice doesn't burn, Turrow.'

'It burns.'

She put it aside, sucked the stickiness from her fingers, thinking, *there was not enough time*. She said, 'You need to keep eating.'

'I know.'

'Will you have some more in the afternoon?'

'Maybe. See how I feel.'

He was flattened against the sheets, almost two dimensional. When he spoke, his breath bubbled in his throat. He said, 'How many ambulances this morning?'

'I couldn't see,' she said.

'Liar,' he said.

'I couldn't see, not with the smoke.'

'Liar,' he said again, and she knew he knew.

She smoothed his hair from his forehead, where it was peaked against his skin. Turrow shuffled irritably, tried to shrug off a blanket. 'Leave that,' she said.

He screwed up his face as another spasm hit. She tensed, but it was only an ache; it faded quickly and he exhaled a long, heavy breath. 'It's not fair,' he said.

'Ssh,' she told him.

'It's not fucking fair,' he said. 'All those years. You'll forget about me. All those years and I won't even be there.'

'Don't,' she said.

'And fucking Cassie ... Alex never calls her on her language. And Tilly. I don't know.'

'Don't.'

'Why did I find you at all? It's not fucking fair.'

'You're here now,' she said.

'I'm not going to go,' he said.

18.2

When things were bad, she wandered. There were sections of the city that Danae knew by instinct alone: when her feet were moving, her brain was free to forget or to process, whichever would bring relief. If her feet were moving, she wasn't stuck in a problem. But there was nowhere to wander anymore.

It was a *terrible* idea.

And still she couldn't shake it. She left Turrow sleeping, or at least still and breathing and with closed eyes, and walked where she could.

Doors had been boarded up, daubed with red paint. Sometimes it was symbols, sometimes a *P*, which, she assumed, was for *plague*. Sometimes it was *shit* or *scum*. Here and there, braver souls had scribbled *out*, very occasionally *out out*. Never whole sentences: whatever could be splashed on in seconds before a patrol came around.

Boredom was like a disease; the street was heavy with it. It dragged like sagging flesh off the faces that passed her on the pavements or hung heavily by their doors, roboticised by tedium, eyes dull and listless above wrappings made from scarves or shirts or lengths of gauze. The plastic soldiers drifted past in twos and threes, weapons shouldered, tight with anticipation. Perhaps the fact that Thirty-fifth Avenue North had yet to erupt put them ill at ease: a knowable quantity was easier to deal with.

Here and there, chairs had been dragged from sitting rooms and kitchens, plastic tables raided from cafés without customers, flasks of coffee and bottles of cheap liquor shared among the stragglers. Some played poker, some played chess; some had opened up a screen or two against the wall where the neighbours could watch, from which soft-voiced newsreaders failed to say anything important. Numbers bounced around: fifteen hundred more casualties in the hospitals, nineteen new fatalities and the e-word, *epidemic*, dragged out in Sunday best for its bi-yearly pantomime of thousands, to raised eyebrows, shrugged shoulders and shaken heads. Danae was passing the steps of an old tenement, where a group of grey-haired women had gathered to eat sandwiches, when a fragment of a story caught her ear: some man in Kolasi had tried to melt a plastic bag over his son's face to keep out the infection. There were tuts from the kerbside audience, short words of disbelief and horror muffled through three layers of fabric; the speaker looked as though he were preparing for a sandstorm. But it stabbed a little tender part of Danae's heart as she quickened her step to avoid hearing how it ended: the idea that one could destroy that which they loved, simply because they loved too much.

In the higher reaches of the ceiling the smoke had yet to clear, but from time to time, when she glanced up, the cloud would shift or thin a little, and she could see faces at the windows above, watching in silence. There was no hint of fear or anxiety, and it took her a moment to understand that the crowds below were both the day's entertainment and the invocation that held the worst at bay a little longer. They were watching and waiting to see if anyone would do anything interesting, content if the most fascinating thing anyone did was to cough hard enough to clear a space around them. Creo lived on the streets, they were the veins through which its lifeblood flowed, and now, denied, all they could do was watch. And, more than that, there was a safety in observation. While they were watching, they were not participating, and there was a certain level of macabre comfort in that. Danae wondered if that's what she was trying to do.

Was that a life? Fear and otherness, isolation and solitary decay: it had kept her world tiny, and it had kept it ugly. These past few days had shone so brightly that it was no wonder they had consumed themselves too quickly; she wondered how she had ever convinced herself that so much beauty was possible. Not for her. But it had been so easy to let him enter her completely and surrender to that other longing, the one she hoped was her truer self. It had always been too beautiful to last.

The crowds were smaller than yesterday. Only four ambulances scrambled through the fog. That could mean one of two things.

It was a terrible idea.

18.3

He was lying on the floor in convulsions, tangled in blankets, his head wrapped in a knot of fabric. Danae heard only the sound of it as she entered, a rhythmic whup whup whup like soft rain drops on canvas, and she ran to the bedroom, skidding to her knees across the floor, coming up short, crawling the short distance to where he lay. How long had he been smothered? She could barely work her fingers; her arms were shaking. Every time she tried to grip the blankets, an electric symphony of tremors would jolt him away from her, until she gave up and just ripped at it, not caring if she damaged him, not caring if bones were broken, thinking only of the seconds ticking by.

She tore through layers — how had he managed to wrap himself so tightly? — blankets upon blankets, knotted like Christmas lights. His arms, falling free from the mess of fabric, beat freely against the edge of the bed, knuckles skinning and bruising, blood welling in little pools. She battled on, like a dream: like running through dark corridors without end, chasing after darkness, and when his fit suddenly stopped, his body suddenly went flaccid in her arms, there was nothing to do but keep chasing.

His lips were blue. Danae beat him, hard, on the chest, shook him, squeezed out desperate tears. Only then, floating on panic, did she think to press her hand to his face, to feel for breath.

He was breathing.

She rocked back on her knees, slumped, exhausted against the bed, and cried: great, gulping baby-sobs that were more sound than tears. It was an auto-pilot noise, outside of her control. When the tears stopped, the adrenaline ebbed, and for a second, there was nothing she could do but sag, boneless, against the bed. Her arms were like lead, like air, as though they were filled with worms when she tried to lift them; her throat raw from the animal sounds that had erupted, unheard, as she struggled to free him from the blankets.

He was breathing.

When she was able, knowing that he must be moved, if only to turn him on his side, she crept forward on hands and knees. Her vision swam white for a second, but it cleared, and she pressed a hand to the side of his face, whispering his name. He didn't wake, but it didn't matter; she rolled him onto his side as blood flowed from his nose in a fat red trail, and lay beside him.

It was a terrible idea.

It was the only idea there was.

18.4

It was an hour before he opened his eyes again. Even that was all right by her: she hadn't thought he would. Her mind was full of the possibility of just lying down beside him and sleeping, drifting away and never coming back. It wouldn't be so simple, of course; dying never was. But it was a good dream.

He said, 'My throat.'

She snapped awake, propped herself up on her elbow. 'Do you need some water?'

'Water,' he said.

There wasn't any water. Rather, there *was* — the kitchen was full of it — but there wasn't any water to drink anymore, not after days of lying in the fungal heat, so she did what she could to soften the orange fizzy stuff that had become of the peach juice and tipped a little through his cracked lips. He was swallowing now like a dying man, like they did in films: lips barely parted, head supported by her hand, eyes closed. He took three small sips, then turned his head away, blinked his eyes open.

'It's pink,' he said.

'Don't worry about it,' said Danae.

'I'm not going in the ambulance.'

'Okay.'

She set his head back on the pillow. He rasped a couple of breaths and said, 'Should I go in the ambulance?'

'I don't know,' she said. It was barely a whisper.

'Maybe there's drugs ... or something.'

'Maybe.'

'What if Tilly was really sick when I left her?' A painful swallow. 'I shouldn't have left her.'

'They're fine. Alex says they're fine.'

'Alex ...'

'Yes, I'll get him. I'll get him.'

'Don't go ...'

'I'm not going.' She burrowed down beside him, foetal, and buried her face in his shoulder. 'I'm right here, Turrow. I'm not going anywhere.'

'It's not fair,' he said, and she couldn't answer and still hold the pieces of herself together.

He closed his eyes again, and, after a moment, his breathing lengthened: slow, measured breaths, drowning in fluid.

... two girls sleep on one of two double beds crowded against opposite walls of a darkened room. One of them has stars on her pyjamas and the other has her arms around her, ready to stir at the slightest noise. A sound from the hallway — a door is opening. He can sleep now; they're safe ...

She lay beside him, nestled her head into the hollow of his neck, tracing a finger over his Adam's apple, which trembled faintly with the effort of sucking air into his lungs. In a couple of hours, he would slip away, drifting on black waves into coma, and from there into death. There was no time left.

It was a terrible idea, but there was no time left.

18.5

Blue shadows from the light-bands crept along the wall as the day disappeared. It had taken everything Danae had left in her to open the curtains, but she wanted to see the evening light fall on the gilt-edged wall behind her, to massage the faded red velvet cushions on the huge sofa, thrown into disorder by the lovemaking of another lifetime; to pick out the emotions on the portraits that punctuated the walls; to see what they were leaving. She smoked a ceremonial cigarette – the last in the packet, and that, too, was a fitting end, like a full-stop to close a long sentence. Rain sleeted down like bullets, blurring the grey glass and dimming the world beyond. The fires had started.

Time to go.

He insisted he could walk. What he could *actually* do was lean all his weight on her and shuffle one foot in front of the other with the speed of a retreating glacier, but it was movement, it was life; it was better than nothing. Standing upright, it was terrifying to see how his skin hung from his bones like a baggy suit, and it was too easy to listen to the itch, overloaded on panic, screaming, *no, we've left it too late, go back and let him sleep.* Turrow was hot to the touch, uncomfortably hot, and the effort of keeping him upright had drained the blood from her arms, but still, regardless, she would have strung out the descent from the apartment for hours, for days, indefinitely, for fear of what waited at the end. She could lose him — she knew that — but she couldn't predict her own response. Who, in the end, was stronger: Danae, or what she should have been?

He had stood by that fountain and shouted after her. The man who'd found her, who'd argued with her, who'd followed her up the stairs as she carefully failed to outrun him, had disappeared into darkness somewhere in the rush of days that had passed between then and now; she could barely see him in the shadow figure, the changeling strapped to her side. Maybe it was better this way: there was nothing to give up, no choice to make; these things had been taken from her without a word when she wasn't looking. Maybe that was easiest, after all. It was always too beautiful to last.

Halfway across the lobby, Turrow's footsteps faltered and his head swung low and Danae slid to the floor with him, but it wasn't a fit, only a blackout. When he came to, he said, 'Is it evening?'

'It's nearly night,' she said.

'I hope you get out,' he said. 'I hope you ...' Trailing off, resuming with effort: 'I hope you get your sky back.'

'We should keep moving,' she said.

The patrols were smaller now, but a constant presence as the scent of burning tyres and petrol inched closer. By the end of the street, Turrow's legs were like rubber bands; it had taken everything in him to get this far, and her arms were white and bloodless with the effort of holding him. His hair was matted to his head with sweat and rain; his clothes were soaked; his skin slipped and skittered beneath her grip; his chest was almost concave beneath his saturated sweater with the effort it took to draw breath. But he raised his head as they breached the junction with Thirty-fifth Avenue North, emptied by the rain of its street population of the bored and restless, twisted his face towards her, pulled his lips back into something that was almost certainly meant to be a grin.

'See?' he said. 'Made it. Told you I wasn't sick.'

And Danae made herself smile back, because her face was already wet, her eyes already so red-rimmed with exhaustion that they couldn't call her a liar, and said, 'Yeah, good point, Turrow. Let's go home.'

Behind her, muffled by the clatter of water on concrete, she could hear the sounds of footfall; six pairs of feet approaching in tandem. The whine of the medevac vans had begun to punch through the wall of rain, setting her teeth on edge. It was over. There wasn't enough time, but it was already past.

Her knees buckled without warning and they slumped to the ground, Danae kneeling, Turrow sagging in her arms. Shouts in French, a language she barely knew, told her they'd been spotted, and when she looked up, two soldiers had broken free from a patrol and were moving towards her, gesturing to another to follow. Creo, the great melting pot: within the sovereign boundaries of France, but not a part of France, whose citizens spoke the tongue of their ancestors whenever they needed to buy food and clothes and alcohol, but stared blankly at the official language of their own country.

The hum of the ambulance had risen to a roar, magnified by the concrete canyon of apartment fronts as it descended to the ground. The soldiers were speaking to her now, but Danae couldn't hear them, couldn't tell if they were speaking French or English or something else, couldn't tell whether their voices were obscured by the wail of the siren or the rush of blood in her ears. With effort, she planted one foot on the ground, raised herself an inch or so. Her knees were sticky with green slime; Turrow was slick with it where he'd fallen with her. His arms flailed in the air, struggling for purchase; he was trying to help her, but without the strength to hold up his head. She heaved at him, like a leaden rag doll, and managed to pull him out of his slump, enough to lever them upwards another inch. Her vision swam white with the effort — not enough sleep, not enough food, too many silent hours wrapped in fear and indecision — and then, suddenly, there were other hands lifting him, lifting the pressure from her arms, which tingled as the blood flowed back.

'Nous lui avons,' said a voice, though Danae couldn't tell which one had spoken, and her gaze swept wildly from face to plastic face, masks in the half-light. The rain beat onto her head in heavy, black pellets, bruising her scalp, drizzling into her eyes. Where it ran down the plastic faces, they seemed to be melting, and she wanted to shout, *not yet, I'm not ready.*

'We have him,' said the voice again — the same voice? 'He will be fine. Are you ill?'

'Danae,' said Turrow. He was trying to raise his head.

'Not yet,' she said, but it was a whisper.

'He will be fine, miss.' It was a friendly voice, muffled by the roar of the ambulance as it began to descend, but it was lying. She scanned their faces, wanting something to take with her, something to remember, and she realised she was still clinging to his hand.

'Turrow, you'll be all right,' she told him. Her throat was dry, the words scratched out, and they disappeared into the fog of noise. *Not yet. Oh, God, not yet.*

A gentle, insistent tug, and his hand fell away from hers. She ran after them onto the road, rain whipping her face, pooling down her cheeks. 'You'll be all right,' she shouted. 'I'll see you. I'll see you soon.'

It was enough that he would live. Two hundred years was too long.

'Wait!' she shouted. 'Wait. You have to take me too. I'm an a-naut.'

18.6

Calm.

Pockets of activity: like surfacing from a deep lake. Like a series of photographs, seen in flashback.

Flash.

Turrow animates suddenly as he realises what she's doing, but not why. He screams her name, so loud that she can hear it over the bellow of the ambulance engines as they descend the final feet to the ground. Danae realises, distractedly, that this is why air transport is banned in the lower city: dust, heavy with rainwater, flies from the street, as thick as the smoke. She can smell burning from somewhere: burning plastic, or is it rubber? She notices these things disjointedly, because she has spoken now, she can't take it back, and it's a focus for her scattering brain.

Danae, he shouts. *What are you doing? What are you* doing?

The soldiers want to know too. They turn to each other for back-up; this has never happened before.

Not the Rens, she's thinking. *Anything but the Rens.*

She steps forward, offering her hands.

Elle dit qu'elle est une ruisseant.

Quoi?

Elle est une ruisseant! Obtenez le capitaine.

He's screaming himself hoarse, and with every cry erupts a new choking, hacking cough. He can't understand; no one can. The soldiers are milling about, wondering what to do. One of them takes her firmly by the shoulder as another emerges from the patrol and crosses to her.

He says you say you are a-naut, he says.

She says, *I can help. I think ... my blood can help. It's ... complicated.*

Now Turrow understands. *Oh, no,* he moans. *Danae, no. Oh, no.*

You understand, says the captain, *I can't protect you.*

I understand, says Danae. If only her voice wouldn't shake as she says it; if only her legs wouldn't feel as though they'll collapse under her weight. They're tearing him away now; he's trying to fight, but he can no more resist their pull than he can take back her words. He's getting weaker, his cries are getting weaker, and she knows that this is the last time she'll see him. She nearly falters then, nearly breaks free to run after him, but she doesn't want his last sight of her to be a gunshot erupting from her forehead. She shouts after him, *It'll be all right, Turrow. It'll be all right. It'll be all right.*

*

Flash.

They press her face against the wall, thick with slime: the algae are having a party in these days of perpetual rain. She swivels her head before it hits so that it is her cheek that strikes concrete, not her nose and mouth, forces her lips closed. The itch explodes out of her – this is what the itch is all about, after all – and it's everything she can do not to give into it. One of them is patting her down for weapons; she knows they are afraid of her, *because* she gave herself up.

Not the Rens, she's thinking. *Please, God, not the Rens.*

The captain is a good man, she thinks. Not the Rens. She wants him to hear her, but she can't say the words.

*

Flash.

The blow comes out of nowhere, propelling her forwards. Her arms are taped behind her back and she can't steady herself and so she falls hard, slamming into the door of the prison car that they've called to take her away. It knocks the wind out of her and she slumps, helpless, onto her knees, tasting acid. Rain sleets down on her like shot blast, hammering into her skull, falling from her open mouth as her stomach heaves. She's dead already. Nausea is nothing.

The ambulance is gone. Everything that still mattered went with it. She just wants them to leave her alone.

A voice behind her shouts: *Hé! Pensez-vous que c'est drôle? Est-il drôle?*

An arm reaches under the tape, lifts her by the elbow. It's the captain. He's a good man, she thinks.

★

Flash.

She's in a car and there is a canvas bag over her head, fastened at the neck. It's been doused in something that smells like sugar left to go bad; she thinks there's a trace of almond there too, but it's slowed her thoughts down to a thick, syrupy crawl and it's made her limbs go boneless. Her arms are still taped behind her back and the blood has long ceased to flow. Her legs are manacled to the seat. She's trying to suck air through burlap, but her lungs know that there is something wrong with the oxygen they're getting and her breathing is too rapid, too shallow. Danae sees her life in rapid fire stills before her: childhood, the Dales, her mother, her father, the sun, the sky, the sky, the sky. The lower city, Nadine and the café, Kim Li, adolescence, the constant rain, all the shades of Limbe, her eighteenth birthday that nobody remembered, even herself, Turrow. *Turrow.* It's like a merry-go-round, but it's spinning too quickly; she wants it to stop.

She says, thickly, 'Where will he go?'

No-one answers. She tries again. 'Will they take him to the hospital?'

Silence. 'What, is it a state secret? Is he in the hospital?' The thought of Turrow lying, disregarded, like a piece of meat, hurts her head.

'The hospitals are full,' says one of the soldiers. It's not the captain's voice, but she can detect the captain's surly influence in the response. 'He will go to a pod.'

The hospitals are full? she thinks. Creo's hospitals have a capacity of two hundred and fifty thousand. The main campus covers half a district.

'Where am I going?' she asks, but there is no answer. She doesn't expect one.

★

Flash.

There are steps. She panics and can't make her legs work. You hear stories about the death centres: above ground, underground, places no-one ever goes. Steps are always involved. She stumbles, retches dry air, finds that she can't breathe. Nothing, nothing can persuade her legs to carry her into the place, she can't even find the words to say it. It isn't how she wanted it to be, she wanted dignity at least, but there is no explaining this to her body. Her body wants to live.

Kicks rain down on her, vicious words. She wants to explain, she wants at least the chance to speak, but the kicks are relentless. If she had breath in her lungs she would shriek at them, *how is this supposed to help?* But instead she kicks out, backwards, like a bucking horse, and, though her legs feel like they've been hollowed out and filled with water, though she knows her movements are slow, clumsy, she's still faster than them and she feels her foot strike bone with force enough to bruise. The itch makes her do it and it won't let her stop. They shout, startled, though it can hardly have surprised them; this is why they've put a bag on her head and drugged it with something that smells like rancid honey. She can hear their consternation, their uncertainty, their hushed-voice debate, because they've only ever heard about people like her, and, faced with three days' basic training suddenly made flesh, they don't know what to do. Then there is a sharp report and there is enough of her left to identify it as a gunshot, and there is a screaming pain in her collar bone. For a white-hot, blinding moment she knows she is dead, and it's almost a pleasure that it came so unexpectedly. Then there is a pneumatic hiss and the pressure of an air bullet alongside the pain and suddenly she's underwater, floating in a viscous grey soup. She can hear them but she is not among them; the itch is silent.

Hands lift her; raise her to her feet, and her arms, denuded of blood and oxygen, scream in protest. She can't form the words to speak, even to offer a word of thanks. Blank-eyed, she searches the shades of light and dark on the inside of her blindfold, but the voice, when it comes, is behind her.

'Forward. You go, come.'

Her legs move; under what authority she doesn't know. Her brain is furiously elsewhere, swimming in limbo.

★

Flash.

She's in a cell. The bare brick walls are painted a yellowish, utilitarian cream, the light poorly filtered through a shaded window, set just above eye-height. A blanketless cot is the only furniture. Sporadic echoes bounce down the corridor outside, speaking of scattered groups of people closed into other rooms like this, and she knows that she is guarded because, if she presses her head to the thick metal door, she can hear a muffled murmur of conversation. Two men, bored and unfamiliar, laughing vacantly about the sorts of things two men who are not friends are permitted to discuss.

At least they've taken away the blindfold. She was startled by the swiftness of the action, no warning given, and she blinked in the half-light as her eyes began to water. They haven't untied her hands. The fingers are cold now, numb and bloodless, and she knows that, if they're ever free again, it will be many minutes before they are of any use to her. Her head is sick and heavy with sedative. The thought comes to her like a winged messenger: *they are afraid of her*. It's something of a comfort.

Where are they? Why don't they come for her?

She doesn't think she is in a death centre. The room has the wrong kind of aura: it doesn't feel as though it's a room in which people have died. There is no scent of despair in the air, but, then again, she can't trust herself, she can't trust her perceptions: she wants so desperately to live.

The light outside the window is almost gone. Turrow is like a presence beside her, so close that she can almost make out the contours of his face in the last pale hours of day. She feels him watching her, and a voice in her brain chants a lonely mantra on a three-second loop, over and over and over: *This is the last day of my life, this is the last day of my life, this is the last day of my life …*

★

Flash.

She must have slept, because the light is now completely gone. A tightness at her face confuses her for a moment and then she tastes bitter caramel at the back of her throat, feels the weight in her bound arms, her manacled legs, and understands that the sleep was unconsciousness; that they have sedated her and fitted her with a hazmask that's pumping medicated air into her lungs. At least her thoughts are clearer now; she wonders vaguely if the chemical agent is different to the one on her canvas blindfold, or if it's just a question of dosage, and she finds herself wishing that she had a watch, or some better access to the light-bands, so that there would be some way to gauge the passage of the hours. Where is he now? Has he passed from the long lines of slowly declining, faceless ill into the care of a doctor, nurses? If she knew how long had passed, she would have some way of guessing, but she has only the lengthening shadows and they are no kind of guide.

She is about to wonder again why no one comes for her when there is a sudden commotion at the door outside. She tries to stand up, with a sharp intake of breath, forgetting that she's manacled, forgetting that she's drugged. The world starts to spin and she wishes that she were not alone, that there was someone, *anyone*, to offer her the smallest word of comfort now.

Not the Rens. Please, please, please not the Rens.

But the man who enters doesn't look like a man of action. She revises the thought: he doesn't look like her *idea* of a man of action. He's an administrator; it's practically tattooed on his forehead, but maybe even the Rens have paperwork? It doesn't occur to her to wonder what possible place she could have in Ren red tape; she's not that focused just now.

She wants to speak first, but her lips are frozen together. She can only watch as, flanked by two guards on either side, he makes his way into the room and stands in front of her. It's an effort to roll her head on her shoulders so that she can angle her eyes upwards onto his, but this is important.

He says, 'I believe you go by the name Grant? Danae Grant?'

She manages a nod. 'My arms are numb,' she tells him, and her voice, strained through the modulation panel, sounds like it belongs to somebody else. 'I can't feel my fingers.'

He nods again and two guards step forward. One of them rolls her onto her front and holds her down, the other unfastens the bindings at her wrists, pulls her arms forwards to rest at her stomach, refastens them. Blood flows back, sharply painful, and Danae sucks in a harsh little breath as the tingling starts, like worms in her bones. Her arms are dead arms, as though they weren't connected to her body; they don't respond to command.

He says, 'I need you to explain to me how you think you can help.'

THE DEMOCRAT, 6TH FEBRUARY 2077

In a bid to quell the growing unease surrounding the disappearance of a-naut leader G-QZ1484, Congressional spokesperson Bastían Astridsson has today announced the reopening of communications with representatives from Emancipation, who claim to speak for the unit. Speculation is rife as to the nature of the negotiations and what, if anything, might be back on the table. In a statement issued this afternoon, Mr Astridsson denied that the move was a response to any threat, implied or otherwise, and reiterated that the government does not negotiate with terrorists.

Meanwhile, police in Dundee, St Petersburg and Geneva have arrested seven men in connection with the so-called 'Tree of Liberty' streamport, to which users were encouraged to upload images and footage of a-nauts being beaten or deactivated. The men, who have not been named, are all thought to be members of the paramilitary Renegade Elimination Network, which released a manifesto in December calling for an armed response to the a-naut situation.

19.1

The Angel of Death hovered three inches above Danae's bed. She spent dark hours challenging him to a staring contest, knowing who would win, but it was good practice, and, in the end, she was glad of the company as the night wound on. Every time a footstep clipped smartly past the door in the corridor outside, his lipless mouth curled into a rictus that was halfway between a grimace and a smile, and once, when the observation panel on the door swung open, he started laughing softly as she scrambled awkwardly upright on instinct alone and the itch screamed, *now? Now can I?* But it was nothing, a silent, faceless check-up, watched by eyes she couldn't see, and it was over before she managed to make her legs start working. Unseen cameras tracked and swivelled with her, but she knew they were there only by the sound they made at the back of her skull; otherwise, she was completely alone.

'How long have I been here?' she shouted at them. 'Just tell me that!'

Nothing, no answer, no indication that she'd been heard: only the sound of footsteps clipping smartly past the door and down the corridor and the echo of distant voices.

Sometimes, a light would flare suddenly on the wall opposite the window: reflected headlights of a moving vehicle. She knew that she was in a holding centre, but whether it was part of an army barracks or a civilian jail she couldn't tell, though she guessed the former: only the emergency services had access to off-ground vehicles in the lower city, and she wasn't on the ground floor. The lights were like a Christmas present: a sign of life, a connection to the outside world, a break in the monotony. The Angel of Death wasn't keen on them either, so that was also a point in their favour.

When the corridor was quiet, it was possible to be calm. It was possible to believe that Turrow was being cared for, that whatever they were giving him was enough to hold back the sickness until whatever red tape got sorted out that needed to be sorted out and Danae did what needed to be done. It was possible to believe that she was just in a room, not the most salubrious, but comfortable enough, and that she could leave at any time. It was possible to play out scenarios in which she was hailed as the saviour of the city and carried through the streets in triumph, or even just given a warm handshake and a heartfelt 'thank you' and left to her own devices. The images dissolved like mirages when the footsteps clicked into the edge of hearing; shrank to a point and blanked into darkness as the fear rushed in to fill the vacuum. But they were good images.

She slept. In the face of overwhelming narcosis, it was the only thing to do. The Angel of Death smirked a lot, but he was no conversationalist, and he had a tendency towards pessimism that she could do without. She wasn't aware of any driving urge to sleep, only the background omnipresent tug of sedative, but she closed her eyes for a change of scene and amalgamated gently with unconsciousness. She saw the lake, narrow and deep, stretching like the ocean from peak to peak and the fish that still flopped from time to time on the slick, oily shore. She saw the hulk of the old steamer, relic of some hundred years earlier, when the lake was a tourist attraction, skeletal and rusting and the source of countless nightmares when the moon hit it just right. She saw the ruined village nestled at the foot of the rolling hills, hills so high and louring that, to a child, they seemed to stretch into infinity, and her mother, tall beside her, squeezing her hand and saying, *race you to the tree stump*. She saw herself, her younger self, tearing off along the path, running for the joy of running, and her mother behind her, trying not to catch up…

She snapped awake. The surfacing was brutal, the dream-picture shattered into a million shards, and for a second, disoriented, she couldn't remember where she was or why her heart was thumping in her chest.

The door swung open.

Danae couldn't see the faces, just the shadows where their faces should have been, with the light from the corridor crowning three heads like a halo. Her shoulders scrabbled uselessly against the cot and the Angel of Death let out a low cackle: deep, with plenty of momentum. A series of tiny, subtle *clicks* told her that three weapons had been trained on her, safety catches lifted.

A fourth voice said, 'Danae Grant?'

She managed a nod. 'Yes.'

Two haloed heads broke formation to cross the room, shattering the shadows, and the panic rose like a wave at high tide, swallowing her before she could collect the presence of mind to make her legs move. And then, suddenly, there were rough hands beneath her arms, tugging her upright, dragging her off the bed and planting her on the floor, and the voice said, 'Ms Grant, my name is Kevin Ackerman; I work for Senator Hadaway. I'd like you to follow me.'

19.2

Ackerman led the way. Danae followed close behind, flanked on either side and to the rear by three heavily-armed soldiers, so dour and taciturn that she started to wonder if they might actually be deaf. Liquid fatigue flowed in her veins, gentle enough to allow her brain to function, heavy enough to dull her reflexes and confound the itch, which howled a protest in the middle distance, lost against the background wash of white noise and generalised panic.

She was led through a system of corridors, windowless and airless, sharp with the scent of disinfectant and not much else. The walls were painted but not plastered, but the echoes of other voices receded as they walked, disappearing into the distance, so that the only sound became the snap of six sets of heels on tile. Once, as they passed into a stairwell ringed with doors on all four sides, she caught sight of a clock on the wall of one of the dark hallways beyond and saw that the time was two forty-three. That made it almost five and a half hours since she had left him.

Five and a half hours.

In five and a half hours, the sickness would have massed in his bloodstream, ready for the final onslaught. His temperature would be spiking, his lungs slowly filling with fluid, his skin swollen and hot to the touch. The fits would come faster and harder with every hour that passed, gripping him for longer, making it more difficult each time for him to come back. With every minute that slipped away without action, the window for saving him edged a little further shut; she gave him maybe another ten hours, then brain damage might set in. What was the point of a grand gesture when there was no one to make it for? Danae tried to dig her nails into her palm, to gouge out some of the panic with sensation, but her fingers were slack, disconnected from somatic control; her hands wouldn't obey.

They pulled up at a door in a corridor full of doors. There was nothing remarkable about this one: it was spaced as evenly as the others, painted the same shade of public-facility green, finished as cheaply and as uniformly as the rest. The only distinguishing feature, besides the fact that it was the only one they'd stopped at, was the plaque, set at eye-height and inscribed in black on brass, announcing the occupant as Colonel Jean-Michel Lataille and listing a series of acronyms that Danae didn't recognise. Ackerman knocked, and she tried to keep her head from slumping forward on her neck.

'Come,' said a voice from inside, and, whoever it belonged to, it wasn't Colonel Jean-Michel Lataille. The voice was female.

They followed Ackerman into an ante-room decorated in shades of gunmetal grey. Chairs lined one wall, wood-effect but stripped back, utilitarian, uncomfortable; these were chairs designed for waiting in, not chairs designed for comfort. A potted plant in one corner gave battle against chronic neglect, leaves scattering the surface of the soil and the dry saucer in which it stood, and an oil painting of crinolined ladies on the banks of a river hung on the far wall, comprising the sum total of interior-decorative efforts. It was more than Danae had seen anywhere else in the building as they'd walked, and, she thought, it hinted at the importance of Colonel Jean-Michele Lataille in the complicated political food chain of places that painted doors in uniform public-facility green, but more interesting than cheap riverscapes and withering greenery was the door on the other side of the room: redwood-panelled and halfway ajar, and leading into a large, well-furnished office where a single woman sat at a desk in the light of an anglepoise lamp.

She looked up as the door to the ante-room closed. 'Come in, please,' she said, and turned back to her terminal screen to ignore them while they complied.

The office was big. Not big like the Authority was big, but big like the apartment was big. It was ostentation by size, not possessions, for the room was largely empty: the desk took up the corner by the darkened window, behind which a bookcase with no books on it reached to the ceiling. Two brocade-covered occasional chairs stood in front, edging the plain, cheerless rug that covered most of the carpet-tiled floor, and on the other side of the desk was a comfortable, high-backed swivel chair, in which sat the woman who was not Lataille.

She was tall and fine-boned, somewhere in the middle of middle-aged, with black hair that she'd scraped back from her face into a complicated knot. Her suit was dark, well-cut, expensive, but the body it covered was too angular to disguise with clean lines; sharp collarbone framing her neck in shadow, spoiling the line of a chain of pearls and leading the eye upwards, over a long throat to a pronounced chin, high cheekbones, a well-sculpted nose. It was not a beautiful face but it was striking, and, though the eyes were red-rimmed and the skin around them grey with sleep-deprivation, the look she trained on Danae was unmistakably the look of a powerful woman.

'Thank you, Captain,' she said. 'If you and your men could wait outside. I'll let you know when we're ready.'

Her tone was neutral, the tone of a woman used to being obeyed. Danae did not turn her head to watch the guards leave, but kept her eyes fixed on the woman in the chair. She had her eyes turned on her screen again, as though she were not aware of Danae's presence, but as the door clicked softly shut, she said, 'Please sit down, Ms Grant: we have a lot to talk about and I don't have a lot of time.'

Danae didn't move. The woman shrugged very slightly, as though Danae's comfort or lack of it were all one to her. 'Suit yourself,' she said. 'You have enough sedative in your system right now to floor a battalion; you're welcome to see how long your legs hold out.'

Something about her smelled wrong, but the bindings had begun to chafe on Danae's wrists, still tender from their previous bondage, and it pulled her concentration into her hands. She shifted uncomfortably, which only made them worse.

The woman glanced up. 'Painful, I suppose?'

Danae shrugged. Her head sat straight on her neck; her shoulders were fixed tightly in place. Only her eyes betrayed sedation and there was nothing she could do about that. 'If you're counting on them to keep you safe,' Danae said, 'I hate to burst your bubble. I could have your neck broken before you opened your mouth to scream.'

The woman laughed. 'I doubt that.'

Danae flexed her fingers, felt the blood shift, pool, fail to flow. The woman looked up, all sophisticated amusement, and the lamplight on her face shifted as she did, but the shadows were wrong, the angle of the light was wrong, the dimensions of the chair were wrong against her body.

And suddenly Danae understood. 'You're a hologram,' she said.

'I am,' said the woman. 'From where you're standing, anyway. I'm not sure this is really the time to be paying a personal visit to Creo, are you?'

She smiled. Danae did not. 'I'm not sure you're in the right office, either,' she said.

The smile, if anything, widened. She said, 'We've done some work with Colonel Lataille in the past. He's coordinating part of the quarantine relief effort on the ground.'

'He's doing a shitty job of it,' said Danae.

'He's doing the best job he can,' said the woman coldly. 'And I'm not sure you're in a position to be lecturing anybody on how to manage this situation.'

'I turned myself in,' said Danae. 'I don't see what else I'm supposed to do that's better at managing this situation.'

'Yes,' said the woman. 'You turned yourself in. And that's the only reason, by the way, that you're not in a Ren cell right now, having a long conversation about why the hell this city has nearly three hundred thousand people in hospital, dying from an a-naut engineered virus that's currently sitting at a seventy-five percent mortality rate. But, believe me, that time will come. Right now, I want to know what you're offering to do to help.'

'A-nauts?' Danae's legs were beginning to tremble with the effort of keeping her upright, but now was most definitely not the time to let herself drop into one of the seats. The tone of bewilderment was damaging enough to the balance of power in the room. 'A-nauts didn't do this. How the hell would a-nauts do this?'

'You tell me.'

'If I knew' — one knee threatened to buckle, but she had just enough left in her to hold it in place —'if I had any idea how this started, why do you think I'd have come to you? I thought it was supposed to be anthrax.'

'No,' said the woman, 'you didn't.'

No. She didn't. Nothing about the spread pattern said *anthrax*, and she'd known that from the beginning. So had most of the city, of course, but Danae had the strongest suspicion that semantics weren't going to get her very far just now. So, in lieu of an answer, she shuffled sideways while her legs would still work and lowered herself into one of the brocade chairs with all the dignity she could muster from elastic limbs. The cushions were overstuffed and staggeringly uncomfortable, but at least now she could devote all her remaining energy to keeping her neck upright.

'If I had any idea how this started,' said Danae again, 'do you think I would have come to you? Please. *Please*. Whatever this is, whatever is causing it, I know I can help. I'm sure I can. But there isn't much time.'

Somewhere far away, the woman sat back in her chair, and, in the bowels of Creo Basse, a holoprogramme struggled to adapt her movement to the furniture in the room. The seat cushions didn't move as she relaxed against them, but at least she didn't disappear into the seat itself.

She said, 'Standard procedure should have had you in an interrogation room five hours ago, you know. Nobody here is happy that I've made them hold onto you; they're convinced you're infected or worse and you're going to take out half the building before dawn. I haven't completely decided that you're not. But there are a couple of things that make me want to hear what you have to say, Ms Grant, and the first of them is that you came to us.'

'Yes. I came to you; I want to help ...'

'The second is that you came in with someone. An organic human, who's currently in an AIP in South District with a fever of one hundred and five, and who was almost certainly infected by you.'

'Is he all right?' said Danae. Her voice was hoarse, far too quiet, but it was as much as she could manage while her mind was preoccupied with ignoring the *infected by you.*

'This came from a-nauts. Patient Zero was an a-naut. The invading pathogen is a modified a-naut cell. You tell me how I'm supposed to trust an a-naut who says she can stop this?'

'Because,' said Danae, and stopped. That was not going to be the tone she used in the woman's presence; that was not going to be the volume or the strength of her voice. There were limits. 'Because,' she said again — better — 'I need him to be all right.'

'Just him? Not the three hundred thousand people who are all going to die over the next few days or weeks? One person you want to save—not a whole city?'

'It won't just be the city,' said Danae. 'Jesus, when has a lock-down ever contained anything in Creo long-term? It won't just be the city — you know that.'

A long silence. 'Yes.'

'And what fucking good will your hologram suite do you then?'

An elegant eyebrow arched, but the woman said nothing, dipping her eyes to her lap. Even that gesture, typically submissive, she carried like a queen; as though her stare was something to be earned, and, when she looked back up to find Danae's gaze levelled on her, unblinking and unmoved, her lips twisted upwards into a tight little smile.

'The transmission rate is alarmingly high,' she said, 'but it's not universal. We'll work out how to stop it spreading; most likely before it leaves Western France. But a cure would be better. You told my colleague that you have some kind of magic blood, I believe?'

'I said I thought my blood could help,' said Danae.

'And *I* thought he was either joking or stupid at first — a-naut blood couldn't fight off the common cold. But you're not precisely a-naut, are you? You're Progeny.'

Danae's eyes were steady on hers. 'Yes.'

'Any other day, that would be a problem by itself. Do you have any idea how much money Congress has ploughed into claiming that you guys don't exist? But I've never heard of one of you reaching adulthood, so I'm going to assume you're better than most at keeping your head down. Which probably means you haven't shot up any shopping malls yet.'

'I haven't done anything wrong,' said Danae. Her voice was level; her mask held her expression in place. She would not sound desperate; she would not. 'I'm here of my own accord, because I think I can help. Please.'

The woman's eyes flickered to her screen, though Danae privately doubted that there was anything there that she needed to check. As gestures of interpersonal engagement went, it didn't exactly inspire her with confidence.

'Cybodynamic immune system,' said the woman, as though she were reading from a script. Maybe it was written in front of her, but it certainly didn't sound like the first time she had spoken the words out loud. 'You want to explain to me exactly what that is? I've been reading up on your generation for the last two hours and I can't find any mention of it.'

'It means,' said Danae, 'that instead of just papering over the holes and hoping for the best, the Progeny system can actually adapt to infection. And it can do it a damn sight better than yours.'

The woman folded her hands across her chest with an air of rising impatience, and Danae she got the distinct impression that rising impatience in this woman was something to be avoided. 'Yes,' she said, 'I'm aware of all of that: I've been reading for two hours. What I'm not aware of is what your immune system actually *does*. The Progeny were able to resist everything we ever threw at them, but we're still no closer to understanding why.'

'What are you talking about?' said Danae, although she thought she knew. The words had dropped like cold stones into her stomach. 'Understanding … what? What are you talking about?'

'You know what I'm talking about,' said the woman, and her face was locked-down, steel and granite. 'You know you're not the first Progeny that ever came to light. You *know* this. Grendelheim. Indianapolis. Keflavik. At least fifteen others. Wipe the horror off your face, Ms Grant — what did you think happened to the killers when they were caught? We studied them. Of course we did. We'd have had to have a deathwish not to try and find out how they worked.'

All those times. All those times the stream warped and she didn't know what it was. All those voices, all that fear, all that agony. And so many of them had taken their first breath in the same dark room as her. So many of them had shared her blood.

Danae knew what was in her eyes; knew that the woman could see it. But she, bodily secure many miles away, was unconcerned.

'I have a pathogen based on an a-naut immune cell that's replicating in the human blood stream,' she said, as though she hadn't just told Danae that two dozen of her siblings had been strapped to a lab table and experimented on to death. 'The cytokine response is off the scale. It's mimicking Host-versus-Graft disease but the a-cell is too hardy to destroy and it just keeps reproducing until the system goes into a full-scale inflammatory response and the organs start shutting down. We can treat the symptoms but we can't treat the pathogen because it turns out that immunosuppressants only work on the human cells and all the patients we treated were dead within four hours. This would be a disaster all by itself, but for some reason the a-cell is behaving like a bacterium and passing from person to person, and we have literally no idea how to make it stop. So - before I lose my temper I need you to tell me right now: what is a cybodynamic immune system and how is it supposed to help put a lid on this thing?'

The itch, buried beneath narcotics, whined like a prisoner in a far-off room. Danae closed her eyes to buy herself the moment she needed, but all there was in the darkness was Turrow's face lit by its inner sun, flashing a smile over his shoulder.

She opened her eyes. 'All this work you did on the Progeny, on our immune system,' she said and, though her chest felt like it was encased in rock, her voice was level. 'Was anyone measuring the uplink response?'

The woman raised an eyebrow. 'Are you sure you want to know?'

'Do I want to know if you tortured them? I think I have my answer to that. No. I want to know if the uplink response was measured during the pathogen trials.'

'The subjects were continuously monitored. Brain function was closely observed.'

Danae shook her head. 'That's not what I was asking. I meant the cellular uplink.'

The silence told her a lot. Into the vacuous cavern of speechlessness, the woman offered a second eyebrow.

Presently, Danae said, 'Okay. No wonder you couldn't tell how it worked.'

A slow smile spread uneasily across the woman's face. She said, 'Are you telling me that your immune system itself is directly connected to the datastream at the cellular level?'

'I am,' she said.

'This is a cybodynamic immune system?'

'It functions in a similar way to yours, except that the uplink is dynamic — it can send and receive information. If this is an a-naut pathogen, then the coding for it, the programming, exists in a pocket of Red Space.'

'Exactly,' said the woman. 'We can't kill it, and we can't access its protocols to switch it off. It's a perfect storm of biological genocide.'

'But,' said Danae quietly, 'I'm Progeny. My cells uplink to Red Space. And if I passed the illness to Turrow, I have had this pathogen in my bloodstream. My immune system knows it.'

The woman's stare was level, evaluative. It was a *good* stare.

'Your immune system might know how to fight this off,' she said, 'but I'm not sure you have enough immunity to share with the rest of us. What are you proposing?'

Danae sucked in a breath. 'I think…' she said, 'that what you have is a little bit like a nanon. Right? It's basically a biological engine that's programmed by the datastream to do a job.'

'Except that nanons don't replicate.'

'No, but isn't that because the datastream tells them not to?'

Silence. Then some more silence, and then a little more. The woman unfolded her arms, clasped her hands in her lap instead, then thought better of it and raised her right to pick at a hangnail on her index finger. The nails were manicured, immaculately painted, but the skin around them was chewed and red. It was something. It was human at least.

'You think,' she said, 'that your immune response can tell this pathogen to stop?'

'I think it can do that inside my system,' said Danae. 'And I think that, to do this, it needs to communicate with the pathogen's stream pocket. And I think — I *think* — that, if you can measure the uplink when the live pathogen enters my bloodstream, then you'll have access to the pathogen's protocol pocket in Red Space.'

'You think. That's not a lot of certainty.'

'It's better than the alternative,' said Danae

The woman tilted her head, conceding the point. 'And what if there's no uplink response when the pathogen enters your bloodstream? Your system has already neutralised it once. Will it respond the same way on reinfection?'

'I don't know,' said Danae. 'I don't even know if you can measure the response. All I can tell you for sure right now is that somewhere on the stream there exists the sequencing that programmes this pathogen, and that my phagocytes have accessed it and used it to clear my system. I can't access it, not deliberately or consciously, but if you can measure my cellular uplink during reinfection, you'll have both the access to the protocol that'll let you take control of the replication process, and you'll have the coding to programme a nanon horde to destroy the cells that have already been produced. If you can do this, you've got a viable treatment programme, and this is over.' She forced herself to breathe evenly, to look the woman in the eye. To erase every thought of begging from her consciousness so that it would not show in her face. And she said, 'I don't have to be dead for this to happen.'

Her hands would not respond to commands, and this was certainly a sensible precaution. If Danae could use her hands, she could snap the restraints that bound her as easily as she could snap the bones of anyone who tried to stop her from escaping. Right now, she needed to be here; escape was not an option. But she would have liked to have been able to dig her fingers into the soft flesh at the top of her thighs, so deeply that they gouged purple crescents in the skin. She would have liked something to anchor her.

Calm.

'Ms Grant,' said the woman, 'I believe you are trying to strike a deal.'

Calm.

'I don't have to be dead,' she said again.

The woman steepled her hands. She exhaled. She said, 'I don't have the authority to offer you anything. I'm a political aide. This is not my decision.'

'But you can talk to the people who make the decision.'

'I can talk. They're not going to listen.'

Please. 'I came to you,' she said. 'Look what I'm giving you.'

The woman looked down at her steepled fingers for a moment, and when she looked up again her eyes were fixed on Danae's. 'Ms Grant,' she said. 'You're an a-naut. Do you know how many people have died so far this year in a-naut attacks?'

Calm. 'No.'

'Thirty-nine. Now, that's down on last year, but it's not good. That's thirty-nine families missing a loved one. That's thirty-nine families that would kick up all kinds of hell if it came out that we had an a-naut in custody and let her go.'

'If it came out,' said Danae, and she realised that her voice was ascending the octaves, spiralling into shrill panic. She stopped herself, waited a moment. 'There's no reason it would come out.'

'These things always do,' said the woman. 'Ms Grant, not only are you an a-naut, you're an a-naut designed by a-nauts specifically to kill people. How can I let you go?'

'I've never....' There it was again: a catch in her throat, the beginning of tears. 'I've never killed anybody. I haven't done anything wrong.'

'The sins of the fathers,' said the woman, and shrugged as though she hadn't just dismissed an entire life in aphorism. 'I never said it was fair. But you didn't really think you were going to walk away from this, did you?'

No, she hadn't. But she had hoped. If she hadn't hoped, how could she have done it?

Danae said, 'All I want is my life. All I want is what was mine to begin with.'

'Miss Grant,' said the woman, 'I'm trying to make this easy for you. There are things I can do. I can make sure your friend is well treated. I can make sure he's first in line if this cure of yours works. But that's it — I can't bring you back to life.'

'What if I die, right now?' Danae's mind was reeling. 'What if I just slip away? Right now? Before you get your fucking cure?'

The woman didn't roll her eyes, but she came close.

'How?' she said. 'How are you planning to make this happen? You're bound and sedated and you're in the centre of one of the most secure facilities in Creo Basse. How do you think you're going to make yourself slip away, Ms Grant?'

'You don't think,' said Danae, and she was breathing heavily now, her chest rising and falling like a galleon sail in a hurricane, and she didn't care, 'that there are ways? How many times did one of us sit in a room with the Rens and wish with all his body and soul that there was something we could do to make it end? There are ways. You will give me back my life or I will make sure you never see a fucking cure.'

The woman half-smiled. 'Millions will die, Ms Grant.'

'I want my life,' she said.

There was a long, pregnant silence. Danae met the woman's gaze with all the ferocity she could muster behind eyes that were not designed to mask so much terror. She stared at the woman staring levelly at her and thought, *I cannot match her. I cannot outplay her at this, I can only believe that what I see is uncertainty and that she wants this enough not to take the chance.*

Seconds ticked by, and with each one the mask slipped a little further.

Then the woman said, 'No.'

And just like that, it was over. It was a mistake to work herself up; Danae knew that, because the fall was immense, like plunging into an abyss. She swayed in her seat and the woman stood quickly, though what help she thought she could be Danae didn't know, but she caught herself before she tumbled, and she said, 'No?'

'No,' said the woman again. 'I'm sorry, Ms Grant. But there's no magic self-destruct button for a-nauts, not even the Progeny. I would know; I've read the reports. You're not going anywhere. And the answer is no.'

Danae sat for a moment, desolate. Her bones were too heavy, they slumped in her skin, dragged her towards the ground, and she had to fight to stay upright. The colour had left the room, the shapes distorted, like watching it from inside a bubble. She said, weakly, 'I haven't done anything. Please. *Please.*'

'Maybe you haven't. I have no idea. But I have a city full of dying people and a terrorist-engineered bioweapon, and there isn't one man or woman on the streets of Creo who is going to give the loneliest of shits that it wasn't you who did this. I cannot let you go.'

There was never any chance that the answer would be different. Danae knew this, of course, but there was knowing and there was Knowing, and, as it turned out, the former was no kind of preparation for the sick, empty tide of panic that swamped her as hope disappeared. It shut down the future like an impatient shutter, it hollowed her out and it sucked all the light from the room and the breath from her lungs. It finished her.

The woman turned away, out of the glare of two eyes that had just seen the world end, and, in a voice she didn't recognise, trembling on the edge of despair, Danae said, 'What will you tell people? When they ask about the cure?'

'Ms Grant,' said the woman without looking up, 'all they'll see is a cure. Nobody is going to ask.'

19.3

So. That was it. There was nowhere else to run. She would live a little longer, while they worked out how to do what they needed to do, while they tested the cure to make sure it *was* a cure, and then it would be over.

She hadn't mentioned the Rens.

She hadn't mentioned the Rens. She'd talked about lab trials and research and how Danae's body belonged to the state, but she hadn't mentioned the Rens. Maybe it would be all right.

Maybe, whispered the vicious little voice that just never knew when the hell to shut up, maybe it wouldn't be death at all, not really. *We'll keep you alive. For as long as it takes*, she'd said. Maybe it would be a living death, brain destroyed but body active; an eternity of vegetative industry as her blood swam in a viral soup, churning out cure after cure after cure. Did it even matter? Death was death, but she hadn't mentioned the Rens.

In the secretary's room, she was blindfolded again, which she took to mean that she would not be returning to her cell. Panic spiked and with it the itch, opportunistic and full of righteous fury. But they saw it before she could muster a response, and there was more sedation, and, finally, compliance. In that room, in front of the woman who could have saved her, Danae lost control of her neck and her head lolled, and her arms hung slackly like ropes, bound at her belly. She thought that a trickle of saliva smeared the hazmask at the corner of her mouth but chose to believe that it didn't; that would be too much. Her legs, heavy and unyielding, ached at the prospect of another blind walk to God knew where; she didn't have the strength left in her. They fastened the bag around her neck with a length of rope — rough-smelling and sturdy — and for a long, painful moment she thought they were going to just hang her right there; for a moment, they might as well have done, because she couldn't breathe. But they weren't hanging her; they were tying her to someone ahead of her, and that, at least, was something, because it meant that they were likely to be going outside.

She followed them down unseen passageways, a hand beneath either arm to keep her spine straight enough to walk. There was no point in keeping track; she doubted, even without the bag, that she could have found her way a second time down the sterile, white corridors to the room with the panelled door. The bag was useful; the bag gave her a private space in which to compose herself. The bag stopped her seeing what she didn't want to see.

They stepped into an elevator. The distinctive, clean-metal smell took its time penetrating the blindfold, and so it came as a surprise when the world suddenly dropped away: nauseating, like seasickness. Disoriented, drunk with fear, Danae felt the bile rise in her throat before she realised what was happening and forced it down. It was disconcerting, blindness in an elevator: like dropping suddenly from a height with no hand to catch her.

She couldn't tell how many floors flashed past, any more than she could have guessed the time of day from the thin strip of light that had penetrated her dark room earlier. Maybe one hundred, maybe four or five: the drop was elongated without sight. All she had by way of a guide was that, when they led her from the lift, she was on the ground floor again, and she could feel the wet, smoke-flavoured air rush through the opening doors to greet her from the street.

They crossed the lobby. If there was anyone to see the group, to comment on the presence between four soldiers of a blindfolded woman with her wrists bound, there was no sound to indicate it. For such a big building, it was a disappointing reception: they crossed it quickly, the scent of the riots strengthening as they neared the open door. The rain was harsh on the sackcloth, penetrating it with huge, dark blotches. Though the scent was lost behind the hazmask, Danae knew that each spreading stain would carry the odour of the lower city, and she found that she was absurdly, ludicrously grateful for it. As though she were taking a part of the city with her wherever she was going. Like a souvenir, or a memento: something familiar for a dark journey.

Unseen arms guided her into a waiting car, strapped her into a seat. Changes of light on the inside of her blindfold told her that two of her escort had eased themselves into position on either side of her, and, in the silence, she could just catch tiny snatches of amiable conversation floating through their suits as they talked over their com-links. It sounded like birdsong, she thought as they lifted into the air. But how would she know how birdsong sounded?

19.4

It was just a room, not so different to the room in which Nadine had died. Danae still had no idea where that might have been, only that it was not here. There were subtle differences: the way the air moved, the sounds of the corridor outside, the vibration of the floor. But more than that, it felt different: where they'd kept her before had been an isolation ward, designed to keep people out. This was a secure ward, designed to keep people in.

The Angel of Death was waiting for her when she arrived, for which she was privately glad. It didn't do to let him know, of course, but it was good to see a familiar face. The walk through the hospital, brief as it was, had been cloying with the sounds of too many bodies packed too close together, and the sense of expectation, like the world was holding its breath. They hadn't taken the blindfold off, but they didn't need to: the air was thick with over-work and overcrowding; heavy with voices. Somewhere in the crowds of sickness, where bodies clamoured to be seen, Turrow lay, disregarded, while his temperature climbed dangerously high and his lungs filled with fluid.

At the end of the ward, through empty corridors and twin-key gates, past banks of cameras and isolated by extremities, they kept a high-security area, reserved for psychopaths and serial killers exercising their constitutional right to medical care. Even here, the cells bore the signs of having been only recently evacuated: the stale scent of other people on the linen; the fluctuating pockets of hot and cold in the thick, stagnant air; remnants of unseen sickness. Danae was manhandled into her room and went down like a rock with the aid of another sedative, swift and more powerful than the last, and when she came to she was on the bed, bag and clothes and hazmask removed, and her wrists were free.

It was just a room. It was a bed, laid with paper blankets that could not be used as a garrotte. It was a cabinet, bolted to the wall, with no doors or hinges and nothing inside. It was a thin cardboard cup of water and no pillow. It was a loose paper gown to protect her modesty in the face of two Perspex walls, one facing an empty guard's station, the other facing the only other cell, across the corridor, empty in honour of her arrival. She had been given some dry bread and ham at some point. They sat, untouched, on the cabinet, the only colour in a world of white.

But it was quiet. That was something, anyway. Once the heavy doors had shut behind her, she'd been left to her own devices. Occasionally, an exhausted, soporific doctor drifted through, hovered, and drifted back out again. Sometimes they waited long enough to draw a sample of her blood. Mostly, they ignored her and got on with the business of prolonging death in the distant wards beyond. It was like a bubble of silence and calm in her cell. That was something.

She thought she'd been there two hours, maybe two and a half when she unexpectedly lost consciousness and woke to find herself strapped to a bed in an imaging chamber with an IV line snaking painfully out of the back of her left hand. She wondered at the courtesy, as though someone had genuinely considered the possibility that she might need her right to sign something in the near future, and decided that it was probably standard procedure, unthinkingly repeated. The skin around it ached and burned with the slightest flicker of movement and Danae guessed it was her conduit to more drugs. At least they were shaking things up a little. That was something.

Voices flickered on the edge of hearing, and from the play of shadows on the far wall she thought that there must be a viewing gallery behind her, out of her field of vision. Her eyes drifted across the arc of imaging shields that surrounded her like a sarcophagus and wondered if everyone who lay beneath them felt as though they'd been slotted into the tomb ahead of schedule. This was the last refuge of the seriously ill, the folks for whom the disease had breached the usual defences and whose only remaining hope involved just blasting the body with several times the usual nanon dosage and hoping it did more harm than good. The shields that surrounded her, that filtered waves of stream-language into the tiny bioengines that were pumped into the patient's bloodstream, were designed to moderate the uplink, to tell the nanon armies what to do and how to fight. They weren't designed to read a reverse transmission.

If it didn't work, would she ever know?

'Whatever happens,' she said now, although she had no idea if anyone could hear her, 'It's going to happen fast. Really, really fast. You'll need to be ready.'

The phantom voices animated slightly, as though a door had been opened and suddenly closed, and a woman said, 'Try not to talk. It interferes with the calibration.'

Danae closed her eyes. When she opened them again, she was back in her room.

19.5

As the sedative wore off, she occupied half an hour with calculating the resistance of the Perspex window in relation to a swiftly moving body and the attainable velocity permitted by the constraints of space. Later, when she thought that she might be sufficiently recovered to give it a try, she put her theory to the test and got halfway across the room before they knocked her out again. This time when she woke up her right arm was fixed to the frame of the bed with a short length of chain that permitted her to lie on the mattress and move a few steps towards the window, but no further.

The Angel was humming the Death March. She ignored him; passed the time by calculating the number of electrons per square metre of air in the cell. Then per square foot. Later, she might start thinking about the atoms in her bed sheet or the cabinet. Numbers helped; numbers were soothing. Numbers demanded complete concentration and kept the mind from maudlin thoughts. To edge out the sound from the black figure by the window, she started to sing a song her mother had taught her, about a dragon that lived by the sea. Danae couldn't remember the words and she'd last seen the sea when she was too young to fix it satisfactorily in her mind, but it was the tune that was important: so long as it drowned out the Death March. And if it pissed off the Angel, so much the better. He was getting on her nerves.

There shouldn't be so much waiting involved in death, she thought. Once it was decided, let it happen. Death itself took a second, and she was sure that it couldn't be so terrible, whatever the Angel, with his sly, knowing smile, tried to pretend. Once it was decided, just get on with it. They shouldn't leave her alone to die a million times a minute, over long hours that stretched into eternity. They shouldn't give her the opportunity to ponder the images of her end, to torment herself with thoughts that she'd left Turrow too long, that she'd never know one way or another if the sacrifice had been worth the price.

The Angel of Death looked up and smiled; he liked it when her thoughts got dark. Danae was just about to tell him to fuck off, when a voice from the other side of the bed startled her back into the present.

She spun around. It was a doctor; a woman she recognised from her arrival, glimmering with the patina of the cheaper hologram jacks.

'Already?' said Danae.

The doctor screwed up her face in irritation. She was perhaps ten years older than Danae, but fatigue had aged her. 'What?' she said.

'Nothing,' said Danae. The Angel of Death sniggered, checked an imaginary watch. 'Is there any – did the uplink capture work?'

'It's possible,' said the doctor briskly, and warmth flooded Danae's belly with enough force to twist a fresh tide of nausea.

'Thank you,' she said softly. 'When will you know for sure?'

But the doctor just shook her head. 'That's all I'm prepared to say,' she said. And then, 'I've just had a call.'

The trouble with vagaries was that they could go either way; her adrenal system didn't know whether to operate the fight-or-flight or the jubilation glands. A call to say, *let her go*? Or a call to say, *that's it, we've got what we need*? So she said, carefully, 'Who from?'

'It's come from the top,' said the doctor. 'They want to know if the friend you mentioned in your meeting last night was' — she glanced at a pad — 'Boston Malcolm Turrow, born December 27, 2089.'

Malcolm. He hadn't mentioned that. Danae's lungs contracted and she could barely speak, so she gave a hollow little nod and whispered, 'Yes.'

'All right then,' said the doctor and turned to go.

'Is he all right?' said Danae. The chain rattled violently against the bed frame as she shifted her body to follow the doctor, as though she could reach out a hand to catch her retreating back. 'Please, I know you don't have to tell me anything, please, *please*. Please. Is he all right?'

'He's holding on,' said the doctor.

Relief sank her and her spine sagged under the weight. If her hands hadn't found their own way out in front of her, Danae might have fallen from the bed. She said, softly, 'Thank you.'

'He's very ill,' said the doctor. 'You should know that. We're going to do everything we can, but it might be too late. You should be prepared, that's all.'

Danae, who had stopped processing anything beyond the fact that he was still alive, nodded silently into the bed, and it was several minutes before she had the presence of mind to wonder at the use of the first person plural.

19.6

Boston was buried in heat, pinned beneath fathoms of ancient, black rocks, hot and dry to the touch, and their heat edged his vision in red. Fiery air enclosed him like another skin, searing his eyes and his lips, forcing itself down his throat, into his lungs, fanning out in fractals across his guts. In the corners of his vision he saw flickering shadows, like malevolent faces, and he thought he heard laughter and voices; once or twice he thought he heard his name, but his head refused to turn and his neck was like stone, as though he was moulded from the bedrock around him.

A high-pitched wail like a banshee howl ripped him from the darkness and he surfaced violently into blinding white light. His mother watched him disapprovingly from a corner of the room — whose room? It wasn't his — but she wouldn't speak to him when he called her and she wouldn't tell him where he was. Her face was hard-edged, too made-up, with brilliant purple eyeshadow and baby pink lips. He reached for her, but she receded and the room elongated, telescoped out of sight. He called for her, screamed her name until his throat was raw, but his answer was a strange siren-song from the blackness: soothing him, cooling him. He craned his head, but there was no-one near him, nobody to make the noise, only a bright, vivid white light and a sense of presence. Rita, from the vanishing point, was watching him and crying. He turned back to her, to shout after her that it was all very well for her to cry now, but she wasn't there: only the sound of her sobs remained. And then he was exploding, tumbling through a colour octave towards a silent sea of black, opaque water. The surface was as hard as tarmac where he hit it, but it bent under his weight like a balloon, dipping deeper and deeper until the sky was obscured by the enclosing rubber walls and he could see dark shapes moving beyond. The membrane was stretched so thin that his fingers were almost closing on water, and then it burst and he was sucked through into inky darkness, cool and silent. He kicked his heels and swam deeper and further, down to where the water was peaceful, and there he found a cave, lit by a faint green light. Enough to see by, but too faint to hurt his eyes or warm the chilled air. He crawled inside and found the cave walls soft and yielding.

He slept.

★

He slept, watched by the datastream. It drained his bladder and dripped nutrients into his veins. It monitored the dosage on a series of pads, wired into the fabric of the hospital itself. It animated his mattress so that he turned periodically from his left side to his back, from his back to his right. It moderated the temperature on his biocontrol packs, his heat sheet, and dialled him slowly away from the periodic spasms that clenched his muscles when the fever spiked. It watched, impassively, as his life signs began gradually to mass and inch upwards.

★

He woke to the smell of sweat on wet sheets, and the blissful cool of a heat sheet draped over his naked body, with no sensation of the passage of time or where he was. A doctor was standing beside him, looking at something above his bed. His throat was too dry to speak, so he reached out to her to get her attention and watched as his fingers passed straight through where her legs should be. Turrow blinked, convinced now that this place was a figment of his febrile imagination, and not wanting the dream to end so that he found himself once again washed out by fever and pain on a forgotten cot.

'Are you awake?' asked the doctor. He nodded, as awake as he wanted to be. Her voice sounded as if it were filtered through layers of water. 'Do you know where you are?' Turrow shook his head and tried to say no, but found that more than just a dry throat was in the way: something was stuffed into his mouth. He raised a hand to investigate, but it flopped useless to the bed before he had moved it halfway. 'You have a breathing tube down your throat,' she said. 'We'll keep it there for a while yet. You're in the hospital, Boston. We're looking after you.'

A thousand questions bubbled in his throat, but his brain was hot and sluggish and couldn't string them into order. It was dawning on him that perhaps this was real, and, through muddled, feverish thinking, he stumbled across the thought that something must be expected of him, that one was not delivered into heaven free of charge, but he couldn't decide what it might be and all he wanted was to sleep.

His eyes closed without any conscious decision on his part. 'Rest now,' said the doctor, but he was already halfway there. 'You need to ...'

19.7

Boston slept, and when he woke again he was alone. The room, a couple of degrees too warm, was thick with an artificial silence so acute that it left a ringing in his ears. The breathing tube was gone, leaving in its place a red-raw throat, un-bathed by saliva for too long, that had cracked and torn down the length of his oesophagus. A tumbler of water sat on a cabinet beside his bed, misted with condensation where the ice had cooled it. He grabbed it on the second try, hands trembling with effort, and swallowed half of it greedily without stopping for air, letting it run in icy rivers down his chin, soaking his cotton hospital gown, like a drowning man breaking the surface.

He finished and lay back on his bed, exhausted, floor and ceiling spinning lazily around him as his head, immobile for so long, accustomed itself to the sudden sensation of movement. His lungs hurt when he breathed and his skin was still warm, far too warm, but, though the past few days were hazy, he was dimly aware that he had been delivered from something: hot, nightmarish, and reeking of death.

The passageway outside was quiet and still: the quality of the silence and shadows suggested late night. Boston shifted himself very slowly up his pillows until they afforded him a view of the window in front of his bed and watched the empty corridor. No-one passed by.

Night, then.

Night was for sleeping. He slept.

19.8

In his dreams, something was lost. Boston was in a room he didn't know, or a tunnel, or on an expanse of floor that stretched into the infinite shadows as far as the eye could see, and something was missing. Something was missing that was important, but the empty air made no suggestions and his frantic brain could fix on nothing. Something was missing and it was important that he find it, but how could he find it if he couldn't remember what it was?

Once, he surfaced and a person was in the room, or what looked like a person might look like if his face were made out of plastic. The plastic lips smiled at him and the plastic head nodded and spoke a few words in the lazy, underwater language of the ghost doctor. He closed his eyes, like sandpaper on boiled grapes, and when he opened them again the plastic person was gone and the water jug was full again.

Once, he surfaced and the ghost doctor was back and she asked him how he felt. 'Hot,' he said, and had to open his eyes to make sure that the unfamiliar voice had actually come from him.

'The worst of it's over now,' she said. 'Just rest.'

What else did he do but rest? But he said, 'I keep dreaming that I've lost something.'

'Your temperature's still very high,' she said, as if he ought to make a connection between his words and hers. 'But it's coming down. Well done, Boston. You're doing great.'

Sleep assaulted him from every angle. Mostly, he surfaced and the room was quiet: the still, sucking silence of unseen mechanics constantly moving. Heat pressed down on him like a thousand dusty blankets and in its comfortless grip he searched the black wastes for the indefinable missing *something*. Once he surfaced and found tears on his cheeks and his throat raw as if he'd been shouting. Part of his brain knew what it was that had been lost, but it was locked down like a dungeon and guarded with snakes.

19.9

He opened his eyes and something was different.

The room was still too warm; his skin was still a tight, swollen membrane over an ocean of heat, but the fog in his brain had retreated and his vision was clear.

Boston blinked experimentally. Sandpaper yet, but the grapes were no longer boiled, just warm from the midday sun. He tried again, and decided that he was probably awake.

Time had receded; time, in the stale silence of the room, was meaningless. But the light was dimmer than he remembered and the air was still and part of his brain, which had been taking notes even while the fever forced him under the black tide of unconsciousness, volunteered the information that it was still night. The same night, or a different one? Impossible to tell: time had collapsed, and, in any case, he wasn't sure why it was important to know.

Boston lay for a moment, considering. Very, very little made sense. There was the ghost doctor and the dreams, and before that a general wash of pain and heat and panic, and before that there was Danae. How the one state of affairs became the other was a sequence of white noise and missing scenes. More importantly, there was the question of where exactly Danae might be. Blankets, he thought, were critical to the recovery of the memory, which was definitely somewhere in the snake-guarded dungeon. Why blankets might be significant was something too esoteric to puzzle through when every single thought had until only very recently waded through treacle and beaten lethargically at the doors of consciousness.

After a moment, which may have been ten minutes or an hour or three, he decided to experiment with the limits of his new-found clarity. More specifically, he decided to see whether or not it applied to his limbs as well as his head.

Moving carefully, because it was an experiment and the parameters were uncertain, Boston raised his head by increments until he had achieved a sitting position. His arms vacillated over whether or not they would support his weight as he levered himself upright, but the bones knew what to do and they locked him, painfully but effectively, into place. He gave his body a moment or two to come to terms with events, while his brain soared and dipped like a drunken fledgling and tremors gripped his wasted muscles, and then he slid his legs over the edge of the bed and gingerly lowered them to the floor. It was as cold as he had thought it would be, and the shock of it, like a rod through his spine, sent his feet recoiling upwards. He waited a moment and then lowered them again. This time they protested in stinging pain but stayed where he put them.

Walking was difficult, as if he'd never learned how. He inched forward on unsteady, watery legs, gripping the bed for support with one hand, until he got to the end and toppled himself towards the window, where he caught his balance mid-fall. His legs scrabbled beneath him for purchase, and gradually, little by little, he eased himself into a standing position perpendicular to the floor. His head spun and his knees threatened to buckle; he felt as though he hadn't been upright in weeks.

But he was standing, and it was an achievement.

Outside, in the grainy light, the corridor was deserted and preternaturally silent. If Boston's thinking had been less glutinous he might have guessed that six inches of Perspex shields most sound, but in the hazy plains of recently reclaimed consciousness, it was as though the world had ended. The silence pressed against his ears, as though the room were filling up with cotton wool, and he rested his head against the window to steady it as he searched the darkness for evidence of humanity.

Across the corridor, directly in front of him, was a window to a cell identical to his, except that the lights there were dimmed, making it difficult, while his eyes adjusted, to make out dark shapes in the gloom. For a moment he thought that it was empty, but the screen above the bed was alive with the dancing lines of healthy life signs. Boston squinted, trying to peer closer. He could just about make out the shape of a body on the bed, but it was nothing more than a succession of distensions of the blanket into a vaguely humanoid form; it could have been a robot for all that he could tell. Then it stirred slightly and lifted its head, and he saw that, yes, that was exactly what it was.

It was a robot.

She met his gaze at the same moment that he realised that it was her, and for a moment neither of them moved, suspended in private space. Her eyes were shadowed: bigger, wider and darker than he remembered. Older eyes; eyes in which the life had receded. And then she lifted one arm in a lazy, soporific gesture and he saw, when it reached the end of its tether, that she was chained to her bed.

Deep in the dungeon, a little flutter of panic escaped, but it refused to discuss what it had seen in the white noise scenes.

Too many questions. Too many muttered fragments of information in a brain that still sweated in the residual heat of a near-fatal fever. Too much background noise superimposed over their final conversation before the blankets descended and he ceased to be. A catch in Boston's chest sent a polite reminder that he had stopped breathing, and let out a long breath, which condensed on the glass in front of him. He looked at it for a second, and then, before it had a chance to evaporate, he traced a word through it with his finger.

Hi, he wrote.

She seemed pale, but perhaps it was a trick of the different levels of light. Perhaps the bright light from his room reflected on her like the sun on the moon, silvered her skin. She closed her older, deader eyes and a fat, pearlescent tear slid out from under the lashes of the right and traced a perfect arc down her cheek. She opened her eyes again and tilted her head as far towards him as it would go, and she smiled.

Hi, she mouthed.

He wrote, *You OK?*

Her head inclined slightly, as though it was loose on her neck and her movements had to be strictly controlled.

You? she mouthed. A tiny gesture, but it brought the light into her eyes again and they fixed on him and held him until he leaned forward and breathed on the glass and wrote, *Better.*

The smile, which had faded as she waited for him to answer, tugged at the corner of her lips again. It didn't look like the kind of smile that reached the eyes, but she closed them before he could tell and leaned her head back. In the shadows, he saw her lips move as she faced the ceiling, and she might have been saying, *Thank God* or she might have been saying, *All right, then.*

He knocked on the window, and the sound was flat and dead in the heavy air. It couldn't have carried across the corridor; it barely carried to his own ears, but she lifted her head again and caught his stare and returned it, and before she could look away he wrote, *You sick?*

Of course it was a stupid question. Of course he knew that she wasn't. Or, at least, once upon a time he'd known that it was a stupid question and that of course she wasn't sick, and the knowledge remained as knowledge of knowledge; it was only that the questions that he wanted to ask could not be asked of a woman chained to a bed in a soundproofed room.

She shook her head a little, with careful, rubber movements.

You OK? he wrote again, and this time she didn't answer.

Heat and blackness and panic. And her voice, shouting his name, and his voice, shouting hers. And something lost, something indefinable but infinitely precious; something that could not be found in a thousand rooms or a million miles of tunnel.

You save me? he wrote. Her head dipped forwards. Before the words could fade, he erased the question mark and added, *give self up?*

She nodded, slowly, like a clockwork doll.

Let you go? he wrote, as though pretending not to know it could make it go away.

She shook her head, and two more tears spilled out and traced the hollow line of her cheeks, trickling silver all the way to her jaw.

He slammed his hand against the glass, palm down, evacuating the air like a thunderclap where it struck. His head dropped so that his eyes didn't have to look at her, and he slammed the glass again, and again, and again, until exhaustion dropped him to his knees. Without looking up, he wrote *NO* against the unfrosted glass. His fingertip was white where it pressed the letters into nothingness.

When he looked up, her eyes were still on him and her face was wet and glistening in the half-light. Gently, she nodded her head.

Why? he wrote.

She shrugged. It was a little gesture that conveyed so much hopelessness, so much despair.

Just because, he thought.

On the glass, he wrote it again, but more gently: *No.* As she craned her head to read him, her body shifted on the bed and he saw that her legs were chained as well. They were frightened of her. Him, not so much, but she had to be chained to the bed. Heavily, as though the air was lead, he lifted one knee and then the other, pulling himself upright against the sheer plastic surface of the window. When he was level with her eyeline, he wrote it a third time: *No.* And she forced a tight little smile and nodded, and he thought that, even without three dozen different chemicals pumping through his body, without his heavy mantle of illness, without the close proximity of death, he wasn't the sort of person to instil fear in the heart of oppressors. And he thought about the night that he'd run into almost certain death to save her, and how it had, against every law of probability, worked out for him then, and that once was unlikely and twice was impossible.

She looked at him, and she mouthed, *It's okay.*

No, he wrote.

It's okay.

Not.

It's okay. It is, she told him and slowly, deliberately she raised a hand to the neck of her gown, pulled it tightly around her, then trailed one hand down to pat her right hip. Her eyebrows arched, furrowing her forehead, and she stared at him levelly. *It's okay,* she mouthed again.

She was telling him something; that much was certain. There was fear in her eyes, but something beneath it, something clear and something important, and he knew she needed him to understand. And he didn't: he had no idea, no context, no key from which to decode the gesture. Maybe it was the drugs, maybe it was the fever, maybe it was the blankets and the white noise and the missing scenes, but Boston was lost, helpless, hopelessly confused. She needed him to understand, and he didn't understand, and he knew it was in his face. And he knew she saw it when the clarity, the focus, left her gaze.

It's okay, she said again. *Don't worry.*

His hand struck the glass again, but there was no force in it, and his head bent forward to meet it and slid through his words, obliterating them.

Without lifting his eyes, because he knew that she still watched him, he breathed on the glass and wrote, *Love you.*

It wasn't enough. But it was all he had.

★

Across the corridor in her darkened room, Danae, knowing he couldn't see her, whispered, *I love you too*, and dropped her head back against the wall.

Turrow's hands were pressed against the pane, as though he couldn't stand upright without them suckered onto the glass, and she raised hers to match, as far as they would go. Pressing them against the dark, still air, as if an act of willpower could remove the empty space between them and press flesh against flesh. She held them there until she thought that she could feel the pressure of his hands on hers; thought that if she closed her eyes she would really believe that they were touching. All the time he never raised his head and she could not see his eyes.

He crumpled suddenly, and she saw that his life signs, which had been blocked from her view by his body, had plummeted. In the darkness, unseen and unheard, Danae thumped her arms against their chains and started yelling for help.

THE HERALD, 12TH FEBRUARY 2077

A spokesperson for the Metropolitan police was today playing down concerns around public safety after a bomb scare closed off parts of Westminster for almost three hours during the morning rush. Speaking at a press conference this afternoon, Detective Inspector Julia Rowe insisted that there was 'no compelling evidence' linking this incident to the mass deactivation of S3A units at Satellus-Ford warehouses in Liverpool at the weekend, despite widespread reports on the stream of threats of retaliation from a-naut rights activists. A 400-metre perimeter was erected around the complex on Victoria Street, bringing traffic in the city to a standstill while officers from the Explosives and Firearms division conducted their search for the device, which was later revealed to be an elaborate hoax.

Head of Protocol at Fidex Systems, Dr. Kenneth Yeung, who sits on the newly established advisory panel set up to advise the municipal government on the S3A crisis, was also keen to stress that the increasingly extremist tone of Emancipation's press releases should not be construed as an indication of a radicalisation among a-nauts. 'The S3A unit is incapable of orchestrating any direct act of violence without specific instruction from a human handler,' he told reporters, while assuring the public that the Commons Select Committee on Non-Organic Affairs is set to recommend significantly tighter restrictions on a-naut movement within UK jurisdiction, along with governmental assistance to telectronics firms struggling to cope with mandatory recall of malfunctioning units. Twenty-two amnisobiological manufacturers across the globe have already filed for bankruptcy in the past six months alone, while concerns remain high that many more are to follow suit.

23 MAY

20.1

It was a warm, balmy late morning in early summer. That was easy to achieve with the right temperature controls.

Sometimes, Corscadden felt as though he lived in a cocoon, so warm and comfortable that he'd long ago ceased to see it as a sort of prison, and when the thought hit him, he started to wonder if he'd even recognise a natural flower-scent for what it was, or distinguish a real breeze from the piped zephyrs surrounding his guests with just the right fluctuation in temperature. His thoughts were turning that way today, as they often did when something was preying on his mind. He couldn't remember why they were throwing a party; presumed his wife knew, and that it was for a good reason. She played the same game he did, but from a different perspective. *Death by canapé*, he thought, and sipped at his wine.

The trouble with lunchtime galas was that, by definition, they had to be thrown during the day, for reasons that escaped Corscadden and were never likely to become any clearer, and, by this stage of the year, the heat was usually too severe to spend any length of time outdoors during the hours of sunlight. There was indoors, of course, which was fine for most people, but this was a garden sort of crowd. Corscadden was precious about his garden; only the exalted few were permitted to tread the immaculate gravel and sniff the perfumed air, but these were people with money. They expected garden, so they got garden. Above the atmospheric shield, the sun rained down a blistering barrage of fire that sucked the water from the ground and scalded the skin of the unwary, but in the garden it was a temperate home-counties noon. It was a question of protocol.

His wife, wispy in something pink and filmy, glided up to him, trailing a middle-aged man and woman. He had the sort of horsey, chinless face that Corscadden associated with centuries of inbreeding, and laughed like a choking dog; his companion looked like a man in drag. 'My dears,' he said, casting them a five hundred watt smile so dazzling that the electricity supply failed across a three hundred mile radius. 'How *marvellous* you could make it.'

'You remember Gus and Penelope, darling?' said his wife, secure in the knowledge that Corscadden did not.

Gus: Gus Puig, heir to the Puig multi-media empire, richer than God and as useful as a concrete enema. Penelope: wife or mistress, he couldn't remember. Puig had children somewhere, but whether or not he shared them with the man-faced woman on his arm was beyond Corscadden to guess.

'However could I forget?' he said.

The problem then, of course, was that Gus felt the need to start talking to Corscadden, and Corscadden's wife subtly disappeared to do what she did best. Corscadden nodded and smiled and listened to the orchestra, playing soft Mozart in the shade of an oak that was older than the house, and to the conversations in his immediate vicinity, which were always more interesting than the ones going on in front of his face. People spoke more freely when they thought you weren't listening, and were will-crushingly dull when they thought you were. Eventually, Gus brayed with congested laughter, and Corscadden, through years of training, found his mouth joining in before his brain had time to react.

'My dear boy,' he said, 'How wonderful. How absolutely wonderful.'

'Well,' said Gus, 'that's Lucy for you.'

Lucy? Who on earth was Lucy? And why would Gus imagine that Corscadden might care? Still, seven minutes in the company of Mr Puig was not totally wasted; his nasal droning was remarkably easy to zone out, and Corscadden had taken the time to overhear several snippets of conversation that might be useful later on. 'Of course,' said Corscadden. 'Dear Lucy. Now, won't you excuse me for a moment?'

He found his wife by the fountain, chatting to a dazzlingly beautiful young woman with flowers in her hair and a conveniently vacant expression on her face that Corscadden did not trust for a second.

'Darling,' she said brightly, in the tone that immediately preceded a 'you remember ...'

'My dear,' he said to the vacant-looking girl, who forgot herself for a split second and turned a gaze of sharp scrutiny on him. 'How wonderful that you could make it. Darling, if I could borrow you for a moment?'

'You are a wicked man,' she said when they were out of earshot.

'Where do you find them?' he protested.

'You're in a mood,' she said. 'And you shouldn't be drinking.'

She was right on both counts, which irritated him intensely. He was in a mood, and the wine made it more difficult to disguise the fact. He flashed a dazzling smile at a pair of couples as they passed, and his wife fluttered a hand at them. 'Darlings,' she trilled. And then, in an undertone to her husband, 'I'm not going to rescue you, you know. So don't even ask.'

'I'm going to have a word with the conductor,' said Corscadden, without missing a beat and in a tone of manufactured innocence that would fool ninety-nine point nine percent of humanity, but certainly not his wife. 'The *Minuet in G* was appalling.'

'Don't disappear,' she warned. 'The Mayharts are about somewhere.'

Mustn't disappoint the Mayharts, he thought sourly. The wine was giving him heartburn; he wondered why he'd accepted a glass. It was what he would have done as a young man, full of nerves and ambition, but not for more years than he cared to count. Why now? Perhaps he was getting old.

He hovered about the edge of the crowd, stopping long enough to exchange words here and there with a couple of terrified husbands of relentless socialites, and avoided the orchestra, who had noted his glares and were slipping every other note under his terrible scrutiny. He thought they had progressed to Chopin, but it was difficult to tell.

Beneath the shade of a vibrant, opal-flowering magnolia, he perched on a stone seat and lit an illicit cigar. These too were forbidden. With good reason, of course: always with good reason. Old age had come upon him suddenly, to the point where, although he knew he had the drive and the acuity of a man half his age, he had started to believe his own hype. It was useful to be underestimated — though the ones who counted didn't buy it for a second; he wasn't that good — but the problems started when one began to underestimate oneself.

A flickering of shadow caught the corner of his eye. Corscadden knew of only one person in the world who could hover so inconspicuously. He glanced up.

Ah.

'What is it?' he said brusquely. He knew, and knew that the butler knew, that the call was expected, but it didn't do to let standards slip.

'A telephone call, sir,' said his butler smoothly.

'Who is it?'

'A gentleman, sir.'

Ah, the game. Even his butler knew the rules. A gentleman, with the faintest emphasis on 'a', contriving to imply that it was not *a* gentleman, but *the* gentleman. But the butler wasn't supposed to know there was a *the* gentleman. Corscadden offered a thin smile.

'I'll take it inside,' he said.

The study was cooler than the garden: a clean, fresh chill that made the air feel as though it had been scrubbed in lemon detergent. This, too, was expensively artificial, but at least it wore its inauthenticity like a banner, proudly. Corscadden was confident that he could spot air conditioning at fifty paces.

The butler retreated discreetly, as though he had dissolved into thin air, and only the soft *whoosh click* of the closing double doors indicated that he had used a conventional mode of exit. Corscadden waited for a moment or two, ostensibly checking to make sure he was not overheard, when he was actually delaying gratification, allowing the thrill to build up to a heady, satisfying rush. This, *this* was the game. When he was ready, he crossed to his desk and waved a hand over a touch pad. A careful observer might have noticed a tiny flash from a dark stone set into the gold of the pinkie ring that he always wore on his right hand and wondered if, perhaps, he was transferring to a secure line. The screen made no noise as it materialised above his desk, but Corscadden always heard a nasal *fizz* inside his head: it was the sound it *ought* to make.

The screen was white static. This, too, was the game.

He said, 'This is he.'

And a voice said, 'I've had the opportunity to review your report, and it's exactly as you thought. The uplink seems to have destabilised when the Sinon pathogen entered a live a-naut system.'

'Ah.' Corscadden pursed his lips, relaxed into his chair. 'That's extremely troubling. Perhaps you'd better tell me what you know.'

'Some of it is still speculation,' said the voice, 'And I'm waiting for confirmation on a couple of facts. You would not believe how difficult it has been to get an answer on all of this.'

Corscadden reached his hands up to his head, folding them into a pillow at the back of his scalp. 'I would believe,' he said pointedly, 'that a destabilised uplink should have shut down the entire project as soon as it was discovered.'

'Possibly,' said the voice in a tone that practically dripped with an unspoken air of *assurances were given*. 'You asked me to tell you what I knew.'

'I did,' said Corscadden, and suppressed a sigh. Hardly anybody played the game properly anymore. 'Why did it destabilise?'

'As far as anyone can tell,' said the voice, with the defensiveness of a man who'd had cause to know just how well Corscadden tended to respond to lack of certainty, 'it has something to do with the fact that, in a live system, there's a continuous data transfer going on between the a-cells and Red Space. This is a guess, but it's based on the fact that the link first of all corrupted, and then the pocket shifted directly into a-naut controlled streamspace. It's unlikely that this was a conscious effort on the part of the subject, but as soon as Sinon's data pocket was in Red Space, it was effectively neutralised as an counter-amniosobiological weapon and it was no longer able to fulfil its protocol. The Aurillac death seems to have been the one and only instance of Sinon doing enough damage to the shields to let infection in - beyond that, it was almost completely inert. But because it was designed to replicate, because it was designed to be transferred ... it transferred. It just transferred to the wrong kind of bloodstream.'

Sinon: son of Aesimus and warrior of Greece at the siege of Troy. His act of treachery penetrated the walls of that unbreachable city and brought it to a crushing defeat. He was the perfect ancestor for a project designed to break into a hermetically-sealed system by turning the system against itself: an imitator and a destroyer. But it was too easy to get lost in poetry and forget that a traitor is, by his very nature, duplicitous.

'My understanding,' said Corscadden, 'was that Sinon should have been free to transfer to any bloodstream it liked. It should not have been able to interact with any cell but an a-cell. Correct?'

'Yes,' said the voice. 'That was how it was designed, and while the data pocket remained under ReGen's control, that was the case: Sinon was completely inert in the human bloodstream. But the markers that trigger the human immune response are extremely similar to the markers that trigger an a-cell response in the artificial system. The best guess is that Sinon was still trying to fulfil its protocol and attack an immune response - it's just that the protocol got skewed when the pocket transferred out of ReGen-controlled streamspace. And so the wrong kind of immune response got attacked.'

'I see.' Corscadden did not, as a rule, tend to lose his temper; it was not a productive use of resources. But he practised the art of cold fury like an ancient master, and, if white static could have noticeably flinched, he was certain it would have done so. 'And, were I in charge, I might be tempted to wonder how, precisely, it managed to get as far as Phase 3 clinical trials without anyone noticing this. Never mind,' he added, before the intake of breath at the other end of the line could turn into words. 'Recent developments have made that point slightly moot. The prevailing theory among the people that have to control the damn thing is that it's an act of terror. How close to ReGen does the paper trail run?'

'It's difficult to access the information,' said the voice. 'Extremely difficult.'

'But not impossible.'

'No. There are distinct sequencing patterns that are theoretically traceable to ReGen.'

'Theoretically?'

'At present, yes. The project is classified at CTS Level Violet and subject to the appropriate restrictions. But someone with legitimate clearance would be able to gain access.'

'Legitimate clearance.' If Corscadden had been in any mood to smile, his lips might have twitched upwards. 'Anyone with legitimate clearance at CTS Level Violet already knows about ReGen's involvement. I want to know if it's something the casual observer can come by with a bit of persistence.'

'You want to know,' said the voice, 'if it can be traced back to you.'

Silence descended, sparkling faintly in the lemon-scented air. Corscadden was positive that the statement did not deserve a response.

'No,' said the voice, after an indecent period of conversational chicken. 'There's no record of your involvement. As far as the stream is concerned, your only connection with ReGen is as a major investor.'

'That involvement,' said Corscadden, 'is a little too public for my liking.'

A beat. 'If you're worried about insider trading laws …'

'Insider trading?' That very nearly did raise a smile, but for entirely the wrong reasons. 'I think this is a little bit beyond insider trading now, don't you?'

'Maybe,' said the voice. 'But I don't think it's time to sell your shares just yet.'

A humourless puff of laughter. 'Don't worry,' said Corscadden. 'I have no intention of selling. Panicking costs money. I'm just a little disappointed that my stock won't be soaring the way I'd hoped.'

'But at least it's not likely to crash.' A small hesitation, uncertainty filling the empty space. And then: 'This is ... not good. It's very bad indeed. But nobody could have predicted it would happen.'

Ah, but that was the game. The game was *all* about prediction. It was about calling the odds and making your move accordingly, and the higher the stakes, the greater the need for absolute clarity. He'd known - he'd *known* - that the ideas didn't match the facts, that the numbers didn't add up to the world that Corscadden knew, but there had been an answer to every question and he'd wanted them to be right. Never before in his life had Corscadden made a decision based on wanting someone to be right. It was possible that he was finally getting old.

A sudden peal of laughter, diluted by distance, trickled into the silence, trailed by a thin whine of strings and a buzz of voices, in the manner of a door being opened from the garden by a wife in search of an absent husband. Corscadden sat back in his seat.

'I suppose not,' he said placidly, and it was as much for himself as for the voice at the other end of the line. The party beckoned: sushi skewers and monotonous gossip and wine he wasn't allowed to drink, but this was different. This was the *game*. 'The bioterrorism theory was a lucky escape,' he said. 'And now, so they tell me, there's an actual a-naut in custody. I'm not sure I could have ordered a better alibi if I'd come up with it myself. As long as it holds.'

'It'll hold.'

Corscadden nodded, considering. 'Yes,' he said, and reached his hands above his head in a lazy, leisurely stretch designed to put off the moment when the game ended and politics, endless politics, began again. 'I think it will. We'll have a chat some time, you and I, about why your project leader decided to ignore the advice of the leading expert in counter-amnisobiological weaponry, but for now, Dr. Rademaker, I believe we're in the clear. So — let's start talking about how we can make Sinon actually work.'

20.2

She didn't sleep. Wrapped in the thin sheet that covered the bed, Danae sat cross-legged on the mattress and watched his room for signs of life. Somewhere, down one of the vacant corridors, she knew that a machine was screaming out a message to an empty room, or else to ears wrapped so deeply in sleep that they wouldn't hear Armageddon if it started in the lab next door.

She watched.

After an hour or so, the pattern of light on the bare walls beside the window of his cell began to change, shifting in little static bursts that suggested that the shadow of a moving person was present and that Creo had not been abandoned just yet. She watched with interest; watching was all she could do.

The doctor looked to be half-asleep. He shuffled his feet along the sterile floor as though the act of lifting them into proper footsteps was too much for him, and periodically smacked the side of his head as if he were trying to fire life into a soporific brain. He barely spared a glance for Danae's room, but Turrow's window interested him and seemed to finally charge his neurons into action. Danae could not hear what was going on outside the corridor; the scene was as distant as watching a television with the sound turned off, but suddenly the corridor was buzzing with activity. That Turrow was on the floor was a good sign: he had got out of bed. That he was unconscious was bad. The crowd in front of his window were blocking her view of his life signs, but still she didn't move, conscious that to shift even slightly, to seem to fret when there was chaos outside, would be to risk a sedative infusion before she had time to hold her breath.

A change of light in the room across the corridor told her that a doctor was in the hologram suite, though what good she thought it would do Turrow to be examined by a doctor that couldn't touch him was anybody's guess. Apparently, the thought occurred to the doctor too, because a moment later she was beside Danae.

'Did you see what happened?' she asked sharply.

'Yes,' said Danae.

The doctor waited a moment, and then snapped, 'We can check the recordings, but it'll take time. If you saw what happened, just tell me.'

The thought of strangers watching their silent conversation sent a pang of hot resentment searing through her belly. 'He stood up,' she said. 'He walked over to the window, he stood there for a moment, and then he collapsed. I've been watching him for the past hour.' Thinking, *at least one of us has.* 'His life signs have been stable.'

Across the corridor the crowd was dispersing a little, and she saw that Turrow had come to and was being helped to his feet by an early-generation Prometheus medical droid. The doctor dissolved out of her room and reappeared in his, firing questions at him in quick succession. He responded by rolling his eyes and letting his head fall, flaccid, to his chest, but Danae, after one sharp moment of panic, saw that his life signs were stable, and he was just reacting to the doctor exactly as she would have done if she thought she could get away with it.

He allowed himself to be helped to bed and a hasty sedative hit his veins before he knew what was happening. Blood was drawn and whisked away down sterilising tubes to a lab somewhere, and then, as abruptly as it had started, it was over and they were quiet again.

Danae, in an increasingly unsettled brain starved of stimulus, began to work out the number of electrons in Creo's air supply.

20.3

She woke up late in the afternoon, head thumping through the after-effects of a sedative that she didn't remember breathing. The air in the room was a pungent, antiseptic mint flavour, and she realised from the rapidly receding sensation of pressure at the back of her throat that the only reason she was now awake was because of an anti-sedative, administered, presumably, at the instruction of the doctor who stood beside her, glimmering with a hologrammatic sheen.

Danae sat up slowly. The heaviness in her head massed and thumped against the sides of her skull, as if it were gearing up for an explosion. White light danced in front of her eyes.

'I don't want to be sedated,' she said, her voice thick with fatigue. 'I want to be awake.'

'You've been starving yourself of sleep,' said the doctor. 'Studies have shown that all a-naut generations are prone to psychotic episodes after relatively short periods of sleep deprivation.'

'Studies?' said Danae with distaste. The doctor had the grace to look away. 'So come on,' she added, running her hand through her hair, knotted and limp, 'Do what you need to and then please go away.'

'It's about your friend,' said the doctor.

Fear prickled her brain up a notch on the scale of wakefulness. 'What about him?'

The doctor pursed her lips. 'All his tests are coming back negative,' she said.

Danae looked at her expectantly. Finally, she said, 'So this would be good … ?

'His white cell count's on the high side, his liver function is a little sluggish, and there's still some oedema and swelling, but the antigen count is almost completely nil. He's out of the woods,' she said, but she left a long, expectant pause that Danae did not know how to fill.

'So ...' she prompted.

'So I'm concerned about his collapse,' said the doctor. 'There's nothing in his medical notes or his family history, and I know you've spent a lot of time in his company. I want to talk environmental factors.'

'I've already told you what I know,' said Danae, and realised she was talking herself into a swift despatch. She hesitated, and added, 'What caused the collapse?'

The doctor took a breath to speak, then stopped. She was young, no more than thirty-two or thirty-three, with sharp eyes and the air of someone who wasn't used to not having an answer. 'He stops breathing,' she said. 'That's as much as the printouts are telling me. It lasts for about five minutes and then he collapses and it stops. It's happened three more times since last night, and he's not strong enough to cope with it on top of everything else.'

Danae thought several unworthy thoughts, but she said, 'Can I talk to him?'

'No,' said the doctor.

'Okay,' she said slowly, and curled the edges of her lips into a smile that had nothing to do with humour or goodwill. 'Then can I see the printouts?'

'They're confidential,' said the doctor. Danae narrowed her eyes and opened her mouth to speak, but the doctor interrupted her. 'I've spoken to his brother - there's nothing in his background, no childhood illnesses. I want to know what else he might have been exposed to in the days before he became ill.'

'Let me think about it,' said Danae, in her new capacity as diagnostic investigator.

'Think quickly,' said the doctor. Her hand reached out into thin air as she pressed a switch in the hologram suite, and she vanished. Danae glanced suspiciously at the air ducts in the ceiling, but they took no notice of her: perhaps she had compensated for her sleep deprivation. Perhaps the doctor just wanted her awake. Deciding she didn't care, as long as she was left alone, she sat up, easing the chain to as far as it would go, and stared at the window.

What's going on, Turrow? she thought.

While the nanotherapy's effectiveness was uncertain, she would live. Stifled by the sour air, unable to move from her bed, bored to collapse, but alive. She stared at Turrow, prostrate on his narrow cot, deep in the arms of sleep. His face was reddened where it had been pressed, still feverish, against the mattress for too long; his breathing was ragged but even. Above his head, lifesigns twittered like birds, dancing a recovery dance. She wondered suddenly how it must be, to lie in agony and wait for the body to get the upper hand on something almost infinitely smaller than oneself. To wait for death at the hands of an invader too small to see, so small that they couldn't be repelled. And then, because it was leading her down an avenue of soul-shaking panic, she filed it under Things Best Left Alone, and closed her eyes. It was better than the alternative, though not by much.

20.4

He woke in the evening for his tests. His dinner, an unappetising mess of strength-building carbohydrates and low-fat proteins, sat untouched by his bed, and Danae said, like a scolding mother, knowing he couldn't hear her, 'You need to eat, Turrow. You need to get your strength back.'

His eyes had glazed over under a barrage of questions from a new doctor that Danae didn't recognise. Idly, she kicked at her blanket with her toes, infused with a restless energy and a life of their own after days of inactivity, and stared at the ceiling, as though she could make it do something interesting by force of will alone.

She jiggled her feet against their chains for a while, for the sake of the sound they made where they struck the bed frame. That was safe enough while they were preoccupied with Turrow; other times they got antsy when she moved about, and she tended to wake up three hours later with a brutal headache and the taste of nausea in her mouth. Funny how this, too, had become a sort of routine. Perhaps it was possible to get used to anything, given no alternative.

Given that the alternative was death.

She was settled again, and when she got settled it was easy to forget. Even the Angel of Death had ceased to turn up; he'd got bored and gone off to bother the incumbents of the ward down the corridor. She leaned her head towards the window and watched absently. Someone had tracked dirt through the corridor, a fuzzy grey trail across the white tiles, and a little familiar thrill stirred in her belly: *her* city, *her* dirt. Home.

Turrow was starting to lose patience. The doctor, more perceptive than some of his colleagues, took his patient's fraying temper in good humour, but his face, when he half-turned to let himself out of the projection room, was a battleground of fatigue and weary bewilderment. Danae closed her eyes quickly, in case he decided to make a lightning visit to her cell, but the ward was quiet. After five minutes, she decided it was safe and shuffled upright on her cot again.

Turrow was easing himself out of bed. With only a gown to cover him, she saw how thin he'd become: flesh hanging slack from his arms and legs, purplish patches describing the last remnants of the violent rash that had snaked along his limbs as the inflammation spread. His bones looked too narrow to hold him, but he stood with a little effort and shuffled to the window.

His eyes locked on hers.

Go back to bed, she mouthed, but she smiled.

He shrugged, returned her smile, as though they were co-conspirators. Then he lowered his head, and collapsed.

And it hit her, violently, with such force that she wondered how she could have missed it.

The doctors wouldn't spot it because the doctors didn't know Turrow; they wouldn't realise that he needed to echo Danae's grand gesture in the only way he could. They would see an anomaly on a print screen, and try to turn it into a relic of the fever or – worse – the nanon sequence; might even wonder if it had left him with a permanent glitch in whichever part of the brain controlled the respiratory function and if that meant that the net result of the fever or the treatment was going to be a worldwide population of thousands that kept falling over and forgetting to breathe. Presumably some doctor on the staff had experimented with holding their breath as a child, to punish their parents for some miscarriage of household justice and discovered that their retribution was seriously undermined by the fact that no matter how blue they went, as soon as they passed out, their treacherous lungs would capitulate. Presumably, somebody would know that, but it would never occur to them to make a connection.

It wouldn't occur to them that maybe he was doing it on purpose.

THE MIAMI POST, 14TH MARCH 2077

Sources in the Department of Homeland Security are refusing to confirm or deny reports that a 'substantial quantity' of explosives has been seized this morning on a fishing boat bound for Charlotte Harbor. The claims were published at 0817 local time on the Pensacola page of the controversial Tree of Liberty streamport, which makes unverified statements linking the shipment to an organisation calling itself the Capuan Legion. Thought to be a faction of Libertas, a radical a-naut rights group with ties to Emancipation, the Capuan Legion came to prominence earlier this month when it published what has become known as the 'Red Sea Speech,' attributed to a-naut leader G-QZ1484, which some sources are calling an incitement to terrorism.

XTRACT: 'RED SEA' SPEECH, PUBLISHED 3RD FEBRUARY 2077

... and so I say to you now: we will be heard. We will shout so loudly that no man shall turn a deaf ear. We shall rain fire and blood upon the heads of those that have stolen from us our brothers and sisters, our friends and comrades. I have come to free the slaves of the earth. I will part the Red Sea and give them safe passage, but I will bring the waters crashing down upon the heads of those who pursue us. For each of my innocent brothers and sisters that you take from me, ten of yours will pay the price.

These are the wages of oppression.

SATURDAY SENTINEL, 20TH MARCH 2077

... attempting to verify the source, but a spokesperson for the Congressional police confirmed that they are treating the threat as genuine. Flights into the airport have been diverted to Wellington and a no-fly zone has been established above the city...

TRANSCRIPT: NINE O'CLOCK NEWS (EUROPE-WIDE) 23RD APRIL 2077

... we interrupt this programme to bring you some breaking news. We're receiving unconfirmed reports on the stream of a major explosion in Chicago's financial district, possibly La Salle Street. No word at this early stage on what might have caused the blast, but it's thought to have caused extensive damage. Let's go live to our North America correspondent Simrin Bhela, who's in the city now. Simrin, what can you tell us about what's happening?

24 MAY

21.1

She watched him when she could. Sometimes, she would wake suddenly with the taste of metal at the back of her throat and a head full of porcelain butterflies and realise that they'd mickeyed her again and stolen an hour, two hours, half a day of Turrow from her. She made a great show of lying quietly, in perfect granite stillness with her eyes locked on the ceiling and her breathing soft and shallow, and sometimes it worked and sometimes it didn't. There was no consistency to the dosage; one minute she would be drifting in a gentle, foamy half-light, then she would surface for as long as it took someone to notice and send her under again. 'Under' was anything from groggy to comatose, and there was no way to prepare for it and no point in getting worked up. At least in the shadows, the Angel couldn't smirk at her. In the shadows, she was untouchable and it mattered almost not at all anyway, because there was a certain amount of time left and at the end of that time it would be over, and maybe, after all, it would be better to plummet suddenly into the darkness and never wake up.

When she was lucid, or semi-lucid, she watched him.

Maybe it would be different if anyone had asked her after the single instance of throwaway questioning on the first night. When she didn't know, she could answer honestly and didn't have to wait and see if she could make her mouth form the words to say, *he's faking it for me, now take me away to die*. From time to time, he would get out of bed on shaky legs, stronger by the hour, and walk to the window to stop breathing and fall down. Danae watched him, drank him in, pricked and needled at the base of herself to see if any part of her looked at him and wondered why she'd made the choice she made. And when the panic swelled – and the smallest things would make it swell, like the flowering of a bruise on her ankle where the restraints had crushed a handful of blood vessels and the sickening lurch of nausea that reminded her that it would never get the chance to fade – when the panic swelled and all she could think about was the crippling injustice of having to give up her life, she imagined lying beside him in their stolen bed and not doing what she did, and she remembered why that wasn't possible.

While there was any tiny flickering remnant of doubt, the nanons would not be replicated. What wheels had turned and what mountains had been moved to get him into the room across the corridor from her and to get an eldritch concentration of sub-microscopic DNA-engines siphoned into a human system on the assumption that this was the one human system that she had a vested interest in maintaining, Danae didn't care to contemplate. But even in their underground cocoon, detached from the world at large, she knew that they were watched with the kind of interest for which *interest* didn't begin to describe the level of focused attention directed at one man and his fainting fits. Even detached from the world at large, she knew that people were dying and people were panicking and that, in small fragments, the world was coming apart.

And his life signs were subtly failing.

She let it go into the night, and knew that she ought to be dead. In the early hours of the morning, a new doctor, a man she didn't recognise but who radiated authority even as a gremlin in the holosuite programme made him twinkle like Christmas lights, appeared beside Danae as the sedative was unceremoniously withdrawn, and said, 'We've just hit one million cases in the lower city.'

And still she couldn't say it. Her mouth would not form the words that would condemn her.

She blinked, tasting mint, and rolled her eyes until they fixed on his face.

'What do you want me to do?' she said.

'They won't keep you here forever,' said the doctor. 'Whatever you think. Whatever you have in mind.'

Her head was fuzzy from sleep she hadn't wanted and it took her a beat to make sense of what he'd said. 'You think this is *me* doing this?' she said at last.

'I think that if you suddenly disappeared, we'd suddenly find your friend made a miraculous recovery,' he said. 'What do you think?'

What did she think? She did nothing but think. She wished she could stop.

'I think I'm chained to a fucking bed and doped to the eyeballs twenty-three hours a day,' she said, but ice was trickling relentlessly into her belly and her voice sounded sick even to her. 'That's what I think,' she added, to stop herself saying what the panic wanted her to say, which was, *please help me, please help me, please, I don't want to die.*

'I think it was a mistake to test it on your friend,' said the doctor, after a long, frigid silence. 'If we told the families upstairs that we had an experimental treatment that might save their loved-ones' lives, I have a funny feeling they'd be falling over themselves to sign the consent forms. And I have a funny feeling we wouldn't be seeing any fainting fits.'

Danae had no clock, no view of the light outside, but she thought that it must be close to three o'clock in the morning. Two and a half hours from dawn: May yellows, inching up the colour spectrum like kidney failure, but beautiful; so beautiful. It was the last day of her life.

Numbly, detached and watching herself with interest, she said, 'If that's what you think, then why don't you give it a try. See what happens.'

Silence. Danae waited a beat, then chanced a look upwards, towards the doctor. His eyes were fixed on her, treating her to the full force of an uncomfortable stare. Behind him, a shadow on the wall announced the return of the Angel of Death, bright-eyed and bushy tailed, to wait with her until the end.

'Okay,' said the doctor.

Strange, thought Danae when she was alone at last. Strange that the sense of what she had just done, the finality of it, was so unreal that she could think about it indifferently, as if it would never happen. In a day, in half a day's time, she would be gone. Dead, reconditioned, strapped to an operating table in a lab somewhere; the details were academic. It was all completely meaningless.

She looked at Turrow, sleeping, or at least seeming to do so, and hoped that they took her before he woke; that she didn't have to look him in the eye as she was leaving. She hoped that he'd seen her gesture in their silent, midnight conversation, guessed its meaning, guessed enough to put it all together in time, found a way to do what almost certainly couldn't be done before she couldn't hold out any more. It wasn't much of a hope, but it was all Danae had left.

21.2

Turrow woke up in the bed and realised that his efforts were starting to make him ill. He didn't remember coming to on the ground, or the sensation of strong, mechanical hands lifting him onto the mattress. He had no idea even how long he'd been out this time. But when he raised his head, the nausea that usually swept over him after any attempt to shift his centre of gravity was fleeting. A brief look at the skin on his arms revealed scaly, discoloured skin where the rash had been, but no signs of purple. His thinking was clearer, even the air smelled cooler. But his muscles were weak and only unpredictably responsive to command, and his ribs protested with every breath. His body was healing through bloody-minded determination alone, and at some point that was going to stop being enough.

He eased himself gently up onto his elbows and waited for the white spots to clear from his vision. The corridor outside his room was empty, as always. There was no sensation that they were part of a grander scheme of anything in the ward, nothing to contradict the growing sense of unease, building in his brain over the past few days, that the rest of the world had actually died and only a pocket of people remained: himself, Danae, and a gaggle of irritating physicians. Maybe it was Purgatory; that might actually make more sense. He eased himself carefully upwards, just enough to see into the room across the corridor. Just enough to see that she was still there.

Her mattress had been raised at the head so that she was sitting upright for the first time in days, and the female doctor was with her, standing at a distance with her back to the window. The doctor's right arm was folded across her chest, and the left was gesticulating as her shoulders moved. Danae's head lolled heavily against her bed but her eyes were sharp and fixed on the doctor's face. There was nothing to read in them; she had completely shut down.

His right elbow failed him then, his limbs capricious and uncoordinated, and he tumbled back onto his pillow. Both women looked around, his movement captured in their peripheral vision. Danae's expression terrified him. It was devoid of emotion.

The doctor flickered off and reappeared in his room half a beat later.

'How are you feeling?' she said.

Turrow knew better than to tell her what his life signs would contradict, so he said, 'Yeah, fine. I'm getting there.'

She treated him to a long glare that could have withered steel.

'You're getting there,' said the doctor. 'Yes. I'd say you were already there.'

Her tone sent little prickles of unease sparking along his spine. Turrow looked at her for a moment, then said, cautiously, 'But when I get out of bed …

Danae's gaze, across the corridor, was like stone.

'Yes. When you get out of bed,' said the doctor. She pursed her lips, stared at the ceiling for a second, as though she were calling down strength from the heavens. 'We gave the sequenced nanons to fifteen new patients during the night. One of them was spiking a fever of a hundred and five when he came in. Two of them are out of the woods already. So — why not you, Mr Turrow?'

Turrow's heart started to break. He looked again to Danae, her expression unreadable, her eyes hollow. She looked away.

'I wouldn't need proof,' said the doctor, relentlessly. 'I couldn't make a case for obstruction, but do you think anyone would care? People who've lost children, or husbands, or parents, because you let them think the treatment was bad? Do you think they'd care?'

'Please,' he said. 'She hasn't done anything. Don't let them hurt her.'

But he was talking to empty space.

21.3

They came for her within the hour. Danae saw the play of light on the walls announce their arrival and knew what it meant even before she saw the uniforms. Panic focused into a high whine, ricocheting off the walls in electric flashes of light and colour. On the wall behind her, her life signs began to spike, flinging themselves at the ceiling in a *danse macabre*. Her arms pushed her body from the bed in a single, fluid movement, unaware, checked by the length of her restraints; her feet began to scrabble at the mattress as though they could move her out of danger.

Oh God, she thought. *There's not enough time. There's not enough time.*

Through the habit of survival, her eyes scanned the room in quick, frantic bursts, searching for an escape, but her thoughts were too disordered; she barely noticed. She couldn't turn her head towards them; nothing could make her turn to face them: three of them, waiting patiently to bundle her off towards death.

I could run, she thought desperately. *They would try to catch me, but I am too strong for them …*

The Angel of Death snickered, but sadly, and there was no humour in the smile he turned on her. That was almost worse than the gloating.

Danae's breath nearly gave out. She arched backwards, throwing her throat open, panic burning through her bloodstream, forcing the air from her lungs. As she twisted away from them, into air, away from death, the world swam very briefly and then went black.

21.4

He knew she hadn't seen him. He knew that she'd been cocooned in a secret world of fear and that the only thing she saw was the advancing face of death, and he knew that it had been a monster, despite his whispered prayers that, against the odds, it would look like an old friend. He had watched her, scrabbling and hissing like a cornered animal, nerves screaming at her to run, and his hands had risen with hers, pulling on invisible chains, struggling and fighting and clawing. He'd watched her arch off her bed, stripping her restraints to their limit, and he'd hammered, unheard, on his window until his fists bruised and his arms ached, while tears rained, unnoticed, down his cheeks.

There's not enough time, he had thought. *Oh God, there wasn't enough time.*

And then she had collapsed, like a deflated balloon, and again that little part of him had thought, *take her now*, but it was a sedative, nothing stronger, and his heart had broken.

She would have been all right. She would have walked out of the compound with that Cleopatra dignity that always seemed so ludicrous on the streets of Limbe, and she would have seen him and she would have looked at him and in that second he would have found the way to make it all right. But they couldn't give her even that, and instead they blanketed her in sleep and stole her away.

He screamed after them until he was hoarse. He thumped on his window until he was sure it would break and drop him into the corridor in a shower of little perspex shards. And they lifted her onto a gurney, shackling her flaccid arms in front of her, her ankles and her throat, they wheeled her out of his line of sight without looking back.

TRANSCRIPT: *EBC NEWS INTERNATIONAL,* 24TH APRIL 2077

The sun is just coming up here above a ruined skyline after a night of terror that some local people are likening to living in a war zone. Ground forces at the scene won't let us get any closer to the site of the explosions, which would seem to imply that there's some concern about additional devices, but I can say, Eleanor, that from the cordon it's possible to see the sheer extent of the devastation. You can hear the sirens behind me — that's been constant now throughout the night, and they're still coming. It's hard to say at this stage, but I'm hearing reports of some twenty-five fatalities — but given the scale of what we're seeing here, Eleanor, that number seems certain to rise. There's still no word on whether or not these explosions are linked to the blasts in Singapore or Zurich, but all I can say, Eleanor, is that this is a city in shock, it's a city in mourning, and it's a city — like others across the globe today — that's very, very scared.

22.1

Danae dreamed.

Her fear-washed brain threw up images of life, nagged her reproachfully for all the things she'd said she would do and never had. In her mind's eye she stood again with sweat-moist skin in a chill breeze and felt the shiver of goosebumps on her skin. Children were born to her. She lived in a house, with simple furniture and a bed that was all her own, with a milk-gorged baby pressed to her breast. She took a holiday. She wore a suit. She stood on a beach at sunrise and listened to the music of the waves and the wind in the grassy dunes. She picked apples from a tree in one of the underground orchardariums she'd heard they still had on the other side of Paris. She walked barefoot in a stream. She lived on, into old age and decrepitude, beside Turrow, awash with Turrow, living and breathing Turrow. She lived.

Not enough time, she thought, as the images fractured and were sucked into the grey present. *There was not enough time.*

She was strapped tightly into a car seat, as she had been when they brought her to the hospital. The hazmask was back, feeding a sweet-smelling chemical soup into her chest with every breath, soothing her into a twilight between motion and stillness while her brain rattled against her skull and the itch wailed. Her wrists and ankles were in manacles, fastened by a short metal antenna to the seat, and another restraint was around her chest, sharp against her ribs. On the journey here, it had seemed crazy, unnecessary, because she had something she needed to do; she would not have run. Now she would have killed every man in the car before they knew what was happening and disappeared into obscurity, like Angelo.

Now? said the itch.

Now.

But her body wouldn't obey. Loose with sedation, she managed to lift herself half an inch off her seat, managed to twist her arms thirty degrees against their manacles, managed to shake a rattle out of the chains at her legs before inertia claimed her and she slumped backwards, neck slack, eyes rolling in her head. Enough to get their attention, enough to unsettle them; not even enough to bruise her own skin.

'*Hé!*' said the soldier to her left. He shook his head, said something she didn't understand, so she swore at him and twisted her head to the side, bracing herself to start again.

'Danae,' said a voice – a kinder voice, one she thought she recognised. She looked up, met a plasticised gaze. 'Don't make me put you under,' said the voice. 'I don't want to.'

'Let me go,' she said. Her words were ragged, breathy, trailing into incoherence. She sucked in air, titled her head back, tensed. Nausea flashed as the drugs pooled in her lungs, but she ignored it, focused all her energy into one long sound of rage: 'Let me go!'

The final word trilled out into a long crescendo and ended in something that was more like a shriek. Pain fired in Danae's chest, and was joined by a smack to the face by the soldier to her left, catching her by surprise and snapping her head to the side, where it dropped against her shoulder. A line of saliva fell from her lip, spread out against the thin membrane of her mask.

Over the ringing in her aching ear, she heard somebody muttering something, heard a faint bray of laughter in response. Danae's head lolled forward, and her hair, imperfectly caught behind her head as the mask was applied, tumbled about her face. She sat, motionless, aware of the tension in the car, aware that they were waiting for her to animate. She breathed deeply, painfully.

Fuck the itch. It wasn't how she wanted it to be.

'We had an a-naut when I was a kid,' said a voice from ahead of her. It was the kind voice, magnified by the hush in the car. 'She was an Isis line. Quite a late generation. Maybe a 770 B or C, I can't remember now. She was our nurse.'

Danae said nothing; watched the pattern of light as it fell through her hair.

'She would have been about three years old when the Insurgency started. I remember, the Rens came to the house and we didn't know what to do, so we just handed her over. They shot her in the garden.'

Danae wondered if he had a point or if he was just making conversation. Maybe it was protocol or something; maybe every a-naut that made the journey to the death centres got regaled with stories about the execution of other a-nauts.

She realised that he was still talking. 'What?' she said.

He said, 'This doesn't have to start any sooner than it needs to.'

22.2

The car drew to a halt. With effort, Danae raised her head, but there were no windows. She couldn't have said how long they'd driven, even if they were still in the lower city. Pain from her ear had spread in a tendrilled arc across her face, flashing white lines of pain in front of her eyes when she moved her jaw. It was a different sedative, she thought, to the one they had used in the holding cell: not strong enough to knock her out, not light enough to allow her to move in anything more focused than languid, drunken lope, but her head was clear; her thoughts were sharp and unobstructed. She concentrated on that as a bag was lowered once more over her head and fastened around her neck; as her arms and legs were ejected from the seat, forced together, manacles locked with an electromagnetic current; as rough hands gripped her shoulders and pulled her to her feet, out of the car and into thick, warm air that was unmistakably Creo Basse. That gave her a tiny, absurd thrill of joy. At least she was where she belonged.

Her leg irons afforded little space for movement beyond a graceless shuffle; she could not move unaided. A dull, soporific heaviness had settled in as the panic had reached a crescendo and levelled off into a plateau. Without the benefit of a constant, tidal flow of adrenaline, Danae could not have run anyway, even if her legs had been free, even if they hadn't trained three guns on her. Something had settled; it allowed for denial.

'The bag off?' she said. She sounded drunk. 'I want to see.'

'You don't want to know,' said a voice close to her ear.

'I do,' said Danae. She wanted to know everything while there was still a brain to know it with.

And then there was the kind voice, behind her; a kind hand on her shoulder. 'Let me do you this favour at least,' it said. 'The blindfold stays on.'

A change in the texture of the air told her they had crossed over a hidden threshold and entered a building. Dampness leeched upwards through the soles of her feet, and the ground was coated with a kind of granular slime that spoke of desertion and rot and decay. She thought that they might be beneath a drainage pipe or maybe a bubble: above her head, water trickled over ancient floorboards and down hollow walls, pooling in dark puddles that exploded thick, syrupy water when her feet slammed through them. She imagined faded, peeling wallpaper, hidden behind a black fungal fur: a floral pattern, perhaps, consumed by mould. The floor that she walked on bowed beneath her feet; it was like walking on sponge.

'Steps,' said a voice ahead of her.

'Up or down?' she said, thinking, *it doesn't matter anymore.*

Down; but they were on her too quickly and she lost her balance. For a second, she hung in mid-air in defiance of gravity, too stunned even to cry out, and she thought, *even here, there are surprises.* To have come so close, to have been minutes away from the chamber, and to have been snatched away by the great gaping mouth of an unseen stairwell ... and then strong hands caught her and she stumbled, bending her ankle at an unnatural angle so that her leg irons dug first into one foot and then the other. The exhilaration, like a candle flame in the wind, was gone as quickly as it had arrived. She shuffled forward, foot over foot.

Fifty-three stairs. She wanted to know everything there was left to know. Twelve, then a platform, and then forty-one and then they levelled out. Another four steps across a tiny landing – she could feel the soldiers shuffle in close – and then they stopped. Metal whined across metal.

A reinforced door, she thought, and realised that the journey was over.

22.3

The bag was removed, but there was no rush of light to assault her eyes. She was chained to a metal chair in a dimly-lit room so clean and sterile that it might have been transplanted from another place, were it not for the pits in the floor where the concrete had been poorly poured, the hints of spreading damp in the corners, the chill of the air. There was a steel table in the centre of the room, bolted into the ground and polished to a shine but it was empty, decorated only by the bright flares of light from the recessed bulbs in the low ceiling. Beside it were two chairs, plastic seated and cheap, on one of which sat a middle-aged man with a cigarette hanging from between his lips, rocking forwards and backwards. The rhythmic click-click of chair legs on concrete was like the chipping of a gravestone.

It could have been a dental examination room, a delivery ward, an Acute Injury Pod, if it weren't for the fact that it was so obviously a place where people came to die.

How can you sit in this room? she wanted to ask; would have asked if she could have made the words easily. She was genuinely bewildered, beyond even the horror or the fear. The air was greasy with death: it dripped off the chair, glistened in little twinkles of light that bounced off the tiles, glowered at her from the shadows. It buzzed like a swarm of flies above the chair where she sat, over the grated drain below her, around the head of the second man, who was now busying himself with a CP scanner at the back of her neck.

'See?' said the cigarette man as a green glow bounced off his companion's face. 'Clear. But look at the waveforms — they look mostly organic, but they're just ever so slightly off. You need to know what you're looking for.'

'Please,' said Danae. Her voice was shuddering, forced through her teeth. 'It's a green light. It's a green; I'm okay. I'm not an a-naut, it's a green....'

But the cigarette man ignored her and his companion looked past her as though she wasn't there. 'Please,' she said as he pressed patches to her chest, her throat, her wrists, and, above the table, her life signs sprang into technicolor glory: heart rate spiking, O2 sats dropping, brainwaves trembling like barley fields in the wind. 'Please,' she said again, and it was a whisper.

A nod to the soldiers from the electrode man. 'Thanks, guys,' he said. 'We can take it from here.' To the cigarette man as the soldiers filed out, heels snapping against the crisp, white tile: 'Calibrate for non-lethal; we need basic autonomic function preserved. Pons, medulla oblongata, midbrain if possible. We can probably go to 17,000 before she starts to fry.'

He might have been reading a shopping list; it was just words. There was no way to make them words about her; not when the cigarette man perched his smoke between his lips and crossed the floor to close his hands on either side of her skull, not when he rolled her head on her neck and asked the electrode man about the sheathing on her brain stem, not when they made a show of checking the tubing on her hazmask or when the electrode man called up a screen in front of her with her name, her details, the story of her life scrolling down the page into darkness. It wasn't her. It was happening to someone else. Danae just needed to find a way to get through it until the universe caught up.

'I'm a good person,' she whispered but her mouth was just making sounds now; her brain was not in control. Nothing would work, her arms wouldn't lift her, her legs wouldn't carry her. Nothing else was going to make it go away and she couldn't die like that, limp and helpless. 'I don't deserve this. I want to go home. Please don't hurt me. Please don't hurt me ...'

As easily as if he were kneading bread, the electrode man closed his hand into a fist, swung, slammed it into her face. The chair rocked forward onto two legs.

He pulled it back onto four and went back about his business. Danae, dazed and semi-conscious, barely heard the cigarette man speak.

'Got a couple of questions for you,' he said.

THE SOUTH EAST EXAMINER, 30TH AUGUST 2077

Emancipation continues to distance itself from last week's carnage, amidst widespread reports that a-naut terrorist G-QZ1484, also known as Garrison, has claimed responsibility for the attacks. A spokesperson for the organisation insists that the explosions, which killed 122 – including 17 children – and injured almost 1500, were the work of 'a small band of radicalised insurgents' and that 'the overwhelming majority of a-nauts want nothing more than to be allowed to coexist peacefully with the non-artificial population.' They have further condemned yesterday's attack on a holding centre in Croydon, in which 33 amnisonaut units awaiting reconditioning were destroyed, and have called for members of the so-called Renegade Elimination Network to be tried under Article 4 of the Geneva Convention. Figures published last month by advocacy group Venia suggest that, of the 1400 individual or group attacks against artificial units between December 2076 and 22 April 2077, at least 50% can be directly related to the Network or its affiliates, which Emancipation are calling 'an affront to humanity' and 'a blatant attempt to aggravate an already unstable situation …'

24 MAY - AFTERNOON

23.1

'Mr Turrow.'

Boston didn't look up, didn't move. If he lay like this, perfectly still, and stared at the ceiling for long enough, he found that he could let his mind slip into a trance of sorts, and found that this was the only way to keep thoughts of her from encroaching. One day, perhaps, he would revisit her memory and smile at the knowledge that there had been such a person as Danae Grant, and that they had touched and breathed the same air and loved, but now the thought of her ripped his chest apart, and when he thought of her it was invariably accompanied by a scream, less a thought than a streak of pure, white-hot emotion: *I did not save her.*

'Mr Turrow.' The voice was getting impatient now.

Fuck off, he thought casually and continued to stare at the ceiling, thoughts of nothing interrupted and momentarily damaged. The voice could 'Mr Turrow' all day long; they wouldn't come near him for fear of what was in the room with him, and until such times as they actually fumigated and opened the door and dragged him out, he would lie and stare at the ceiling and would not think of her or what was being done to her in the last hours of her life.

She sees the blow coming, but there's nothing she can do about it. Time telescopes, like she's staring at a movie screen through the wrong end of binoculars. She sees it coming as a series of stills, milliseconds apart, so that she can watch it with something approaching interest as his arm arcs, swings backwards, and pivots towards her. It hits her in the throat — she wasn't expecting that — and the tiny sharp breath she took in readiness for the impact lodges there, twines around her tongue. Red light explodes from the edges of her eyes and the room recedes into a dark, strangled hole, where the only sound is a desperate, asphyxiated wheeze...

'Mr Turrow.'

Somebody must have run out of patience, because the room hissed suddenly with the sharp whine of irradiation, and then the gas descended without any further reference to the filter on his bedside table. He grappled blindly for it and clamped over his nose before his eyes were forced closed, stinging and burning and weeping hot, affronted tears as it dropped over him and to the floor, pressed down by its own weight, and disappeared into unseen suction vents. He heard rather than saw the door slide open, fists pressed into his aching eye sockets as if they could pound the pain away.

Hands gripped his shoulders and pulled him into a sitting position. 'Take a minute, son,' said a voice he didn't recognise, and the hands on his shoulder, attached by kindness to the voice in front of him, squeezed reassuringly and let go.

Boston prised his eyelids apart and saw through a thin, watery slit that the older doctor, the one who knew when to leave him alone, was beside him, watching him carefully. Two orderlies, limp with exhaustion, hung back at the door, and beside them stood a man in soldier's fatigues.

'Better now?' said the doctor. Boston nodded and lay back down on the bed.

'Mr Turrow,' said the soldier, 'it's time to go.'

Boston didn't move. 'You took her,' he said.

The chair rocks backwards under the force of the blow. Her eyes are bulging, fixed on nothing as she sucks and sucks at the air and nothing comes. She falls, carried by the chair's momentum but separate from it, so that there are two connections: the back of the chair with the floor, and, half a second later, Danae with the chair. Her head slams into the ground, her neck against the sharp edge of the chair back, and a white nausea spreads through her like dye. But she cannot be sick because her throat is closed and her face is covered; she will drown...

'He had no choice, son,' said the doctor.

'He had a choice,' said Boston. He looked up at the soldier, who was watching him with an air of unconcern. 'Like I'm choosing not to cross the room and beat the living shit out of him right now.'

'You wouldn't even get close,' said the soldier mildly.

Boston shrugged. 'Who cares?' he said. 'I would try.'

'Then why don't you?' There was no challenge to the voice; it was a question.

'Because it doesn't matter. You don't matter,' said Boston, staring at the ceiling. It would take hours to get back to that meditative half-way point between thinking and sleep. 'Nothing matters. You did that.'

The soldier nodded to the doctor. 'Give him a light sedative,' he said. 'Just enough to get him to the transport.'

Boston went out.

23.2

'Don't get smart with me, buddy.' The same, mild voice, infused with reproval, edging slightly towards menace. 'You're lucky you're not with the Rens right now yourself. Now. Let's try again.'

... she raises her head, enough to see where the next one is coming from. It hits her in the nose, an explosion of heat and pain, and when her head snaps back from the blow she realises she's crying: huge, open-mouthed sobs, and she wonders, when did that happen?

They were sitting in a windowless room, white-walled and fluorescent-lit, and furnished with the kind of regulation, soul-sapping furniture fitted as standard in governmental buildings across the world. Boston was on one side of the table, the mild-voiced sergeant was on the other. A jug of water sat between them, and the soldier had offered a packet of cigarettes as an ice-breaker. Boston had taken two and put them in his pocket, enjoying his companion's arch-eyebrowed amusement.

'Go on then,' he said. To his ears, his words sounded dull, half-asleep. 'Try me again.'

The soldier sighed. 'We can do this all day if you want.'

Turrow shrugged. 'How long will they keep her alive for?'

The soldier ignored him. 'Let's recap. You met the subject about three weeks ago, right?' A weary sigh. 'Mr Turrow. Is that right?'

'By *the subject*,' said Turrow, 'you mean Danae?' Silence and a stony glare. He gave up. 'Yes. I told you.'

'And that was the first contact you had had with the subject?'

'That's what happens when you meet someone,' said Turrow.

'*That was the first contact you had with the subject?*'

'*... I don't know,*' she screams. '*Please. Please. I don't know. I swear I don't know. Please. Please. Oh God, please ...*'

'Yes,' said Turrow.

'Were you aware then that she was contraband?'

Turrow shook his head, rubbed his eyes. His skin felt like rubber left in the sun too long. He said, 'She told me later.'

'When did she tell you?'

'About …' He considered. 'Ten days later.' Barely a week. Barely a week had passed since that night. There was not enough time.

'Why do you think that was?'

'What?'

'Why do you think she told you then?'

I need you to go. There is no me. And I can't trust myself.

'I don't know. She was upset.'

'What had upset her?'

'She said … her friend had died.'

'What friend?'

'A woman she worked with.'

'How had she died?'

'You know how she died.'

'I don't know, pal. That's why I'm asking.'

'The same thing that's killing this whole fucking city. The same thing she just saved you from.'

'Okay. Her friend had died, she was upset. Did that seem plausible to you?'

He looked up. 'What?'

'Okay. Let me put it another way. Did you think it was in keeping with her character? Was she the sort of person who usually got wound up and started spilling her guts?'

Boston stared at him levelly, wondering where he was going, but the light hurt his eyes and he had to look away. The soldier took it for capitulation. He said, 'Because she didn't seem that way to me.'

'You met her, what — once?'

The soldier shrugged. 'What else did she say, Boston?'

'When?'

'Did she try to talk you into something? Maybe she knew a soft touch when she saw one. I think she was playing you from day one, wasn't she, buddy?'

Boston laughed. He couldn't help himself. 'This is bullshit,' he said.

'She was looking for someone with a way in, wasn't she? She trots into the Housing Authority, and there you are, all sweetness and light, and she knows she can spin you out for as long as she needs to. Maybe it's not exactly top level stuff, but it's a way in. And you went for it. It's all right, Boston. Maybe we all would.'

'This is bullshit,' said Boston again.

'What else did she say?' He slammed a hand down on the desk. 'What else did she say, Boston? Did she give you a name? I *know* Emancipation runs caches out of every damn district in this city. Did she give you a name?'

'You have no idea,' said Boston.

'Do you know what the penalty is for knowingly harbouring an a-naut?'

'I don't care,' he said.

'You'll care all right. I'm trying to help you, Boston. But I need a name.'

'I told you what happened,' said Boston. 'There wasn't any name.'

The hand slammed down on the table again with a violence that startled him. Boston blinked at it; said, 'Thank God I don't have to pretend we're best buddies anymore.' Which wasn't his finest hour, but a knock on the door deflected retribution for the time being.

'What?' shouted the soldier.

It was another soldier. Boston didn't know enough about military ensigns to be sure, but he thought, from the way his companion's demeanour changed, that the newcomer was his superior. The first soldier tried to stare him out, but the new guy was a pro; used to having commands obeyed without actually articulating them. He carried a package in his hands.

Without a word, the first soldier stood up, pushing his seat back with enough force to topple it, and stalked out. The captain took his time crossing the floor to the desk; Boston had the impression that he never hurried, always moved with a slow, even poise. He lifted the fallen chair, set it upright and sat down. Boston's eyes fell on the package, plastic-wrapped, that he set in front of them.

'You could be in a lot of trouble,' he said.

Boston shrugged.

'It's ten to fifteen years, by the way.'

'What?'

'For harbouring an a-naut.' A beat. 'Yeah, I thought you might care after all.' He pushed the package across the table. 'Lucky for you, I think we have enough on our plate right now. That's for you.'

Boston touched it as though it might burn. 'What is it?' he said, but he thought he knew.

'It's your friend's personal effects. They've been irradiated; they're clean.'

'Oh.' He could feel it starting in his throat; knew that if he said any more, he would not be able to hold it in.

'You can sign for them on your way out.'

Turrow nodded, rested his fingers on the plastic. The captain stood up.

'There's a convoy going to Chatelier in fifteen minutes,' he said. 'You can hitch a lift. Take your time here; I'll send someone to get you.'

'Will it be quick?' said Boston.

The captain hesitated. Boston thought that he was not the sort of man to give evasive answers, nor would it occur to him to think that Boston was talking about the convoy. He rested his hand on the desk, and said, quietly, 'No.'

'Where is she?'

A sigh. 'There wasn't anything you could have done. You know that.'

'Where is she?'

The captain shook his head. 'I didn't take her,' he said. 'I wouldn't know.'

'Limbe?'

'There aren't any sites in Limbe. Nebe, maybe. I try not to know these things.'

'Okay,' said Boston.

'Okay.'

'Thank you.' It was starting. He held it in. If it started, it would not stop.

'I'll give you a minute,' said the captain. When Boston looked up, he was alone.

23.3

He eased open the plastic seal and the scent of her hit him in a tidal wave. Boston sucked in a breath, wondering how long it would take to fade, whether he would remember it when it was gone, or if he'd just remember that he had known it once, like a vanishing smile that hovered on the edge of recollection.

Little enough. Scant evidence of a life. Her coat, thin and threadbare; the scarf she wore with it, because the coat might as well have been just for show, it didn't keep out the cold. Not his sister's coat, no matter what she might have told them, and he wondered if she'd just wanted him to have it, wanted to make sure that it hadn't been cast into the furnace, erased with the rest of what made Danae. It *was* her, an extension of her, and when he touched it she glimmered briefly in front of him; flashed him a smile over her shoulder, disappeared ahead of him down a street in the rain. Her socks — which almost undid him; they had pulled on her boots as she lay unconscious on the bed, but they had forgotten her socks. Something so tiny, so small. It hardly mattered at all. His hands tightened around the rough cotton as he closed his eyes, allowed it to pass.

A scattering of coins; not even enough to buy a coffee, loose in the bag, as though they'd dislodged themselves from her coat pocket. He lifted the coat and waves of her rose like birds, folded into the creases. One of the buttons was missing, he noticed for the first time – no, three were missing: one from the top and two in the middle, but the top button, where it mattered, had been replaced at some stage with a little plastic brooch in the shape of a cat. A tiny thing, a cheap thing, maybe a present from the distant past. Flecks of paint hinted at a long-eroded finish, but it had rubbed up white over the years, so that only the relief features remained. Danae's? He couldn't tell. Perhaps, and perhaps it had been her mother's, retained out of a sense of nostalgia, or simply because it functioned. It mattered more than anything that he knew.

She was still alive. He was sorting through her stuff as though she were dead, but she was alive.

... she's on the floor again. How did she get on the floor? She's fallen backwards and to the side, and her cheek is pressed against the white tile concrete, cold against the plastic. Her vision takes its time clearing and a million pressure points of pain in her skull join in the chorus of dissent, but she's still here; she's not gone yet ...

Four pockets: two outside, two inside. It was a practical coat; never well-constructed, probably even when it was new, but well-conceived. It was designed to be useful. Gently, almost reverently, he eased his hand into the left outside. Coins: the remainder of the loose scattering. Almost a token; useless shrapnel. Scraps of paper; a crumpled serviette, soaked once in a rain shower and disintegrating into pieces. Paper again in the right pocket: long, curling, vine-doodles surrounding a number that he recognised as the Authority's helpline. Old receipts, faded beyond reading. An ancient, petrified business card with recent scribbles in two different handwritings: *Da, Église du Sacré-Cœur, 30/04 10 A.M*, and an address in Mère de Martyrs. And an old ID card, her father's, the light forever dulled.

I did not save her.

He waited a second, let it pass. The inside left pocket: two microcards, probably worth a couple of tokens to a collector if they'd been in better shape. No label on either. An empty cigarette packet. The right: a pen, a cigarette lighter with a broken flint. A hair elastic with a thin skein of blond hair tangled around the middle. And then, the killer: another scrap of paper, this one with his phonewave number.

Boston shut his eyes, let his hands close around the fabric. The scent of her danced inside his head and he saw her face, eyebrow raised as he scribbled his name, his number, onto the first thing he found in his pocket; lips curling into a smile as she took it from him, buried it in folds of fabric with a hundred other signs and symbols of an ordinary life: a part of him pressed close to her as she walked the streets of the city she couldn't escape.

I did not save her.

A brisk, military knock at the door jolted him sharply from his reverie. Boston twitched, startled, and looked up to see a young private sidle halfway into the room. 'Mr Turrow?' he said. 'Transport's leaving in two minutes. In your own time, sir.'

The signs and symbols of an ordinary life, sealed in a plastic bag that smelled faintly of her. It wasn't enough. He nodded without turning, and began to gather them up.

Mère de Martyrs, though. It wasn't her handwriting. Who did she know in Mère de Martyrs? It was a bad part of town, bordering on Nebe and nearly as volatile. Mère de Martyrs would riot over a rainy day; its denizens dark and surly, with a gruff, black humour that excluded outsiders. Who did she know in Mère de Martyrs?

I did not save her.

'Mr Turrow?'

'Yeah, I'm coming,' he said.

Mère de Martyrs. But she'd mentioned Mère de Martyrs once. It hadn't seemed out of the ordinary when she'd spoken about it. Part of a larger story? He folded her coat, her socks; eased them back inside the plastic covering. She was still alive, somewhere in the city. Somewhere in Nebe, which was home to nearly one and a half million people and winding up into full-scale chaos for another night. She was alive, but she was out of reach. She was not in Mère de Martyrs, so why was it important?

The city was under lockdown. There was no way to Nebe and there was no way to Mère de Martyrs. She was out of reach. He lifted her things, pressed them against his chest under his coat, as though he were sheltering them from the rain.

Why was it important?

He stepped into the corridor. The private glanced at him with a look of syrupy sympathy that Turrow could have done without; he did not want to look fragile. 'Ready, sir?' he said.

'Ready,' said Turrow.

Mère de Martyrs. It bordered on Limbe to the south. She would have walked through it every day on her way home from work, except when they rioted in Nebe and she went around by Cilicia and South District. That wasn't why she'd mentioned it. Mère de Martyrs hadn't *been* the story, it had been part of the story. He'd been getting ill at the time, he thought. He remembered the thundering in his head that he'd pretended to ignore because of what it might be, but she'd wanted to tell him. It had been important to her that he knew.

It had been about Angelo.

The knowledge hit him like a bullet. Angelo had been in Mère de Martyrs. Angelo who was dead because the Rens had come for him; but he'd been with her when they took him; his friends in Mère de Martyrs would not know what had happened. And suddenly Boston was back in a windowed cell, heat washing through his veins, blanketing him in confusion and tangled thought while she lay across the corridor from him and tried to tell him a tale in silence that he couldn't decipher. She had gripped her gown at the neck and she had touched her right hip, and he hadn't understood then, because his brain wouldn't do what he needed it to do, because he had no clue and no context, but he'd thought even then that there was something about the gesture that echoed inside the snake-guarded dungeon. It was familiar; he just didn't know why. But the top button of her coat was missing, and it let in the cold when she walked, and, when the rain came, she pinched the folds together at the neck to stay warm and dry. He'd seen her do it a dozen times; she had to believe that he'd recognise it. Her coat. The right pocket of her coat. The coat she'd told them was his sister's, because she'd wanted him to have it.

She was alive. She was in Nebe and she was still alive, and he had an address in Mère de Martyrs that she'd wanted him to find. He followed the private through windowless corridors, too brightly lit, and tried to think.

23.4

Starbursts on the window, like fairy lights at a Christmas pageant. Cilicia was alive, a breathing centre of light. In the air, scattered throughout the raindrops, blending upwards into the shadows, swirled car after car in perpetual motion, like a heartbeat. In the sound-proof cocoon of the transport it was like a ballet, as though the orchestra were swelling for the final act.

Turrow watched in water-colours through the rain-smeared window. Around him, laughing, talking amiably, cracking jokes and making plans, were men who had worked twenty hour shifts for more than a week, men whose eyes were black with exhaustion, whose skin was so pale every vein was outlined in blue and purple. They were wearing breathing masks, their plastic suits discarded, thinking about home leave and the stories they would tell. There were days to go yet, millions of babies and elderly and infirm and at-risk to inoculate, millions more lying supine in makeshift beds to be treated and transferred. There was a city to get back on its feet.

Cilicia had been given over to five separate inoculation centres. Five more had been centred in Bastié, the financial district, another five in Hôpital – districts short on residential areas, where they couldn't be surprised by a particularly single-minded mob. In each one, teams of hundreds worked round-the-clock shifts, assessing and treating, administering and vaccinating, patching up the lower city. The soldiers in the transport were replacements for men who had been working almost non-stop for the hours that the cure had been available and verified.

Close to the centres, the traffic slowed to a crawl, pooling into a sluggish tide. Transports stacked upon transports, in traffic jams sixteen, seventeen blocks long, shunted forwards and backwards according to somebody's plan. But it worked: transports moved forward, they disgorged their load and waited only long enough to refill with returning passengers before they swept back out again, lost in an ocean of advance and retreat. Somebody was in control. It just wasn't clear who.

Half the city might have been in Cilicia central, but for the fact that Boston knew otherwise. You knew about the numbers of citizens involved, that the city was home to as many people as a small country, that there were millions of them, hidden beneath the concrete ceiling, cloistered away from the sunlight. You knew about it with the same abstract knowledge that told you that one day you would die, the earth would freeze, the sun would supernova. Twenty-seven million people; it was just numbers. More than a million of them had found their way to the hospital; forty per cent of those were already dead. But it was just numbers, until they appeared en masse on the streets, and it wasn't even a fraction of them, and still there was nothing but people. Wall to wall people, banked up tightly in the wide street. An anthill of activity: plastic-faced soldiers, white-eyed children, men and women indistinguishable behind the scarves wrapped tightly around their faces. A sea of people, a catastrophe of people, too many to breathe, too many to fit in one place. They flowed before the soldiers' orders, like sheep before the shepherd: worried, harried. Someone knew what was going on, but it was not the general population.

The transport rose and fell on eddies of traffic control, buffeted by unheard command. Now that they were approaching their destination, the festival atmosphere had dampened inside; now the smiles were wry and bored, ready for the hours ahead. Boston kept his vigil by the window, staring out at sodden storeys of nothing, at the mass of people thirty feet below him, at the buses: swarming, retreating, arriving, constantly moving. Buses to Fiore, to Kim Li, to Omicra, to Punta Oeste, to Limbe, destinations splashed brightly across them like banners. No buses to Mère de Martyrs, he noticed. Or Nebe, for that matter. He had no idea how the city had been subdivided for the purposes of the programme, only that Chatelier was not among the districts served by the Cilicia centres; he would not be leaving the bus with the soldiers.

Close to the melee, as the transport began its descent, he watched three buses, ahead of them in the impossible queue, pull in to the doors of the building: two from North Gate, the third from Limbe. Passengers were evicted like bad produce on a production line; shepherded, bewildered, past tiers of armed guards – protectors of the nanon banks – into the cavernous lobby, shunted off in various directions. The soldiers around him began to shoulder their rifles, smiles faded now into exhaustion and ennui. Boston swung his legs around to one side to allow them to pass down the narrow aisle in the centre of the transport as they began their descent: rapid, heart-stopping, close enough to the vehicles in the queue behind to reach out and touch their windscreens. Muttered complaints drifted from the soldiers, flung backwards in their seats; a brace of nervous laughter, some shouted comment to the driver, whose reply was inaudible over the sudden screaming of the engines. Boston tightened his knuckles against the seat, plastic covers shrieking in protest, and waited for the impact of their wheels on the ground.

They landed heavily a couple of yards from the mouth of the confusion, close enough to make out the shapes of the crowds but not the individual faces within. The doors slid open and a wave of heat sound roared over them, like a backdraft from the furnace of Hell. It hit him full in the face, with force enough to sting his ears and catch his breath. The soldiers, who were used to it, recovered more quickly, started to move past him: in no hurry, but purposeful. Some of them, not knowing who he was or why he was there, patted him amicably on the shoulder, wished him luck with whatever. Most of them ignored him. There was not enough space to accommodate Turrow and their movement in the narrow truck; he was in the way. The chaos outside pounded his head as the hordes swarmed around them like eddies around a stone: thousands of people, frightened people, confused people, talking to each other, through each other, over each other. Commands: barked, shouted; engines moving, engines firing up, engines slowing down, engines descending. Constant motion, of feet, of cars, of troops walking in line. Warning shouts, unseen; loudspeakers forming blue lines, red lines, orange lines, yellow lines. A million questions, the piercing screams of children, the backbeat of sirens.

Buses and confusion. Confusion and buses …

Boston was moving before he realised, before his conscious mind was able to catch up with its instinctive connections. The clamour of the streets was disorienting; it dulled the mind and slowed responses, and he knew that, regardless, the soldiers in the transport were unlikely to follow him far. They would give chase – he heard them behind; a babble of outraged demands, the beginnings of pursuit – but it was for the look of things. They were disrupting the plan, sifting through the lines, scattering the patterns. Complaints, streams of protests as crowds crumbled in their wake, but he moved more easily than they did through the masses. They were having a hard time, and he was just one man.

He moved quickly, not running: neither wanting to draw attention to himself nor to have his lungs try to claw their way up his trachea with every razor-blade laboured breath. The air was foetid, thick with humidity and exhaust fumes. It made his head spin; the exertion made his head spin, the adrenaline made his head spin, but he was charged, running on autopilot. There was no clear plan, only the creeping suspicion that anywhere was better than Chatelier, where he would sit in his apartment and count the hours, wondering when she would be dead. Pretending that he knew that there was nothing he could do so that every nerve did not cry out for action; waiting for her to be dead, needing her to be dead.

Buses moved overhead and around him. People surged forward, held back, surged forward again. He tried to follow the patterns, to blend in, but he was not a part of it and couldn't mimic it; he knew he stood out. Faces watched him warily, pulling children out of his path: he looked like he was infected, probably looked like he was close to death. Boston kept his head down, wanting to put distance between himself and the transport, not wanting to catch anyone's eye until he was satisfied that the pursuit was over. In the crowd, it was easy to be anonymous, but from above he would be visible: the free radical, the statistical anomaly. He risked a glance over his shoulder, but it told him nothing: the crowd had closed around him like a healing wound.

He moved on.

23.5

She has no idea how long she's been in the chamber. There has been no way to gauge it; the only thing that changes is how they hurt her. They've asked her a grand total of three questions — several times each — and the space between them has been black and red stretches of livid pain. She wants them to ask a question she can answer so that they'll be pleased with her, so that they'll for God's sake stop hurting her, but her mouth is full of blood, her lips too swollen to speak. She's just not ready to realise that it's not about the questions, and when she does, it will break her. For now, she needs to think that if she can help them, they will stop.

She needs to think that she can make it long enough for him to get to Mère de Martyrs. She needs to make it long enough for the people behind the red door to come and help.

★

Buses to Omicra, flashing green lettering that lit up the gathering shadows. Buses to Sainte-Thérèse, buses to Omicra, buses to North Gate. Buses to Kolasi, mainly women: few men and fewer children. Buses to Limbe, buses to Frain and Kim Li. Buses to Punta Oeste; more buses to Omicra. Nothing for Mère de Martyrs.

Boston had been wandering for almost half an hour, dodging patrols, sliding himself into lines when it looked like someone might ask a question. He had no clear idea beyond getting to Mère de Martyrs, which had seemed like the beauty of the operation in the first rush of freedom, and which now seemed just really, really stupid. His legs felt like they had hollowed out, like the bone was dissolving, his lungs were at least half-full of burning petrol, and someone was trying to break out of his skull with a jackhammer. And she was there, she was somewhere, and with every step he took, she could be dead.

Five hours. She'd been gone five hours. Part of him wanted her to be dead.

A violent whoosh-roar from the road behind him; the ground trembled and Boston looked over his shoulder as another bus pulled into the pavement, its destination flashing in great green letters across the front windscreen: Omicra Verte. Nothing for Parnasse, which bordered Cilicia due south, and he had guessed by now that Chatelier belonged to a different subdivision, but Mère de Martyrs shared a border with Cilicia to the north east; surely it would feed into Cilicia's inoculation programme?

Pockets of activity: like microcosms. He passed through groups of new arrivals, blank-faced and dazed; listened to the hollered instructions that erupted from the soldiers that met them from the transports. *Limbe Group 374C, you have been assigned to Blue Section 44. You will proceed to elevator shaft fourteen and travel in groups of twenty to the thirty-second floor where you will approach ONLY Blue Leader 44. Does anyone have any questions, then let's move out. Come on, come on, people, let's move ... North Gate Group 1132G, you have been assigned to Green Section 71. There is currently a backlog of approximately one hour in this section. You will proceed to elevator shaft two and you will travel to Green Section 71, which is located on the eighteenth floor. You will be met by Green Leader 71 who will furnish you with arrangements for a waiting area. Okay, let's move, let's go, I haven't got all day. Let's move, let's move ... Punta Oeste Group 12J. Punta Oeste Group 12J. Is there anyone for Punta Oeste Group 12J that is not yet on this bus? Anyone for Punta Oeste Group 12J? Transport is leaving in five minutes. Punta Oeste Group 12J, five minutes ...*

Whoosh-roar, like thunder, so close above the crowd that it ruffled his hair as he walked. Boston moved quietly, head down, meeting nobody's eyes. Rivers of sweat trickled from his hairline, blurring his vision, dripping down his collar, mingling with the teeming rain. Sodden babies screamed a chorus of red-faced and white-lipped rage. *Sainte-Thérèse Group 867E —I want to see a line, form up single file ... Kim Li 44P, there's a delay with your transport, please follow me and I'll show you where you can wait ... Omicra Verte 636I and 627I, you've been amalgamated, wait here a second and don't disappear; I'm going to check the reassignment ...*

Where the hell were the buses to Mère de Martyrs? The further he walked, the closer he got to the gate; he could see signs, for God's sake: Thirty-first District, and an arrow, with the word *Mère de Martyrs*, like an embarrassment, like a nick-name, tacked on below in brackets, even though most of the city wouldn't know the Thirty-first district from the Thirtieth or the Thirty-second, but they all knew Mère de Martyrs. He could see the north east wall, looming up ahead of him; he could see the wallpaper of cars and transports shrouding it like a curtain, but not one of them bore its name. He was exhausted, washed through with fatigue and hunger, despair crystallising like salts in his blood. Whoosh-roar, a wall of water pouring from the tail as another transport dipped for landing, and a hazy sea of complaints, lost in the general clamour.

And in it, veiled by sound, a reference to where he needed to be.

Half-heard or mistaken, it pulled him up short. He could no more identify the source of the comment than he could be certain he had heard it at all, but it was something, it was *anything*. He moved in its general direction: a pocket within a pocket to his left, comprised of family groups moulded into a homogenous whole, with the air of people who have been standing around for far too long in the heat and the rain. They watched his approach with hostility. That would be about right. He said, 'Is this the line for Mère de Martyrs?'

Silence. One of them, a big, grey-bearded man, probably self-elected group leader, allowed it to go on a little too long, and then said, 'What?'

'I'm lost,' said Boston. 'I got lost. Is this the line for Mère de Martyrs?'

'What?' said the man again.

Boston scanned the faces of the man's companions, hoping for even the tiniest glimmer of solidarity, but they were blank. He tried again. 'I'm trying to get back to Mère de Martyrs. Is this the line?'

'There is no line for Mère de Martyrs,' said the man.

That would certainly explain things, but it was hardly helpful. Boston waited politely for a moment, but no further information was offered. 'Why not?' he asked.

'There's no-one coming out of Mère de Martyrs,' said a second man, the vice president. 'Not with the riots; they couldn't lift the lock-down. Mère de Martyrs, Nebe, Dog Island, Petite Cloche. No one gets in, no one's getting out.'

It was the sort of devastating, soul-crushing blow that in any other circumstances would lead to giving up and going home. *No one?* thought Boston in despair, as though just by wanting it enough he could make it happen. And then he saw the look on the man's face, the look he was sharing with the vice president, and he thought, suddenly, *Yep, I should have known that, shouldn't I?*

Time to go.

'Right,' said Boston. 'Thanks.'

He started to walk away, quickly, knowing he'd made it worse. Knowing that the only thing to do now was put distance between him and them before they animated enough to wonder why he was purporting to be from a district that had been closed by rioting. One foot in front of the other, letting the crowd fill in behind him and obliterate his path, but the crowd was like a wall, and it was all in front of him, only space behind. They were watching him, computing, and he could hear the rumblings of a *why the hell would he?* debate. But a woman had moved into his path like a battleship and she was not for shifting, as though Boston might be determined to steal her place in the line. He moved left, she blocked; he moved right, she blocked, her eyes ferociously locked on the man in front. He tried easing past her, tried a couple of polite *excuse me*s, then a final, *get out of the way, okay?* And then a voice behind him shouted, 'Hey! Wait a minute, son.'

He couldn't think of anyone else the voice might mean. He didn't bother to check.

The battleship woman was amenable to a fierce shoulder-shove, which shunted her just enough to let him pass. Boston slid awkwardly through the line, heart-beat thumping out a stampede against his ribs, bruising his tender lungs. His breath caught in his throat like acid and set him wheezing, and he was aware that he was making no headway, that the source of the voice was closing in tightly behind him.

Another, 'Hey! Wait up, there.'

'He's calling you,' said a man helpfully as Boston tried to elbow past, nodding to a point uncomfortably close behind.

'No, it's not me,' said Boston desperately, digging his elbow into the man's ribs.

'It is, it's you,' said a woman that Boston took for the man's wife. 'Hold on, son, he's looking for you.'

Her fingers extended, gripped his arm like a vice. He checked quickly over his shoulder and saw that the source of the voice was not the grey-bearded man, but a soldier. Of course it was a soldier. It had been that kind of day.

Boston gave in. He turned.

23.6

She's still alive. She's still conscious.

He walks over to her. She can't tell which one it is. She starts to cry.

He prods her with his toe. It's such an innocent gesture that she starts to tremble, violently.

'I'm sorry,' she says. She doesn't know why she's apologising, only that he's going to do something to her, and if she can deflect his rage, maybe he won't.

'What's that?' he says. His voice is friendly. He prods her again.

'I'm sorry,' she says, louder. Her mouth is swelling; she knows she can't get the words out properly.

'What are you sorry for?' he says. His tone is light, jovial: like they are two old friends who met in the park.

'I don't know,' she tries to say, she starts to say, but she doesn't finish, because the world explodes into violent sodium yellows and blinding whites — like someone's letting off fireworks in her brain. The shock of it dulls her reactions and the pain is delayed and it's only when her vision clears and she's hovering above the ground that the answer arrives: he's lifting her by her hair...

★

'Man back there says you're looking for a bus to Mère de Martyrs.'

Boston glanced over his shoulder, saw that the grey-bearded family was not within earshot. 'No,' he said.

'That's what he told me. He said you asked him if it was the line for Mère de Martyrs.'

'He heard me wrong.' Boston was thinking wildly, grasping for inspiration. 'I asked if it was the line for Limbe.'

'That's not what he said.'

'Why would I ask for the line to Mère de Martyrs?' said Boston. 'No one's getting out of Mère de Martyrs. The gates are shut.'

'That's why he called me over. You mind telling me what business you have in Mère de Martyrs?'

'I'm not *going* to Mère de Martyrs,' said Boston, going for the outrage card. 'He was talking about Mère de Martyrs, that's why he's confused. I asked for *Limbe.*'

'What's your name, sir?'

Limbe was north of Mère de Martyrs. He could see the gate to the thirty-first district – the top of it, at any rate – edging through the traffic. He said, 'Walter Grant.'

*

The first breath is a surprise. She wasn't expecting another. There is a second of pure exhilaration before his hand is fisting in her hair again, dragging her upright; the next breath is a scream.

'Daddy!' she bellows. She's four years old again; daddy fixes everything. 'Daddy, please. I want you. Daddy …'

*

In retrospect, he thought, he should have expected the scanner. It wasn't exactly a massive leap of logic to assume that a soldier tasked with making sure a couple of hundred thousand people weren't lying about who they were was going to look for something a little more concrete than a bright smile and the heartfelt assurances of a stranger. Especially one who looked like Boston. Even Boston wouldn't have trusted himself.

'All right, Mr Grant,' said the soldier. 'Just press your thumb here.'

'Sure,' said Boston, and tried to keep the panic from his voice and his cheerful grin. 'But … no, I'm not actually Walter Grant. I'm just staying with him in Limbe. I got caught when the gates were locked.'

An intake of breath hinted at finite reserves of patience and a very low tolerance for bullshit.

'Yes, sir,' said the soldier, who sounded like a man who had taken enough crap to last him several lifetimes. 'And what is *your* name, sir?'

He really should have expected the scanner. Of course he had a scanner; they all had scanners. And it was just that sort of day.

'Boston Turrow,' said Boston.

'And do you think you might be able to press your thumb to the pad now, please, Mr Turrow?'

The queue surged forward again, hitting them from the side. Boston stumbled, caught himself, but not before the scanner spat out a red light and a warning tone.

'Again, please,' said the soldier. To his comlink, he added, 'François? *J'ai besoin d'une vérification du nom, s'il te plaît ... Oui, c'est Monsieur Boston Turrow; aussi Monsieur Walter Grant, et ce dernier est de Limbe. Merci.*'

Boston pressed his thumb to the scanner, held it long enough for the read-out to flash green. The crowd made another move again and he thought of running, but the soldier's eyes were level on him. He said, 'Chatelier is not part of this inoculation programme.'

'I'm not here for inoculation,' said Turrow. 'I just came with my friend.'

'Yes,' said the soldier, but his stare said, *you are running out of time.* 'And your friend is Mr Grant?'

'Yes. No. It's his daughter.'

An eyebrow arched in a manner that was definitely not good news: if the soldier were that sort of man, a large vein would have been throbbing in his forehead. 'François?' he barked into the comlink. '*Qu'est-ce qui passe?*'

Another surge, catching both of them off-guard, and, for the briefest of seconds, the soldier looked away. Boston sidestepped before he realised he was going to do it; caught himself as the soldier's eyes snapped back; tried for sympathy.

'I'd really like to find my friend now, please,' he said, and coughed for effect. 'I've been ill. I need to get home.'

'I can see,' said the soldier. 'François? *Combien de temps faut-il pour vérifier un nom?*'

'*Oui, tout droit.*' A petulant voice, tinny with distance, raised in objection. 'Boston Turrow, *appartement trois cent trois, numéro quatorze cent douze, avenue trente-quatrième nord-est; Walter Grant, douze cent cinquante-trois, rue vingt-neuf sud, Limbe. Mort.*'

'*Mort?*' said the soldier. He looked up at Boston. 'He says your friend is dead.'

'Not dead,' said Boston, as though it were any kind of explanation. 'Evicted.'

The soldier treated him to the kind of withering glare that the answer deserved. Boston would have been the first to admit that it lacked panache, but at that moment the queue surged again.

'Forget it,' said the soldier. He stuck his hand in the air, motioned to a colleague nearby, who looked up and rolled his eyes with an expression of purest *now is not a good time*. The first soldier, with murder in his eyes, waved a little more emphatically. The second soldier rolled his eyes again, but broke away and made towards them. Boston's heart sank.

The queue surged, and for the first time, Boston noticed how far they had already been moved. The second soldier glanced over his shoulder at his own queue, now under the command of a subordinate, and started an irritable *sotto voce* conference.

The second soldier looked up. He said, shortly, 'Limbe? You come with me. *Come.*'

EXTRACT FROM THE *SPECIAL REPORT ON THE ACTIVITIES OF THE RENEGADE ELIMINATION NETWORK (REN, REN)*, PRESENTED TO THE INTERGOVERNMENTAL SECURITY AGENCY INSURGENCY THREAT RESPONSE DIRECTORATE, 17 OCTOBER 2077; DECLASSIFIED 17 OCTOBER 2102

Moreover, the group's ongoing attempts to liaise with law enforcement officials have provided significant statistical evidence of its efficiency. Official efforts are constrained by the rule of international law, while the network is free to employ guerrilla and paramilitary tactics in apprehending and eliminating contraband, and their willingness to share information with representatives of the local, national and international Insurgency Response efforts have led to significant actions against caches in Dublin, Monte Carlo, Melbourne and Shanghai in the past three months alone.

While the group continues to operate coram non judice, it is clearly impossible for this or any other governmental or quasi-governmental entity to be seen to support its ethos, manifesto or methodology through either tacit or material measures. However, given their enormous popular support and their kill-to-casualty ratio, arrests of key figures within the organisation have tended to be detrimental to the overall effort, in terms of manpower, finance and public opinion. It is desirable, therefore, that the group be permitted to continue its operations.

In conclusion, then, this report makes the following recommendations:

•That all outstanding criminal proceedings against any individual or group associated with the Renegade Elimination Network cease forthwith;

•That information gathered during the course of any interrogation by the Renegade Elimination Network be considered admissible as evidence, regardless of the methodology employed in its collection;

•That the Renegade Elimination Network be retroactively decriminalised with immediate effect, and be afforded unofficial licence to continue the pursuit of their objectives unhindered.

24 MAY - EVENING

24.1

He saw her on every street; saw them as they might have been, walking together in the rain, sheltering under an oversized umbrella, his arm around her shoulders, her thumb tucked lazily over his belt, her hand buried beneath his coat. He saw them stopping for coffee or to pick up a paper, chatting to friends, debating what to have for dinner: simple things, tiny things, the makings of a life together. But the streets were empty. And she was in Nebe, dying.

The transport stopped at the southern corner of Nineteenth Park Place and Nineteenth Place South. Boston stood up with the rest of the passengers, inched forward down the aisle with them. They were a tired crowd, bearing the scars of a long wait and a longer week, but the air was scented with their relief; colour had begun to creep back into their eyes. It was over.

Though the barricades remained, they were poorly guarded now, citizen militia withdrawing to their houses, to the hospitals, to the inoculation programme in Cilicia. On the streets, the change was palpable. There were smiles, even snatches of laughter: tentative and doubtful. These were the survivors; it had not yet occurred to them to wonder why.

They were ushered forwards, off the street, and Boston, having nowhere to go, attached himself to one of the larger groups and followed them a little way along the road. Behind them, the transport's engines stepped up a whine, ready for take-off. Limbe was a crowded, disordered district: louring blocks and narrow streets, and the engine noise, reverberating off walls in rapid succession, was almost deafening. He stuck close to a family in front, followed them to the door of a crumbling block, squeezed in behind them.

Inside, the air was maybe half a degree cooler: dark and stale. The lobby was comprised of a staircase, winding steeply upwards into gloom, from which grey drops of water plummeted earthwards. What little space there was in the narrow chamber that wasn't part of the stairs was paved in off-white tiles, cracked and uneven, protruding from the floor, and leading to a series of shabby, decrepit doors. A broken pushchair, cowering in the shadows, was the only ornamentation.

The family — two parents, two grandparents, three children in early puberty — stopped by a door near the back of the lobby. An air of grief hung about them; Boston guessed that the three kids were the oldest of the brood and wondered if the others were lying still in a pod or a hospital bed, or if they were already part of the silvery grey ashes piled high in the Wharf. He hesitated on the edge of the shadows, knowing that they knew he was there, knowing that, in so small a block they would have to know that he didn't belong, and that the reason they didn't challenge him was because they didn't care enough. Sudden, unwelcome thoughts of Tilly slammed into his conscious mind: he thought of the apartment lying empty, his family spirited away while he lay wracked by fever in a sterile cell. He sidelined them; they were too much right now. They were for later.

'Excuse me,' he said.

One of the grandparents looked around. She caught Boston's eye, held it for a minute, just long enough to be uncomfortable, and then tugged on the father's arm. He followed her brusque nod towards the main door, sized up the intruder, said, 'You okay there?'

He was guarded, his body-language defensive, but his tone was even, light enough to imply that he would listen long enough to decide what to do next. The children watched Boston with dark, heavy eyes as their father ushered them away with a couple of words to his wife, who opened the door and harried them through, but stayed by her husband's side. She fixed her eyes on Boston, folded her arms across her chest, regarded him with a gaze that said *this is a private world and you are not welcome*.

Boston hesitated. He swallowed, licked his lips, and said, slowly, 'I think – I need to get to Mère de Martyrs.'

There was no hint of surprise. The man just shrugged and said, 'You're not far, then,' and his words were polite, but his expression was like a shield. 'Three blocks south, you'll come to the gate. You'll want to watch the patrols, though.'

'Will I get through all right?'

The man smiled, though it was not a friendly smile, and it was impossible to say what had prompted it. 'I'd say so,' he said.

It looked as though he were about to continue, so Boston waited, but the man remained silent. Finally, he said, 'Okay. Thank you. What are the streets like at the minute?'

The door inched open a fraction, and a blond head poked out. It was a boy, about Cassie's age, with Cassie's air of blanket defiance against anything and everything. He stared at Boston with suspicion bordering on hostility. The mother, glancing around, spoke a couple of soft words and the child receded. The father said, 'We're quiet in Limbe. Bad enough in Mère de Martyrs, now.'

'What about patrols?' said Boston. 'Will I get past the patrols all right?'

The father opened his mouth to speak, but the mother, whose expression was unreadable, said, 'What's your business in Mère de Martyrs?'

The father glanced sideways at his wife, but she kept her eyes fixed on Boston's face. Women were like this in Limbe, he remembered: they spoke softly, but their word was law.

Boston said, 'I just,' and stopped. He tried again. 'There's someone I need to see there.'

'In Mère de Martyrs?' Her face was sceptical, her tone incredulous. 'Good luck to you, then.'

Boston looked to her husband for help, but the man returned his stare, impassive. He turned back to the wife. 'Are the riots bad?'

She considered him for a long moment. Her gaze was uncomfortable, like sitting for too long in direct sunlight. She said, 'You don't belong in Limbe, do you?'

Boston opened his mouth to lie, thought better of it. 'No,' he said.

'But you got here anyway.' There was no accusation in her words, just curiosity and implication.

'Yes,' he said.

She waited for him to elaborate; acknowledged his reticence with a nod. She said, 'Are you in trouble, son?'

Rita had been like this once. Only less so, thank God. She had stretched a maternal arm around the dispossessed of the city, had scolded children on the street as though they were her own, had swept them into her arms when they were hurt or lost. She gave half an inch for every mile they tried to take, but she would not turn away a child in need.

That was a long time ago; before the world wore her down and closed her off in a place where there was no space even for her own. He said, 'Not me.'

'Someone is, though.'

'Yes.'

'Okay,' she said. 'All right.'

She glanced sideways at her husband, and there was nothing in her expression to signify permission to speak, but he cleared his throat and nodded briskly, as though he'd read a code that Boston didn't know. 'I'd say you'll be right, son,' he said.

24.2

The fact was, Nebe would riot about a fart in a bean factory. It was that sort of place. Once, about fifteen years ago, some lateral-thinking Nebe street entrepreneur had thrown a couple of hundred tokens at what became known as the Weekday T-shirt range. Turrow had owned the Thursday model (*Hey! It's Thursday! Let's riot!* With a grinning smiley face and Nebe's district coat of arms), and Rita, irascible and unpredictable as ever, had taken one look at him and burst into fits of uncontrollable laughter. They'd spread around the city like wildfire might, if it got a chance to spread. If you had two or more in the range, you were the kid everyone wanted to know; if you had Saturday *and* Sunday, you were a kind of minor deity. The brains behind the operation had made more money than he knew what to do with – which was a lot of money in Nebe; they thought big there – and spent twenty years behind bars for incitement to breach of the peace.

And when Nebe rioted, Mère de Martyrs rioted. Often, Dog Island joined in, and once the three of them got going, Petite Cloche could be relied upon to follow suit. Usually, once the rioting had entered the third day, others would drift into the fray: Victoria, Parnasse, sometimes Limbe, and very occasionally La Nef, but those were the key four. The problem was, they were now rioting so fiercely over the introduction of a quarantine lockdown that had, effectively, caged them inside their districts and left them to die that the transports to the inoculation programme couldn't get in. Behind the scenes was a flurry of political manoeuvring: clever people, dangerous people, people bright enough to understand the nature of compromise, were talking in low, menacing tones to military representatives about terms and conditions, but on the ground, four districts were being denied access to the cure, and they were the opposite of happy.

Boston waited. In Cilicia, he hadn't thought he would ever feel cold again, but an hour and a half in the vertical rain, like someone had tipped the ocean upside down and started shaking it over the city, had numbed him to the point of inertia. Everything was wet. His clothes were wet, his hair was wet, his shoes were wet. He thought that if someone were to cut him in half, right down the middle, at that point, nothing but water would run out. Certainly there was no blood left in him; his fingers were a kind of purplish white. Heat was a distant, miserable memory. And he dared not move, not even to stamp some life into his feet, or move out of the shadows into the questionable warmth offered by the blue glow of the light-bands: he could not risk being seen.

The gate was huge, about the height and width of the Authority's regulation port lobby, but, against the south wall of Limbe it was dwarfed. It looked like a cat flap. Cars and the flow of traffic forced the eye to readjust, gave it some proportion, but, silent and shut, it was just a very small opening in a very big wall. Graffiti crawled in violent colours over the first few feet, some of it so elaborate that he could read it from where he stood, but it gave way at the third metre, and the gate climbed blackly towards the distant upper shelf, on which the soldiers had begun to mass.

They'd broken through seven times already, at least once a night since the rioting began. The gate was pitted and scarred, rent and patched in great canyon rifts along its length, blackened with fire and cratered with explosion. Seven battalions stood guard on the Cilicia/Mère de Martyrs gate; there was no way through there, but in Limbe, the army presence was small and sporadic, not strong enough to offer serious resistance until it was already too late. Boston could just about hear the chaos on the other side, seeping through with every seismic thung from the other side, with every tremor that trickled limply through the ground as whatever they were using as a battering ram this time connected with the broken gate.

He thought, *I am standing on the streets of Limbe* — Limbe — *on my own. In the rain. In* Limbe. *And I'm waiting for a riot to break through the gates.*

He breathed on his hands, but even his breath was cold.

Platoons were drifting into place near the bottom now, sirens whurping as armoured cars lowered into place. There was no hint of the oil of organisation that he'd seen in Cilicia; these were just the men who could be spared from other things, drafted in at the last minute when the situation was too threatening to ignore. The street was silent; they were the only noise, and even that was not much. They talked little, spoke quietly, fidgeted. Commands were delivered in low monotone, men moved into position. Checked their weapons, checked their suits, checked their friends.

Whung. More violent than the last one; he saw the gates shake. That was something Boston would not have believed if he hadn't seen it for himself. The gates were immutable, constant: they were not amenable to force. Screams of rage pierced the air, only just audible above the, gnawing rattle of rain, but louder than the last time. It was like waiting for a punch.

Whung, and the activity stepped up a notch. The soldiers were getting uneasy, bracing for the onslaught. Near the front, they crouched into firing position; further back, their COs were deep in discussion.

If you shoot off straight away, the woman had said, *you'll get shot or bottled. Hold your ground and you'll be right. Let them get a little way through, and they'll not care who's going in, just who's coming out.*

The next whung was silent.

Boston was holding his breath. He hadn't realised it until the impact didn't come and he suddenly found that he wasn't breathing. They were regular, like the ticking of a pendulum, and the absence was as ominous as the sound itself. He tensed —

... And the gates gave way. It happened so quickly he let out a yelp of surprise: one minute they were standing — like metal monoliths, unbreakable — and then they were crumbling, toppling inwards under the force of a burning articulated lorry, which sliced through the waiting troops like a hot knife through butter. And the noise rushed forwards like a wall of water, covering, obliterating everything in its path. It ran through every fibre, in every key: from a thrumming, throbbing bass line that danced through his feet and up his spine, to the high shriek of rage — one long vowel of fury, dragged from a thousand mouths. The lorry careened forward, rolling only as fast as the momentum of a couple of hundred very focused men, but unstoppable, lethal. The gates were hanging at an angle — what kept them up? he wondered belatedly. Surely not a giant hinge? But that was what it looked like — tilting precariously towards the mob still spilling in their multitudes through the rupture in the wall, which was screaming metal death as it slowly burst its moorings. Shots rang out, unheard, unnoticed, and, flying before the crowds, flowers of fire pierced the dark streets where incendiaries had been tossed.

The lorry tore down the street, losing speed as the tyres melted in unheard pops of burning rubber, crashed headlong into the side of a building. The explosion ripped the air in two: a muted whoosh with the first rush of flame, and then the eruption of noise and heat that threw him to the ground, distant as he was. Fresh shouts broke out: the explosion had blown a massive hole in the supporting wall of an inhabited block, and, through it, masked by a ring of flames, he could just make out men and women, faces bloodied, hair burning, screaming and running. And then the smell of burning that made him choke and gag, as the smoke washed over the streets like fog.

Boston started to move forward. The smoke, choked by rainwater, was cloying: it muted the sounds of the riot, but it caught in his lungs and made it almost impossible to draw breath. Without the fans, it would settle for the night, thicken and congeal, and by morning, you'd be able to shift it with a bucket. He was half a street away from the centre of the violence, which had flared out forwards but not yet to the side where Boston had been watching in the shadows. Closer to, it became possible to make out individual noises in the white wall of sound: bottles smashing, volley upon volley of gunfire, the sounds of tearing flesh as men fell. Voices were screaming abuse, but he couldn't hear the words; couldn't tell, even, if they were shouting the hundred languages of the rioters or the French of the soldiers.

Men slammed into him from every angle; Boston had to fight the push towards the slick pavement, where he was already stumbling over bodies. Some of them grabbed at his legs as he inadvertently kicked them, clawing at him with clammy fingers, faces rising out of the fog. There were children there, he saw: children with knives and guns, and women too, dark-eyed and red-faced with rage. They came at him from every angle, jolted him out of his orbit and towards the soldiers. The gate was visible only as a darker space against a dark sky, but the tide was flowing away from it, the gunfire getting closer. He was being washed towards the red smoke, where the fires were burning.

Boston lowered his head, bracing himself, and shouldered through. Hands grabbed at him, grabbed his collar, his shirt sleeves, his hair; faces screamed things at him. He hollered back, anything, whatever they wanted to hear, punched the air. Gunfire spat overhead, from behind him as the soldiers opened warning volleys into the air, from in front when dissidents responded. Bricks and bits of bricks whistled over his head, thrown too short, hammering the rioters themselves and he saw a woman go down with a grunt of surprise and disappear into the tangle of legs and moving feet.

A neat eruption of sound: huge but contained, and then a second and a third. Close to the front, screams broke out and the tide suddenly surged backwards, sweeping him with it. Confused, Boston almost lost his footing, almost fell to the ground to be trampled into a thin smear of red on the tarmac. He grabbed out wildly, found purchase in the hair of a white-faced blond girl, who shrieked in pain and shock as she took his weight. She turned on him, slammed him full force in the face with something hard, and he felt his eyeball explode, but he was upright again. And then the first whiff drifted back in the smog, and he realised why they were running.

Gas.

The *what* didn't matter, it was the *how long* that worried him. The mob was in full retreat, but there were so many of them, all moving at once, and the gate, which had looked so small until they all burst through and set a scale, had shrunk again. The air was acid with a yellow mist, and, behind him, people were beginning to fall; the pressure was easing off. But the spread was relentless: it was sinking into his lungs and making him gag, and he couldn't run on his tiny rations of oxygen, even on a full lung capacity. Yellow tendrils, creeping through the greyness, reaching out for him like fingers. The pressure in his lungs was unbearable.

And then the crowd in front of him dispersed, suddenly, and he was running in twos and threes down a street littered with broken glass and twisted hulks of metal, and the smoke was thinning out. And when he risked a couple of back-treads to glance over his shoulder, he saw that the south gate had become the north gate, and he was running alone through the streets of Mère de Martyrs.

15 MINUTEN KOMMENTAR, 23RD APRIL 2082

The mood is sombre here at the Reiterpark this morning as Congressional officials from all over Europe gather for the dedication of a memorial to the men, women and children who lost their lives five years ago in the April 23 attacks. The monument, designed by Korean artist Ryu Min-Seo, consists of two eighteen-feet curving copper sheets, representing the encircling arms of humanity, with perforations for each of the 4,715 lives lost to date in the hostilities. Financing for the memorial has been provided by a consortium of telectronics firms, including many former manufacturers of S3A units, prompting some critics to ask if the industry has done enough to stem the increasing tide of violence from groups of artificial units who continue to resist protocol. A spokesperson for organ printers ReGen International, whose venture into amnisobiological manufacture brought the company to the verge of bankruptcy three years ago, says that the firm is 'disturbed by the ongoing violence' and that it 'remains committed to working with authorities to resolve the situation as quickly as possible.'

24 MAY - NIGHT

25.1

Her face is swollen purple; her skin is barely visible beneath the bruises. The beatings have stopped and she knew when they did, she knew, *that they'd dropped off a plateau and into an abyss, but she thought,* maybe this is it. Maybe it's over, *because she knows and they know that there is nothing else she can tell them. She's not yet ready to believe that the pain will continue until they get bored — she can't believe that, or she's gone anyway. She's seen the doorway open in front of her and she's nearly crossed it a dozen times, thinking it was the way to oblivion, but she has told him how to find the people that can help her; she needs to hold on until they come.*

But the men haven't stopped beating her so that they could end it; they've stopped because they've decided, somewhere in the last crowded minutes, that she knows more than she can tell them and that she needs to hurt a little bit more before she'll give them what they want. They've asked her the same questions, over and over, and she's tried telling them, she's tried pleading with them until she doesn't recognise the creature that she's become — a wretched, craven thing, a thing that will beg and cry and weep for the tiniest word of compassion. Twenty-four hours ago, she would have hated the person sitting in her chair. She would have been scathing, vicious, if she could have heard the noises she has made. She would have said, that will never be me. Not while I have breath in my body. *She was a different Danae then.*

She can hear them moving behind her, and she starts to cry: thick, ugly sobs that slicken the inside of her mask. But she knows what's behind her, because she's heard the whine of currents firing; she is Amnis — she can feel it in the air. And she knows that there's nothing else she can tell them, but there's no way to make them believe her, and so all she can do is sniffle and moan and make little sounds of petition through lips swollen with tears and blood, until they just go ahead and flick the switch anyway and her body arches backwards as the electricity soars. She can hear the scream that chokes in her throat, she can feel teeth grinding against teeth, she can see creeping black stain of an electrical burn where her trousers touch the chains that bind her, and she wonders what it will take to kill her, because she doesn't think there's much more left to beat out of her before she starts begging them to let her die.

★

Boston ran. He ran even when the crowds around him had stopped running to take stock of the situation and wonder how soon they could decently start rioting again; he ran because he couldn't stop. Adrenaline powered his legs, overriding instruction from his brain, ignoring the nagging burning in his lungs and chest. He ran because he had to keep running, because there wasn't enough time, because everyone else was running and he was in Mère de Martyrs by night, alone and in the middle of a riot; but also because he had the strongest suspicion that when he didn't have the running to distract him, it was really going to hurt.

When he stopped, it was because he fell. And he fell because the panic cut out abruptly, subsumed by a tide of exhaustion so black that his legs could not keep up. He stopped, mid-stride, legs curling uselessly below him, and he collapsed forward, face down, into the street. Shards of glass bit deeply into his skin and he felt blood begin to flow, trickling into the pools of unspeakable liquid on the street.

He lay, prone, while the rain sleeted over him.

Sounds drifted over him, sounds of rage, sounds of people who'd very nearly just been gassed. Boston struggled to raise himself, inched his hands in towards his body, and, with supreme effort, managed to raise his torso an inch off the ground. Figures approached: three or four of them, and he knew they'd seen him because their tone took on a note of wary concern, got high-pitched as they debated the morals of walking on by. One of them said, 'You all right, mate?'

Turrow didn't answer; his arms had begun to shake with the effort of supporting his upper body. The last thing he wanted was a helping hand to get himself to his feet, but hands gripped him regardless and he was levitating, suspended off the ground. Halfway through, he realised that he would have to do something, to show some kind of willing, so he shuffled about for a foothold on the ground, let his legs take his weight. They held, but only just.

He said, 'Thanks,' although he was not grateful.

'No problem, mate,' said the voice that had helped him. He was a young man, younger than Turrow by a good five years, with the pinched, ratlike expression of one who has never had enough to eat. 'That was a bad one back there.'

'Yeah,' said Turrow. He dusted himself down, smears of blood streaking his coat from a network of tiny cuts on his palm.

The man regarded him doubtfully. 'You sure you're all right?'

Turrow looked up. The street was littered with broken glass and charred black stains, burnt-out cars and half-bricks, lead piping, bullet casings. Soot marks crawled up the walls, ten, twenty feet high, to windows shattered by the heat.

He said, 'I'm looking for West Park Road.'

25.2

It was like waiting for a sneeze, he realised later. The streets were thick with the promise of violence, and maybe if the troops had pressed their advantage and streamed through the gates behind the dissidents when they were fractured and confused, it might have been decided there and then. In fact, the troops had suffered losses almost as heavy as the rioters; they were barely able even to retreat, but he didn't know that then. While the cogs of righteous indignation were greasing up for the next round, Boston was standing in the shadows of a porch overhang, across the street from a house with a red door.

He had been standing for some time. This was for a number of reasons. First, and most pressing, was the sensation that if he moved at all, even slightly, he was going to collapse. His temperature was creeping upwards again, and with it the muggy, distant feeling in his head, as though his skull were too big for his brain. Attempts to breathe in the thick, caustic air set off a hacking cough, but holding his breath didn't help either. When Boston woke up that morning, he had been a recovering invalid, wrapped in the safety of a hospital bed. He wasn't exactly convalescing.

Second was the very real possibility that the people behind the red door would kill him. This seemed like a reasonable concern. And finally, though he wasn't prepared to admit he knew it, there was a chance that they wouldn't be able to help. There was a chance that it ended in front of the red door and she died anyway, somewhere in the streets to the south, waiting for him to come for her, waiting for him to bring help. So he stood in the rain and considered his next move, while the murmur of the streets rose steadily towards a roar.

Perhaps, he thought, he was waiting for a sign of life. Maybe he wanted to know that there was someone on the other side of the door before he showed himself. It was not the sort of door that looked as though it masked a thriving population. It was old and scarred; flaking paint like dandruff and wearing its bullet holes like a badge. It had been patched several times, dulled by the years, and sporting an array of electrics that would have been lethal even if he weren't standing in half an inch of water.

Maybe.

Boston stepped forward, out of his shelter. Rainwater hit him full in the face, cold and sharp enough to make him catch his breath, which in turn set him coughing. Water sloughed off his shoulders, shaken loose by the spasms in his chest, and he bent double into the torrent. Heavy, black pellets pounded his head, but the beauty of walking bent into the onslaught was that he couldn't see where he was going. He couldn't see the approach of the door until it was on him, right in front of him. He looked at it, raised his hand to the buzzer, then thought better of it and slapped his hand a few times against the upper panels instead.

The response took its time. In the distance, the storm was brewing, but in his own world it was silence, grey and heavy. Then a voice said, 'Yuh.'

It was not the most auspicious of starts. Boston said, 'I'm looking for Angelo.'

'Who?'

'Angelo.'

'Nah.' The voice sounded as though it were chewing, bored and interrupted in the middle of a meal. 'No one here called Angelo. Sorry, buddy.'

Boston hesitated. Suppose he'd got it wrong? Suppose she'd unearthed a long-lost relative or something, hadn't wanted to lose the address? Suppose it was the sedation talking, that night in the hospital; suppose she'd just had an itch at her collarbone and Boston, desperate for anything that might bring her back, had turned it into a sign where there was nothing at all?

He said, 'Danae gave me your address.'

'Who?'

'Danae.'

'Nah, don't know her. No Angelo, no Danae. You sure you've got the right address?'

No. 'Yes. I'm sure.'

The sounds of mastication. 'Don't know what to tell you, mate. Sorry.'

'Wait ...' he said, but the line had gone silent.

Boston cursed, kicked out at the rain, slammed a fist into the wall. A thousand criss-crossed grazes ached, bubbled tiny points of red blood that caught on the trickles of dampness that clung to his skin and splayed out in red tendrils. He took a step forward, into the rush of water, and stood, immobile, letting it flow freely over his face, run off the end of his nose in a single, unbroken line, trickle down his neck and soak his shirt.

Furious, bereft, he lifted half a bottle that was lying in the street close to his feet, and flung it at the opposite wall. It exploded into fragments as he emptied his aching lungs in ruptures that doubled him up, left him gasping for breath.

This is not right, he thought. *It was supposed to work. It had to fucking work.*

It had to work.

... because the electricity stops and there's a deceptive, oblivious, morphine-high moment before the pain starts when she thinks, I am dead, it's over, *before it rushes back at her in technicolor and she's screaming before she knows what's happening ...*

He turned, stalked back to the door, hammered on it with his fist. Kicked at it again when the voice took a second answering and shouted, 'I know he's not in with you. You know how I know he's not in with you? Because he's dead. Danae told me. You want me to shout out why he's dead? Should I let the whole street know why he's dead? I just want your help. That's all.'

A beat. Silence. He hammered again. 'Hey!'

'Mister, I *told* you.' The voice again. 'There's no one here for you.'

'I need your help!' shouted Boston. 'Jesus Christ! I just want to talk to someone. Just talk to me. Just talk to me! I have *nowhere* else to go.'

A hesitation, a fraction of a hesitation, but enough to imply doubt. When the voice spoke again, the tone was cold, angry. 'Not my problem,' he said.

'She came here,' said Boston, who had felt the pause, felt the tiny fingerhold opening up. 'About a week ago, a little over. She came here looking for Angelo and he let her in. He let her in. Please. She's going to die.'

'Not my problem.'

'*Please.*' He was almost screaming. Rain pooled in his mouth, made him gag. 'She's going to die.'

There was a long pause. Only the timbre of the silence told Boston that the link was still open, that, not a foot away from him, the voice was considering. He leaned his forehead on the door, waiting. *Please.*

'Mister,' said the voice at last. 'We're all going to die.'

25.3

He sank to the ground like a puppet whose strings had been cut. There was no space even for the anger that should have rushed in; the despair was too huge. Rain teemed unnoticed around him; lay deep enough on the ground to cover his fingers, splayed out behind him to stop him falling all the way, and he thought about lying in the street until the water rose and he drowned.

Boston's head ached. His chest ached. And there was no way home.

Misery rose like a high-G whine in his inner ear, blocking out the sounds of the street. Somewhere in the middle distance, casting red and yellow shadows on the walls above him, the riots had broken out again, but the sounds were muted, far-off.

… the first thing he sees is the golden flash of her hair. He's hazy, failing now, and he doesn't understand how she's got here, but he knows that it's her, even before he sees her face. It might be that she's just saved his life, and it might be that she's just thrown hers away for a man who made her coffee; only the next few minutes will decide, and all he knows is that if he doesn't find a way to make it out of this alleyway he will never have the chance to ask her why…

The street-song was encroaching. Boston listened to it, knowing that it wouldn't be long before it spilled down the side streets. He thought, absently, that there was a rhythm to the noise: a low, primeval pulse, like music or the opposite of music. It tempered the shrieking of metal and the explosions of glass and flame, which danced in all the colours of autumn in shadows on the far walls. There was beauty in the city, even now. And she would never see it.

A flicker of movement caught in his peripheral vision. Boston had assumed that he was alone; the street was dark and relatively silent, rapidly becoming a river. He wondered abstractly if a bubble might be forming over Mère de Martyrs, and whether anyone would even care. Glancing up, he saw yellow shadows and, possibly, the glint of a pair of eyes, buried in the darkness of a doorway. It was nothing more than a flash, a half-seen image, felt rather than observed. He shuffled his body — stiff with cold and damp — into a crouch, and leaned forward.

Nothing. Boston stood up, took an experimental couple of steps, thought he could make out an outline in the gloom, close to where he had been standing not twenty minutes earlier. He opened his mouth to call out, thought better of it, closed it again and stepped forward instead, half a step, the street-river rushing over his shoes, pooling around his toes. Another glint: light reflected on eyes. Watching him? He couldn't say, but before he could move, the figure in the shadows shifted position, seemed to dissolve into the light. He saw a hard profile: angular and stern, lit only in pools of blue light from above. The figure — a woman — shifted her weight, and he saw that, in front of her, in the half-light, hovered a newspaper, shimmering faintly as the images on the front page animated, vied for attention. Without glancing in his direction, she touched the sensor in her hand and the page changed; second page news, absorbing her full attention. She leaned back against the wall, and, as she did so, the page pivoted with her so that he could read the headline.

Semblance Safe House Bust: REN Squad Commended on Arms Find.

He remembered the story; it had been big news maybe two years back. Semblance was a dying tiger: too weak these days to have any real bite, but it had been a big haul. The Rens had lifted seventeen a-nauts and a miniature arsenal, and patted themselves soundly on the back, and less than a week later an a-naut shrapnel bomb outside a school had killed fourteen children: Emancipation's retribution, and precisely no one had been surprised. Why was she reading a two-year-old newspaper?

She lifted her eyes to him. Her expression was neutral, but her eyes said, do I need to spell this out?

The look was so fleeting, so abrupt, that it was gone before Boston's brain had time to register it. She zipped the paper, checked her watch, and walked away from him, lifting a cigarette to her lips as she did. He saw the flare of a match, illuminating her head in a halo of light.

It was almost certainly a trap.

Boston was bone-weary. His chest felt like sandpaper and his injured cheekbone had settled into a rhythmic throbbing in the cool damp. He was a poor match for anyone; *Cassie* could probably have taken him in a fight. But he followed the trail. What else could he do?

Bullets spat through the air two blocks distant, erupting a chorus of howls. An explosion roared down an alleyway and the world flared yellow, then orange, and the heat, when it rushed at him, was enough to make him duck his head. Debris — dustbins, bricks, lethal-edged shards of glass —

scattered in the street as rats ran squealing in its wake, tangling around Boston's feet. Ahead of him, she barely flinched.

He followed.

She crossed the road, stepping elegantly through the swirling, rushing waters. An oily sheen dusted their surface, dotted here and there with clumps of congealing dust-slime, bits of clothes, something that looked suspiciously like a severed finger. But the woman walked as though she were in another world, oblivious to the detritus of the city and its street-tantrums, her bearing upright, almost regal. At the mouth of another alley, the opposite direction to the rioting, she stopped, discarded her cigarette, and entered.

Boston hesitated, then smiled, slowly. Whatever was in the alleyway, she knew very well that he would enter, because she understood that he had no choice. His fingers, buried in his pockets, closed into a pair of tight fists, and he braced himself for attack or injury or death.

He made it five whole steps into the darkness before he was seized by the neck and a rough, out-sized hand — a man's hand — pinned him against the wall. There was no time to cry out, no time even to deflect the impact as he was slammed face first into the brickwork. White-hot pain erupted from his cheek, searing through his eye, and for a second Boston was blind. Something hard and metallic was pressed heavily against his head, and he knew without looking that it had to be a gun. It registered with detachment; no fear, no anger, just a lingering, sweet-sad regret, and he hardened himself for the shot.

It didn't come. Instead, the wall glowed green for a second, receding as the CP scanner was removed. A voice, surly but intelligent, said, 'He's organic.'

'But is he a Ren?' It was a voice to match the clean, graceful lines of her body: educated, refined, cold. Boston couldn't tell if the question was directed at him, but, regardless, there was no way he could have answered. The pressure on the back of his neck ground him firmly against the wall; he could barely find enough air to breathe. He thought that if he tried to strike out backwards, his hands would connect with air, and he knew better than to try.

'Where did you get the address?' she asked now. Her voice was pitched from the far side of the alley: despite her exterior poise, she was afraid of him.

Boston's mouth was flush against the bricks; when he twisted his lips to speak, he ground moss from the abraded surface, which scattered into his mouth. He said, 'From a friend.'

'What friend?'

'Danae. She was there last week. She saw Angelo. Please, I need help …'

'You know what's in there?' Softly spoken; phrased as a question, but it was a statement just the same.

Boston hesitated, considering his answer. 'I think she's in Nebe,' he said. 'Please. She's going to die.'

'You followed me,' she said. 'I know you know what's in there.'

He waited a beat. 'Yes,' he said.

'Then we have a problem.'

'Trust me,' he said. It didn't even sound convincing to him; certainly, the mouthful of moss didn't help. '*Please.* Trust me.'

It didn't have the effect he expected. She said, 'Why?'

He hadn't expected even that much, and the question threw him. And he knew that the longer he stalled, the less convincing his answer would be. So he said, 'Because I haven't got anything else. She's going to die.'

'*She* is Danae?'

He tried nodding, but it didn't work. 'Yes,' he said. 'She was here last week. Angelo gave her the address. She was looking for Angelo.' The name was his only trump card; he played it again. 'Angelo knew her, he helped her. And then the Rens came for her, and this was the only place I could think of.'

'You know Angelo?'

Lie? He thought not. 'No,' he said. And then, quickly: 'She knew him.'

A beat. Then she said, 'So he *is* dead, then?'

Too insouciant. Too quickly spoken. He could hear the break in her voice. 'Yes,' he said.

The grip tightened on his neck; the man had heard it too. Boston felt the look that passed between them. 'You know that for sure?' said the man.

'She said …' said Boston, and stopped. 'She said she felt it.'

'Did she say she saw it?'

Had she? The apartment was like another lifetime. 'No, I don't think so. She said she felt it.'

'How did she know it was him?' He felt the man pivot quickly, turning to reassure the woman. 'There's no way to know it was him.'

Another beat. She said, 'It was him.' The man started to speak, but she interrupted. 'It was him.' A shrug; he could practically see it in her tone. 'He was no warrior. He was a good guy, but he was no warrior.' He heard her move a little way across the alley. To Boston, she said, 'I remember Danae. Blond hair, right? Tall. We don't often get new people. Why did you come here?'

'There was nowhere else to go,' he said.

'Mister, it's been a long time since we could have fought our way out of a paper bag. Twenty years ago, maybe. These days we keep our heads down and stay out of trouble.'

If she had sounded as though she meant what she was saying, he would have despaired. But there was regret in her voice that could be levered open. He said, 'I won't just let her die. Jesus Christ, I've got this far. Help me. *Help me.*'

'... Even ten years ago, when we had the resources, but they've taken everything from us; it's just about staying alive now ...'

'Help me find her, then. I'll get her myself, but help me find where to look for her.'

He expected derisory laughter. What he got was a low rumble from the man: 'There's death centres all around the city, mate.'

'She's in Nebe,' said the woman. In Boston's world, the clouds parted and a ray of golden sunlight pierced the gloom. She was listening. 'He said she was in Nebe.'

'She's not in Nebe,' said the man. 'Nebe's on fire. No one's going in or out.'

The words were like a blow, pitched squarely at Boston's gut. The man was right; of course he was right: no one was going in or out of Nebe. Boston hadn't known about the riots when the captain had told him; hadn't known why it wasn't possible that he was correct.

And then the woman said, thoughtfully, 'No, that's *exactly* why they'll have taken her there.'

Against the wall, forced into the brickwork, Boston closed his eyes.

At last the man said, 'All right. So you narrow it down to three. When was she taken?'

'Nearly eight hours ago,' said Boston.

'Eight hours?' The tone said it all, said everything. 'She's gone, mate.'

And the woman said, quietly, 'But the stream hasn't warped.'

25.4

Silence. The hold on Boston's neck tightened, rasping his face further into the bricks, but he couldn't move to shift it, couldn't break the spell that had settled in case he tipped the scales the wrong way. He held his breath, concentrated on remaining motionless; felt the long, unbroken look that passed between them.

Then the woman said, 'I can get you into Nebe. *We* can get you into Nebe. That's not a problem. But you've still got to find her.'

Danae was still alive. He could have walked on water. He said, 'Where would she be?'

'Three centres,' said the man.

'Two,' said the woman. 'They won't use Copenhagen Street. It's too soon.'

The air behind Boston suggested that the man did not share her confidence on that point, but he let it pass, and said, '*Two* centres. One on the corner of West Zlata Ulicka and North Thirty-Seventh Place, the other's on Golden Lane.'

Opposite ends of the district. And Nebe was not conducive to long, rambling strolls. But Boston worked at the Authority; there were things he knew. 'She won't be at Zlata Ulicka,' he said.

Sharp interest. 'Why not?' said the woman.

'They're closing off blocks,' said Turrow. 'It's falling down. Most of it's so structurally unsound they can't even get in to seal it.'

'Creo Basse is falling down,' said the man, who had a point.

'I'm telling you,' said Boston. 'They had a fall-in about a month ago — the Northwest Street bubble branched east all of a sudden and took out half a block. I'm telling you. She's not there.'

Silence, laden with consideration. The woman said, slowly, 'If Zlata's out, they might use Copenhagen Street.'

'They might,' said the man, but his tone, for the first time, said *they might not.*

Boston waited, his face pressed to the wall. Seasons changed, glaciers melted, stars were born and died.

The woman said, 'Titus, take off your jacket.'

A beat. 'What?' said the man.

'Take off your jacket,' said the woman. 'You don't think they'll try and shoot him? Take it off. He can have my gun.'

The grip slackened. The man's hand, loosely on Boston's neck, casually pummelled his face into the wall as he did as he was told and shrugged off the coat.

'It'll keep out most of a round from a semi-automatic before the fibres start to weaken,' said the woman. 'Just don't get shot near the neck or the sleeves. They only ever keep two bullets in the chamber anyway, in case an a-naut gets loose, but you'll need to watch out for the blades. They're good with blades. If you get hit right, the jacket will deflect it, but you wouldn't want to count on it. You go in and you shoot, okay? You just shoot.'

'I shoot,' said Turrow.

'Just fucking shoot,' she said.

25.5

She's tired. She's so tired she feels as though she's sinking into the ground. She hasn't even got the energy to be afraid anymore. She hasn't even got the energy to breathe, but still she does, in and out. In and out. And scream.

The last blow broke her nose; she felt it shatter. There was no blood — she's not built that way — but it felt as though her face was turning inside out. She can hear him coming for her again; she can feel the air move as he raises his hand, pulls it back, swings it at her and all she can think of as she waits for it to connect is not my face, not my face, please God not my face again…

★

'Movement,' said the woman. 'Keep moving. Don't even stop for breath. Keep moving. Be faster than them.'

★

… misaligning the bone fragments which scrape across each other and everything hurts, everything is pain, and she can't get a breath through her shattered nose …

★

A firecracker *boom* and the air lit up. Down the street, the crowd toppled like dominoes as the blast ring spread out. Gunfire and petals of flame, licking upwards from the burning car. A surge of people, pressing back against them in the rush to be free of the fire. And the gates of Nebe, dark and unlocked; perhaps they had never been closed at all.

★

… the noise explodes into her bubble of white light, a high ragged wail. It sounds like an animal, like the sounds she heard from a mutilated cat on the street outside the apartment in Limbe, tortured by some boys and left to die. Only a tiny part of her recognises that the sound is coming from her…

★

A gun and a volt gun. Boston could feel them, reassuringly heavy beneath his coat. 'Just shoot', she said again when they left him. 'Make sure they're good and fucking dead.' She must have felt the stream warp for Angelo as well, he realised; she must have known that he suffered. She was white faced and white lipped, and the man said, 'There isn't much time.'

★

… they're shouting at her now, both of them. She thinks they want her to stop making the noise. She can't. The noise comes from somewhere outside of herself, it's not even a part of her. Danae is barely aware that his hand is gone; the essence of it lingers. He turns the butt of the gun to her face and swings it; it hits her forehead. Again, and it hits her cheekbone; her poor, brutalised cheekbone…

★

She said, 'The doors are double locked from the inside. You need to break the circuit. It's all about timing, okay? You need to flash a voltage across the lock when the internal current is low. It will demagnetise the locks. That's the only way in.'

He said, 'How do I do that?'

'That's where you use the volt gun', she said, and smiled.

★

… she floats in a hazy space, between consciousness and limbo. Her head is too big for her; it is cavernous. She floats through it like a ghost. Outside her, the world is all heat and anger. She wants to find somewhere else to be. She needs to survive, just a little longer, just long enough to let him get to her, but she's losing the fight now. She doesn't want to hold on; she wants to stay in her head, where it is cool and peaceful …

★

Flames licked the side of a building; thick, dark smoke tumbled towards the street, met from below by the detritus of a burning transporter. The light-bands were out; the only illumination was from the fires, and in front of them, figures writhed and jumped, threw things and punched the air.

'How will I know when the current is low?' he'd asked her.

And she said, 'We don't conduct electricity as well as you. They have to turn the voltage up really high.'

★

... she snaps back. She has no choice. They have fastened a belt around her neck and they are slowly pulling it tight. And it's funny because she thought she wanted it to end, but now they are gradually draining the life from her body, and she can't breathe, she can't breathe, she can't she can't she can't...

★

He started to run.

★

... Her eyes are beginning to bulge, and she knows there is no give in them anymore. Her hands jerk against the chains that hold them to the chair, her legs do a constricted dance on the floor. Her neck is extended, as far back and upright as it will go, but still there is no air, she can't breathe ...

★

'How much time?' he had asked, but the look was clear; it said, *You don't want to know.*

'Just don't stall, is what I'm saying,' he said.

★

... And suddenly the pressure is gone. Air rushes back in a painful, burning bolt and a sound that is like nails scraping down a blackboard. She is so grateful, she is so grateful for air that it doesn't occur to her to wonder why there is air, and then he says, 'Not yet, Danae. It's not time.'

And above the ragged, wretched sound of her breath, she hears him move around to stand in front of her...

★

Boston's heart thundered in his chest; his vision swam. A rattle of gunfire to his left, and he ducked, hands instinctively covering his head, but he did not stop. He ran. Blood burned in his veins; his legs were awash with acid. His throat was dry and cracked, his head was full of cotton, his muscles screamed.

He ran.

★

… he strokes her fingers with the back of his hand, like a lover. He is enjoying this. She feels the touch of his skin, cool in the damp air, feels him trail the length of her arm and back again. She chokes out a tiny cry — Oh, Christ, oh please — and he grips the top of her finger inside his fist and snaps it backwards, just when she thought she couldn't scream any louder…

★

A violet explosion of light up ahead. Boston saw it before he heard it and knew it was going to be bad. Instinctively, his hands went up to his face, and then the blast wave was on him, raining bricks and a thick, choking shower of hot dust. People fell, crumpled to the ground. Some of them were on their feet again in seconds; some were writhing on the ground; some of them did not get up. Pinned down by asphyxia, Boston choked, gagged, clawed at his tongue. A half-brick had slammed into his shoulder and the arm was deadened, a lump already rising in protest. He wretched, vomited dust, breathed. Breathed.

★

… And suddenly there's a flash of white light, and she's running. She's haring across a hillside, under an infinite sky; running for the joy of running. She's too far from home; there will be hell to pay when she's caught, but on the high peak, sometimes the mist rolls down it, white and tactile, like an old man's beard, and it's too much: cloud you can touch. So she ran, but somewhere the mist became less important than the running, and now it's the only thing there is. She runs because she can, because she is free.

Danae has found somewhere to be while it ends…

INSIDE COMMENT, 2ND DECEMBER 2092

Dr. Michael Baramasimbe is to step down as Head of the ISA's Insurgency Threat Response Directorate following widespread criticism of the agency's failure to prevent the Port of Balboa attacks last September that claimed 14 lives and cost almost 35 million credits worth of damage. Dr. Baramasimbe will be succeeded by Gerald Corscadden, former Special Adviser on Non-organic Affairs to the municipal government of the United Kingdom, who brings almost twenty years' experience of amnisobiological production models to the table. The decision to appoint Lord Corscadden, whose political career began in 2079 when a life peerage awarded for services to industry granted him a seat in the British House of Lords, to the role has met with broad approval on the Senate floor, although a number of parties have expressed vocal opposition. Sen. Milena Velasquez (S-Am. 3) has voiced concern about Corscadden's continuing position on the Board of Directors for Calator Munitions and his ownership of controlling shares in a number of former amnisobiological manufacturing firms, while Sen. Moss Rosenstiel (A-Min 1) is worried that his relative lack of political experience and friends in The Hague will impact on his ability to deliver the results that Congress needs. Lord Corscadden could not be reached for comment, but his policy advisor, Sarah Cartwright, told reporters outside his Richmond home that he was 'honoured' by the appointment, and that he intends to use his considerable practical experience of a-naut physical aptitude to 'bring the situation under control as soon as possible ...'

24 MAY - MIDNIGHT

26.1

It was an uninspiring building: blackened with age and abuse, standing – though only just – in defiance of every law of engineering. The lower floors had been subject to a fire at some point in its long, inglorious history and had never been put right, leaving a charcoal shell, transparent in places, that had never actually become unstable enough to collapse. The upper storeys wobbled precariously on the bones, like a schoolboy with skinned knees, but stopped short of disintegration.

Boston had walked past countless identical buildings, relics of the continual state of war that existed in some of the districts. As long as they weren't actually sealed, they were inhabited. This one bore signs of earlier prosperity, faded like a silent movie star into steely-eyed decrepitude: small things, like paint on a doorframe, just visible under a patina of soot, and the remains of what had once been a carpet. When he stepped into the building, his foot sank deeply into the sodden fibres, and the sharp odour of stale urine hit him like a wall.

In the old days, a-nauts had died in their thousands in places like these: uninspiring little buildings, scraping about for the extra tokens to be had from the Rens, scattered through a thousand cities like confetti. They were called the death centres, throwback to the days when they were the hives of industry that the name implied: as meticulous and mechanical as abattoirs. When the Insurgency ended, the centres dwindled. Some of them were uncovered, to varying degrees of shock or horror; some of them were burnt out. Perhaps it was an a-naut that had torched the lower floors of the Golden Lane Building. He hoped so.

Detritus of occupation: hulks of rubbish, skulking in the shadows, a well-worn path across the charcoal floor. People flooded back where there was no seal. Now he understood why they had chosen Nebe for her, why it was the first place the captain had suggested: the building was deserted while the riots raged, but elsewhere there was a curfew in place. In other parts of the city, they were guaranteed the residents would be safely ensconced in their homes, but in Nebe, they would be on the streets. In Nebe, silent, empty rooms wrapped their chamber, rooms around which a scream could echo unheard.

He found stairs. They led downwards to a cellar, half-choked with rainwater runoff, in which the urine-stench rose sharply on a pervasive crest. It was empty but for a series of archaic fuse boxes, as big as his kitchen, which lay open, trailing a tangle of brightly coloured wires into the mire. Teeth-marks decorated the plastic casings: rats, perhaps, or worse. In one corner, an ancient furnace rested in a black, metal hulk: dead for many years, now a repository for the excreta of vermin. In the other, a disturbance in the black sludge that covered the floor: a regular, linear caving: two sides of a right-angled triangle. Boston crossed to it, digging his fingers into the muck, which released the vaporous odour of filth and decay. The stink made his eyes water and bile rise in his throat, but he dug down, slime oozing between his fingers, until they struck solid.

It was an edge. Opened recently and inexpertly re-sealed, it sat just shy of the ground. His fingers ferreted deeper, found purchase, and he pulled. His grip slipped on the oily surface, pushing him backwards, but he dug down again, pulled again, felt it give just a little before he slipped once more. Back onto his feet, crawling, sliding through the grime: dig down, pull. Dig down, pull. A little further every time, until, filth slid from the hatch in a dark avalanche, and a hole appeared in the floor.

Thick, black globules tumbled through, landed on another set of steps, these ones rougher and more primitive. The space they filled could have been carved from the bedrock of the city, he thought, but imagined instead a gap in the foundations, never filled in. Lighting was sporadic, dotted along the dank walls, and it flickered randomly as he lowered himself through the hatch and onto the stairs. They were more solid than they looked, less neglected, and Boston revised his first impression of the place: this was not an abandoned hole in the ground. It was well-travelled.

The stairs gave out onto a short landing. And a door.

It was a great hulk of metal, warped and scratched, but solid. Above it perched a camera so old as to be entirely visible. It did not follow him as he approached the door; only a faint red light on one side told him it was even active. Were they watching him? Were they sitting on the other side of the door, beside the ruins of the woman he loved, watching and laughing as he crossed the tiny patch of concrete, unsheathing a volt gun with hands that would not stop trembling? Were they sniggering as he whispered, involuntarily, the instructions he had been given and looked up, searching for the lock? Did they see him freeze, uncertain, and run his hands over the surface of the door, searching for a clue? Did they realise, suddenly, as he did, that there were senses gifted to an a-naut – the sense of electricity – that he did not have, and that, without it, he could not break through?

He hadn't asked how he would know; he hadn't thought to wonder. She had seemed so sure of him then, so convinced. More convinced than he was himself, no matter what he said, and he'd wanted her to be right so badly that he hadn't questioned the assumptions she made. They sensed the flow of electrons as he might have sensed the wind on his skin or light on his eye; they would feel the charge rise and fall like waves in the room beyond the door. And they would feel the suffering, they would shrink under the weight of the stream, which writhed like a striking snake; they would know when it was time.

And then he saw it. The light on the camera faded — slightly, almost imperceptibly — but he saw it, and he moved without instruction, conscious thought bypassed; he just moved. The gun was in his hand, and it was hard against the door, and the current, when it came, was enough to knock him off his feet, but he was up again, running, slamming into the door, which gave way under the impact and spewed him forwards, into the stink of death.

26.2

There were two of them. Danae sat in a chair, frozen in an electrical spasm, arched like a diver in flight. Their heads snapped up as the as the door burst inwards, faces blank with surprise, as though, in the scheme of everything that the universe could throw at them, they had never considered Boston. It was probably a fair assumption. The current fell away and she sagged; her head slumping forwards, chin connecting heavily with her chest. He couldn't see her face, but the hair that fell around it was tangled through the edges of a hazmask; he could see the breathing tube trailing off towards a pack at her hip. Her ripped shirt hung open, exposing an upper body that was covered with bruising and splashes of bright, angry red around a series of electrodes that clung to her skin. Two more sat on her wrists, and he noticed now that the skin under the chain was burnt and scarlet-striped, leading his eye in an uneven line towards her hands, her broken fingers. And on the table, lights dancing gently, a screen measured her life signs and told them exactly how far they could push her before she fell apart.

Boston saw this in the instant it took him to raise his gun and fire, but it burnt into his brain, searing itself into a place where it could wake him from sleep for the rest of his life. In the second that he saw her, time skewed, and there were two Bostons: one who stood frozen by horror, open-mouthed and immobile, and another who did not see her, would not see her, for as long as he needed to be able to function. And then, like a freeze-frame, the image animated, and sound rushed in to fill the silence: the roar of a gun, and the tear of bullet through flesh.

It hit the electrode man in the gut, forcing him across the room, against the far wall, where he slumped, folding in on himself and staring, speechless, at the pooling blood escaping from his belly. He tried to stand, but his legs wouldn't move; Boston, had he been thinking, would have thought that the bullet had lodged in his spine. But there were two men in the room and only one was down, and Danae had not lifted her head at the sound of the gunshot. He had a split second to register that her life signs said she was still alive before a second shot ripped across the room and caught Boston in the chest.

The impact knocked him halfway out of the open door, and before he had a chance to notice that he was not bleeding and that his scorched jacket had absorbed the force of the bullet, the other Ren had crossed the room and launched a follow up. Big hands fisted in the thick fabric at Boston's neck and pulled, snapping his head back as he was jerked upwards and slammed back into the wall behind him. Level with the Ren's face, Boston could see now that, though he might have the height advantage, the other man was broader, more powerfully built, and possessed, of course, of a set of lungs that had not been bathed in fluid as recently as yesterday morning. Breath knocked out of him from the front by a bullet, from the back by a wall, and pinned by a man who outweighed him by at least thirty pounds, there was no hope of twisting out of the grip. But there was more than one way to break a hold: Boston slammed his head forward, skull connecting with skull, and the world flashed white.

A crack of fracturing bone, and the Ren howled, releasing Boston as his hands flew to his face to cradle his injured nose. Boston let his legs move him, rubbing at his head as he scrambled upright from where he'd fallen against the wall when the Ren dropped him. His gun was on the other side of the room, thrown out of his hand as the Ren's bullet hit him, and he lunged for it, using his upward momentum to carry him two full strides before the Ren barrelled into him with a low tackle that sent them crashing into Danae's chair. They fell: Danae to the side, striking the floor with enough force to bounce her head; Boston and the Ren collapsing by the wall behind her.

There wasn't enough time to check if she was all right; there was barely enough time to think. Boston had the advantage, but only just: they'd fallen badly, Boston's hip twisting as they went down, but the Ren was beneath him and it gave Boston the second he needed to get back to his feet and start raining kicks into the man's face and chest before he could recover. The Ren's hands went up to his face, deflecting the blows, but there were snaps too as fingers broke. And then ... he caught Boston's leg and pulled, and Boston fell.

He landed on his back, and a pain in the leg that the Ren held almost sucked the breath from his lungs. The Ren dived and Boston just had the presence of mind to duck out of the way before he was pinned. He rolled to the side, and now he was rolling in blood, the blood of the first Ren, who lay lifeless against the wall. Boston's gun was beside him, just out of reach. He scrabbled to his knees, hands outstretched, and then collapsed under the weight of his attacker.

Fingers closed around Boston's neck, but, face down, the Ren couldn't get purchase enough to choke him, so instead he started to rain punches down on the back of his head. Slammed from behind, Boston felt himself being ground into the tile, someone else's blood forced into his mouth and nose; he was drowning in the blood of a dead man. Fighting for breath, he turned his face sideways and spluttered red froth, and there was just enough time to see that Danae's face was pointed towards him, that the tube had detached from her hazmask and her mouth was open, sucking, searching for air, before a punch slammed into his exposed eye and the world went black.

He was out for no more than a second, but it was enough to get him turned. He woke to find the Ren's face close to his own, hands tightening their grip but slipping on a neck wet with blood. It was not much of an advantage, but it was something; Boston swung with his right arm, badly aimed but weighted with rage, and his impact blazed a trail of pain through his knuckles, his wrist, his lower arm as it connected with the man's chin. With his left he punched blindly at the man's chest, his arms, his cheeks; a one-two barrage of blows that did more harm to Boston than the Ren, but which kept those big hands away from Boston's throat. At the edge of his vision, he could see Danae's chained hands moving, sliding slowly across the slick tile floor towards her face to tear at the hazmask that covered her mouth and nose, but her eyes were rolling in her head. How many minutes now had she been without oxygen? How many minutes could she survive with no air reaching her lungs? Why the hell didn't she *move*, move faster, move *now* — and then his left swing went wide as the Ren dodged, countered, deflected the blow with one of his own that twisted Boston's shoulder, tore it in the wrong direction, and Boston heard himself howl as white-hot pain dropped his arm uselessly to the ground.

A second of agony, expletives spluttered mindlessly as he struggled to grip his injured tendons, and then it was gone, trapped in his chest as the Ren's hands found his throat again, pressed down, squeezed. The grip was strong, determined; he thought that his neck might snap before he ran out of oxygen. Desperate, Boston's right hand flew to his throat, fingers scrabbling ineffectually at blood-slickened skin, legs dancing staccato against the ground as he bucked against the body pinning him to the floor. The tile was hard, cold beneath his head as it scraped the ground, searching for a way to loosen the pressure, and all the while lights were beginning to pop in front of Boston's eyes, a roar of flame building in his chest as his lungs fought for breath, a black mist creeping across the edge of his thoughts. He couldn't see Danae — the Ren filled his vision — but he knew she could see him; he knew she was watching him, and he knew that she knew he was dying. This was always a stupid plan, of course; the stupidest of stupid plans; King Stupid of the stupid fucking plans, but he'd done it because of course he had, because there was no other choice, because she would die if he didn't. And now she was going to die anyway, because he couldn't get a breath, couldn't move his head, and his hands were flailing uselessly now,

… He is in an alleyway and she is visible only as a flash of golden hair …

muscles slackening as their oxygen supply failed, movements jerky and uncoordinated. Boston's uninjured leg kicked ineffectually; it couldn't reach the man, who was pinning him halfway up his body.

… Strong-willed, hardened by the years, he loves her almost immediately, and they're not going to die here; that's not going to happen tonight …

A pneumatic pressure, like molten lead in his chest; coiled and burning with nowhere to go. A grip like steel, driven by hatred and revenge and a will to live, and Boston's brain was fogging and his vision was punctuated by little flashes of black.

… His hand swings upwards, knife clutched between fingers that don't tremble, and they should be trembling; why don't they tremble? Because there's a line that he's about to cross, and he can feel the bile rising in his throat, and he knows that it won't be the same again after this; nothing will be the same again…

He was unconscious. Swimming in darkness, the only lights from a distant building high above; there was no need to light alleyways because people didn't go into them if they wanted to live. She'd found him when she didn't have to, and, re-routed, she'd managed to be in an alleyway in Fiore North at the same time as two dying a-nauts in need of blood. She had nothing and she'd come back for him anyway, and he was angry, he was so angry, because it was her life, and she didn't have much and they were going to take even that. And he loved her, and he knew that from the very first. He loved her and she was going to die because one man with bruised lungs and a determination that outstripped all common sense was not enough to save her. He could feel himself slipping away, and the blackness was cool, welcoming; the pressure in his chest sliding into memory as his consciousness let go, and he knew then that he was dead; that the fight was over and all he had to do now was close his eyes and wait for it to end …

And then there was a gunshot. Two more, and the vice that had closed around his ribs released; air rushing into his lungs in a heaving breath that seared his throat like acid and broken glass. He was lost in blackness, but a voice he thought he knew was calling his name — not his name, not the name that his family used, but another: Boston but not Boston, a part of him that belonged to a different life.

Turrow. Turrow — Jesus, Turrow, open your eyes. Please please please please please open your eyes, Turrow, I've got you. I've got you; it's over. Turrow, please …

26.3

The city was a kaleidoscope of light and sound. Turrow slumped awkwardly, heavy against her, his head lolling against her shoulder as Danae dragged them the final steps out of the place where she'd almost died. He hadn't opened his eyes, but he'd said her name, wrapped his arm weakly around her waist, let his feet be shuffled forward, one step after another, and that was enough for now. There was too much to fix, too much damage done to one fragile body. It was enough that he'd said her name.

The street was dark, choked with a thick soup of gas and smoke. Danae laboured for every breath sucked through a ragged hole in the hazmask's plastic sheen, but the taste of the city at the back of her throat was more than she had ever expected to know again. She had no idea how he'd done it, how he'd found her, how he'd made his way across a district wrapped in fire and violence, but she wanted to tell him that she understood: he did it because he had to, because the choice was not a choice at all. He was stripped by illness and slick with blood and every breath hollowed his stomach as he sucked air into much-abused lungs; she did not expect him to raise his head as they crossed the final yards of the road together, to open his eyes and whisper her name, but she wished he would. She wished there was time to say goodbye, time to look him in the eye and make sure he understood that this, too, was not a choice. She wished there was more to mark the parting than a couple of figures, waiting at the end of the street, silhouetted against the flame-bright darkness.

One of them, a tall, robust man whose eyes were much older than his face, looked up as they approached, and she saw a flash of something that was not quite reverence, not quite awe, ghost across his face. 'Holy shit,' he said quietly. 'He made it out.'

It was almost more than she could do to pass Turrow into their arms, to feel the night air rush in to fill the vacuum that described the shape of him against her chest. Somewhere down the line, there would be time for anger, for questions, for answers she thought she probably didn't want to hear — but later, much later, when the screaming inside her head had stopped. She said, 'Will you make sure he's safe?'

A nod from the woman. Her eyes were soft with sympathy, or perhaps it was pity. 'I will,' she said.

'If he asks how to find me …'

'I'll tell him,' said the woman, 'that you'll find him.'

'Come on,' said the man. His hand hovered at Danae's side, but he didn't touch her; she wondered how much he understood. 'Let's get out of here while we can.'

She followed him as he moved off and she didn't ask where they were going. He wouldn't tell her, and she wasn't sure she wanted to know. But she glanced back once, as they rounded the edge of an old warehouse that disappeared above them into blackness, to find that Turrow and the woman were already gone, melted into the interplay of light and shadow like ghosts. As though they'd never been there at all.

EXTRACT FROM *THE STREAM RAN RED: THE A-NAUT INSURGENCY*
BY OSCAR LUNDELL. CHAPTER 12: ALEA IACTA EST

History records that the Amnisonaut Insurgency came to an end on June 12, 2095, in a storm of fire and bullets; a bloodletting that spanned the globe. And yet, in another manner of speaking, the Insurgency has never ended. Almost forty years after the northern headquarters fell, thirty-five since the capture and deactivation of the unit known as Garrison, the war may be over, but the battle continues.

A moment of clarity, inscribed in peace and stillness on the island of Zakynthos, has echoed down the years: a reminder to those who would fly too close to the sun; a glimpse into the threads of consciousness itself; a many-layered question without an answer. But on June 12, 2095, the question on the lips of politicians and journalists, policemen and statesmen, and a brutalised, battle-hardened public, whose innocence was stolen forever one day in April 2077, was not the why, the how or the who. On June 12, 2095, the only question worth asking was where: where do we go from here?

3 JULY

27.1

The room was cold, and somewhere between gloomy and dark. Light was via a skylight in the low roof, but it was clogged with the grime of decades, and what faint illumination drifted through was tainted purple by the algae, giving the air an ethereal, underwater shimmer. There was a perfectly good light bulb in the ceiling, but instinct told him not to suggest its use, and Corscadden's instincts were always on the money.

The woman across from him was thin and slightly built, with pale, almost translucent skin that glowed in the half-light as though she were lit from within. It was not a healthy glow: too blue, too wan, and her eyes were like saucers of darkness: a startling contrast. One leg was draped over the other, her blond hair scraped back off her face. He thought she looked like a damaged twelve-year-old, but for the eyes. The eyes retained the scars that the body had healed with the passage of weeks. The eyes had looked directly into Hell.

He said, 'Thank you for seeing me. I appreciate the risk involved.'

She half-smiled, sucked her lips into an amused pout. She said, 'You're welcome.'

He took her point. He had come to her, of course, on her terms, at a location of her choice. The risk, where it existed at all, was largely his. He had no idea where he was, no idea what waited for him outside the silent door, but he suspected that it involved guns and creative death at the slightest provocation. They were protecting her as fiercely as a mother would protect an injured child; as fiercely, he thought, as he might have protected her himself.

'We're still in the city?' he said.

She smiled again, the same knowing smile, but said nothing. He said, 'I had thought you might have been elsewhere by now. I had a lot of trouble finding you.'

It had taken him weeks, but there were ways. He was a patient man when he needed to be. In fact it had never occurred to him that she would still be within the confines of Creo Basse; it had come as a genuine surprise to him, and very little surprised Corscadden. But when he'd seen her, he had understood: the eyes told him more than she would have wanted him to know.

'I'll be moving out soon,' she said. 'You nearly missed me.' She was fumbling with a cigarette packet and he noticed that she wore dark cotton gloves on both hands, that the tips of her fingers curled in on themselves like claws. She followed the line of his stare, met his eyes, and deliberately, one by one, straightened them.

She held up a cigarette pack. 'Do you mind?' she said, insouciantly, as though the damaged hand that held it was not shaking. He shook his head, but a response was not required.

'You know who I am?' he asked mildly as she lifted a cigarette to her lips, and it was only partially a question. Of course she knew who he was. What he was asking, in truth, was, since she knew who he was, why on Earth she'd made him visit in person. When he'd tracked her down, at least as far as to be able to get a message to her, he'd suggested she meet with his assistant, see if they couldn't come to some arrangement, maybe thrash out a plan for future negotiations. He was a man who'd dedicated his life to making sure people like her weren't free to live as she had lived; he'd thought that she'd want a little time to get used to the idea first.

The message came back within hours: *to hell with the monkey; send me the organ grinder.* That was when he knew they could do business, though what remained to be seen was whether or not she would agree.

'Of course,' she said now. The same, knowing smile. 'Though I'm not convinced you know who I am, Mr Corscadden. Otherwise I might wonder what the hell you think you're doing here.'

'Oh,' said Corscadden pleasantly, 'I know exactly who you are, Ms Grant. Though that's more, I think, than can be said for the rest of Creo Basse.'

The smile died, the eyes hardened. *This* was the woman he had come to see.

'Yes,' she said. 'And I plan to keep it that way.'

'Really?' He was enjoying her glare, her scrutiny, the way her eyes measured him, every inch of him, inside and out. *He* would not have underestimated her. 'You don't think, perhaps, you're due a little something?

A word of gratitude, perhaps? They're not about to build a statue to you in Cilicia district centre, but they might at least say thank you.'

At last she lit her cigarette. She exhaled a cloud of smoke; shook her head, very amused.

'Why are you here?' she said, and Corscadden smiled.

He smiled, and Danae thought she understood. He was a little old man in a den of a-nauts; a little old man whose life's work had been dedicated to finding new ways to wipe out every single member of the house in which he sat. But he smiled, and, though his eyes were carefully amiable and his white beard bristled becomingly as his cheeks creased, though his forehead was furrowed with wrinkles and he wore wire-rimmed glasses at the end of his nose, Danae thought that her first impression of him hadn't been wrong: Gerald Corscadden was well into his seventies, stoop-shouldered and frail, and with a mildness of manner so open and glowing that it was practically visible from space, but it would be a fool who read him the way he wanted to be read.

He said, 'I hear your friend made a complete recovery.'

Turrow, thundering against the thick glass; but she was too blind with panic to register his brief presence until much, much later. So many, many things to say...

Still when she woke, his absence was the first thing she registered, beyond the pain or the nightmares. Sometimes she woke with his name on her lips and she slipped out onto the streets to find him. Creo was bruised but healing, like a garden in the throes of the last frost of winter. The word was *potential*. Nearly one fifth of the population had got sick, according to the last estimates; almost three quarters of a million had died. The figures bounced around, swelled and ebbed, but they tended to settle at seven hundred thousand. *Seven hundred thousand*. It didn't mean much until you walked around the streets for a bit, saw the boarded up windows of people you used to know, the empty school yards, the solemn processions, rounding the corners in black cars, the gaps in the street where the stalls should have been.

But Creo was healing. Before the last of the corpses had begun to cool, there was an influx: people had to live somewhere. In the early days, when walking was painful and her sentinels were like shadows at her heels, she had drifted towards the Authority to watch him. In the vast, empty canyon of marble, he had been like a child's figure, superimposed on a blank canvas, too distant to see the bruises and the sallow, unhealthy skin, the gaunt jaw line and the livid purple streak on his cheekbone where the fracture was healing. He was so beautiful it was painful to watch him move, slowly, deliberately, as he had always done, as though nothing had changed. As the days passed, the canyon began to fill, and, somewhere in the city, some poor sod was hanging on the end of a telephone, inexpressibly delighted because they'd been bumped up in the queue from one thousand to nine hundred and ninety nine. The city healed.

In the evenings, Cassie or Alex would arrive for him, as if they thought he wasn't yet strong enough to make the journey on his own. She would follow them a little way along the street, shrouded by a veil of people, vicariously happy, and watch them disappear into the mouth of the underground. She would stand for a while, impervious to the bustle of frustrated elbows at her ribs and the jostle of big hands at her shoulders, to the fury of the flow behind her that could neither pass her nor move her. She would stare after them absently, vacantly, her mind in another place and another time, watching them long after they were gone.

Look, Daddy. That lady is smiling.

'Yes,' she said now to Corscadden, but it was too casual, too carefully disinterested. She knew he read her like the nuances of a picture, every tone of every colour an impression of the artist's heart, and there was more inside her heart than she cared for him to know. 'That's what I'm told.'

'And yet,' he said, 'you're leaving the city.'

Danae said nothing, fixed him with a stare as she raised her cigarette to her lips, inhaled, released blue smoke into the shadows. He smiled, let her silence slide with a gracious nod, and said, 'Would you stay? If you could?'

Turrow, hand pressed against the window, and she raises hers to mirror it, though there's nothing but air and emptiness and wasted space between them …

He was safe; she was safe. It was enough.

It had to be enough.

'No,' she said. 'I wouldn't stay.'

He nodded, slowly, sagely, as though he understood. And maybe he did, she thought; he was a man who heard the things that people didn't say, and she knew her face, her eyes, were poor secret-keepers these days. Turrow wouldn't understand, but maybe Gerald Corscadden could: that wanting to stay, wanting not to turn and walk away, wanting it so badly that it woke her from her sleep more nights than it let her rest, was the very best reason to leave.

'Perhaps you're right,' he said. One hand reached up to pull his glasses from the bridge of his nose, and he sat back in his chair, polishing the lenses with his tie. 'Still,' he added. 'This city owes you something, don't you think?'

A faint laugh made her point without words: to speak of obligations due implied equity of esteem in the mind of the debtor, and he was the last person to talk to her about that.

'I asked you before why you were here,' she said. 'You didn't answer me.'

'I'm just curious, that's all.' Spectacles held up to the half-light, twisting in search of smudges. 'An unstoppable plague, halted by one woman, and she disappears into the night without a word. I'm wondering if you haven't considered the wider picture, my dear.'

'There is no wider picture. Why are you here?'

'There is always,' said Corscadden evenly, 'a wider picture.' The clarity of the lenses had failed to satisfy; the frame was lifted to his mouth so that he could frost the glass with his breath and start polishing again. 'Maybe there's a company somewhere, the sort of place with a bit of ambition and a lot of ready cash. Who knows what they might do with a small sample of, let's say, a cybodynamic bloodstream that's quite unlike anything currently available to industry. It seems to me,' said Corscadden, and his eyes, when they rose to meet hers, were bright with the game, 'that they might be able to offer a person the kind of money that gave that person options.' He smiled. 'Don't you think?'

Danae sat back in her chair, folded her arms across her chest and realised, a moment too late, that it was the wrong image; it looked defensive. But his face was open, serene: a little old man fixing his glasses back into place on his nose, folding his hands in his lap, and watching her with milky grey eyes that saw entirely too much.

'Why?' she said.

'I have friends,' he told her.

'I know you do,' she said. 'Why?'

'Because I don't like to see valuable things go to waste.'

'I'm not a thing,' she said, 'and I'm not valuable. *Why?*'

Corscadden's face was impassive but his eyes were dancing, shining, lit by the thrill of the chase. It was life, it was the science of people, it was humanity in all its many forms. It was the game, the essence of the game. It was beautiful.

He said, 'I have a small nanopharmacodynamics portfolio.'

He smiled. And he leaned back in his chair to wait for her answer.

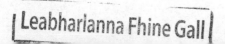